Seeing Beings is Believing

Rise of the Sisterhood

Written & Illustrated by E & K. Kim

I0592969

E & K. Kim
Seeing Beings is Believing - Rise of the Sisterhood
ISBN: 978-0-6458397-9-1

About the Authors

E & K. Kim were born in Box Hill Victoria, Australia. At a young age, both sisters were interested in fantasy genres. As they got older they became even more captured by different books and movies. They started to write their own stories about beings such as vampires, wolves and creatures that are mentioned very often in popular culture.

E & K. Kim live together on a farm with their animals. They love the rural aspect that comes with living on a large property. Still being young themselves, they wanted to create a book that contained a collection of stories that aren't heard of except inside these stories that intertwine with each other.

Both sisters wish they could have read a book like this when they were younger. However, now that they get the chance to write their own stories, they hope that everyone, especially younger people never lose their creativity or the imagination they had during childhood. They both believe imagination is the key to creativity and without it the world would be a duller place. Belief in yourself and belief in something is what led E & K. Kim to come up with Seeing Beings is Believing - A Hidden World of Mythical Creatures and now their sequel Seeing Beings is Believing - Rise of the Sisterhood.

Every tale has secrets to be unravelled.
Mysteries and truths to be uncovered.
Wolves, Magicians, Vampires or famous legends.
Many creatures will be challenged.
To overcome the problems that lie ahead.
Until the very end.

Have you ever wondered what creatures lurk in the dark? What creatures do you really know about? In this book, there is a collection of stories of a funny, dark or mysterious nature. Delve deep into the world of mythical beings. Map & Mythical Creature Glossary are on the next page. So, turn the page if you dare, as you can choose where to begin or end. The stories have been set out for you in chronological order, but this is a book with a difference; it is a collection of stories of the wonderful and obscure, and you can choose where to start or end.

Magical Beings here and there.
Hidden Creatures everywhere.
Show your true identity.
As you are now real to me.

Table of Contents:

Map & Mythical Creature Glossary

Banshees - Country of origin: Ireland (E.g. Thomasin Dullahan)

Bunyip People - Country of origin: Australia

Succubus/Incubus - Species of demons known to fool humans. Also able to remove energy from lifeforms and magical objects/items. Country of origin: Middle East (E.g. Aisha Gregory)

Vampires - Country of origin: First Vampires originated from the Middle East; and the most famous Vampire from Romania (E.g. Vlad the Impaler)

Cat People - Country of origin: Egypt; also migrated to Australia and South America, see brown spots on the map, (E.g. Cleopatra Philopator)

Zomon - Zombie/Demon Hybrid created to serve demons. Place of origin: the Underworld (E.g. Groady)

Pookas - Species of waterhorse. Country of origin: Ireland

Nickurs - Species of waterhorse from Northern countries. Country of origin: All of Scandinavia

Kelpies - Species of waterhorse originally from Scotland. Country of origin: Scotland

The Ancients - Country or place of origin: Unknown

Werewolves - Country of origins: Stories based from many countries indicate that werewolves originate from and/or have no single country from where they are believed to originate. As they are popular in many cultures around the world. (E.g. Siegfried)

Witches - Country of origin: Universal mythical being. Known throughout the world and all witches are governed by the Witches Covenant.

Mute Beings (or aka as mutants. Beings that were born of a human bloodline with some or little mythical being gene. The type of mute beings with genes or which circumstances they were born from vary depending on the types of the mythical being gene they have.) (E.g. FOG, Levi Virazio and Maximillian Tillman)

The following creatures are mentioned in the 1ˢᵗ book: - Dragons, Grim Reaper/Reaper associates, Merwolf, Phoenixes and Gargoyles.

Will-o-wisps - Country of origin: England (E.g. Lord Gruesome)

Headless Horseman - Creature similar to the Dullahan. Country known to be of origin: North America also known to Ireland

Ghosts - Spirits are well known around the whole world.

Fae species - (Fairies, types vary) Country of origin: No specifics

Demons - Many demons lurk in the Underworld. Origin point of demons: the Underworld (Ruler of the Hidden Empire; located in the Underworld, the Demon King)

Meerpeople - Creatures of the sea. Place believed to be origin: Atlantis/no specifics (Poseidon, King of Atlantis)

Elves - Species of beings similar to the Fae. Country of origin: Specifically based in Europe.

Heretic witches - Origins of the creator (Brynhild, the Red Blood Queen; founder of the Sisterhood) of Heretic witches: Germany

Zyclops - Zombie/Cyclops hybrid. Country of origin: None since it is a hybrid species.

Dullahan - Being that runs amok at night, creating disturbances/destroying anything in its path. Country of origin: Ireland

Kitsunes - Country of origin: Japan

Hu-Hsien - Species similar to the Kitsune. Country of origin: China

Celtic Wolf - Country of origin: Germany (E.g. Fane Halfdan)

Gemstone Chart

Moonstone:

Where found: Europe, Sri Lanka, Brazil, Madagascar and USA.

Name Origins: Called Moonstone because of likeness to the moon. Also known as Selenite, from the Greek 'Selene' meaning Moon or Adularia a variety of Moonstone found in the European Alps.

Ability: Werewolves use it to help weaken the effects of their transformation and to hold their powers in balance. In certain cases the stone can also enhance/strengthen werewolf powers.

Sunstone:

Where found: USA, Canada, Madagascar, India and Norway.

Name Origins: Named Sunstone because of it's aesthetic appearance. The ancient Greeks saw it as a symbol of their Sun God 'Helios'.

Ability: Vampires can use the stone to ward off the effects of the sun for only a few hours a day.

Actinolite:

Where found: Australia, China, Germany, Italy, Scotland, Norway, Uganda and Tanzania.

Name Origins: Named in 1794 Actinolite meaning ray stone.

Ability: The power to hold energy. Can also radiate energy and due to it's high stimulating energy it can be used as a healing stone for the whole body.

Amber:

Where found: Baltic coast, Lithuania, Poland, Germany and the Dominican Republic.

Name Origins: The English name for the stone Amber is derived from the Arabic word Anbar.

Ability: Due to it's rejuvenating properties it has the ability to nurture and prolong ones soul and physical body if enchanted properly.

Obsidian:

Where found: All countries where there have been volcanic eruptions.

Name Origins: Name Obsidian is derived from the Latin word 'Obsidianus', derived from the name of a Roman named Obsidius who allegedly discovered the stone in Ethiopia.

Ability: Protects the wearer/user from harm to themselves or from others/negative (bad) energy.

Apatite:

Where found: Sri Lanka, Burma, India, Canada, Mexico and Brazil.

Name Origins: Named in 1788 using the Greek word apatao meaning 'I am mistaken.

Ability: Can stimulate intuition and aid in finding a form of truth. Is used in the daggers of hunters of the 'World Hunt Organisation'.

Magnetite:

Where found: Sweden, Norway, Elba and Brazil.

Name Origins: Officially named Magnetite in 1845, however, was called Magnetis by the ancient Greeks.

Ability: It is said to have positive and negative function; it is a natural magnet which enables it to be used as an electricity relayer/conductor.

Dracul Voivode; Dark Eclipse Part 1

adu speaks:

'At first, in this world... there was only fleeting darkness... a darkness that eventually subsided and hence came the light. So we say without light there is no darkness and without darkness there cannot be light.'

'From the darkness we once came, to there we shall return... perhaps.'

Turnu, Wallachia, 1431 AD:

Vladana was pacing back and forth continuously in her long white nightgown. She knew it wouldn't be long before her child would come. But the child was taking it's time. She was pregnant and had been for nine months. Now it was time for the child to be born. She was humming a song she had been taught in her childhood. Vladana's husband was off fighting a war against another country. He had left her, a pregnant woman be regent over an entire castle and over Wallachia in his stead. Vladana did not know if her husband would come back victorious. Her son Radu was fiddling with the tapestry that hung on the wall.

She lectured him: 'Radu, stop doing that.'

He had a smirk on his face.

Radu said in a cheeky tone: 'When will father come back?'

Vladana yelled: 'Go to your room, Radu I can't deal with your despicable nature right now!'

A servant came in and pushed Radu out of the room. Vladana screeched because of the pain. Another servant came in.

Vladana asked impatiently: 'Is the man coming?'

The servant asked: 'What do you mean?'

Vladana shouted in a strained manner: 'Go get the man, his name is Lucien, he is a healer of sorts, he should be able to help... he should be on his way here!'

The servant hastily scurried off to find a man that went under the name Lucien.

Vladana laid herself down on the makeshift bed that was made out of haystacks. She prayed that her friend Lucien would come. Three months ago a strange man arrived at the castle. Vladana had come to an understanding that this man had need of a place to stay which she allowed in return for his service at the castle. His name was Lucien. He called himself a traveller and was seeking a certain homeland for his people. He was able to magically ease Vladana's pain during that time of her pregnancy. Before he left, the two had formed an unlikely friendship and he told her that if she ever required his help again, then he would return for the last time to repay the debt. She only needed to send out a letter to summon him. Vladana didn't understand how he could know exactly when she required help if he wasn't there. But she did understand that Lucien was a miracle worker. He would just know.

Strangely her plea for help would not go unanswered. The servant from earlier came marching back into the room with a confused expression on her face and Lucien standing behind her wearing a long coat. Vladana was overjoyed when she saw Lucien standing there. Lucien went over to the bed and took his friends hand.

He asked: 'I came when summoned to repay my debt to you, how can I help you Vladana?'

Vladana smiled in a painful manner and said: 'My child is on it's way... but it isn't coming... what do I do, what if my unborn child is dead.'

Lucien touched her womb and concentrated, he replied: 'The baby is not dead, do not fret Vladana, the child still lives but not for much longer.'

Vladana grabbed his hand and looked him in the eyes.

She begged with a pleading look: 'I beg of you, help me bring this child into the world, I don't know how but there must be something you can do... I know you dabble with magic so I beg of you, save my child, please if you are still my friend, the only man I could truly trust.'

Lucien shook his head and then said: 'Vladana, there is not really much I can do, I myself am still trying to control my powers, I know that I've existed as this being for a long time now but there is still much I have left to learn about what I can do and the consequences that go with it... even if I did try something... your child would be cursed.'

Vladana asked: 'What do you mean Lucien?'

Lucien said in a low tone: 'Anything in this world that is unnatural is cursed.'

Vladana said: 'Are you saying that you as a witch is unnatural.'

Lucien: 'In a way, yes.'

Vladana insisted with tears forming in her eyes: 'You are not a beast, you aren't cursed, you are a living breathing creature just like me, the only difference being that you are not truly mortal.'

Lucien smiled slightly and said: 'Dear friend, you always see the good in me when some see nothing or only little... I knew someone like that... never mind... Vladana, if this is what you want, even if the child is on the verge of death, there is one thing I can do, but this is unbecoming of me, you must drink from my blood.'

Vladana asked: 'Your blood?'

Lucien explained: 'Once, an incredibly long time ago, I was a free spirited being, free from attachments or magical restraints, but after I was sent here to live out my punishment, I needed to evolve in order to stay alive, this evolution nearly killed me and all that I once was, was gone, I could no longer heal people just by touching them, I had to give them something that consisted of the magic that I once had. The magic I once had... that once ran in my veins is now not magic but my blood, only the ravages of my blood may heal such damage.'

Vladana nodded in understanding and said: 'I understand, that you must be conflicted and agitated by my choice, but what would you do if you had a child... I think you would do the same... you would be willing to go to extreme lengths to save them.'

Lucien glanced at her with a saddened look as if he could relate to how she felt. He than saw Radu peer into the room.

Lucien said to Vladana's son: 'Come here Radu.'

Radu grinned and ran over to Lucien. He hugged Lucien.

Lucien remarked: 'You are a handsome little man, I will make sure that from now on you will be called Radu the Handsome... now little man, do you understand what is going to happen to your unborn sibling?'

Radu said: 'No, I don't think it matters.'

Radu ran off.

Vladana yelled: 'Watch your manners around this man!'

Vladana apologised: 'I'm sorry, he's always like that, not a care in the world, he'd make a terrible ruler, that's what his father said which is why he wasn't called Vlad III.'

Lucien somehow created a cut on his wrist using magic and so Vladana drank Lucien's blood in hope it would save her child.

Lucien eventually took his wrist away and the cut healed by itself.

He asked Vladana: 'How are you feeling?'

Vladana coughed and replied: 'Like I'm about to be sick.'

Lucien chuckled softly and said: 'One feels like that when one partakes in something vile as such.'

Vladana coughed more. Her body began to shiver.

She said to Lucien while grasping tightly onto his arm: 'No, I'm being honest, I really don't feel good.'

She fell off the bed and collapsed onto the floor. She began to tremble, shake and shiver. Her legs kicking uncontrollably.

Lucien shouted: 'Vladana... wake up!'

Vladana's eyes were filled with fear and confusion. This was the last time her eyes would have life in them. Lucien yelled to the servants to help their mistress. But it was too late. She was dead. However, a life was exchanged for another. Lucien learned that day that his blood only worked for the undead and not for the living. His blood was tainted with demonic power of death not of the living. As a consequence Vladana who had been alive, had died due to the negative affects of the blood. But her child who had been on the verge of death was now being born.

The servants noticed that the child was on the way. They pulled out the infant from the deceased mother. The child was healthy and alive. The servants huddled around the child. One of them eyed Lucien suspiciously.

Lucien clenched his teeth and held his friend in his arms. His friend, one of the only mortals he trusted now gone, a lifeless corpse. Suddenly he heard the baby's wailing. He pushed the servants out of the way and stared at the child who had been the offspring of his human friend. The child who's mother risked her own health to save it.

One of the servant's said: 'It's a boy...the next prince of Wallachia, Vlad III.'

Radu stood there in the archway, listening in on what was being said and was jealous of his brother who had been just born. His brother who had only existed for a mere few moments already was hated by those that should love him. Radu was jealous because his mother had gone extreme lengths for his brother when she had never done anything for him. His mother never loved him and he decided then and there that his brother would never be loved either. Lucien saw Radu run away again. Lucien followed the boy's presence till they were in the very courtyard of the castle. Lucien was about to yell at Radu for his lack in brotherly hood when a trumpet was blown.

The guard yelled: 'The Voivode has returned!'

The castle gate was drawn open. A man came riding in on a horse. The horse cantered in but the rider fell off the saddle. He had an arrow pierced through his chest. Radu looked in horror at his father. The guards rushed to lift up Vlad II and carry him inside. Inside, Vlad II was brought to his bed chamber. The Voivode shouted out due to the pain. Radu ran to his father's bed chamber and wanted to greet his father for his return to Turnu. Vlad II pushed away his son and gave him an angry glare. The castle's healer, took a heated blade and held it to Vlad II wound. The skin made a strange sizzling sound. Radu had been showed out of his father's room. Later, he heard the healer discuss his father's condition with the castle guards.

The healer said: 'The Voivode has had quite the ride back from Bucharest, apparently, he's been involved in a bad skirmish with some Boyars there...he was intercepted by the Boyars whilst on horseback on the way back from somewhere from Turkey with his small group of troops... his horse collapsed into a trench after being frightened by the unexpected actions of the Boyars.'

One of the guards asked: 'Is his condition stable?'

The healer replied: 'He is rather fortunate to be alive... he however fractured multiple bones in his legs and ribs, the arrow that nearly was shot through the heart left a big wound... it will take a very long time to recover... how long it will take I cannot tell.'

Lucien who was still outside, shook his head in disappointment and looked towards the starry sky. The moon was reaching an eclipse. The wild wolves howled in the distance. Lucien was now aware that he had created another mess.

Future Radu speaks: 'And thus, my foolish brother was brought into this world, the legendary Vlad Tepes, the impaler who was a mass murderer and the cause of the uprising of the undead army that led the dark rebellion, an event unknown to humans, the grand Dracula one of the first born vampires in existence, or as few of the Romanians call him to this day *Draculea* meaning in our language, devil.'

Vlad II would be bed ridden for the next fourteen years.

Targoviste, south of Turnu Wallachia, 1441 AD:

Vlad was riding a horse in the forest. He was 10 years old and his brother 17.

Radu shouted to his brother: 'Don't wander off too far on that horse of yours or you'll get an injury and die while leaving the throne to me little brother!'

Vlad shouted back: 'Good, have the throne and I'll spend the rest of my life in this forest with my horse!'

Radu frowned and yelled: 'Well I can't, I wasn't given the heir title Vlad III, I'm called Radu the Handsome, I might as well be called Radu the idiot.'

Vlad and Radu shared hateful, discriminative looks with one another when a man said: 'There's no need to quarrel over such silly things.'

Vlad's frown vanished and was replaced with a smile.

He rode towards the man and shouted: 'Father!' Vlad jumped off the horse and hugged Lucien.

Lucien said: 'I still don't understand why you call me that when I'm not your father.'

Vlad grinned at Lucien and said: 'Well, who else am I going to call father?'

Lucien pushed Vlad away and stated: 'I'm the worst person to choose for that role in your life...besides, your actual father is still alive and also I think your mother would agree... I'm just here to check on the two of you as a favour to your mother, Vladana, she was a close friend of mine, nothing more and nothing less.'

Radu: 'Mother was a fool, giving up her life for a nearly dead child, even though she had the right one standing right in front of her... and now my brother is a walking, talking and breathing born demon.'

Radu took the horse and headed back to the stables. Lucien took a short stroll with Vlad in the forest.

Lucien asked the young boy: 'Your brother, does he know about your secret?'

Vlad shrugged his shoulders and replied: 'Hmm, it's not like I have demonic control powers like you but he thinks I'm like you because when I was born I nearly died but came back to life.'

Lucien said while pushing Vlad and holding him against a tree: 'Vlad, you must take this seriously, you cannot let your brother find out anything about you; that you can smell things better than normal humans. That you can see and hear things as well as have better speed and strength than normal humans. I'm telling you that when I used my powers to bring you back at the time of your birth, it reflected onto what I am, a demon, that means you were born partial demon... I have no clue about what powers and weaknesses you truly have.'

Vlad asked with a hint of confusion: 'So what are you asking of me?'

Lucien said: 'Just to be more careful... this world isn't exactly friendly.'

Lucien released Vlad and kept on walking.

As they walked up the hill and over the bridge back towards the castle, Vlad asked Lucien: 'Are there others out there like us?'

Lucien: 'If you mean demons, then yes, if you mean witches and mythical beings then also yes.'

Vlad's eyes widened then he asked: 'So I would be considered a type of demon... are there more like me?'

Lucien stopped walking and looked at Vlad while saying: 'To be honest, yes... but only a small handful scattered across Europe so far... the humans call them vampires.'

Vlad said: 'But I thought you said that you didn't know what I am.'

Lucien said: 'That's because you're different, the other's were turned into vampires by other vampires, but you were sired by my blood directly and you were born a vampire. A vampire that can naturally walk in the sun, a vampire who has double the amount of strength than a normal one... and from my knowledge there is only one other born vampire that my people know of... he was born in Norway during the 9th century.'

Vlad said: 'By your people you mean the Hidden Empire?'

Lucien said: 'Yes but I still haven't found the home for my people.'

Vlad and Lucien headed into the castle. Lucien remarked as they walked through a corridor:

'So this is the seasonal palace, I'm guessing your family comes here for winter or specific times of the year.'

Vlad said: 'Yes, the Targoviste palace is much nicer than the one in Turnu.'

They walked past a long wall that had a vast family tree painted on it. It said: Tepes.

It went from Vlad I and his wife then Vlad II and Vladana as well as their two children Radu and Vlad III Tepes. The line from Vladana though was labelled with a word that said: Cousins.

Lucien looked at the family tree with Vlad and asked: 'Your parent's were cousins?'

Vlad said: 'Seems like it, they were apparently cousins through Vlad I sister Bela.'

Lucien said: 'Your mother had a sister too.'

Vlad said: 'Yes, her name is Vlaadia and she has a daughter, although her daughter is sick a lot and prefers to be locked up in her room most of the time. My aunt is a widow and is current regent as well, she rules in my father's stead till he's made a full recovery.'

Lucien and Vlad continued to venture around the palace and eventually met up with Vlad's forty year old aunt Vlaadia Tepes. Vlaadia Tepes seemed like a quiet but intellectual woman.

She greeted her nephew and said: 'Ah you look more and more like your mother... such a shame that she died from childbirth... Radu is as irresponsible as always.'

Radu sat in the corner sharpening his dagger using a rock and said: 'I'm not deaf aunt Vlaadia, you people sometimes seem to forget that I even exist.'

A girl that sat a few meters across from him laughed very quietly. Radu gave her a frustrated glance. She stopped immediately.

Vlaadia asked the girl: 'My daughter, might you go see to it that my nephew's friend here has a room here for the night?'

The girl nodded and ran off.

Vlaadia said with a sigh: 'My daughter is such a fragile creature, tragic, my only child with such a foolish heart and mind.'

Lucien asked Vlad as Vlaadia left to her bedchamber: 'Who is that?'

Vlad answered: 'She's Fenna, my cousin.'

Radu got up and left the room. Lucien noticed that the ever growing rift between the two brothers would only get worse.

As always, Lucien's forecast would become true. The rift would only worsen.

Turnu, Wallachia, 1445 AD.

Vlad was at his writing desk, he was reviewing some language scripts his tutor had given him. It ha d been four years since he had seen Lucien. His brother suddenly came into the room and gawked about.

He mocked his younger brother: 'Look what we have here little brother, trying to learn to speak Italian, French and Latin... how interesting.'

He snatched the papers off from the table and looked at them. In these years, Radu hadn't changed at all. He was still the picky bastard that persistently mocked his brother in everything. Vlad who was 14 and a little bit shorter than his brother chased after Radu.

He shouted: 'You, give those back... if I lose them, Istvan won't be too happy with me!'

Radu snickered and said: 'If you want them back then you'll have fight to get them back.'

Vlad yelled: 'Coward, bring them back now!'

Vlad jumped onto Radu and pounded him onto the ground, he did it with surprising strength.

Vlad had a slight grin on his face when he had successfully grabbed what his brother had stolen from him but froze on the spot when a voice said:

'Ahem, boys, might I ask what is taking place here?'

Vlad said: 'I was practising combat with Radu... sorry to bother you Istvan.'

Radu freed himself of Vlad's grasp and then retreated out of the corridor.

Istvan inquired: 'So, Vlad, I know you were lying to me, what did you and Radu really do here in the castle corridor?'

Vlad showed Istvan the tattered teaching notes.

Istvan sighed rather loudly and said: 'Good god, I swear your brother is going to make me rip my own hair out one day.'

Vlad said while walking with his tutor: 'I'm sorry I let Radu damage them, I know those notes were important to you, after all you're a travelling tutor for noble families and you need those notes to tutor people.'

Istvan said to him: 'It's alright, your aunt Vlaadia pays me to tutor you, I will find other ways to teach you, and with my knowledge, we'll turn you into a smart and outstanding Voivode.'

Vlad forced a smile (Voivode means warrior prince).

Istvan said: 'Don't let your brother make a fool of you, Wallachia needs a good leader after the circumstances of your father.'

Vlad asked Istvan: 'But what if I don't want to be the Voivode of Wallachia, what if I wish to seek out my own path?'

Istvan said: 'You are the only viable legitimate heir remaining from Vlad II.'

Vlad complained: 'But what about Radu, can't he replace me!'

Istvan said: 'Your brother is a moron and spends most of his time talking to female servants in the castle or brushing his hair... he doesn't dedicate himself to his studies in any way.'

Vlad said: 'So just because I'm more capable to be the next Voivode...I have to be stuck on the throne against my will even though Radu is the older brother.'

Istvan said: 'Well, your parent's declared you heir to the throne because they knew that Radu wouldn't be the rightful heir.'

Vlad continued his lessons with Istvan for the day. But was summoned by his father later on in that day. Vlad normally didn't visit his bed ridden father because his father refused to see anyone, let alone his own children. The castle in Turnu was huge. The bed chamber of Vlad II was in the other side of the castle.

As Vlad was at the door of his father's room, he hesitantly knocked on the door. Vlad saw his father on the bed. Vlad's father sat upright in bed and stared emotionlessly at his son.

He said: 'You've grown so much.'

Vlad said: 'You haven't really seen me in these last fourteen years.'

He said: 'You are correct, it is not of importance anyway... I wanted to talk to you about a certain letter I received from the Sultan.'

Vlad frowned.

He replied: 'Maybe you should tell me what the letter contains.'

His father said: 'The letter speaks of an invitation to celebrate an event with the sultan, the current head of the Ottoman empire... but coming out of that war fourteen years ago has made me ponder much about this letter.'

Vlad insisted: 'Perhaps you should ask Radu for advice on this as well.'

His father tossed the letter to the floor and said: 'No, your brother is not fit for such matters, his mind thinks of other less important things.'

Vlad asked: 'I don't know, this sounds too risky, what do you want to do father?'

He said: 'I think we should go, if we don't the Turks might think we intend to conspire against them, I don't want Wallachia's reputation to sink to a new low.'

Vlad agreed in a hesitant manner and left the room. He dared not speak up against his own father. Vlad didn't hate his father, they just shared an unexplainable father-son relationship.

He met up with his tutor who was jotting down something on bit of parchment. Istvan stopped writing when he noticed Vlad push open the door to his room.

Istvan pointed out: 'Vlad, what are you doing here... it's late in the evening, I don't do lessons around this time of day.'

Vlad said: 'I had to go see my father regarding matters with another country.'

Istvan asked: 'How did it go?'

Vlad said: 'Terrible, my father asked me for my opinion but out of some sort of fear, I struggled to voice my view point on the matter.'

Istvan: 'Don't lose heart Vlad... you're still going to be just fine someday.'

Vlad said in a bothered manner: 'But I can't even voice my opinion on such a small matter, how am I going to handle and rule over an entire country someday... I don't think I could pull it off.'

Istvan said while attempting to calm down Vlad: 'Now we've all had trials of hardships in our lives but we must always try our best to fight our way through those hardships.'

Vlad calmed down a bit and asked: 'Istvan, what was your father like?'

Istvan's thoughts wandered off for a moment, after that he said: 'My father, was a cruel man who treated me and my brother with the utmost disrespect...he loved his dog more than he cared about us. Eventually I noticed that me and my brother would only have a future that was filled with filth and squalor of living on the streets...we were born and raised in Hungary and we only ever had each other. If it hadn't been for my talents, the royal family would never had tried to seek me and my brother out... but Vlad... that's all in the past and I try not to be belittled by it as I am getting older than 30.'

Vlad asked: 'What kind of talent's would the royal family of Hungary be interested in?'

Istvan said: 'Well, I lived around people that came and went, here and there from many, many countries during my poor upbringing, as a result, I was exposed to a vast variety of languages, after a while I could speak adequate German, Latin, Italian, French and my primary language Hungarian... so because I was well versed in those languages, the royal family hired me as a tutor to mentor and teach their children those languages.'

Vlad asked out of curiosity: 'That's the only talent's you have?'

Istvan raised an eyebrow.

He chuckled and said: 'Nothing that should bother you but something that could protect you if need be... now I believe it's time for you to go and rest.'

Vlad went to his room and wondered what Istvan had meant by that.

The next following morning, Vlad the II and his two sons left Turnu, crossed the Wallachian border and headed to a place in Bulgaria that was called Edirne.

Edirne, Bulgaria, 1445 AD:

After what seemed like a long journey, Vlad II and his sons arrived at a Garrison at Edirne. Vlad though was still sceptical about the entire idea of meeting with the Sultan. Istvan reassured Vlad that he would stay safe. Suddenly multiple men on horseback surrounded the Tepes family. They forced the Tepes family inside of the garrison. They were greeted by an odd looking man. He wore robes and a turban. He had this sadistic smile and a remarkably ugly long beard that reached down to his hips.

The man realised his disturbed guests wouldn't understand Turkish or Bulgarian, so he spoke their language.

He introduced himself as: 'Welcome to Edirne, My name is Saalyin Aaamand, I am the head of this garrison.'

Vlad's father asked: 'We got a letter to join the Sultan in the celebration of something... may I ask where he is?'

Saalyin said: 'I'm afraid you've been played for a fool... the Sultan laid this trap for the three of you, it seems to have worked...now here's how we shall go from here, the Tepes Voivode shall be set free some day to return to Wallachia and rule as the face of that country but as hand of the Sultan and your sons will stay behind as leverage.'

Radu blurted out: 'You mean to say as hostages!'

Vlad II rolled his eyes at his sons bickering. The soldiers put Vlad II in his own cell. But Vlad, Istvan and Radu were forced to be separate.

Vlad was pulled from his horse. He tried to shake off the soldiers that held him but knew if he did something reckless, he would get his brother and tutor killed before he would even be able to save them.

Later, Vlad was put in a cell and shackled to the wall. The shackles burned his skin. Vlad didn't understand why the shackles were made of silver. Lucien had once explained to him that silver was dangerous to all demons alike. But Vlad didn't know how Saalyin would know about the fact that he was a vampire. Naturally, Vlad could have used his vampiric strength to break out of the cell which is what he had intended to do in the first place but now, the silver shackles weakened his powers. He couldn't do anything at all.

Saalyin walked past the cell and said: 'I do hope the two of you make yourselves at home...no harm will come to the two of you as long as your father acts accordingly... oh and don't break those chains, they cost me a fortune... I overheard from some rumours once that Vlad III was born but had nearly died. The son of the devil they say, as well as that silver repels evil and holy water weakens them so I had those types of shackles fitted just in case.'

Vlad narrowed his eyes at the man. Then he exchanged glances with Radu who was chained up on the wall across from him in the cell.

Radu asked him: 'So little brother, what do you think they are scheming?'

Vlad said: 'I have no idea.'

The next day:

Vlad woke up to see Radu missing. Two guards opened the cell and brought Vlad outside. They forced him to his knees on a wooden platform next to Radu. Vlad became shocked when he saw Istvan kneeling down on the ground. Istvan stared at Vlad.

He pleaded: 'No, don't let them see this, Vlad's just a boy!'

Saalyin nodded to the guard who drew a blade and beheaded Istvan on the spot. The head remained intact for a brief moment then proceeded to slowly slide of it's neck. The head smacked the floor and made a disgusting *thud* sound. Saalyin pointed at the head and laughed meanwhile, Vlad had watched back in horror as his beloved mentor had been killed so mercilessly.

Saalyin joked: 'Coming around asking who's the head of this garrison makes me want to laugh my own head off, get it!'

The guards laughed with their commander.

Vlad was truly horrified at what he saw now. Istvan had been the only person in Vlad's life that made sense to him. A wave of hatred arose in Vlad. He despised Saalyin for what he had done.

Saalyin walked up to Vlad and said: 'This demonstration was a warning for both of you boys, you might be our guests, but we won't treat any retaliation lightly.'

He yelled: 'Bring them back to their cells!'

Radu and Vlad were brought back to their cells just to be shackled up again and treated as prisoners. Later they tossed Istvan's head into the cell. It rolled around on the floor for a brief moment then reached a standstill. The empty eye sockets seemed to gaze at Vlad. Though the empty cavities lacked eyes, it awfully bothered him to have a dead face look at him so. Vlad imagined Istvan's face now in each and every memory he had shared with Istvan. But in each memory, Istvan looked at Vlad without eyes. Vlad closed his eyes. He thought to himself: 'My friend, they removed you from my memories, you who was one of the only friends I had in my upbringing, the times I was forced to advise my father or train to become the next Voivode which involved learning to use weapons for brutality even though I was but a child... you reminded me of Lucien and guided me on how I could be better in those times, you were my teacher in all things...I promise to remember you as the way you were and not your dead component, I will avenge your death, somehow...after all, blood must have blood as death must have death.'

Over the months, Vlad was given only little water and food to eat. Radu was so weak he couldn't even speak. During the day, they heard the cries of prisoners being killed and executed. Some days they even made Vlad and Radu watch as they killed those people for sport. Saalyin insisted for them to watch the cruel inhumane acts so that the next Voivode of Wallachia would be perfectly trained to deal with people, to know how to punish them the way the Ottoman Turks did. Vlad saw how they would impale people by using lance like weapons or long sharp poles made out of wood. They would pierce the pole through the stomach, upwards and out through the other side of the victim's stomach or from the front of the stomach toward (the back side).

However, they would remove the body afterwards and dispose of the body just to impale another. A different torture method was hammering people to walls, sawing people in half or stretching their body onto a strange wheel which Vlad was often forced to operate. The wheel would pull the person further and further apart until the body would split in half. Those were the barbaric things that Vlad had to see with his brother for five whole years. At the first year of captivity, Vlad II was released from the garrison and was allowed to return to Wallachia with his two sons remaining behind as hostages for the Ottomans.

Bulgaria, Edirne, towards the end of 1450 AD.

Another day filled with death and misery. Vlad was in his shackles practising impaling on an innocent when a person rode into the garrison and handed a guard a letter. The guard motioned for the others to follow him to Saalyin's room in the garrison. Even though the gate of the garrison was closed, they had forgotten to leave someone behind to watch their so called guests. Radu eyed an axe one of the guards had left behind. He grabbed it and attempted to break his own chains. He failed.

Vlad said: 'Give it to me!'

Radu passed it to him. To his amazement, Vlad had broken the chains off himself rather quickly. He helped Radu get off his chains.

After that, Radu suggested: 'We should grab some food rations, two horses and get out of here before they find out that we're trying to escape!'

Vlad said: 'No, not before I complete my errand... the one thing that kept my mind clear and sane all these years, my promise to avenge Istvan's death... and to kill all those that have wronged us here.'

Radu complained: 'Vlad, he's been dead for five years, we should leave the past in the past.'

Vlad said: 'He was unrighteously killed for no reason at all, unlike you, he meant something to me, he was my friend, much more dearer than you will ever be.'

Radu frowned as he watched his brother run off towards the barracks of the garrison. Radu would try to leave without his brother. Vlad slid into the room via the conveniently open window. The guards who were discussing something with Saalyin saw Vlad sitting patiently on the windowsill with an angered smile on his face. Radu suddenly heard screaming and saw bodies being chucked out of the window. He saw disassembled arms, heads, legs, feet. Vlad came out of the building, he pulled Saalyin behind him. One soldier was trying to run away from him. Vlad held a lance in his other hand. He threw it in the soldier's direction and it ran right through him. The man collapsed. Vlad pulled Saalyin out in front of him.

Saalyin pleaded: 'Please don't kill me!'

Vlad asked: 'And why should I adhere to your request?'

Vlad said to him: 'You were the one that killed my friend and held me and my brother captive for no reason...I should kill you so terribly... but I can't bring myself to such cruelty as I believe I've done more than enough of that...I will simply kill you like my friend was executed and that will be the end of that.'

He pulled Saalyin's head upwards with one hand and pulled downwards at the neck with the other. Saalyin screeched very loudly. He ripped off Saalyin's head and threw aside the rest of his body. Vlad saw his brother who was sitting on a mount, gaping at him.

Vlad asked him: 'Were you going to leave without me?'

Radu answered quickly in a startled manner: 'No, of course not, I was just preparing our mounts!'

Vlad said while swinging about Saalyin's head using his beard: 'I am deeply disturbed by all this...to believe that I was capable of such horrible things, perhaps it was the effect of being held captive by monsters for five years that made me capable of this.'

The soldier who had been attacked by the lance whimpered: 'Master Aaamand!'

Vlad frowned and said: 'Here's your master, the head of the garrison!'

He hurled the head at the wounded man. The wounded man screamed at the head.

Vlad shook his head, he sighed loudly and said: 'I've had enough of this.'

He stood over the wounded man and said: 'Goodnight.'

The man screamed again but was silenced when Vlad twisted his head.

After that, Vlad said: 'Let's return to Wallachia shall we?'

He got on his mount.

Radu noticed that in these years, Vlad had changed somehow. He became more judgemental and self aware. When Vlad and Radu returned to Wallachia, they caused an uproar with the Boyars (Wallachian middle class people). Apparently, Vlad II had been assassinated by Vladislav the seconds army a month ago because he crossed the border. The Boyars who barely supported the regency of Vlaadia Tepes, were rejoicing that Vlad and Radu returned to Wallachia in hopes that they would overthrow the current female regent as the Boyars did not find it to be right for a woman to rule over Wallachia. There was no Voivode title for women. Even though, Vlad returned and greeted his aunt. Seeing a member of his family again seemed to ease the murderous, dark evil things he had seen for the last five years. When his aunt questioned him what had happened during his years of captivity. He would only say that he didn't wish to speak about it. He only mentioned having seen many people die or be tortured. So it came to be that to everyone except for Radu and Vlad, the horrendous events of those years spent at the garrison would be shrouded in mystery.

Lake Snagov Wallachia, in the future.

Radu stood by the side at the lake. He remembered how he had taken trips here with his mother in summer. A boat rowed towards Radu and stopped there. Radu got on to the boat and told the people to row over to the island on the opposite side of the lake. The boat rower though refused to go more than halfway. Radu got off the boat and swam the rest.

The man who had been on the small boat yelled out something in the Wallachian language to Radu.

Radu ignored what the man on the boat had said. Radu said in his mind: 'Telling me in the language here not to go to the island, I intend to go there, I'm not afraid of some old buffoon rotting away in a tomb.' A thought went through his mind: 'Vlad has apparently been dead for a while now... not regarding the mystery as to how he died... I want to see his resting place for myself... just because I'm curious enough and besides, it's too late for revenge, he's dead.'

As the boat sailed away. Radu created a fireball in his hand so he could see. Fire after all was his vampiric speciality. He felt the moss covered ground for a certain lever. Once he found it he pulled it. Open went a hidden door covered with patches of grass. Radu went down various steps and into the inside of the tomb. There was text inscriptions on the wall. They were in the language spoken in Wallachia. Radu glided his hands over the words.

He said some of the words he read: 'Voivode, means warrior prince, Tepes means impaler... my these burial words certainly suit you... brother!'

Radu's gaze rested on the decorated coffin. In a complete fit of rage he tore open the lid. However he looked within with a surprised expression.

Turnu Wallachia 1452 AD:

Vlad woke up in his room in the main castle and found a servant there standing with a letter in her hand. Vlad rubbed his eyes and took on the letter in a tired manner. On the letter was a seal with the emblem of the royal Wallachian family of Draculesti. When the servant was gone he opened the letter to see his aunt's handwriting. The letter said:

My dear nephew Vlad, after recent events that took place over two years ago I am aware that my letters are the least you might want to read as I understand that those events were cold, cruel and disturbing. This letter was written a day before my demise. I want you to ascend to the throne now. You are more than worthy of it. You are older than most throne successors since you are now the age of 21. I was regent for the past 11 years because I wanted you to grow up a bit first before you take on those burdening family matters. Of course, your brother should be the one to rule since he is the older one, sadly though your mother and father gave you the title of the heir of the throne, Vlad III. You will also inherit the palace in Targoviste. I know that you've been fond of it since the age of ten. Please make sure to watch over Radu and I have a request to make, please make sure that Fenna ends up somewhere safe so that she can live out the rest of her days in peace. As the sister of your late mother I implore you to do so.

Sincerely,

Vlaadia Tepes.

Vlad dropped the letter and got dressed for a horse ride. He was never truly close to aunt Vlaadia. His brother on the other hand didn't care at all. He seemed to have gotten a letter as well and he shoved it into Vlad's hands in that morning.

Vlad bickered to his brother: 'Our mother's sister just died and all you can do is not care at all!'

Radu threatened: 'Don't talk to me like that little brother!'

Vlad shouted: 'If you're the older brother start acting like one!'

Radu wanted to shout back when he noticed his brother was now the leader of Wallachia and so he must not disrespect the new soon to be Voivode. Radu kept his mouth shut.

Vlad said: 'Since I am a grown man, you and I have our own lives now, you can live here and I'll go and live in Targoviste... in fact I'm going there today.'

Radu said: 'But that's a few days ride from here.'

Vlad said casually: 'And.'

Vlad got his food pack ready, his long lance, fur coat and rode off on his horse north of Turnu towards Targoviste.

At Targoviste a few days later:

Vlad arrived at the castle. He was quite exhausted from the travel and the ride. He brought the horse to the stables. But as he went up into the castle, he saw the view. The snowy forest. The various trees covered in blanket's of snow. The cloudless sky and the fresh breeze was what made Vlad happy to be back in Targoviste. He went through the various corridors. He remarked on how the elegant carved arches and awnings in the corridors hadn't changed a bit as well as the wall painted features and hung Tapestry's looked like they had been made only yesterday. In a certain room there was a woman who seemed to be crying. She sat on a stool and covered her face using her hands. The room had been Vlaadia's bedchamber. The woman noticed him standing in the doorway. She looked up and had a confused expression on her face.

Vlad asked: 'Fen, is that you?'

Fenna replied: 'I told you a long time ago not to call me that.'

Vlad scratched his forehead.

He replied: 'Now that you mention it, I do remember you saying that, 11 years ago.'

Fenna rolled her eyes. She crossed her arms and blushed. Vlad noticed that even though she was grown up, she still acted like a child.

That was his first impression till she said: 'Well don't bother talking to me, I'm no child any more, my mother's dead and since I'm a woman I'm going to have to keep my wits about me.'

Vlad began to laugh hysterically.

He said: 'I'm not here to talk to you, your mother left this castle in my care, I'm here to live here.'

Fenna said: 'I suppose this is just going to be like old times, no difference.'

Vlad said: 'One difference is that my brother won't be here.'

Fenna said: 'Not to mention you have other problems than your brother, the King of Hungary has already challenged you as the new soon to be Voivode of this country, there are rumours surfacing that Vladislav II is challenging your hold on your position, he is allied with John Hunyadi who intends to help get him the title of Voivode of Wallachia... then there are the Turks with unsettling requests from you.'

Vlad: 'Where did you hear this Fen?'

Fenna said: 'Some royal advisers here.'

Vlad muttered: 'Why must my lifetime be spent in trauma...always something.'

Vlad frowned as he remembered the assassination of his own tutor, killing all those Ottoman Turks at the garrison. His hatred hadn't fully subsided. It still remained like a moving ocean tide, having it's highs and lows, always moving, never leaving, always unphased. He hated having become the way he was, all that blood shed. But he would have hated himself even more if he had only let himself stand by and watch as those soldiers would have killed more and more relentlessly. Vlad's existence was only truly pleased when he satisfied his need for justice. Everywhere he went, he saw the unfair acts of others against the innocent. Those people that suffered needlessly for no reason, just like he had for five years.

He set his heart on this belief and decided that his place in life was only for him to choose. He wanted to stand out from the rest, he wanted to make a difference for the people of his country to the best of his ability. His country that had been robbed of certain things like pride, robbed by the Ottoman Turks. He swore to fight for the honour of his father's legacy and those that came before him. He swore to avenge the deaths of those he had lost and to fight against the Ottomans for as long as he willed no matter if it was a complete suicide mission, his heart writhed with resentment for the past and what all those corrupt and vile soldiers had done to him. His final oath was to avenge his own suffering, and in the future, kill everyone that either crossed him or betrayed him.

Vlad now had the first official duty to take care of. What most weren't aware of was that he was going to battle his way through this with an iron first. Literally.

In the year 1452 Vlad decided to ignore negotiations with John Hunyadi as well as the Ottoman Turks and challenged them to war. He decided he wouldn't bend to anyone's will. In the year 1452, the Hungarians collided in a battle against the Ottoman Turks on the plains of Kosovo. With the Hungarians were the Germans and Bohemians. The Hungarian forces were led by John Hunyadi and the Ottomans were led by Mehmed II as his father Murad had died from a stroke. Mehmed was not to be messed with, he was after all to become known as, Mehmed II the Conqueror. Vlad took this chance of diversion to rid Wallachia of his contester, Vladislav II. Vladislav was of the second noble faction of Wallachia called Danesti. The Draculesti faction (where Vlad had been born into) and the Danesti faction had always had an unfortunate tension about. Though, Vlad's supporters in his faction weren't enough and his small army wasn't enough to defeat the huge army that Vladislav had gained through the support of Hunyadi.

Vlad the Impaler

Vlad was forced to flee to a Saxon town called Sibiu. After the loss against the Ottomans at the plains of Kosovo, Hunyadi had heard that Vlad was staying in the place known as Sibiu. Hunyadi seized Vlad with his own troops and decided to take him into his service. Hunyadi did this because he was suspicious of Vladislav's actions.

Apparently there were rumours that Vladislav was having 'talks with the sultan'. Hunyadi was not pleased by this and decided to use Vlad as a replacement as a Voivode of Wallachia. First though to make sure Vlad would remain loyal, he brought him all the way to the Hungarian capital to pay homage and swear fealty to the King of Hungary. Vlad was forced to leave behind all his family back in Wallachia and as a hostage, he was taken to Buda.

Buda (Modern name is Budapest) January 1452 AD, Hungary.

Vlad was tied to a rope. He was quite fed up being held hostage all the time. His rope was tethered onto some soldiers horse. Vlad had only witnessed multiple days pass, he didn't hold count of them passing. The army had arrived at the capital. They were crossing a wide long bridge and heading to a large castle like structure. Vlad had a little bit of annoyance directed at Hunyadi. He didn't have a clue as to whom Hunyadi was in this army filled with many men. He felt like wanting to plunge a weapon through this so called great Hunyadi. But Vlad's impression would change a bit soon.

Vlad's rope was untied. They shoved him into a room in this castle where Vlad was faced with an odd looking soldier. He was fitted with heavy metal armour from top to bottom. The room Vlad was in was long and narrow. The soldier had a very deep voice. The armours helmet muffled his voice.

He said in Hungarian: 'You will stay here till my uncle has decided what to do with you.'

He marched out of the room.

Vlad was now a hostage of Hungary. He frowned at that thought, walked up to the window of the room and looked outside. He was ashamed of himself. Back in Targoviste he had sworn to avenge his past and for those he had lost. He realised how he had tried to use the war in Kosovo as a diversion to rid himself of Vladislav II, but he had failed, epically. It was because of his overwhelming, renewed pride in himself.

He admitted now to his losses. With his own strength, he could take down many but he can't go showing his true self to others in the process. He saw that if he wanted to defeat Vladislav, he needed to submit his loyalty to Hunyadi and the King of Hungary. Vlad understood that even though Hunyadi had given Vladislav II the power, he was not the one that had killed his father, the death of Vlad's father lied at the fault of Vladislav the second. This notion seemed to make it easier for Vlad to make his decision. Hunyadi seemed to be a person who always put the welfare of King's country first no matter what. His actions lied on his diplomacy for the better of others in his home country. Because of that, he shared a similar interest and shared a similar resentment for the Ottoman Turks, and so, this enabled Vlad to decide what to do. Vlad would come to swallow his pride and to rely on the help of an army dictator of another country. Vlad hated compromising. Through constant losses and being held hostage, he forced himself to always rely on himself, this didn't cause him pain but deep loneliness. It was a void he filled with his need for the suffering of those he hated. Vlad decided that in the future he would have the help of allies but on his account and if they didn't agree with him, he would kill all of them.

Vlad stayed in the room, of course he didn't want to make a scene so he agreed to wait for the audience of John Hunyadi. He waited till noon. The clouds were dispersing and the sky was turning grey. Vlad was still looking out the window when he heard footsteps nearing the room he was in. Someone barged into the room. This person was accompanied by the same soldier from earlier who had put Vlad in the room in the first place. The man whom Vlad hadn't seen before had a broad wooden shield that had a coat of arms painted onto it. Vlad gazed at the shield. He recognised it somewhere before. Istvan had once shown many coat of arms of various noble and royal families. Since Istvan had been from Hungary, one he spoke fondly of was the house of Hunyadi. Their coat of arms consisted of a blue and white design. It had two ravens, each holding a ring. It also had two lion like creatures that each held a crown. Vlad knew now that what he was looking at was the Hunyadi family crest. The person with the shield placed his shield against the wall and went on to remove his helmet.

Vlad narrowed his eyes at the man as he was confronted by the face of an elderly man.

The elderly man spoke in a stern manner and said: 'This is not the reaction I was expecting from Vlad III, the man who clawed his way free from the Ottoman Turks, our common enemy.'

Vlad stated: 'I wasn't expecting to meet an old soldier when John Hunyadi was the one that supposedly wished to discuss something with me.'

The elderly man said: 'I am John Hunyadi, of course my appearance must be terribly disappointing.'

Vlad said in a forced respectful manner: 'No, I apologise, I forget sometimes that the wisest people are those that have lived a while on this earth.'

John chuckled and said: 'Yes, I like that, very well put.'

He glanced at the soldier next to him and said: 'Shall we get down to business Ilona?'

The soldier said: 'I believe so uncle.'

Vlad frowned at the soldier who was addressed by a woman's name.

John noticed Vlad was distracted in their conversation and pointed out in a bold manner: 'Vlad, I will have your assistance to destroy Vladislav the second, I have reason to believe that he might otherwise have deeper unacceptable relations with the current Sultan...if we don't act now, Vladislav II might allow the Sultan to pass through Wallachia to invade Hungary and neighbouring countries.'

He added: 'I believe you have distant relatives in Moldavia, a distant cousin called Stephen... he too might be in danger of the Ottoman Turks.'

Vlad asked: 'How do you know of all this?'

He explained: 'I am a trusted adviser of the King and as such I have many connections to nobles and royals... I have overheard that a supporter of Vladislav the second called Petra Aaron, is currently usurping his brother's throne, your cousin, Stephen is being held hostage by his uncle.'

Vlad scoffed at the word 'hostage.'

John said: 'I do hope we can come to some sort of agreement...that bastard Vladislav must be put down before we have even more problems.'

Vlad debated in an annoyed manner: 'How dare you pretend to be a virtuous person, if you hadn't supported Vladislav in the first place, nothing would have come down to our situation now!'

John grabbed his shield and explained in a tired manner: 'I admit that I have made a mistake in that instance but I believe in due course you will understand what it means to sacrifice and fight either knowing risks or going in blindly, we never know what life is like the next day which is why we must use whatever skills or knowledge we have to fight back. At the time I couldn't determine if I could trust you as the new Voivode of a neighbouring country.'

Vlad only replied with: 'Perhaps I might understand a little of what you mean... but I will learn how to plant my own roots in this world.'

John sighed and said: 'Alright Vlad... it seems we have come to an understanding, tomorrow you'll meet the King and then we shall go from there as allies.'

John left the room with his companion.

John and Ilona led a conversation on the way to the guest quarters.

He said: 'Dear, that was quite the conversation... Vlad was very difficult to converse with... it was almost as if he lacked a soul.'

Ilona said: 'I don't agree with that, I think he's just bothered by something.'

He said: 'I can't believe that someone as open minded as you and kind as you is the daughter of my idiotic friend Michael Szilagyi.'

The next day, Vlad was awoken by the sounds of galloping horses. He woke up from his chair and went to the window. He gazed out the window and saw two horses galloping in a circular formation. The horses were beautiful. Their finely combed manes and tails swaying in the wind as they went. But it was not the horses that truly caught his attention, it was the young woman that was on one of the horses that made him watch closely. There was something enchanting about her. She laughed and continued to freely ride her horse. A young man on the other horse laughed with her.

This sound of laughter made Vlad feel the bitter isolation of his existence. He hated that feeling so he rid himself of it. The feeling that made him feel vulnerable and useless. Once more he was a slave and hostage to something.

Someone knocked on the door. Vlad turned to see who it was.

The person said: 'My name is Michael, I believe you and John have an audience with the King.'

Vlad followed the man until they reached the place where the royal court of the Hungarian King took place. John waited for Vlad beside the throne.

John greeted him and said: 'I see you've met my in law, Michael Szilagyi, he's going to be our tactician between our armies, he's also the count of Beszterce.'

Michael nodded. Vlad bottled up his annoyance at all the formalities and went on to swear fealty to the King, Vladislav the fifth.

The rest of the evening, Vlad was free to wander about the castle. Though he heard absurd commotion coming from a dining hall. He opened the door to the long room and was greeted by an odd looking man. He had similarities to the man he had seen earlier on horseback.

John who spotted Vlad by the door said to him: 'Vlad, why don't you come and join us... I'm sure you wouldn't mind celebrating with us.'

Vlad frowned and asked with a hint of confusion: 'I don't really understand what all this festivity is for.'

John awkwardly raised his cup and said: 'Oh humour me, we might as well be celebrating gaining you as an ally.'

Vlad had a very unhappy look on his face as he sat down at the table.

John yelled at someone: 'Laslow, play some music for us!'

Laslow played a flute and proceeded to dance around the table like a drunken fool. Michael, John and the man who had invited Vlad into the room, clapped repeatedly. Vlad rested his chin on his hand and tried very hard to ignore the madness that was shown in the room. This fortunately didn't last long as a soldier dressed in armour entered the room. It was the soldier known as Ilona. Vlad strangely looked up to glance at this Ilona. Ilona removed her helmet. To Vlad's unexpected surprise, he was confronted with the face of a woman. She winked at him and smiled.

She stood upright and spoke in a clear voice: 'Uncle, I have urgent news to relay.'

Michael sprang up from his seat and asked: 'Ilona, what is the meaning of this?'

She begged him: 'Please father, this message is crucial!'

Michael argued with John: 'Is this your doing... have you been dressing my daughter in something only men should wear!?'

He added: 'How long has this been going on behind my back?!'

Michael plugged his ears with his fingers and stomped out the room.

He said to his daughter in a disrespectful manner at the doorway: 'What you do brings disgrace to your mother....both you and your sister cannot and never will truly be able to fit in to the Hunyadi family nor that of Szilagyi.'

John said to Ilona: 'Don't try to get so wrought up over that niece.'

He asked: 'So what was it that you must report to us?'

Ilona said: 'Well, I rode to the nearest post and got message from a guard that the Ottomans are nearing a city in our neighbouring country Serbia, I believe it was Belgrade.'

John stood up, and pointed out: 'But that's so close to our border!'

He grinned and said: 'We have a problem to take care of... if we don't deal with it, the Ottoman forces will gain free entry over the Danube... if that happens, our pride in our country will fall!'

He charged out of the room and said to the two others: 'Mathias, Laslow, arrange an audience with the King at once, I will go look for Michael.'

He said to Ilona: 'You must look for your sister...see how she will do and tell her that her fiancé Laslow is going to ride off with us to Belgrade.'

Ilona sighed.

Vlad asked: 'And what am I to do?'

He said: 'You will be asked to join Michael to discuss arrangements for our troops.'

With that, John left Vlad and Ilona in the room.

Ilona plopped down onto a chair and covered her face with her hands. Vlad stared at a wall not knowing what to do now.

Ilona asked him: 'Could you please leave the room?'

She added: 'I could really use some space right now.'

Vlad wondered what her problem was.

He said to her: 'If it's space you need, I respect that.'

With that he intended to leave the room. Ilona had a quick change of heart.

She tugged his sleeve and said: 'Wait... don't go!'

Vlad was about to argue with her when he saw the troubled look on her face. It reminded him of how lonely he had felt as a child.

He sat down next to her. Staying by her side felt wrong but something changed Vlad that day. A feeling he thought he would never show anyone again, kindness.

Ilona observed Vlad's reaction.

She said: 'I'm sorry for wasting your time, I won't bother you again.'

She looked at him but got no reply.

She said: 'I apologise for my father's over reacting, he's always like that... no matter what, he never changes.'

Vlad asked her: 'And why is he like that?'

Ilona said: 'Maybe he blames me for mother's death, I just know that I'll never be good enough for him. I'm not your typical loyal lady who stitches and wears dresses as well as leaving family matters to the men but my uncle in law, he saw I had potential, he saw that I was good with horses and knew my way around most weapons.'

Vlad said: 'I know how you feel.'

Ilona asked him in a curious manner: 'How so?'

Vlad said: 'My father was bed ridden for fourteen years, it began since the day I was born, in those fourteen years, I never so as much as heard him say my name nor look at me if I was summoned by him until he was killed.'

Vlad's eyes flashed with anger.

He went on to say: 'Killed by those scum the Ottomans.'

Ilona asked him in a confused manner: 'I thought you hated your father, that was my impression from the way you speak of him, though why is it you wish to avenge his death?'

Vlad's angered expression faded.

He stated: 'Even if he was the poorest example of a father, we are still bound as family, no matter the time that separated us or his death that challenged my bond with him.'

Ilona smiled.

She said: 'I suppose we both have had troubled relationships with people in our families.'

Vlad had an astonished look on his face. He didn't know how to respond to her statement. She seemed to be the first outsider in Vlad's life that he could relate to.

Ilona smiled. Her smile captivated him. He was rendered completely speechless. But it felt wonderful to be needed by someone else, that is what Vlad thought. All troubles and feelings of hatred or loneliness seemed to fade to nothingness. A simple bond was formed that night.

Vlad thought: 'I don't deserve this kindness, I have not righted any wrongs... what am I saying? I thought that killing those that opposed me was righteous, am I wrong after all? No, those evil and insolent Ottomans made me this way... I have no reason to explain myself. No reason at all, I am arrogant, though the roots of that was the constant, pointless rivalry between me and my own brother. I understand that I am a dark soul, tainted in every way possible, though my lament of the truth is not convincing to anyone; I never believed there would come a time in which when other people judged me, someone who did not do so, convinced me to judge myself. So why, why does my conscience now weigh so heavily on me?'

The next morning Vlad awoke in the room he had been appointed in the castle. He heard fanfare and commotion outside. He got up and wanted to exit the inner castle to see what the commotion was for. But when he pushed the door to leave the inner halls, a certain voice shrieked: 'Hey, watch it!'

Vlad frowned to see a young lady get up from the floor. She dusted off her garment.

Vlad asked: 'Can I help you?'

She complained: 'Of course not... instead of slamming a door in my face, knock first, imbecile.'

Vlad frowned even more.

He said: 'I didn't hear you.'

She tapped her foot on the floor and asked in an annoyed manner: 'Do you hear my foot... or are you deaf?'

Vlad said: 'I can hear you very well.'

She stated: 'You lunatic, switch your head on, maybe I should knock your head in... see how you like it.'

Vlad was about to reply when Ilona came walking up to the two of them.

Ilona exclaimed: 'Sister, there you are, I've been looking everywhere for you.'

She said to Ilona in a mocking tone: 'Oh there you are sister, I've been avoiding everywhere of you.'

Ilona asked: 'Jona, what is it with you today?'

Ilona added: 'You're normally so calm and quiet.'

Jona's angered expression vanished and was replaced with a saddened look.

She said: 'Yes, you're right... I just didn't sleep well last night.'

Ilona laughed and said: 'Where did you sleep, outside in the garden again... father will be furious when he hears what you have been doing last night... you know what, forget about it, uncle John is back, let's go talk to him.'

The two sisters hurried off happily together.

Vlad noticed that this Jona was very secretive and only behaved normal around her sister, Ilona. He remembered that Jona. His frown vanished as he remembered that young woman on the horse from yesterday morning. The peaceful way she had rode that horse had somehow distracted him from his own bothersome affairs, in that time, she had given him solace. She had been Jona.

Later that day, John had requested to speak with Vlad. Vlad met with John in a drawing room in the castle.

John addressed the conversation.

He said: 'So this all seems rather confusing to explain and because of that, I've asked my son, my eldest, Mathias, to join us.'

Vlad nodded and replied: 'That is fine with me.'

John explained everything about what happened.

He said: 'My younger son, Laslow, is still on the way with troops to Belgrade, I on the other hand, have received a letter from the sultan himself stating that the attack on Belgrade has been called off for now... I don't trust this man let alone the fact that he addressed this matter in a letter... it seems somehow suspicious, because of that, I've told Laslow to

42

continue his journey to Belgrade with troops so he can help aid the Serbians if need be.'

He chucked a letter at Vlad and requested: 'Go on, take a look at it.'

Vlad snatched the letter and read it. After reading it, he shook his head in disbelief that the Ottoman Turks would be so foolish and cheap in their schemes.

He asked John: 'So what now?'

John said: 'I've asked the King for consent to make you the guardian over Transylvania in case the Ottomans decide to threaten another neighbouring country. If I had to go there to fight with my troops, I could have you watch over Transylvania in my stead... the King has agreed to this proposal.'

Mathias handed Vlad a sort of stamp.

He said: 'Show this to the people in Transylvania to prove to them that you are the sole guardian.'

He added: 'Only use this if need be.'

Vlad rode off to Transylvania at the behest of John Hunyadi. Michael and his two daughters went with Vlad to help Vlad familiarise himself with the people of Transylvania. It was in Transylvania that a major aspect of Vlad's life would change.

Transylvania, Hungary, 1452, Grand house of Hunyadi.

Vlad and the others had arrived at the Hunyadi house in Transylvania. The house was huge. It had carved stones and well placed stone walls. Around the back was an old looking well and the stables. Towards the end there was a grave yard. Vlad questioned himself as to why the grave yard was so close to the house of Hunyadi. The landscape and hillsides reminded him of his own homeland.

Ilona asked Vlad as she got off her horse: 'What's wrong?'

Vlad shook his head and replied: 'Nothing.'

Vlad was estranged having lived in multiple places over the years that weren't his own home. He felt out of place every where he went, a constant looming cloud over his gloomy and desolate existence.

At night, in the large house of Hunyadi, he couldn't sleep. He would gaze out the view of his room. Through the window that overlooked the paddocks that were camouflaged in the dark. These nights seemed long and yet the next day would come upon so fast. However, on one of the strange nights, he spotted someone that resembled Ilona run outside in her night shift, holding a small lit candle.

Convinced it might be Ilona, he followed her. He went outside into the dead of night. In the distance, he glimpsed the flickering light of her candle. He followed the light, the light that led him to the small grave yard. He saw her standing in front of a headstone.

She gasped and turned to look at him in a startled manner.

She asked him with a hint of annoyance: 'What are you doing out here?'

He replied: 'I might ask you the same thing, Jona.'

Vlad realised it had not been Ilona but her sister whom she shared much likeliness with, Jona.

Jona said to him: 'What I do out here is none of your concern, besides, my uncle, John Hunyadi, who owns this family home with his sons might only be my uncle in law but I am still a member of the Hunyadi family and that means I can do here as I please whereas you are a guest in my uncles home and lack bedside manners!'

Vlad said: 'Very well, think as you may.'

He walked away.

Jona said: 'You must be very fond of my sister to be able to mistake me for her and then follow me out here.'

He turned to her again and said in a slight surprised tone: 'I suppose I do.'

Jona grumbled: 'Suppose you do... bastard I see the way she smiles at you... my sister likes you know.'

He said: 'How observant of you.'

He suddenly caught sight of a claw like scratch on the side of Jona's neck. Jona noticed this and was quick to cover it with her hand.

Vlad asked: 'Who did that to you?'

She said: 'N-nobody, a dog did it to me.'

Vlad sighed and said: 'It may be true that I am in many ways cruel, unkind and ignorant but one thing I cannot abide to...the suffering of those around me, those that lead a simple way of life, those that refuse to inflict needless suffering on others.'

She looked at the headstone she stood in front of and remarked: 'No, I'm not innocent or a kindhearted person.'

Vlad asked: 'Why do you keep looking at the headstone in such a sad, longing way?'

She said: 'That's not something you have to know.'

Vlad replied: 'Fair enough but you know more about me from your uncle then I know anything about this so called Hunyadi family.'

He added: 'Not that it matters.'

She huffed and said: 'Alright, I'll tell you, the truth about everything, including where I got the scar from.'

Vlad listened to what she had to say.

Jona speaks:

In one time of the year during a harsh winter in the year 1443 in which I was 14 and my sister was 15, both of us, our father and mother as well, stayed with our cousins, our aunt and uncle in law John. We stayed in the Hunyadi house. I vividly remember those days and what happened back then.

She reflected on the past.

Transylvania, Hungary, 1443 AD, Grand Hunyadi House.

Jona stepped out of the carriage and onto the stone path that led to the house.

Her sister walked with her and asked her: 'Aren't you excited to see uncle John?'

Jona whined: 'No!'

Michael scolded her: 'Stop acting like a child...you are old enough to behave like an adult.'

A woman next to him said: 'Stop it already Michael, you've been acting like a madman since we first got in the carriage!'

Michael motioned for the guards and carriage driver to leave.

After that Michael bickered with his wife: 'Andreea, it's been a rough journey here!'

Andreea shook her head in a disappointed manner and debated: 'It's no excuse to treat our children like they are worthless peasants!'

Andreea pushed her daughters encouragingly towards the house and declared: 'Onwards we go, today will be a fun and exciting day amongst family!'

Once Andreea and her daughters were inside the house, in the entrance hall, a boy around her own children's age came up to her.

He smiled and said: 'It's good to see you again aunt Andreea!'

Andreea exclaimed: 'Same here Laslow.'

Ilona asked: 'How have you been doing Laslow and where is your brother?'

Laslow shrugged his shoulders and said: 'With our father, discussing family matters.'

He rolled his eyes and said: 'He is the older one after all.'

Jona crept behind her sister. Laslow laughed at Jona's shyness.

He stated to Jona: 'I'm only two years older than you, I'm not some big bully or something.'

Ilona said: 'It's okay, our father scolded her this morning so that's that.'

Laslow said: 'Well that's not the point, she's always like this when all of you come to visit.'

John came marching down the stairs with his eldest son Mathias who looked quite annoyed.

John ruffled Laslow's hair and said: 'Go get your mother, she's out by the old well.'

Laslow nodded and ran off.

Mathias stared at Jona. As if she was so interesting.

Ilona didn't like it so she asked: 'Why are you staring at my sister?'

Mathias brushed it off as something normal and went back upstairs. Later that day, Andreea's sister who was also the mother of Mathias and Laslow (the only way Ilona and Jona are linked to the boys as cousins) joined the two girls and their mother for lunch.

They sat outside by the old well on the grass.

Andreea's sister sighed and remarked while holding her arms up towards the faint sunlight: 'Ah, in this winter, I'm happy to even find a few rays of warmth.'

Andreea commented: 'Sister, we haven't seen each other for three years, that's all you can manage to say all the time.'

Her sister saw the two girls discuss something with each other. She went over and hugged her two nieces. Ilona and Jona complained.

They both said: 'Ugh, stop it!'

Their aunt said: 'Aw but you're both so adorable!'

Jona said: 'No we're not!'

Their aunt said: 'So I'm just a doting aunt eh.'

Their aunt added: 'Ah, Andreea, you're so lucky, you have two beautiful daughters, while I have two useless, worthless, annoying rascal sons.'

Andreea stated: 'But your son Laslow is so obedient and kindhearted.'

Andreea's sister complained: 'Sister, you are incorrect as my son Laslow spends most of his time practising the flute.'

Andreea remarks: 'But all our children are as ridiculous as we were when we were younger.'

Jona overheard her mother and aunt discussing things from their own childhood. For some reason, that Jona could not explain, she always wanted to know more about her Mother's upbringing and heritage. Because her Mother had never truly revealed anything about her past to her or her sister.

Jona asked her Mother out of curiosity: 'Mother why didn't you ever tell us about your life growing up?'

Andreea replied: 'Because my past has many things that I am not very fond of talking about and the less you know the better.'

Andreea's sister stated: 'Oh, why didn't you tell your children about their heritage? Because I told my sons all about theirs.'

Out of curiosity Jona asked her aunt for the answers she had been looking for: 'Aunt do you know anything and what was your past like, because Mother won't tell us anything.'

Andreea grabbed her daughter's hands and said to her sister: 'Don't you go around telling my daughters about our past.'

After that she left with her daughters and headed back to the house.

Finally it was night-time and Jona was lying in her bed that was across from her sister's. The room was cold because of the winter weather and even though it was chilly she decided to get out of bed. Then walk around the house. She wandered aimlessly, trying to make herself tired. But all she could think of was her Mother still kept many things hidden from her family. She decided that she would go and speak with one of her cousins. Jona quietly made her way to Laslow's room, trying not to raise any suspicion. Once she reached the room, she gently pushed open the door and then whispered his name without trying to startle him. Laslow awoke and slowly sat himself upright on the bed. Through the darkness he noticed the presence of someone who looked like Jona standing next to the door. Laslow slowly moved towards the door and saw for himself that it was Jona standing there. Jona closed the door.

In a calm manner she asked Laslow: 'Could you tell me anything you might know about your Mother's past?'

Laslow nodded in a sluggish manner.

He replied: 'Of course, I can tell you a few things I know.'

Laslow who sat on the bed and Jona who sat on a chair began to discuss the details of their family history.

Laslow said: 'My mother once told me that before she married my Father John Hunyadi, she and her sister Andreea came from the outskirts of Bistri which is close to Transylvania, their family consisted of a group of people that were called the travelling folk or as my mother preferred to call them, travelling people that went where the road or work took them.

My mother and her sister grew up with many constant ordeals and challenges filled with hard work and labour... the life she led with her sister only changed when she met my father, John Hunyadi, who was a wandering army dictator in his younger years.'

He continued: 'On one of his conquests to help the people of Hungary, he came across these travelling people who were in dire need of help... upon meeting these people he fell in love with one of the women...that woman was my mother... although marriage wasn't really allowed with outsiders, my father vowed to these people to support them as a folk and certain aspects of their culture... after that my parents got married in the capital of Buda, my mother's sister, Andreea, went to their wedding and met my father's tactician, Michael Szilagyi, both of them married later on as well. My parents moved together into the family home of the noble faction, Hunyadi, a year later in the year 1422 my brother Mathias was born, he was named Mathias Corvinus after my grandfather, Corvinus Hunyadi. Then five years later, I was born in 1427 and was named Laslow, after a deceased friend of my father... that is all I know about our family history.'

Jona had a strong look of disappointment. She asked herself: That's all mother wanted to hide from me? She shook her head and without exchanging another word with her cousin, she left the room.

The next morning, she woke up more confused than ever, she couldn't understand why her mother would hide some simple family history that was harmless. Jona hurried outside to go for a stroll to clear her mind when Mathias charged at her and shoved her against the stone wall.

Jona screeched: 'Leave me alone!'

Mathias shouted at her: 'You need to tell me what you are!'

Jona asked: 'Tell you what?'

Mathias frowned in an angry manner and said: 'I know you're like me... so why won't you show me.'

Jona stated: 'I don't understand what you mean.'

Mathias scoffed and said: 'Your mother didn't tell you... otherwise you wouldn't be so clueless.'

He stepped back and said: 'You're a werewolf, idiot... but a special one, like me... every single time you and Ilona came here in the past, I sensed something unique about you, but my brother and your sister, I never noticed anything of the sorts.'

Jona said: 'I don't believe you.'

He said before walking off: 'Both our mothers are also werewolves, so go ask your mother about it.'

Jona ran off in panic being convinced that if she didn't do something to distract herself... her world would crumble to nothingness with no hope to latch onto in her existence, the existence she thought was real. In her panic she accidentally bumped into her mother.

Andreea caught Jona to break her fall. Jona gazed at her mother with a questioning look.

Andreea sighed. She realised her daughter had discovered something she should have left buried in the past.

Andreea said: 'I knew it... you spoke with your cousins.'

Jona demanded to know: 'What does Mathias mean by werewolves?

Andreea thought she would never hear that word again. She never wished to hear it again. Andreea's eyes trembled with sadness. Tears began to gather in her eyes.

She said: 'It's true...I am a werewolf... so are you and so is my sister.'

Jona shook her head.

She yelled at her mother: 'I don't understand what a werewolf is... is it a monster... why won't anyone explain it to me!'

Andreea said while covering a necklace that hung around her neck: 'A while back, before you were born, I committed a crime, a friend that died by my hands, that's why I wear this moonstone necklace to this day to help prevent the same thing from happening again.'

Jona still couldn't understand what her mother was trying to tell her.

Jona ran off. Her mother shouted out her name but she wouldn't listen.

She hid in the stables till night time. It was dark there, shadows cast everywhere within like a deep and vast web cast across the ground and walls. There was one window in the stable from which Jona could glimpse the eerie moon from afar. Though this moon was white and full, standing out amidst the shining stars. That moon, there was something adequately disturbing about it. On the cold stable floors, Jona tried to scoot away from the pale moonlight but no matter the effort, the moon seemed to follow her every movement.

Suddenly, she felt her heart beating heavily like it was made of iron. A rush of pain and adrenaline pulsated through her body, through every bone and vein she could feel some abnormal shift between the change of time and reality. Those bones began to creak and twist rapidly like her form was changing to something else. The pain was true agony. She screeched.

Andreea had heard the familiar sound of a howling wolf. She feared for whom that might be. She ran outside towards the stables. Andreea's sister ran after her, concerned for the life of her own sister. As they both stood in front of the stables, a scary scratching sound came from behind the door. Like sharp claws scratching on the wooden door. *Scratch, scratch.*

Andreea pushed her sister behind her and said: 'Stay back.'

Her sister asked in a concerned manner: 'What are you going to do?'

Andreea said: 'Remember that time, when I lost control in my own wolf form and you brought me back from the clutches of my own prison?'

Her sister nodded.

Andreea remarked in a saddened tone: 'But today will be different...sister I need you to go back to the house and make sure everyone is okay, tell them it was a false alarm and make sure they stay there, I don't want John or Michael to discover our family secret and I don't want Ilona to come to fear her own sister because she isn't in her human form.'

Her sister hesitantly returned to the house.

When Andreea saw that her sister was gone, she said in a calm tone: 'Jona... I know you're still in there, I'm going to help you.'

She thought: Though I didn't think it would be so early for you to turn... I wonder what triggered this transformation.

She slowly pushed open the door. Once the door was open, Andreea stepped back for a moment. She was confronted by a wolf with dark fur and flashing white teeth. A beautiful but terrifying creature.

Andreea very slowly held out her hand in front of her.

She said in a soft tone: 'It's okay, it's me, your mother -I.'

Her sentence was cut short. The wolf growled at her and bit into Andreea's arm. The wolf's teeth bit deep.

Andreea screamed at first. A large quantity of blood trickled onto the ground. Steeped in blood, she quickly wrapped her other arm around the wolf. With her injured arm, she put the moonstone onto the wolf's forehead. The wolf growled even more. It bit into Andreea's hip and threw her against the stable wall. Before the wolf could finish off Andreea, it suddenly whimpered as if it was in a great deal of pain.

Suddenly the wolf began to change. Until the body of the human it had once been, collapsed onto the ground. Only Jona's sad eyes gazed up at Andreea. In a weakened state, she slowly crawled to her mother's side.

She cried: 'Mother, what have I done to you!'

She saw her mother lie there with no movement or signs of life. The sickening smell of blood she inhaled, it was her mothers. Once she had woken up to the reality of the horror that had taken place, her eyes widened.

She screeched: 'Mother!'

Jona moved away from her mothers body. Noticing that she lacked clothing. In the stables she found old rags that used to be used for horses.

Wrapping herself completely with those rags she went to the open barn door and glimpsed her aunt run down to the stables with Ilona and Laslow.

Ilona mad dashed towards her sister and hugged Jona tightly.

She asked her sister: 'Are you alright?'

Jona's blank and empty gaze made Ilona sad. Jona didn't reply to her sister's question.

Jona only blurted out: 'I-I killed mother...I wasn't willing to believe mother about our heritage and she paid the price.'

Ilona was confused at what her sister said and proceeded to bring back her sister to the house. But as Jona looked back at the stables while leaving with her sister, she spotted a hateful and judging look on her aunt's face.

As Jona and Ilona's aunt went into the stables, crying was to be heard.

Later that night, John was raving all about how he wanted to find the wolf that had killed his sister in law. Mathias explained it to Jona. Jona's mother told her sister to stay away from the barn and keep everyone safe meanwhile, she used every ounce of bravery to help Jona transition back to a human form but because Jona was only a fledgling with the power of the wolf, simply talking her out of it wasn't enough. Andreea was forced to use her moonstone to come in contact with Jona's presence to shatter the wolf form that Jona took on. Andreea's sister told her husband that a wild wolf had broken into the stables whilst Andreea was tending to the horses with Jona. Jona managed to break out of the stables and make it to safety. That is what Mathias told her behind closed doors.

He asked her mockingly: 'Do you understand now?'

He added: 'After all, your mother had to die so that you could understand how to control yourself.'

Jona twisted her mouth.

She said: 'I didn't ask for any wolf powers... I didn't want to kill my own mother... Mathias, how do you think that makes me feel!'

He stated: 'Life does not care for petty feelings neither for what anyone wants...I had a rough time learning to control my powers and I still haven't got a grip on them.'

He said: 'I learn to control it to protect myself, my brother and my mother as well.'

Jona asked: 'How did you learn to control it?'

He pulled out a moonstone necklace and pointed at the one that hung around her neck.

He said: 'Werewolves transform every full moon, but using this, we can weaken the effects of the moonlight...that is how my mother and your mother could hide their secret for many years without having to endure a great deal of pain.'

He eyed her suspiciously and said: 'But you... you're different... your transformation was triggered by something else...just like when I transformed for the first time.'

He added: 'If I could ask my mother what this is supposed to mean then I would but she refuses to speak to me... maybe she hates me for telling you about the history of werewolves in our family...I wouldn't know...just avoid asking questions and try to figure it out yourself but remember, do not take off that necklace especially on the night of a full moon.'

Jona solemnly looked at her necklace and said: 'I won't ever take it off, I will continue to wear it as a token of the shameful thing I have done and as a reminder of the person I will never ever see again.'

Jona's aunt entered the room. A deep tension was about. Jona could sense it. The hate emanating from her aunt. Her aunt walked up to her. She stared at Jona as if she was considering something. Then unexpectedly, Jona's aunt raised her hand and hit Jona in the face. Her aunt clenched her teeth.

She said: 'You are unbecoming of a wolf, you are a disgrace to everything your mother stood for and me and your mother's people...even I managed not to kill my own sister when I was a wolf... I see you for whom you are, I won't take my eyes off you now that I am so near to the truth.'

She went on to say: 'The truth that you are a cold blooded killer...you're not my sister's daughter, you don't belong anywhere... to believe that I protected your secret from John at the risk of revealing my own son...don't ever make me regret my decision.'

She trudged out of the room.

The next day, that morning where the cold winter breeze blew into the room, Jona just slept and kept on sleeping in the hopes that she might drift off and never wake up again. Ilona jumped on Jona's bed and rattled her sister to wake her up.

Ilona said to the half conscious Jona: 'Sister if you leave the window open like that you'll catch a cold!'

Jona said in a tired manner: 'Leave me to rest.'

Ilona pulled her sister closer to her and said: 'No, I am the older sister here, and I'm not going to abandon hope on you just like that.'

Jona asked: 'Aren't you tired of me?'

Ilona smiled and shook her head.

She replied: 'You are my sister, a part of me and we are a part of each other; I will never tire of you.'

Jona said: 'Then you need to promise me that it will always remain that way.'

Andreea Szilagyi was buried in the Hunyadi grave yard. Jona and Ilona left with their father Michael and returned to their home in the capital of Buda. But something changed that day. Jona grew more distant often sleeping outside at night or hiding from people during the day time because she was afraid. Afraid that she might kill her sister or father even if she wore that necklace. Like always, her being remained a mystery to even herself. Even Michael was different after the death of his wife.

Reflection over.

Transylvania, Hungary, 1452 AD, Grand House of Hunyadi.

The hand that covered Jona's scar trembled. She looked away from Vlad.

Vlad said: 'The headstone that is privileged by your longing gaze is that of your mother.'

Jona replied: 'Yes, here lies Andreea Szilagyi who was killed by a wild wolf...that creature that my uncle and cousin refer to as scoundrel was none other than me... I killed my own mother....so that should convince you enough...that I am a criminal.'

Vlad casually replied: 'I see, well from my experience, everyone has different view points...there are people in this world that wish to cause no harm nor ill fortune... even though I was born into this world, I've been given nothing but hatred, that of my own and others...you aren't a criminal unless you choose to be... unlike me, you still walk a path amongst the light so don't fret about the past, but in this case, my understanding for past suffering of both you and your sister shall not diminish.'

Jona smiled.

She said: 'My sister would swoon if she heard you say that.'

Vlad frowned and said: 'There's nothing else you can bicker about.'

Jona ignored his remark and said: 'Thank you for putting my thoughts at ease for now.'

Vlad said: 'Well nobody thanks me for things so don't bother.'

Jona muttered: 'Haven't you ever felt connected to someone before, someone that you share a mutual bond with...it's just you seem so vague.'

Vlad: 'Over a year ago I made an acquaintance with someone that came close to being a friend...but that does not matter.'

Jona stated: 'Earlier you asked me about the scar on my neck...my cousin Mathias did that to me over a year ago before you came to Hungary...we got into a fight about something back in Buda, but that's not something I want to talk about.'

Vlad asked her: 'So if you're a werewolf, shouldn't that scar have healed already?'

She explained: 'Wounds take longer for werewolves to heal when we're in human form.'

Vlad yawned and said: 'It would be best for me to retire for now.'

Jona

Szilagyi

Jona simply smiled to herself as he left.

The next morning, Jona approached Ilona and Vlad who were seated at a table and were discussing something with each other.

Jona waved about a letter.

Ilona noticed and asked her: 'Is it from Laslow?'

Jona replied: 'Yes, I'm surprised he even has time to write in Belgrade with the potential threat of the Ottomans.'

Ilona got up from her seat and took the letter from Jona.

Jona protested: 'Sister, that letter has personal details in it!'

Ilona read it in a quirky manner: 'My dear Jona... he called you dear, how sweet... next is, I long to see your face again, even though we've only been separated for a few months to me it feels like eternity... so my brother in law to be is a romantic, how nice, and continuing the letter is, the days are empty without you even though you and I weren't close growing up, there wasn't a time I couldn't regard you as a friend only in the last year, when my father, your uncle betrothed each other to us... I make a promise that upon my return we shall get married in the Hungarian capital.'

Ilona stopped reading. Jona had a look of embarrassment.

Vlad forced a humorous smile and said: 'You'll get married soon, congratulations according to that ridiculous love letter.'

Jona said in a defying manner: 'No, it's a heartfelt letter, considering this whole marriage thing between me and my cousin was arranged we put all our time and dedication into our relationship to make it work.'

Jona began to become teary.

She said: 'But after he and I get married...other things won't matter any more...I'll be forced to part with my sister to live somewhere else as newly weds... I won't ever truly get to see my family again!'

Ilona tried to calm her down and then said: 'But that won't matter, for sure as family we'll always find a way to see each other.'

Ilona slowly approached her sister but Jona stepped back.

Jona remarked: 'At that very day you remember the pact we made with each other, you said to me that I was your sister, a part of me and a part of each other, you claimed that you would never tire of me.'

Ilona reassured her: 'Yes, that's true, that pact will never vanish between us.'

Jona replied: 'I don't believe you.'

She hurried off.

As the night sky approached, Ilona stood out on a balcony and held Laslow's letter in her hands. Vlad couldn't ignore her sad demeanour.

He stood on the balcony with her and asked her: 'What is the matter?'

Vlad felt like a stranger to himself. Asking people if they were alright then tearing people apart. Hatred fuelled by violence and old resentful blood lust, a beast of the night. Now wrapping his arms around a warm and kind being.

He found that light or the hope that Ilona gave to him offered him the ability to show kindness and sympathy to the outside world. These fragile feelings that he hated, the ones he had rid himself of and torn the wings off it like a foolish child does to an innocent butterfly. Those feelings that made him weak but at the same time, it nourished his hatred, that hatred he felt like a relentless ocean, all vows of vengeance and memories of past sorrows dispersed like pollen in the wind, nothing else mattered. This hope was so dear and beloved to him. He wanted to keep it close and cherish it forever, he wanted to cherish Ilona forever. He realised for the first time in his life, he had attached himself once more to a mere mortal, he had fallen in love.

Ilona said to him: 'Vlad...there's no need to hug me, I'm alright.'

Vlad gazed at her face. She cried. Ilona wiped away the tears in an embarrassed manner.

Vlad said: 'If you feel sad, I can try to help you overcome that sadness.'

Ilona said: 'Oh, I'm not sad, I just don't know what to do with Jona any more.'

Ilona added: 'We used to be so close, now she's so distant and I have no understanding of why, what secrets she holds locked away, punishing her heart and weighing heavily on her conscience...I don't want that for her.'

Vlad asked her: 'Then what do you want?'

She replied: 'I want her to be honest and open with me...because she's right, when she gets married, I might never get to see her again...I just want some honesty.'

Vlad said to her with a frown: 'Then you're talking to the wrong person.'

Vlad sighed and said: 'Ilona, the time I have spent here, has opened my eyes to what I've always wanted and that's unconditional-'

Ilona cut him off and said: 'Love...seems strange, especially for you.'

Vlad said: 'No, I meant loyalty, all I've ever wanted or asked of life was someone to stay by my side, go through life's hardships with me and never lead my trust astray, unwavering loyalty but even that was not given to me in life.'

Ilona stifled a laugh; she said: 'You have had a dreadful life, Vlad, I can't help but feel deeply sorry for you... perhaps if you and I had met before, then I could have been there to hold your hand, be there for you to lean on when life took it's toll.'

Vlad said: 'You're the only one that listens to what I have to say with an open mind and a kind heart and this experience to have met you was the most memorable time of my life... but I wouldn't want you to come too close to me lest my darkness snuff out the remaining light in this world.'

He gently ruffled her hair and said: 'But I don't deserve forgiveness for the horrible things I have done and for the countless evil acts I am yet to do... you are the last person I'd want to see get hurt in the process.'

Ilona hugged him tightly and said: 'Stop being so hard on yourself... it's nobodies right to deem what is evil or good, there is no such thing but the choices we decide to make.'

Vlad murmured: 'Ilona, you are very dear to me...but I cannot burden you or myself with these uncanny feelings, please leave me be.'

He pushed away Ilona and stormed off the balcony.

Ilona could not help but feel guilty for forcing his hidden feelings to show.

The next midday, Vlad was told there was a war brewing in Moldavia and that with some help from John Hunyadi's forces he should go and fight in the hopes of overthrowing the usurper Petra Aaaron who was holding Vlad's distant cousin hostage. At this time, Vlad was about to depart with his men when Jona came running out of the house.

Vlad refused to look at Jona. He was in truth ashamed of his connection to both sisters. To Ilona he felt bonded together, giving each other the strength to survive but with Jona he felt like he stood in a bottomless hole filled with darkness or perhaps two festering moths that desperately search for the light. He was drawn to her darkness, her sorrow.

Jona shouted to him: 'Vlad...that night what you said to me in the grave yard...I hope you meant what you said.'

Vlad thought about what he said: 'I've been given nothing but hatred, that of my own and others...you aren't a criminal unless you choose to be... unlike me, you still walk a path amongst the light so don't fret about the past, but in this case, my understanding for past suffering of both you and your sister shall not diminish.'

Vlad said: 'I meant every word I said, I meant that very much.'

Jona asked in a demanding tone: 'Does that perhaps also mean that our relations to you won't diminish?'

Vlad replied: 'My bonds to both of you shall remain.'

He added: 'Jona, I promise that I will always remember the time I have spent here.'

Jona asked in a rushed tone: 'Will we see you again?'

Vlad did not answer her question. He simply rode off with his men. Jona knelt down on the stone path and tried repeatedly to fight back her tears.

Vlad wouldn't see Jona or Ilona for a good two years. In one year, he spent his time fighting off the supporters of Vladislav the second. It was a long war, it's expense was the loss of many countless lives. During this time, the true Vlad showed. Death was everywhere. All places Vlad looked and touched was decay of life. Most civilians in Moldavia began to believe that the lives of people seemed to be trivial matters to him, something to squash like a bug. A monster that has no feelings and kills like all acts of cruelty are premeditated.

Finally after utter loss and destruction, all the supporters and forces of Vladislav the second had been driven out of Moldavia and Petra Aaaron killed, Stephen was able to presume the role of Voivode of Moldavia. In the very last month of that year in 1452, Vlad met up with his cousin after Stephen offered soldiers to help fight against the Ottomans. Vlad considered it but only as an alternative in the future. He left his cousin to rule Moldavia. Only having just left Moldavia, he was summoned by the army of John Hunyadi to join them in the attacks on Belgrade. Upon hearing this, Vlad felt feelings of bitter hatred swell in his heart. No matter how much Vlad tried to fight against the idea of what his life had become, he couldn't overcome it, how his life had turned into an infinite battlefield.

Already had the next year begun. During the first month of this year, Vlad had arrived at the settlement site for the Hungarian troops. The army resided outside of the city, Belgrade. Apparently, John Hunyadi and his two sons were currently here as well. Vlad was shown to the dictator's tent and upon entering it he was greeted by John.

John inquired: 'Why are you looking so glum... are you alright?'

Vlad held his hand to John and said: 'I do not wish to discuss what horrors I have caused back in Moldavia.'

John sat down on a stool. He was seated at a small table that had a map on it. John was eyeing the map.

Mathias stated: 'I believe there was something you wanted to talk about with my father... I will go and see to it that the horses have their mounts prepared, make sure all weapons we can find are at the ready, all ready for combat.'

Mathias left the tent. A gust of wind shook the tent.

John's candle light dimmed.

John grumbled: 'Goodness sake, we've been fighting off these nasty Ottomans for a long time with the help of the Serbians but they just keep trying to invade Belgrade... we might win Vlad, I feel victory is within our reach but it has cost us many lives and I cannot even keep some random candle lit!'

 Vlad said in a monotone manner: 'Don't be so sure about that, Hunyadi, I've seen with my own eyes at the front of all this...what the enemy is like.'

Vlad closed his eyes in such a woeful manner. He thought to himself: 'That's right, I'm no better than them, those barbarians... Ilona, you have made me see the truth, you have made my eyes that were clouded by lies so clear... is my past enough to justify the cruelty of the things I have done back in Moldavia? Ilona and Jona, both of you have said to me many times, one is only evil when one chooses to be or that there is no right or wrong, only the persons intent to make it so. I don't understand myself any more. Those civilians I killed, the ones that tried to drive me out of their country with their pitch forks and soldiers... I was fighting a war within a war, trying to drive Vladislav II forces out of Moldavia to protect the simple people, the people I decided not to kill stood against me for no reason at all and in the end I killed the people I was supposed to safe guard. They feared me or feared for their lives...'

Vlad thought on: 'Am I actually choosing to be evil?'

'Like the promise that binds me to the dark side, to kill everyone that opposed me, my confession, I found it sublime, the killing of those that opposed me but I feel a disturbing tug towards my true dark feelings, a feeling that if I could, I'd kill everyone who forced me to endure and partake in this senseless war. Poisoning wells, spread of famine, money and homes taken and destroyed, livelihoods crushed, trenches dug making land barren and useless. I am exhausted with this life, that is the truth, it had always been so, fed up with betrayal, ignorance, neglect, jealousy and now all that is left is regret, the regret that I couldn't stay by Ilona's side.'

A sickening smell wafted into the tent.

Vlad frowned and asked John: 'Hunyadi, what is that smell?'

John replied in an agitated manner: 'Well, it is war against the Ottomans to keep them away from Belgrade and in war, people die.'

Vlad reproached him: 'I know that already...so people died, I smell smoke so I'm asking you what it is!'

John insisted for Vlad to stay. Instead, Vlad hastily left the tent in an angered manner. It was then that he inhaled the foul, rancid smell of rotting flesh melting away in a fire. Vlad looked towards where he saw heavy black smoke ascending into the grey sky. He saw a huge fire, in which he could see that bodies were stacked and piled atop each other. He saw guards and soldiers cough from the overwhelming deathly smell. More bodies were carried to another pile. One soldier was so injured that he could barely walk.

Vlad narrowed his eyes with a hint of sadness in them. He thought: 'This senseless war.'

Vlad continued to aid John and his forces against the Ottomans who wanted to invade Belgrade. The battle was harsh and unpredictable. Mehmed the conqueror's strong artillery and soldiers fought against John Hunyadi's tactical weapon wagons. Hunyadi's men would then be able to take cover to shoot down any enemies and use cleverly dug trenches. The war lasted the rest of the year in 1453. Incredibly, the

Hungarians held out but suffered catastrophic casualties. The Ottomans retreated.

Serbia, Belgrade Hungarian army settlement, end of 1453 AD.

A certain sense of tragedy lingered in the hearts and survivors of the war. Even John was grief stricken when he heard his son Laslow had been killed in a stronghold raid.

Vlad remembered that Laslow's last words were: 'Tell Jona that I am sorry for not being able to meet her at the other end of this lifetime and that I did love her.'

Vlad promised to tell Jona Laslow's final words. Mathias did not speak about seeing his own brother get killed in front of him. It was as if Mathias was somehow connected to his brothers death. Vlad knew about Mathias' wolf secret but did not think it necessary to bring it up as he had other problems to deal with, Vladislav the second was leading a rebellion against Hunyadi. Apparently, Vladislav demanded an immediate alliance and surrender of the Hungarians, in addition he strongly requested recognition as the Voivode of Wallachia. Hunyadi allowed Vlad to head to Wallachia with some men to deal with the problem.

During this time, the anger continued to posses his heart, the anger that was caused by his exhaustion that he had, had enough of fighting as he already had enough of that in his own family. The anger rose within him and with it, a deep desire to kill Vladislav, a strange idea that if he would kill him, some of his inner feelings would be put laid to rest.

Towards the end of this year to June in the next, he travelled to the mountains and foothills in the north to the plains in the south to gain support from the Wallachian Boyars to end Vladislav the second. He did so till his support was strong enough to battle once more.

Wallachia, Near Targoviste, June, 1454 AD

Finally after much support gathering, Vlad and his forces were able to corner Vladislav the second. On this day, the armies faced each other. Glares of fear, anticipation of being killed were what the soldiers exchanged with each other. The sky was grey and in the distance it thundered.

Vlad saw the man who was called Vladislav the second. Yet again, his inner resentment took hold of him.

Vlad yelled: 'Vladislav the second, of the Danesti faction I challenge you to a one on one duel to the death.'

A grin spread on his face; he added: 'Whomever wins, wins this entire war.'

Vladislav thought on it. In the distance he was seen on a horse. He hesitantly rode his horse towards Vlad. Eventually the two stood face to face. The man who felt like he had been battling against his entire life now stood against him. Vladislav narrowed his eyes at Vlad. He attacked first and so the duel began. The armies were not allowed to clash with each other.

In rapid moments which seemed like in the blink of an eye, Vlad cut down Vladislav. Vladislav knelt on the ground badly injured. All that Vlad had to do was deliver the final blow.

Vladislav peered upwards at Vlad. He laughed in a deranged manner.

Vladislav muttered: 'Do you think you are avenging the death of an honourable man?'

He added: 'Your father was far from that, the atrocities he committed, heh, why do you think the Danesti faction hates your family so much and now here you are thinking that your so called honour calls for the death for the one that wronged your life in so many ways possible.'

He scoffed and said: 'Go on kill me, plunge your lance inside me, fill yourself with mad hatred.'

Vlad asked: 'What do you mean by my honour?'

Vladislav said: 'Well, you want to show all of Wallachia what a brave man you are for taking me on in single combat and you want to honour your family and avenge your fathers death, so poetical and bold... but now this, my death alone will not be enough to win over the trust of your people for they have feared you and always will no matter the risks you take for them.'

Vladislav said: 'Now finish it off.'

Vlad was infuriated with Vladislav's statement. He threw his lance aside and grabbed Vladislav's head in a violent manner. Then intending to crush Vladislav's head with his bare hands, he was then prevented from doing so when feelings that did not belong to him came rushing forward. Sequences of thoughts and memories being displayed in his mind.

Bucharest, Wallachia, 1424 AD, Danesti tower.

Vladislav approached his sister who was embroidering something. Catalina smiled. Her rosy cheeks blushed.

Vladislav asked: 'So sister, I wonder why you prefer spending your time in this small, dreary room and why are you blushing?'

Catalina giggled; she said: 'Because you look ridiculous, brother, you need to clean your face, you have ash smeared on your face.'

Vladislav said casually: 'On the way in I re-lit the fire.'

Catalina smirked; she said: 'You're lying to me.'

Vladislav boasted: 'No I'm not.'

Both of their facial expressions changed when the guards shouted out the name: 'The Voivode of Wallachia, Vlad II Tepes and his wife, Vladana Eupraxia Tepes wish to enter!'

Catalina wanted to question her brother when he hurried out the room. Vladislav and Vlad met at the castle gate. He welcomed in the two.

Vlad greeted Vladislav.

Vladislav replied: 'So what brings you both here?'

Vlad said: 'Nothing, me and my wife were just passing through.'

He glanced at Vladana who looked away in a bothered manner.

Vladislav said: 'Ah, Vladana, it's been a long time since I have seen the two of you...I'm guessing both of you are experiencing marriage difficulties.'

Vladana turned her back to Vladislav and her own husband.

She said: 'Vlad and I rarely have the chance to spend time with each other, these are troubled times as is.'

Vlad whispered to Vladislav: 'Me and her don't mesh well in marriage, you know she's a grudge holder.'

Vladislav laughed very loudly: 'Aha aha hah, I believe that, you can come inside and join me and my family for dinner, then you can tell me all about these so called troubled times.'

Vladana sighed with a hint of annoyance and unwillingly followed the two men inside.

She murmured: 'How I wish I could spend these days with you, Vlaadia.'

Inside, an old man sat at the table.

Vladislav said to him: 'Grandfather, two people from the Draculesti faction have decided to come visit us.'

The old man seemed to be blind; he said: 'It does not matter, the Draculesti and Danesti were once both the Voivode of Wallachia through Basarab the Founder, whatever will come, our two divided factions will always be connected.'

Vladislav pointed out: 'Don't mind my grandfather, he clearly hasn't been the same since my parents were killed in a robbing incident.'

All sat at the table now. Vlad II explained how the Dragon Order strived to keep the Ottomans out of Wallachia, Serbia and Hungary to keep out the enemy faith. He told everyone how he befriended the founder of that order, the King of Luxembourg.

Vladana only stared at her food. But the excitement was interrupted when a little boy came dashing towards Vladislav.

Vladislav exclaimed in a surprised tone: 'Kazaan, what are you doing down here, you should be upstairs and in bed.'

Kazaan continued to gaze at Vladislav.

Vladana's attention seemed to be caught by the child.

She asked him: 'Oh who is this charming young man?'

Kazaan smiled at the lady.

Vladislav explained: 'He is my grand cousin, sadly his family was killed by an Ottoman attack in Giurgiu and now the only family he has is me, my grandfather and my sister.'

He said: 'Quite a curious four year old.'

Vladana offered the boy a piece of bread. He frowned and stepped back.

She asked Vladislav: 'What's wrong with him?'

Vladislav replied: 'He refuses to speak or trust people after what he probably saw when his parents and other family were killed.'

He added: 'He was a sole survivor.'

Catalina walked into the room. She pulled Kazaan away from Vladislav.

Vlad abruptly stood up from his chair while gazing at Catalina. Vladislav looked at Vlad then back at his sister.

He asked then with a hint of confusion: 'Do you two know each other?'

He added: 'Because I happen to leave my sister out of most affairs.'

Catalina said: 'No, I don't know him, he just happened to stare at me.'

She left the room with Kazaan. Vladislav felt suspicious about Vlad.

Later on, Vlad and his wife were allowed to stay in Bucharest for the night. In fact they stayed in the room opposite to Vladislav's. The entire night, fighting and yelling was to be heard from the room.

Days passed. Vlad refused to speak with his own wife and she with him. Catalina received flowers from an anonymous person every morning and night. Vladislav questioned her in regard to where she had gotten all the flowers from. She only said that she didn't know.

Vladislav knew his sister had many admirers, after all, she was known as Catalina the fair but did not expect all the fake tributes to his sister. He decided that if he found out who was sending his sister all those things, he would confront him and threaten him to leave his sister alone as dozens of measly flowers weren't enough to ask for her hand in marriage. She was after all dear to him, the only close family Vladislav had left. It was one day that Vladislav was reviewing a map that a cartographer had drawn up for him that he had heard screaming from his sister's room. He hurried to get to his sister. By the time he reached her, she was on the floor, backed up to the wall; with a scared and traumatised look on her face. When she saw her brother enter the room, she broke into tears.

She cried: 'Vladislav, brother, I-'

She yelled in a broken tone: 'Get out of here, I don't want you to see me like this!'

Vladislav sat down at her side. Catalina buried her face in her lap.

He asked her: 'Whatever is the matter sister?'

She sniffled and said in a quiet tone: 'Don't ask me, the sheer thought of that ghastly man touching me, wrecks me and crushes me to bits.'

He inquired: 'By what do you mean by a man touching you?'

Catalina spoke the name so specifically, like gentle dust settling somewhere.

Vladislav's eyes grew with deep anger. He had a scowl on his face as he rushed out of the room.

As he saw the one he directed his anger towards, outside the castle grounds he jumped at Vlad (Voivode of Wallachia and leader of the Draculesti faction) and pounded him to the ground.

Vladislav (leader of the Danesti faction) clutched Vlad's shirt tightly. Vladislav balled his hand into a fist and held it above Vlad's (Vlad II is Vlad III Tepes's father, is the Voivode of Wallachia and leader of the Draculesti faction and lives in Turnu, Vladislav is the leader of the Danesti faction, Vladislav lives in Bucharest) nose.

Vladislav said in a disappointed tone: 'I thought we were friends... why did you; what brought you to act the way you did?'

He practically yelled at Vlad: 'Why did you defile my sister's honour and betray my trust? You traitor, you filth, you deserve to live in the mud with pigs and rats, now I truly despise you.'

He ordered the men of the Danesti Tower to have Vlad and his wife sent back on their way to Turnu.

To this, Vladislav's excuse was: 'My guests have simply over stayed.'

But ever since that day, a tension between the factions, Draculesti and Danesti was brewing.

Two months passed, another complication struck the Danesti faction when Catalina discovered she was with child. It was a chaotic and saddening time, where Vladislav was forced to sent to send his sister to a nunnery to have her child somewhere unknown to all. There was no other way, Vladislav was too weak to kill his own sister and innocent unborn child. Neither could he allow his sister to suffer from poisons and concoctions made to kill unborn infants. He struggled in convincing himself that it was the best thing to do. Six months later, Vladislav had an envoy convey a message to him that his own sister had taken her own life after child birth. A shocked Vladislav made haste to the nunnery.

At the nunnery, he found his own sister hanging from the ceiling. Her body strung up by tied knotted together bed sheets. The nuns refused to remove her body, claiming it was a harbinger of evil. The nuns would touch their foreheads to make crosses and walk out the room.

Vladislav had Catalina's body taken back to the home of the Danesti faction and buried there. The baby was abandoned by it's mother and not known of by it's own father. Vladislav took the bastard child with him. The baby stayed with Vladislav at the tower for many days. Vladislav was at a loss as to what to do with the baby. It might be part Danesti but it was also part Draculesti. Over these days, Kazaan would smile at the newborn baby. Even attempt to speak with it.

On one lifeless day, Vladislav knew what he had to do. He snatched the baby away from Kazaan.

Kazaan said: 'But, he not belong anywhere else, he never be accepted anywhere else cause he bastard.'

Vladislav frowned at his cousins attempt to speak.

He stated: 'No, he doesn't belong anywhere, least of all with us.'

Kazaan said: 'Radu won't grow up to be good person if he surrounded by bad people.'

Vladislav asked: 'Where did you get that name from?'

Kazaan replied in a nervous tone: 'Was name of my younger brother, he's no longer alive.'

Vladislav ignored Kazaan and bolted out the door.

Vladislav and a group of his men rode to a castle in Turnu. The castle in which Vlad the second of Draculesti lived with his wife.

When Vladislav arrived there, he forced his way through the barely open castle gates. He demanded to speak with the Voivode. Vlad the second walked out upon request.

He said while trying to calm down Vladislav: 'Friend, please tell me what brings you here.'

Vladislav replied in a vicious tone: 'Don't call me that, traitor!'

He shoved the baby into Vlad's arms.

Vladislav said: 'He belongs to you, your property, your petty bastard.'

Vladislav boasted in a daft manner: 'Hah, a bastard for a bastard, seems perfect.'

Vlad frowned. Vladislav's men laughed.

Vlad's guards pointed their weapons at Vladislav, however, the potential skirmish was brought to an abrupt halt when a woman who looked like Vladana came running towards the two men.

Vlad gave the infant to his wife in a frustrated manner.

Vladana said in a surprised tone while holding the baby: 'Where did this baby come from?'

Vladislav threatened: 'Both of you will take in this child... or else I will tell every single Boyar in Wallachia of the treachery and deceit you have committed against my family, then they will refuse to support you, with it you will lose your title as Voivode of Wallachia.'

Vlad sighed and said: 'Very well.'

He intended to force his wife back inside.

But Vladana turned around one last time before heading inside and asked Vladislav: 'What is the baby's name?'

Vladislav carelessly blurted out: 'His name is Radu, a name my young cousin suggested.'

Vladana mouthed the name Radu.

Vlad commented: 'It doesn't matter what his name is as long as he doesn't bear the name that marks the heir to the throne, after all, he isn't a legitimate child, only a bastard of mine.'

Vladana was about to question her husband what Vladislav had meant by bastard child. Vlad only said he would explain everything once they were inside.

Vladislav could not rid himself of his hatred towards Vlad, because of him, the very man he had once trusted had become the reason his life felt empty and dull, the reason his sister killed herself. Vladislav vowed then and there to get vengeance on the Draculesti family and claim the title that was rightfully his, the title of Voivode, that title that had been stripped from his own family for generations.

After getting what he wanted, Vladislav left Turnu.

Wallachia, Near Targoviste, June, 1454 AD

The immediate rush of overwhelming feelings dispersed. Vlad knew now what he had seen as he had touched Vladislav's head, he had somehow established a psychic connection to Vladislav's mind. He knew everything his enemy knew and had seen everything he had seen all in that brief moment, those flashes of memories felt so real. They also revealed the truth about Vlad's parents. Especially his father. Vlad felt sick just thinking about how Radu was his half brother, how his own entire childhood prepared him to become the next Voivode.

As a boy, Vlad had constantly prayed that the burdening title would be placed on his older brother, he never understood because in every royal or noble bloodline, the eldest are always in line to the throne. If Vlad had known the truth about his brother, some of his hatred towards Radu would have been dimmed. But Radu would never be allowed to the throne because once a bastard always a bastard. The true ideal that bothered him was that everyone who knew the truth about who Radu really was, was told to keep it a secret from everyone and to act as if Radu the Handsome had always been the son of Vladana Eupraxia Tepes and Vlad. One who knew was Istvan. The one person Vlad thought of fondly in his memories, was in truth the person who kept telling him the biggest lies. Istvan kept saying how Vlad was the legitimate heir and as a quick excuse to Vlad's complaints was that Radu was not fit to be a Voivode, he was too idiotic and stupid. In truth, Radu would never be able to rule because he was a bastard son.

Now, Vlad understood why he was the one to be named after his father. Finally, Vlad understood everything, how his life up until now had still been teeming with lies, but he decided to not tell anyone about this truth, the only thing that mattered was to use this as a peace of mind and help recover from the lies, finally he understood the story behind his brother's estranged and humiliating existence. Though right now Vlad intended to end this feud once and for all but not to honour the vow he made to his father; a vow to eradicate all that crossed him. Nothing else mattered.

Vladislav said in a voice that lacked emotion: 'In the end, I failed to uphold the oaths I had made to myself...looking back I wished that I had killed Vlad II on the spot rather than endure these pointless charades, I also wished to have killed Radu the Handsome the first second I held him and had him in my grasp, that abomination.'

Vlad (Vlad the Impaler) huffed; he replied: 'I pity you, in some way... I know the words, I just can't explain how I can relate to you.'

Vladislav scoffed; he said: 'Don't pity me, you should keep those pitiful feelings for yourself.'

His eyes gazed so specifically at Vlad.

He added: 'One day, if that day should come to pass, you will become just like me, consumed by hatred that knows no bounds, lonely to no end, desperate to set ones ravenous hands on vengeance by killing innocents in the hopes that someone will kill us and end our misery or someone to understand us. Since the light that once lived in our lives was either taken or severed... blissful and a true living hell...I can feel the same doors open for you, like the ones opened up the path of hate for me, they are opening slowly.'

Vlad frowned; he said: 'I have always come to terms with who I am, as such, I am aware that I am a monster already, I cannot succumb to darkness if I've already succumbed to it and with that I am going to end you.'

Vlad held his lance firmly then he thrusted it into Vladislav. Vladislav coughed blood. Blood gushed out of his wound. Vladislav's eyebrows twitched. In Vladislav's last moment, the final expression on his face was that of drifting to sleep. It was as if Vladislav truly waited for someone to kill him.

Vlad ripped the weapon out of the body. Vladislav crashed to the floor. He was dead.

The soldiers that had joined Vlad were cheering him on. Vlad only asked himself: How does it always come down to this... when I kill for the better of my people, they watch onwards with frightened looks...they know I would never harm them without reason and yet when I kill with no true intentions, the onlookers cheer me on and applaud me... I don't want to be this way, a killer yet with every heart beat, I feel immense joy at the suffering of others even when I choose not to... there's no denying that I truly am a monster, that is the only thing that remained the same so far.

The other forces retreated. Vlad breathed easily for the first time in ages.

Vlad reported back to John who had returned to Transylvania. Upon Vlad's arrival in Transylvania, he pondered over what he could have done with the last two years instead of taking part in some random and pointless wars. Vlad still had his suspicions about the fact if he was truly free of his war time. Vlad arrived at the house and rode up towards it. That was when he remembered that he had promised Laslow to deliver his final words to Jona.

Vlad now felt the fact as to how much he really had missed hearing the two sisters speak with each other. As Vlad got off the horse, he could hear and sense someone running towards him.

She cried out in a cheerful manner: 'Vlad, you came back!'

Vlad immediately sensed it was Ilona. He didn't even have to focus on any other detail or turn around to look at her. He could telepathically sense her. He asked himself whether his telepathic powers were getting stronger. Still Vlad didn't know much about his own powers. If only Lucien was there to explain it to him. Now he realised that he even missed Lucien though it was not much.

Vlad turned to see Ilona standing there with a smile though there seemed to be more to it. Her smile was almost nostalgic. Vlad could sense her feelings were somehow sad.

Ilona said: 'I am grateful that you are here...I don't know what I would do without you.'

Vlad asked her: 'Ilona, what is the matter?'

Ilona explained while breaking into tears: 'My uncle, he died over a week ago...while you were fighting against Vladislav in Wallachia, nobody was able to relay a message because of the war... he died of the plague, he must have contracted it back in Serbia...I don't know what to say.'

She covered her face using her hands.

Vlad wrapped his arms around her and said: 'He was quite important to you even though he was only your uncle in law.'

Ilona said: 'He was the only man that treated me with respect other than Laslow who is also dead, he was the supportive father I should've had.'

Vlad noticed Michael walk towards them. Michael had a serious look on his face. He looked cross.

Vlad pushed away Ilona and went inside.

Ilona wondered what Vlad had to discuss with her father. Then it dawned on her, Vlad came here to be pardoned from serving the Hungarian forces. If he is allowed to return to his home land, she won't be able to see him too easily and there were still many things she wanted to tell him. She ran into the house to find Vlad talking with Jona. Something about Laslow's final words. Jona seemed to be affected by every word she heard. After Vlad's discussion with Jona, Jona simply shrugged her shoulders and went upstairs.

Vlad felt like he had made Jona sad. He himself felt confused. Vlad felt glad that for a moment in his life he didn't have to kill someone. But something, a feeling was making him feel confused.

Ilona walked up to him and said: 'Before you return to Wallachia, I must ask of you one favour.'

Vlad's confusion wandered.

He told her: 'If it's one person I'd do a favour for it would be only for you and your sister.'

Ilona said: 'There's a small town nearby in which there is a tavern situated... there away from prying eyes and ears I'd like to discuss something personal with you.'

Ilona smiled nervously and walked away.

Later that day, Vlad did as Ilona had asked of him and went to the tavern. The tavern reeked of foul old food and sour drinks, because of Vlad's heightened sense of smell, he could smell everything just like he could read the thoughts of everyone there. One man thought of punching someone and another thought about women. Vlad was disgusted to be able to read peoples minds like a book. Vlad asked the tavern keep where a woman named Ilona might be. They only said that they've never had someone under that name in the tavern before. But then suddenly a woman that sounded like Ilona said his name. Vlad glanced at the person who had said his name.

Ilona sighed, she looked relieved; she said: 'Vlad, there you are, I've been looking everywhere for you.'

Vlad replied: 'I've been looking for you as well.'

He asked her: 'May I ask why you wanted to meet me here... in this dirty and overcrowded place?'

Ilona rolled her eyes casually, she smiled and gently pulled Vlad out of the tavern.

She remarked: 'Foolish Vlad, I didn't mean the actual tavern.'

She pulled him to a secluded room and closed the door behind them.

Vlad asked her: 'Did you hire this room?'

She replied: 'I paid the bar keep to use this room for a few hours.'

She sat down on the poorly made bed and went on to say: 'Look, I wanted to talk to you about the entire situation.'

He sat down next to her and asked her: 'What entire thing?'

Ilona sighed with a hint of annoyance, she sprung up from where she sat and paced back and forth.

She bickered: 'You never change, you're so close to me yet so distant, even now you wear your suit of armour as if there's another battle to be fought!'

Vlad said to her: 'Ilona, I wear this to be able to fight, I was part of a bloodied war that lasted nearly three years...it is not of my choosing.'

She calmed down and said: 'I know and I'm sorry...I shouldn't have hurt your feelings like that.'

She explained: 'It's just that...well every single time I reached out to someone in the past I got hurt, I must be such a fool, I never experienced what it feels like to be cherished by someone and ever since that accident with my mother and the rift that causes distance between me and my sister, those feelings of love or compassion have faded.'

She added: 'The only person that makes me feel like I exist is you Vlad, instead of talking to a wall.'

She sighed and said: 'There I said it, I have feelings for you, now don't lie to me, I know how you feel about me, I know how many times you told me of how terrible you are and every time you and I spoke to one another, those feelings came to light, you barely wanted to be around me because you were afraid that something bad might happen to me.'

Vlad confessed: 'You are right Ilona, I myself have said to you that I did not wish to burden you with my uncanny feelings for you...but I never lied or hid my feelings for all this time you knew how I felt about you...there is a reason though that I cannot let myself be overcome by my feelings for you...I am a criminal, even if you might not believe it... others do, it does not matter to me as I continue to slaughter innocents but what matters to me is how you see me... your kindness makes me feel like I'm the worst person alive no matter what the intention behind my actions, yet I wish to be a better man... these feelings only grant me confusion, they tear me apart, these pesky feelings that constantly nag me.'

She explained: 'I see you for who you are, it doesn't matter why you're like this or what people think of you, both you and I have had our difficulties... I am and always will be in love with you.'

Vlad shuddered at the word 'love'. It is not something someone had ever said to him before.

He asked: 'Would you still feel that way if I told you my darkest secret?'

Ilona smiled and said: 'Try me.'

He revealed: 'I am a born vampire.'

Ilona's smile faded; she then replied casually: 'I believe you.'

Vlad was astounded. He did not expect her to believe him that easily.

She said: 'In my family, my aunt once spoke of a certain witch... she often spoke of this witch as if she had truly existed...her name was Olga the Wise, I of course never fully believed in this tale until one day I came across my aunt's moonstone necklace... I had seen it gleam once so beautifully as if magic had been bestowed upon it.'

She added: 'Now I believe this witch truly existed, so if witches exist, why shouldn't these so called vampires exist as well.'

Vlad pulled her closer in a tight hug.

He said to her: 'Ilona, why must you always make everything so difficult for me...you know now how precious you are to me but with every word you say, every word of love or passion makes me suffer.'

Ilona mumbled: 'I don't understand.'

Vlad said: 'When I'm around you I feel this light but it causes me pain knowing that a man like me doesn't deserve your attention.'

Ilona stated: 'But I told you that I have feelings for you and you told me that you feel the same way.'

Vlad said: 'Well I suppose I could give into those feelings just this once.'

He kissed her. Ilona was surprised at his action. She kissed him back. Both in that one moment could no longer resist each other. When the intimate moments had passed, Ilona and Vlad put back on their clothes.

Ilona smiled at him.

He said to her: 'I have to go and you have to return to your home as well, otherwise your father will worry.'

She scoffed, got up and got dressed in her plain coloured garment.

She replied: 'My father never worries for me or my sister.'

After both were dressed and ready to leave, Vlad insisted: 'I will accompany you back home.'

Ilona frowned.

She asked him: 'Do you think I can't defend myself and return home on my own?'

Vlad did not reply.

She sighed and said: 'Alright, I'll return back with you on horseback.'

Vlad and Ilona did not speak with each other on the way back. A sort of tension that they might not see each other again prevented them from speaking with each other.

Vlad dropped off Ilona at the front of the old Hunyadi house. She let go of his hand and smiled sadly.

Vlad said to her: 'What we shared, I will cherish in my heart for a long time.'

He hesitantly left Transylvania and embarked on the journey home.

In the war that nearly lasted three years, countless people were killed. Vlad impaled some of them. In the end all that had opposed him were all killed. He did it for two reasons. A warning to the neighbouring countries not to underestimate Vlad Tepes III and because the war tormented him. As he killed each and every person, he thought about the possible lives he had destroyed. Eventually he began seeing things on the battlefield, a world being burned in an engulfing fire. The body count continued. The merciless and needless bloodshed continued into the dark days. Towards the end, a war that nearly lasted three years between Wallachia, Hungary and the Turks, Vlad had become just like his ancestor Vlad I, the first Tepes, the first Impaler (In the Romanian language Tepes means Impaler).

When the tiresome war was finally over, Vlad returned to Targoviste after nearly three miserable years.

Targoviste Wallachia, December, 1454 AD:

For the first time that felt like forever, Vlad was allowed to sleep on an actual bed again without his lance.

Although, at night, Vlad barely got an eye shut for the ghosts of his past tortured his mind. In the morning, the sunlight that filtered in rays of light from the window, blinded Vlad. Neither way did he get good sleep. Vlad remembered, it had been only six months from returning from the battle field. He had not heard anything from Ilona or Jona. He woke up in this specific morning to find Fenna standing in the castle corridor at a clothes rack.

Fenna noticed Vlad yawn. Fenna's face lit up with excitement.

She said: 'Oh, good morning Vlad!'

Vlad rubbed his eyes and asked in a tired manner: 'Is it truly... a good morning?'

Vlad muttered: 'I remember it seemed like only yesterday that it was the most horrid morning and days of my life.'

Fenna tilted her head in confusion.

She remarked: 'Vlad, you look awfully tired, like you've got no energy at all, oh you're too restless, now go back to sleep Vlad.'

She pointed into his room. Vlad eyed travel outwear.

He asked her: 'What are you doing with my outwear?'

Fenna traced with her hand, the stitches on the outwear that hung on this rack and explained: 'Sometimes I feel like you hate me, all I've ever wanted to be is a helpful friend, I do so many deeds and clean up work here but not that anybody notices it, so if it's one thing I can do for you, maybe, just maybe I won't be taken for granted... so I'm mending your clothes so you can wear it again.'

Vlad smiled a bit, just a little.

He said: 'Nobody takes you for granted Fen, and I don't hate you... it's just, you and I have never been close, not really enough to even consider you as family...it's just that with my side of the family, it's always been lacking with the term family.'

Fenna exclaimed: 'Well, Vlad, nobody really appreciates your efforts you do for this country... so maybe that's one way you and I can relate.'

She added: 'Despite the rumours about you.'

Vlad stated sharply: 'Fen, I am fully aware of those rumours, that I am a barbarian and demon born child... just don't be bothered by them.'

Fenna said in a nervous manner: 'Um, o-okay, sorry I said anything.'

Vlad nodded in all seriousness; he said to her: 'They aren't true.'

But all Vlad wanted was to convince Fenna not to believe in those rumours, since she was from his inner family circle, he didn't need these rumours that were actually true to reveal the truth about him and infiltrate his family.

Vlad was about to return to his room when Fenna abruptly said: 'I don't believe in those rumours for a second, I don't believe you're a monster like people say you are.'

Vlad ignored what she said and returned to his room. He slammed the door shut behind him.

He muttered: 'So you say... Fen you know nothing of the world that I must bare witness to every day I breathe.'

The next day, Vlad gathered the war council to discuss creating support for his voice amongst the people using the power of the catholic church in Wallachia. He decided to have various churches and monasteries built and have Wallachian priests not foreign ones, one example of a monastery he would have built is the one at Snagov lake which is located near Bucharest. Vlad dealt with these things to strengthen his reign as Voivode. But soon along came another pressing matter. Vlad received multiple messages from the Ottoman Turks. Requesting passage through Wallachia to attack Hungary or to send payment or trade of Wallachian resources to the Ottomans. Vlad strongly and firmly stood to his own principles. He refused to do anything they demanded from him. Soon after all that, the Ottomans sent two envoys to speak face to face with Vlad. Vlad of course pretended with the fake gestures of inviting them to Targoviste to have 'talks', with the Voivode.

Targoviste Wallachia 1454 AD, court of the Voivode.

Vlad sat upright in his makeshift throne. He eyed the two Turkish envoys suspiciously. They wanted to speak but dared not.

Vlad now beckoned for them, to speak.

One of them spoke in Wallachian: 'We have come to address that the Sultan wishes an audience with you in Constantinople.'

Vlad stated: 'Whatever your sultan wishes to speak, he could have said through the two of you.'

Vlad thought back on what had happened to his father back when they had gone to Edirne.

The envoy replied: 'What the sultan wishes to discuss is something to discuss behind closed doors.'

Vlad tapped a finger on his arm; he replied: 'If it's one thing I've learned in a war that lasted nearly three years is not to trust other countries especially the Turks, they are liars and rats in all things.'

The envoys glared angrily at Vlad's statement, taking it in as a direct insult.

One of the envoys said: 'Don't insult the Ottoman ways.'

An adviser of Vlad tried to suggest something but Vlad grew tremendously annoyed with the Turkish envoys.

Vlad stood up angrily and his voice boomed: 'What I find insulting are your hats... it is a direct act lacking respect, nobody in my court is allowed to wear such tacky things to undermine my status as ruler... in addition, I hate those hats due to the fact that both of you might be hiding daggers underneath them!'

Vlad sighed angrily.

He demanded: 'Take them off.'

The envoys refused.

One of them said: 'In the Ottoman ways, we men hold these hats sacred, they are special to us.'

The other said: 'It is not us who lacks respect but you who cannot stand the Ottoman religion.'

Vlad threw himself into his throne.

He muttered: 'So your hats make you special, more than anyone else in this world, they are so special that you can't even walk into a room without them and not be hailed a saint, like the whole world will rot and die, the end of the world itself if you take off your hats for even a second.'

Vlad stated: 'Men, I have seen enough loss of life, tragedy, plundering and decay of life and land... I don't feel inclined to compromise, nor show compassion for anyone... enough of my life time had been squandered in that war... I lack patience.'

Vlad motioned for his guards to seize the two envoys, and for another to bring two hammers and a hand full of nails from the torture chamber.

Vlad explained with a dry sense of humour while crossing his arms: 'If they wish to feel so special, I alone will grant them a once in a life time opportunity to never have to remove their holy hats again.'

The envoys were forced to their knees. They had frightened looks on their faces.

Vlad rounded up the people in his court and declared: 'People... a special... Vlad edition demonstration...specifically reserved for the people that choose and claim to be special, those that do not have common understanding of how the world here by me works... anyone defies me, they die.'

He added: 'Also, a portrayal of my respect for the Ottoman faith... they wish to keep their hats on, they can keep them on forever.'

The other guard returned with the hammers and nails.

Vlad announced: 'Six nails hammered through each hat.'

The guard gulped knowing he was forced to do so while the envoys still wore their hats. The guards held the envoys tightly whilst the one with the hammer proceeded to hammer the nails in.

Fenna who was scrubbing castle floors could hear screaming coming from the Voivode's court. Fenna wondered if she would oppose Vlad in any way... would he have her punished as well? She questioned how far Vlad's brutality may go in the future. 'To what length would he go? To what person had Vlad become?' Fenna shrank back at her own questions. Trying to convince herself that there was nothing wrong with Vlad. Vlad was her friend and cousin, that's how she tried to see it.

Later on, Vlad had the heads of the envoys severed, wrapped in old rags and tied together by ropes that were knotted together in a bow tie formation. The packaged heads were sent to Constantinople.

Just as Vlad had finished dealing with another matter, another problem surfaced. A Boyar was rebelling against the Draculesti faction, joining sides with the other Boyars and fallen nobles.

Vlad had a simple idea to deal with these traitors. He rode to where the Boyar lived and had him and his entire family impaled. Nobody escaped.

With the problematic Boyar dealt with... other remaining Boyars were poisoned against Vlad. Vlad invited them for a banquet under the false belief that he wanted to reward his loyal supporters. The Boyars had heard of Vlad's extensive list of notorious acts yet chose to ignore it, knowing the danger, they went with their wives and children to this banquet. When the banquet was nearly over, the Boyars were convinced that no ill fortune would come upon them, how wrong they were. Vlad stormed in and interrupted the ending of the banquet. He had each and every person there, dragged out by force only to be impaled outside in front of the castle in Targoviste. Though he had the children separated and kept as slaves for future investments. Vlad even partook in the arts of impaling and strongly lectured the guards who had helped him how to impale correctly.

Once all were impaled, Vlad commented: 'How remarkably plump some of them still look... must have been the food they ate before being impaled.'

He now laughed hysterically and said: 'Bah hah, and the way they still twitch, it's hilarious!'

One of the guards faces turned pale. He frowned at Vlad.

Vlad noticed and scowled: 'Stop staring or you'll be next to be impaled!'

In the evening on that same day, Vlad felt tired, he felt so that way that he thought he might give up staying awake and crash to the floor. Fenna who was still cleaning up in the castle noticed the distraught Vlad walking down the corridor. Fenna saw he was about to collapse so she ran to brake his fall.

She said while heaving him up and bringing him to his bed chamber: 'Hey, it's okay, I'm here for you, you know... if you want someone to talk to I'll be just around the corner.'

She sighed and was about to leave the room when Vlad abruptly replied: 'Fen, thank you for your kind gesture... but the last thing I intend to do for the rest of my life is talk about my personal issues... I have other matters to deal with that weigh heavily on me each day... so please don't make me your obligation, don't waste your time on the likes of me.'

Fenna left the room.

She said in her mind: 'With my mother dead, what am I to do these days...marry an old man who might be worse of a man than my own barbarian cousin...I believe the safest place is to be around a barbarian rather than an abusive man, at least the barbarian acts with reason though with cruelty, I do not make you an obligation Vlad... you just happen to be the last family I have that I care about.'

Vlad read Fenna's thoughts. He knew what she had said in her mind.

Vlad replied: 'The shift between good and bad is tiresome... forgive me Fen but it is not you in whom I would seek comfort but in that of someone else who cannot be here with me...I guess I'll never change, the good and bad in me will always be the same.'

Vlad drifted into a deep sleep.

Targoviste Wallachia, January 1455 AD:

Time shifts, we love we hate, why is it that I can only hate, is it perhaps because it's the only true emotion I've ever come to know? Vlad pondered over this in his sleep.

A woman in a long grey dress came into his room and had the servants get him ready.

She said: 'Rise and shine cousin!'

Vlad sat upright in the bed with his pillow balancing on his head. He had this awful glare towards Fenna.

Fenna pulled back her medium length hair and complained: 'Your brother is coming here to congratulate you on your war victory and for both of our sakes, don't make a scene, we don't want Radu telling the war advisers that you were not acting like a warrior prince.'

Vlad sighed with a hint of annoyance: 'Why must this life plague me with that bastard...where on earth was he this entire time while I was going tooth and nail to keep everything in Wallachia straight!?'

Fenna smiled in an awkward manner and asked him: 'What, you don't remember?'

Vlad asked with greater annoyance: 'Remember what?'

Fenna stated: 'You sent Radu on a conquest to make a deal with the people of Braila to found a church there of Wallachian catholic belief... you strictly told him that through the power of that religion it could be your voice amongst the common people...you also sent him to deal with insubordinate priests in Bucharest.'

84

Vlad replied: 'Yes those arrogant priests that continued to ignore me even after various visits to Bucharest...in the end, I was too occupied to deal with the them so I sent my stupid brother to do exactly what was needed to be done.'

One of the servant's handed Vlad his white shirt.

Vlad miserably put on the white shirt the servants had given him and muttered: 'I wish I could give it all away... except for this castle.'

Vlad buried his face in the pillow and he said in a muffled tone: 'This beautiful castle.'

Fenna stated while thrusting the pillow away from him: 'Now one day you can marry the castle but today, you pledge yourself to your royal duties... now come!'

Vlad followed Fenna into the meeting room where he met up with someone he hadn't seen for 14 years. Something that had seemed like eternity. Vlad's frown faded. No surprise was to be seen on his face but a look of sadness.

Lucien shook Vlad's hand and greeted him: 'Vlad, I haven't seen you for a long time... it's good to see you again old friend.'

Vlad took his hand away and said: 'The man I used to call father refused to visit me in the last 14 years and now here you are in my castle greeting me... seems a bit idiotic.'

Vlad said: 'You leave my life for so long, don't bother to find me to talk... as much as I hate it, you have always been a part of my life, because of you I am still alive...yet there have been times I felt exhausted of this life making me wish I wasn't born in the first place...but at the same time, I cannot bring myself to hate, for you still remain the most important role model to me and I would not have that aspect any other way.'

Lucien said: 'Complain all you want Vlad, I could not come because otherwise people would have seen my lack of ageing, you are the only person that knows what I am and why I don't age...that's my true reason... now all that matters is that I am here now.'

Vlad and Lucien frowned at each other. Vlad's mouth curled into a smirk.

Vlad asked while sitting down on a large wooden chair: 'How long do you intend to stay?'

Lucien said: 'A month perhaps, I have an errand to run in another country after that.'

Vlad laughed and asked: 'What criminal is the Hidden Empire chasing now?'

Lucien was about to reply when Radu said: 'Now now, might I pry into this conversation... I overheard something like the Hidden Empire.'

Lucien placed his hands onto Radu's shoulders and began to hypnotise him.

After that Lucien said: 'Do not remember what Vlad had just said or what you have overheard.'

Radu shook his head and said after that: 'So brother, enjoying your first official year out of war.'

Vlad ignored what Radu had said: 'What do you want brother... of course there's always something with you.'

Radu explained: 'Only to report to you that the process to build the church in Braila is on the way.'

Vlad rolled his eyes and muttered: 'Oh really....took you long enough to get back here.'

Radu interrupted Vlad: 'Now I don't wish to talk about that.'

Vlad said: 'What I wish is to no longer have to speak with you.'

Radu shrugged his shoulders. He desperately tried to change the conversation.

Lucien crossed his arms.

Radu said: 'Well, don't you think it's time you got married... I think it's about time you do and in fact, I have a few suggestions for you.'

Vlad grumbled: 'No, I shall find my own wife.'

Fenna came back to the room with a tray of mead.

Radu saw her and remarked: 'Ah if it isn't the little Fen all grown up.'

Fenna frowned and out of embarrassment she dropped the tray and retreated from the room.

Vlad said: 'If you want her to be understanding, you shouldn't call her that, apparently it repulses her.'

Radu said: 'She sure did grow up into a beautiful woman... why don't you marry her?'

Vlad scoffed: 'Ach, enough with marriage, it's annoying to my ears... Fenna is twenty seven and I don't exactly have a connection with her, she's just always so awkward around me.'

Radu stated: 'You fool, maybe she likes you.'

Vlad: 'You've always been the ladies expert, besides she's my cousin.'

Radu: 'Our parent's were also cousins so what's the harm?'

Vlad stood up from the chair and left for his work with the war council.

He said: 'Brother don't get up to anything stupid, I must head to a meeting.'

Fenna was in the castle kitchen stirring a hot meal in a pot that hung over the fire at the cooking spit. Radu went to the kitchen and leaned in the doorway.

He asked her: 'Why are you still here... shouldn't you be married by now and have children?'

Fenna said in a quick tone: 'This doesn't regard you.'

Radu said: 'What if it does...'

He pushed her against the wall in the kitchen and whispered into her ear: 'I'll be watching you from now on.'

He grinned at her and left the kitchen. Fenna was left standing there confused holding a wooden spoon.

Weeks passed at Targoviste. Radu spied on Fenna and Vlad did not notice his brother's behaviour. He was busy ruling and trying to make up time he had lost with Lucien over the years.

Towards the end of Lucien's stay, a peculiar woman arrived at the castle. She claimed to have met Vlad Tepes III in the final year of the war.

On this day Fenna rushed up the stairs with the woman following her to where a council meeting was held.

Fenna barged into the room saying: 'Vlad, there's a woman outside of this room that urgently needs to see you.'

Vlad asked Fenna: 'What's her name?'

Fenna said the woman's name was Ilona. Vlad's eyes widened with surprise upon hearing that name.

Ilona shoved Fenna out of the way and said: 'No need to introduce me damsel in distress, I am a proud woman and can represent myself.'

Ilona was a high spirited, strong willed woman with long dark wavy hair and very dark eyes. She had a well curved face and held her head high.

Vlad covered his eyes with his hand in an annoyed manner and asked the woman: 'What are you doing here, Ilona?'

Ilona fumed: 'Are you blind, look what you did to me, look!'

Vlad looked at her round belly. He raised an eyebrow.

Radu who was partaking in the council said while clapping his hands mockingly: 'Congrats brother, on creating your first bastard child.'

Vlad pulled Ilona out of the room and somewhere private.

He bickered with her: 'What on earth are you doing here!'

Ilona smiled and replied: 'I thought you wanted to see me again...especially now.'

Vlad said: 'No, you can't be pregnant, I am part vampire... it should be impossible for me to sire children.'

Ilona shouted: 'Are you presuming that I'm a slut!'

Vlad asked: 'Are you sure that's my child?'

Ilona said: 'I can prove it to you, from an old trick I learned back in my homeland.'

Vlad wanted to gouge his eyes out.

He muttered: 'If the people of Wallachia discover that I had relations with a woman from Hungary, one of the enemy countries, I am going to be dethroned!'

Ilona placed her hand on her hip and said casually: 'Definitely not my problem.'

Vlad placed his hands to her face and said to her: 'Yes, you could have gotten rid of the child with one of those tricks your people taught you... it's also your fault.'

Ilona said: 'Why should I poison my child and risk poisoning myself.'

He shook his head and replied: 'I'm sorry Ilona, I shouldn't have said something so cruel...I cannot expect you to harm yourself for anything.'

Vlad said: 'So why did you come here?'

Ilona said while gripping his hands with her own: 'Back in Hungary you said you loved me... I thought maybe you were being honest... seems all men are lying fools here like in own my country.'

Vlad shook his head and said: 'No, don't you say that, I did not lie to you Ilona, you are the most beautiful and interesting woman that I have ever met, I really did fall in love with you... I still do.'

Ilona asked: 'So you slept with me for my looks... typical answer... so how many other women have you been with?'

Vlad felt ashamed of himself. He looked away. Ilona gasped.

She said: 'So there was another!'

Vlad told her: 'Yes but it was a complicated relationship based on feelings on an abyss of loneliness.'

Vlad said: 'She was a servant at the castle back in Turnu, for the time, she clarified many things for me and helped me overcome my suffering after having been held captive by the Ottomans, but other than that, there was only you, Ilona of course I love you more than her, I did not even love the other.'

Ilona saw that he was not lying.

She sighed and said: 'Alright, but I want you to prove it.'

Vlad thought on it for a moment then replied: 'If you were to marry me, nobody would doubt your origins, people would respect you not question you.'

Ilona said: 'Okay, now this is getting somewhere, do you want to see the trick I learnt from my aunt?'

Vlad asked: 'Does it work... does it prove that, that is my child?'

Ilona pulled out a wrist amulet from her pocket. She told Vlad to wear it.

She explained: 'If the colour of the stone goes red, then it isn't your child, if the colour goes white then it is your child.'

Vlad looked at the colour of the stone. It turned white.

He asked: 'According to this it is my child...Ilona, where did you get this magical item?'

Ilona grabbed the amulet off him and said: 'It was passed down to all the women in my family... technically it isn't really a stone but the blood of my ancestor preserved with an enchanted stone, a certain witch had created it and given it to my distant grandmother, my aunt gave it to me since she lacked a daughter of her own... she even said that the witch, Olga the Wise was the one who had given the amulet to my family.'

Vlad said: 'You know that I am a vampire, so that when you talk about witches I believe you.'

Ilona grinned and said: 'I remember when you and I met in that tavern that day because I asked you to, on that day you simply said to me, I'm a vampire and I said that I believe you.'

Vlad said: 'Then we had to say goodbye to each other.'

Ilona said quietly: 'A vampire that falls in love with a mortal, that's not something you see everyday.'

Vlad admitted: 'Okay I did miss you.'

Ilona smiled.

He said: 'A lot.'

Vlad wrapped his arms around her waist and said: 'That's what I love about you, that you know about my secret and that you believed me when I told you I wasn't human... so are you going to marry me or not... you didn't exactly say yes.'

Ilona smiled in a cheesy manner and said: 'Sure, I'll marry you Vlad Tepes.'

Later on, Vlad and Ilona came out of the room holding hands. They both had smiles on their faces. Fenna noticed that the person she had always loved was now in love with someone else. She noticed that a certain amount of jealousy arose in her heart. Soon a month later, Vlad and Ilona got married. She would give birth to twins, a son and a daughter.

Radu had seductively said to Fenna at the wedding: 'So cousin, your childhood sweetheart is now married to someone else, a woman of nobility and yet here you are standing unmarried, unwanted and there she is, a beautiful woman with her husband and the two future heirs to the throne in her and her husbands arms... tell me Fen, what will you do now?'

Fenna said stubbornly: 'I still have a claim to the throne.'

Radu said: 'As a woman and a plain descendant of another woman in the Tepes family... you are standing alone without a husband and without the help of your former friend Vlad... his attention is directed and will always be directed at another woman, you are irrelevant, Vlad will no longer care for you or look over you... soon you'll be married off to an old man and bare him children.'

Fenna shoved him away and looked him in the eye.

She said: 'Shut your foul mouth...you just want me to marry you... why I ask... you'll gain nothing.'

Radu said: 'We will both gain something, we will be able to strengthen our ties in the family and create our own status...besides, I'm not an old man, I am still young, I am Radu the Handsome.'

Fenna said while tapping her finger on her arm: 'I'll consider it.'

Radu said: 'Great, you won't regret it, I will make you a happy woman.'

To Vlad's surprise a little while later, Fenna declared that she was going to marry his brother. Vlad saw that she was desperate but he understood it.

Future Radu speaks: 'Another part of the story was over... yet a new page had turned, Ilona the wife and two children Varen and Hanna as well as my wife Fenna, a wife who would never bare me any children other than one, my daughter Dahlia.'

At the end of March, 1456, at Turnu, Wallachia:

Radu & Fenna

Fenna stood at the window and peered outside. It had seemed just like yesterday that she had been at Vlad's wedding but in truth fourteen months had passed. As Radu's wife, she was bound behind these large and cold stone castle walls. She was with child again and she had a very young infant to still care for. Her husband came walking down the hall. He saw her standing there, looking out at the gloomy, rainy wet scenery. Radu wrapped his arms around her from behind and stood with her, watching the weather take its course.

He said to her: 'I don't think that standing out in the cold is good.'

Fenna said: 'What does it matter... the world remains dead anyway.'

Radu took his coat off and hung it over Fenna; he said: 'Rather I freeze to death than the mother of my child.'

Fenna sneered at him: 'You've always been so kind to me yet I repay you with the cold shoulder.'

Radu said: 'I haven't exactly been better than you either.'

Fenna insisted 'Yes you have, meanwhile I have been neglecting our daughter even as we speak by just looking out of this window all the time.'

Radu smiled at her in the best loving way he could. When suddenly she shrieked.

Radu asked her in a concerned tone: 'What's wrong?'

He asked again: 'Fenna?'

Fenna said: 'The pains have begun... go get the midwife.'

Radu told the servants to assist his wife to their bedchamber. He hurried off to find the midwife.

Radu had brought the midwife to the bedchamber. Meanwhile he was talking to his daughter who was asleep in the cradle. It went on for half an hour till the midwife returned.

She said to Radu: 'I'm sorry, sire but the child was born too early and is...'

The midwife was too depressed to finish the sentence. He barged into the bedchamber and found Fenna crying. He saw that his unborn child was dead. The unborn child had died at just four months old.

Radu stormed out of the room and went to a nearby tavern, he didn't return until the next morning.

Radu gambled on and on. Not knowing how to think let alone speak about the premature death of his child. Ah, always so selfish, thinking only of his feelings.

He thought: How must Fenna feel... I should go back to her, maybe she and I need to talk.

For once, Radu was about to do the right thing, but just as he tried to be better, a man punched Radu on the shoulder and pounded him back into his seat. A masculine, strong built man with a square like face, sat down across from Radu.

He introduced himself: 'My name is Dan the third...I believe you to be Radu the Handsome...though I did not think you to be so naive.'

Radu said: 'There is nothing to speak of.'

Dan said with a hint of firmness: 'You are going to help me and my accomplice here to defeat Vlad the third... there are rumours of two brothers that resent each other so much their ties are dull.'

An old woman sat down next to Dan and said: 'Now is not the time for this Dan, we best get down to telling him the truth, then he will help us of his own free will.'

Radu asked: 'What truth?'

The witch introduced herself as Olga.

She explained: 'Long ago, I worked for a noble family in Hungary, I am as you see a witch, and you my friend are not the son of Vladana Eupraxia Tepes but the bastard child of Catalina of Danesti and Vlad II.'

93

She had said while burning a strange herb over a small candle. Radu frowned.

He said: 'It's not true.'

She said: 'Maybe, maybe not, it depends whether you choose to believe it.'

Dan said: 'Radu, you are my nephew's nephew... I am Vladislav's uncle, someone he thought to be dead... I work for the Dragon Order for whom I was forced to fake my own death...since the death of Vladislav, many things have been changing, there is a very common feeling of wanting Vlad the third, your half brother dead... he killed one of our members, it is only a matter of time before he goes to even further lengths to stand in the way of the Dragon Order...seems absurd considering you and your brother's father once worked with us in the Dragon Order, it would only seem right for his sons to follow in his footsteps.'

Dan added: 'However, the rumours that your half brother is demon born... the true purpose of the Dragon Order cannot accept that.'

Radu asked: 'What do you mean by demon born?'

Dan said: 'Interested are we...if so, Olga and I have agreed to allow a further meet up at the Sacred Grove.'

Olga stopped burning the herb and put it away. The smoke rose upwards.

Olga asked him: 'So what do you say Radu?'

Radu remembered his promise to ruin Vlad's life...but a part of him couldn't help but feel the truth why his mother never truly accepted him. Was it because he was not of her own blood? Why his mother sacrificed her life to save a half dead baby. Was all of what these two strangers were saying true? There was only one way to find out. Radu had to go to this Sacred Grove with Dan and Olga.

Radu said: 'Alright... but I'm guessing that in return you both want to know all I know about Vlad in exchange.'

Dan said: 'Yes, that indeed, whenever you are ready to go with us, Olga shall appear before you.....I've heard that of recent there is a conflict surfacing between Hungary and the west Saxons...I have a hunch that Vlad will be pulled into yet another time consuming war, you know how stubborn the Saxons of Brasov and Sibiu can be... that time is the time we shall use to come up with our schemes to defeat Vlad.'

Radu asked: 'Might I ask what you were burning, Olga?'

Olga replied stiffly: 'I was burning sage, sage when burned disperses negative emotions but if altered with magic, it can disperse sound within it's vicinity, meaning that no one has heard a word of what we have been discussing.'

Radu asked: 'Where is this Sacred Grove?'

Dan said: 'That is a secret, like I said, when the time comes, Olga will appear before you to accompany you to that hidden place.'

Dan and Olga left Radu alone to think. Meanwhile someone was spying on Radu far away hidden behind high bushes.

This person muttered quietly: 'I will not let them harm you, Radu, do not go to the grove, oh I have a bad feeling about all this.'

When Radu returned to the castle in the morning, Fenna ran outside.

She shouted: 'Where were you!'

Tears flowed from her eyes. She punched him. He caught her fist.

He said: 'I received a summoning at Targoviste, I have to go... you ask where I was, I was at a nearby town wasting money on gambling.'

Fenna shouted at him as he left on horseback: 'Don't come back... bastard!'

Meanwhile in Targoviste:

Vlad was standing by a window reviewing a letter the new King of Hungary had sent him. It was signed by both Michael Szilagyi and Mathias Corvinus.

Ilona entered the room cradling a toddler; she asked him: 'What is the matter Vlad?'

Vlad exhaled deeply. As if the letter had cut open the wounds in his heart once more.

He wanted to hide the letter from Ilona when she eyed the letter in his hand.

She begged him: 'Vlad, as your wife, I need to be able to help you and I can't lend you support if you hide things from me... read it out to me.'

Vlad forced himself to read the letter to Ilona. His voice was shaky, and as he read, his voice stumbled over the words.

Vlad Tepes, it has been many months since I last saw you let alone saw my father alive... as we both know, my father John Hunyadi died of the plague and my brother was killed in a raid during that war, much of what I am going to mention in this letter stems from current conflict. Previous events after you were pardoned from fighting with the Hungarian forces, you returned home and later married my cousin, both of you were blessed with two children, whilst I have been undergoing sour luck, the King Vladislav the fifth of Hungary was assassinated. Of course the King had no close relatives nor offspring, naturally, the position of King was handed to the noble family of Hunyadi, the closest to be considered as family for the late King, soon after I was named the King of Hungary and was forced to marry my other cousin, Jona Szilagyi who is expecting our first child, my uncle and tactician Michael, suggested that as a grand notion to expand my reign and to gain the trust of my people, I should do something to demonstrate my power as King and expand Hungary further onto Sibiu and Brasov, that has been mostly upsetting to the west Saxons. They have taken it as a direct insult and threat since we Hungarians were the ones that allowed them to live there in the first place so that Hungary could prosper from the foreign presence and influx of new merchandise for trade...but the Saxons are angry and are highly capable of dangerous things... so Vlad, in times like these I turn to someone as reckless and loyal as you, you served my father well and I expect the same in return... the Saxons are rebelling and it is up to you to take radical action at the rebellion in Bistri and take care of them.

Signed Mathias Corvinus, King of Hungary.

Michael Szilagyi, tactician to the King.

Ilona said to him: 'You don't have to do anything he says.'

Vlad ripped up the letter and tossed it into the fire.

He said: 'He is the King of Hungary and I am married to his cousin, that forces me as his ally no matter how much I try to deny it.'

Ilona suggested: 'Maybe you should consider talking to him.'

Vlad said: 'No, I've come too far to rebuild my life...going against the King will cause more problems and I might lose you and our son and daughter, all my life I've been fighting, at least now I have something to fight for.'

He added with a hint of sadness: 'Something worth dying for, you are worth more than anything I could've asked for...perhaps I am already dead... then it won't be so terrible to die once more, if only for you Ilona... and either way I might lose you, I won't make fate easier to steal you away from me, that I know.'

Ilona screeched as Vlad walked away: 'Vlad, I beg of you, don't just walk away!'

Vlad replied as his eyes slowly turned black: 'I'm sorry, spare your complaints at me when I return... and when I do, please find it in your heart to forgive me...I am sick and tired of fighting and I have had enough with making a stand when I know that there is no way out for me.'

He walked away.

He muttered: 'If the King wants blood, he shall have an abundance of it...I will show him... my inner recklessness.'

It took three days to arrive at Targoviste. Radu stormed inside the castle to meet up with Vlad's wife Ilona. Ilona was wearing a long green dress. Her long hair was tied back in a plat.

She flocked to Radu and asked him: 'Have you heard of your brother, anything at all?'

Radu asked her: 'What do you mean?'

Ilona: 'Your brother recently left to fight against the Saxons, but there was no messenger sent back... I fear the worst... I fear he might be dead.'

A tear rolled down her cheek.

She said: 'Curses, what would I do as a widow and a mother of two toddlers... I can't comprehend this any more.'

Radu tried to calm down Ilona and said: 'Alright, we don't know what the status is with Vlad but I do know that he is a tough fool and strong barbarian on the battlefield.'

Ilona asked him: 'Brother in law, you look sad, what happened back at your castle in Turnu?'

Radu: 'My second child died...it never even had life for one second in this world.'

Ilona asked in a concerned manner: 'What about your daughter Dahlia?'

Radu said: 'She's alive and well, a healthy four month year old baby.'

Ilona smiled gratefully and renewed her attention towards her children who simply wouldn't stop crying.

Radu saw that Vlad had everything like always. The happy family. The content wife. He decided he wanted to change that somehow like he had vowed to do so when he was seven years old, to make Vlad lose everything and never be loved. Radu then remembered, Olga and Dan's offer. Radu decided he was going to speak with them first at the Sacred Grove and then make the next decision.

Nothing was heard from Vlad for multiple weeks and during that time, tragedy struck. One day, Ilona was found cradling her daughter. Now the lifeless empty body that had once been a bundle of joy. Radu walked in on her.

Hanna Tepes had died before she could really learn to walk, she had died from a fever.

Ilona wasn't herself any more. She often sleep walked at night in the castle. Forgot to eat on some days. Meanwhile, Radu stayed at the castle in wait for Vlad's return, he watched Ilona disappear. Her strong spirit perish.

Upon one night, Radu was in a temporary room trying to sleep. He couldn't sleep as he heard Ilona sleep walk through the corridors. A slow shuffling and scraping sound was to be heard.

Radu thought about the Sacred Grove. Abruptly a glowing figure appeared at the foot end of Radu's bed. It looked like a fuzzy, faint, see through representation of Olga.

She spoke: 'Radu, if you wish to seek the path to the Sacred Grove, you must help me focus my grip on this plain, currently I am astral projecting, I am there and am not at the same time, now repeat with me these words.... fellow friend or acquaintance of mine walk with me on this fine

98

line, together we are connected by a tether, hand in hand I pull you through the nether.'

Radu mumbled the words. Suddenly, the figure became clearer. She grabbed his hand and pulled him through the glowing figure.

Now Radu was somewhere else in an instant. He rubbed his eyes because he didn't believe where he was. Radu was standing on a small boat.

Olga glanced at him and said: 'Sit down, it'll be a while to get there.'

Radu sat down before the small row boat began to rock.

He asked her: 'Why am I on a row boat with you?'

Olga explained: 'The Sacred Grove is a place that is hidden on a small piece of land along the Danube but in order to get there we have to get there via the Danube, on land it is too difficult to reach.'

Radu began to row the boat. He thought over why a witch would work with the Dragon Order that was founded on the Christian belief. He thought: Doesn't Christianity dislike and scorn witches?

He asked her: 'Why is a witch like you working with the Dragon Order?'

Olga frowned. She rubbed her hands together.

Olga replied: 'Believe me, I hate the Dragon Order and they resent me, a shrivelled old woman with a broken heart... my story is far too long, I don't think you'd have any pleasure in listening to it.'

Radu said: 'Maybe I should know more about the people that want me to work with them.'

Olga said: 'I suppose I could tell you how I came to work with the Dragon Order.'

Radu listened to the old woman.

Olga began to tell her story: 'A long time ago, I belonged to a witch coven in which dark magic was practised vigorously, it was what made my coven special, the last to practice that type of magic...till they were wiped out by an indestructible force, the night the warlock came, I was to be announced the next coven leader as I was the descendant of the first leader, I had a firm grip on the future that was laid out for me, I even had a daughter to follow in my footsteps and a son to help guide her...I never thought that everything would be turned to ashes, the time of the Apheseus coven is long gone and my son Corvus and daughter, Voica are still alive, out there somewhere...soon after, I disappeared from the empty plains that I had once called home and retired to live in a place my ancestors had held sacred since the dawn of time, the last site that proved my coven had once existed, after a while, I had made a discovery of ancient inscriptions hidden in the grove, they spoke about a powerful relic called the staff of Eterna...it was forged and made with the flames of an ethereal dragon and with the magic of the red blood queen.'

She added: 'It is rumoured to have been passed down to my first ancestor and the founder of my coven as a sign of trust between the two witches, this staff is perhaps imbued with the power to erase everything from in this realm, a strong power that is not to be meddled with...in the hopes of finding this staff I returned to the place I had known all my life only to be faced with my not so lost daughter, Voica... she told me that the staff of Eterna was indeed very real and was stolen by the Dragon Order... apparently, instead of upholding Christianity, their true, sole mission is to steal items and lost relics from all over Europe to prevent mythical creatures of establishing an understanding of long lost wisdom from various cultures... Voica also told me that a new age has begun, the new age to revise the prophecy to restore the balance and that the staff might be used to destroy that what the red blood queen had fought so hard to maintain...Voica spoke about the existence of a group of witches she had joined, they called themselves the sisterhood, a group of Warlocks, mainly witches that exist to one day, replicate that very prophecy at the command of their leader, the red blood queen...before leaving that day, Voica told me that if the prophecy is not restored, vampires will wreak havoc and the creatures of the night will be forced to stop at nothing to kill them, it would be an all out war between the two species, soon after she left.'

Olga continued: 'With nothing left but past grief, I pondered much over the insight my daughter had told me about but couldn't decide for myself what to do, I couldn't trust strange witches nor could I trust the Dragon Order...on my journey back to the Sacred Grove, a flickering light appeared, between the hovering flames, a face made up of fire spoke to me this:

Thou old witch, I beseech you to listen and understand the things I am about to explain to you... the Red blood Queen does indeed exist, the one and only who sent me on a journey of vendetta, now listen, hither lies the truth, she is not only a witch, she is far more than that, lest you wish to be killed or be at her mercy, I suggest you find yourself go astray, go forth to the place your ancestor once served, the place your loved one died and the place you will find a piece of the puzzle.'

Olga spoke: 'The flames had poofed away and I was left to contemplate what the speaking flames had meant... that was when I remembered, the place my ancestor had been, the first Olga the Wise, and the man I had met to whom I had two children with, Corvinus Hunyadi... that was when I knew what I had to do, I had to relocate the Hunyadi family, I knew now that through my daughter's warning and the strange man in the fire, I had to play my part in putting an end to this madness, the Dragon Order had the staff of the Red blood queen and because of that, the prophecy of the sisterhood could not be fulfilled...or perhaps the Red blood Queen had other intentions...she wanted to get back the staff to eradicate the Dragon Order... I only had a hunch that the man's warning was true somehow.'

Olga continued: 'I ended up travelling to Hungary, to Transylvania where I made the acquaintance of a young man called Istvan Kosovic, he revealed to me his biggest secret, he too was gifted with magic, he though had only served the royals and nobles as a tutor to their children, he lied to the Hunyadi family so that I could work for the family under the guise that I was a healer of sorts... during those years of John's conquest for Christianity, before he had married, I had been coming to terms that his father, the man I had once known, had died, of course, John Hunyadi had never known about his half brother or half sister...Corvinus had made sure of that.'

Radu interrupted: 'You knew the grandfather of one of my brother's allies?'

Olga said: 'Yes, but how him and I came together, that is not a story that concerns you.'

She continued to speak: 'I stayed with the Hunyadi family for a while, eventually John Hunyadi had met a woman and he married her, the sister of his wife married his tactician though the origins of these women were a mystery to me till one day, Andreea Szilagyi came to me saying that she knew what I was and accused me of practising witch craft... she said that if I did not help her, she would tell her husband and her brother in law about me... in the end I decided to help her at the cost of her telling me how I could help her...that's when she revealed to me that she

101

was a werewolf... a word I'd never thought I'd hear... I had only heard of tales of such creatures in which they used moonstones to weaken the effects of their transformation every full moon... so I did just that, interestingly, Andreea's sister was also a werewolf, I was required to make more than one enchanted moonstone, from those times, things became more difficult to understand when John Hunyadi had two sons with his wife and Andreea had two daughters, one of whom is Vlad the Impaler's wife, you know how the rest went, when you were seven, your brother was born... technically half brother after what me and Dan told you... but that's not important...the exact day after Vlad's mother mysteriously died after childbirth, an absurd letter appeared in my hands... a letter written in my son, Corvus' handwriting it said:

'Dear mother, I am aware that you are plotting to stop the actions of the sisterhood and the Dragon Order but what you are doing is dangerous, you don't even know what the sisterhood is planning...even Voica who corresponds with me from within the sisterhood circle has no clue... but she has managed to pass onto me, old scripture of the prophecy.'

'I turned the letter over and read; Under a blood moon must the two oldest Ancestors come united, of their own volition at the decreed, ancestral site of the Sacred Grove, the blood of the oldest wolf and of the oldest Vampire must be spilled into the large pit, the weight of the spell must be bound to a creature that reflects on the same quantity of power like the two Ancestors, moonlight must be captured and the essence of light, replicated, that power must then be channelled and bound to the blood that had been shed during the end of the initiated blood moon. The incantation must be sealed with blood magic so that the prophecy may only be repeated by the chosen Ancestors.'

She continued: 'The incantations are; in the dead of night, ends the centuries worth of the endless fight... not to be forgotten or for naught lest the one hate for what she fought... one species tied to the sun and the other to the moon, this pact is sacred and must be for eternity to avoid impending doom... no more does the light fade or darkness encroach upon us... that sadness shall be but a memory seldom be, it does not beget what had once beget, to the beginning to the end, we must remain hell bent.'

Olga continued: 'Back then, I had no understanding of all those riddles, but after Istvan had been sent to Wallachia to tutor the sons of Vlad the second, I became suspicious and began to connect the dots... all this madness began when the mother of Vlad the Impaler had died, I began to think that there was more to the Tepes family then just rumours... I dug deep and discovered that Vlad the third was demon born, a baby that had actually been destined to die had come back to life and born like a normal mortal though these rumours were risky to believe... I remembered that the speaking fire had told me that amongst the Hunyadi family I would uncover another piece of the puzzle... I asked myself what puzzle?'

Olga said: 'The children of Hunyadi have wolf blood coursing in their veins and Vlad the Impaler may be demon born as in vampire... then there was the relic that the Dragon Order had stolen from the Apheseus coven, a relic itself forged by the flames of an ancient dragon... dragon-Dragon Order, the relic created by the red blood queen...the leader of the sisterhood who had been hiding in a foreign land, most members of the sisterhood are heretic witches, part witch part demon, the word 'heretic' resembled an old witch tale I had once learned when I had been a child... the story of the trinity, a back story that explained how a witches power identifies... the story of the trinity explains the life of an old witch who's name was Gothel but to outsiders, her name was Olga, she had three daughters, one a witch, one a wolf, one a snake like creature though that is uncertain to say if it was true... these three sisters grew up together living in harmony, this idealism of ignorance was ruined when the third sister was bitten by a disoriented creature whilst travelling in the woods.'

Olga continued: 'The third sister lost control and turned into a deadly creature nearly killing her older sister Lillith, Gothel was forced to put her youngest daughter into an eternal slumber, never to awaken unless her eldest daughter Brynhild found a cure to reverse her sister's state, this was a witches test to her daughter to challenge her bond to her sister... Brynhild of course, who had been a battle maiden most of her life, had no fears, she travelled into the forest where her sister had been attacked and using her power of future sight avoiding all danger, on that day, she came upon an unusual looking man who confessed to being a werewolf after being threatened by Brynhild's deadly magic, she forced him back to her village, intending to question him. Gothel lectured her daughter for bringing the wolf into their home. Lillith, Brynhild's younger sister expressed how she hated men, how she loathed the man whom had turned their sister into a monster. Lillith would always live in the present with her hatred, always continuing to hate... soon, the third sister who had been put to an eternal rest by her mother was found in a body of water, she had been drowned, the daughter who had lived in the past, empty life resumed in the same state of mind in sleep. Brynhild questioned her mother if she knew anything about the mysterious killer of her sister... Gothel's stoic nature shattered as she was forced to tell the truth that none of what they led in their lives was as it seemed.'

She went on: 'Since the day all three daughters existed an evil presence lingered... apparently, Gothel was fated to create true power, the power of three, Gothel had been forced to live under three names, her past name Grendel, her present name Gothel and her future and alias name, Olga, also, she had three daughters... it was when Gothel revealed that the three sisters were all half siblings that Lillith became infuriated... Gothel went on to explain that she had once had relations with a dark warlock who had the ability to take on the form of a dragon, she met this man after Brynhild had been born, this man was the father of Lillith... but this man had a certain dark side, a darkness that went beyond that of a warlock and with this darkness came consequences, he had become obsessed with Gothel and her child that she had from him... Gothel had no other choice but to find a way to rid herself of him... she found that the only way to do so was to make him feel disgusted by her, she met another man and bore yet another child... upon discovering this he was brimming with jealousy and hatred... accusing Gothel of being unfaithful... Gothel said that she was a woman in her own right and that her loyalty and devotion belonged only to herself and her children, after this, Gothel shot a poisoned and enchanted arrow at the man who had turned into a dragon.'

Olga continued: 'The dragon had been shot and the weakened warlock returned back to his normal form, heavily wounded, he said to her that one day, the day that he had regained his strength and obtained his pawns, he will come back and kill every daughter of Gothel's in cold blood, one by one. Gothel then did everything as necessary, she bound the magic of her two daughter's together and bestowed upon each an aspect of her power... Brynhild being gifted with the future, Lillith with the present and the power of the past to Brynhild, after this, Gothel no longer possessed any magic as she had given it all to her daughters so that if she died, her power would not die with her... having told her two living daughters the truth, the man who had confessed to being a werewolf had overheard Brynhild's conversation with her mother and sister, the word Dragon seemed to have more of a depth as the man remembered the significance of that very word, the man decided to share his secrets with the three witches so that they knew of what exact danger they had brought to themselves... his name was Siegfried and before he had been in that forest he had been a hired mercenary, he fought and slayed for the people that hired his strength, he went where the work took him, one day, he had been summoned to work as a guard for a certain princess that lived in a castle by the river Loreley, her name was Lorelei and she had become ill, many feared she would succumb further to this strange sickness...'

Olga explained: 'Lorelei told Siegfried to go forth to a hidden lair that was hidden deep within a certain forest at the very heart in that lair there resided an old dragon, he should then sneak in and cut off a scale... Siegfried did not know whether the princess was just being silly or whether she truly knew the existence of mythical creatures, Siegfried only pretended to fill out the request without acting as if he believed there was an actual dragon, Lorelei said that dragon scales are infused with healing properties, upon this, Siegfried realised that this was an attempt to find something that could cure her illness so he went to the lair, however, something followed him there, when Siegfried had sneaked into the dragon's lair, he was attacked from behind... Siegfried dodged the attack and saw it was his snitch of a step brother Beowulf... Beowulf grinned at him and said that he should leave the lair and leave the found treasure for him... the two went on to argue when a gigantic scaly winged beast with red glaring eyes roared at them, Beowulf with a pathetic and frightened demeanour tried to taunt the creature whilst Siegfried used Beowulf's ridiculous stunt as a distraction to sneak closer to the dragon... the dragon became instilled with anger that was caused by Beowulf's irritating presence, the dragon opened it's mouth and a fiery beacon of flames burst towards Beowulf, who was scorched and torched alive, Siegfried had cut off a scale from the dragon, upon this, the dragon bellowed in pain and hit away Siegfried with its tail, Siegfried ran out of the lair just in time and away from the reach of the beast.'

Olga continued: 'Soon after, he returned to the princess and gave her the scale, the princess thanked him, paid him and sent him on his way but when he was on his way to the next destination, Siegfried had a chill run down his spine as the magic he had sensed around that dragon was now somewhere close by but in a different form, because he felt threatened, he turned into a wolf and hid in the same forest that he had gone to search for the lair earlier... a few weeks later, Brynhild and

Lillith's sister happened to wander through the forest, that was when she had been scratched by Siegfried... after listening to Siegfried's story, Brynhild guessed now that the dragon that had been tormenting Siegfried, was the same warlock that her mother had told her about, the warlock that had the ability to turn into a dragon, the one that had killed her and Lillith's younger sister... now with the help of her sister, she created a weapon that had the potential power to destroy this vile dragon, it was a sceptre like object that was forged using the flames of her sister Lillith, and imbued with the remaining magic of their mother, Gothel, though the ritual was too powerful and too demanding of the life force of Gothel, Gothel had sacrificed and given every ounce of her remaining magic for this cause to protect her daughters, after the ritual, Gothel simply died so mysteriously just like she had lived... the mishaps of life, to this Brynhild said such; empty words have no meaning, life that is filled with words of many things are nothing short or sweet of being deceiving... those words were Brynhild's last thought to her mother.'

Olga (present day Olga) cracked her knuckles and glanced at the shady water that seemed to have shadows dancing on the rippling surface.

She went on to continue the story whilst Radu continued rowing: 'Soon after the demise of their mother, Lillith went to a place their ancestors had once been to hide the sceptre and escape from the wrath of the dangerous and unpredictable dragon meanwhile, Brynhild stayed behind to prepare for the actions of the dragon and with the help of the werewolf, Siegfried, they created a trap for the savage creature, the trap was ropes that had been laced with a type of poison... the poison had been a finely crushed powder which was procured by Siegfried when he had once befriended a certain dwarf. Though the warlock did not come as intended in Brynhild's vision, he went to Wallachia and killed Lillith. Luckily, the warlock had not gotten his hands on the sceptre... Lillith's companion who was the father of Lillith's daughter, searched for Brynhild to deliver to her the sceptre and the news that her sister had been killed. Brynhild who had been on her way to Wallachia to save her sister from certain doom, was stopped during her journey to Wallachia by the man who had known Brynhild's sister. He told her about Lillith's death which devastated Brynhild upon hearing it, the deep and tantalising words that symbolised the start of Brynhild's fall from good, that realisation that she would now be alone forever without family.'

Olga (present Olga) rubbed her hands together and stated: 'I would refer to this term for this part of the story as a violent separation...anyway,

Brynhild scorned herself for being so careless having stood by and had let her sister leave her side in the first place...such shame she carried that she cast a shadow over her existence but her work was not complete... in the end after so much loss and sacrifice, Brynhild successfully found the cruel dragon and put an end to his rage though this conquest was not without it's risks, Siegfried had nearly died that day in the line of fire if a certain mysterious someone had not appeared in front of him... at the same time another man appeared and wielded a strange dark magic in his hands... this man said to the Dragon; Morgoth, your time is at an end.'

Olga (present Olga) continued: 'Brynhild watched as this person pulled the magic out of the dragon...during this, the dragon slowly broke down until nothing but a heap of bones was left... Brynhild had seen a simple man conquer a dragon using nothing but his hands and magic, something that was far from a simple feat, the man had introduced himself as Lucien and explained that he had been searching for the dragon for a long time and Brynhild did not care nor pity the two strangers, the other man who had saved Siegfried's life was an old vampire who's name is not known; he seemed to have a lack of emotional control around Siegfried, the two hated being in each others presence... Brynhild had become tired of all the chitter chatter of her life, the overwhelming turbulence that had crushed her hopes and dreams, she intended to kill herself on the spot... Siegfried ran to stop her, the old vampire's face finally flinched a little at Brynhild's sad expression, even he tried to stop her but Brynhild created a shock wave from her magic that sent both of the men stumbling and falling, Lucien folded his arms and watched Brynhild with anticipation... Brynhild magically made the sceptre appear in one hand and a sword in the other, it's smooth metal glistened underneath the pale moonlight, Brynhild held the sceptre with a tight grip as it began to glow, suddenly she disappeared and her presence transcended onto a windswept hill, atop she stood and held the mighty sceptre upwards, channelling the sceptre's magic, the magic that her mother and Lillith had put there in the past.'

Olga continued: 'Brynhild said these following words; one day, after life, death, your souls may come to stay and be united with mine in another lifetime, through terrors not numbered and untold, we shall meet again, may our former vessels fade and our souls bare witness to each other's glory and lifeblood.'

Olga spoke: 'A glowing circle appeared around Brynhild in which she attempted to drive the swords blade through her heart, she did not even cry out, not a word, just bizarre silence, she did not remove the blade, all she did was collapse into a heap of surrender... Siegfried and the two others rushed to her aid, the vampire begged Lucien to do something, anything at all, Lucien immediately recognised the magic that she had cast onto herself, re-incarnation magic, that was a type of necromancy that had more depth than re-animating a dead body, this spell that she did would strip her body of her own soul and when called upon the essence of remaining spiritual life force, she could reunite her soul with that of the spirits she had called upon to be one day, reborn into a human vessel, which is why Brynhild had a blade in her heart, according to the magic, in belief, if the one who wishes to die and transition to an alternate ghost form, the core of ones being must be prevented from keeping one's body alive and in order to bring ones body to death, the heart must be silenced so that the body may die... Lucien pulled out the sword and Brynhild's eyes sprang open as he forced her to drink his blood, her eyes glinting with hatred, life being restored to her body, being healed, but since Brynhild's soul had been transitioning to a shallow state, her components of her original soul had not completely disappeared, but as her body had awakened as a new being, her soul had been drawn back into her body, fusing with the new creature that she had awakened as.'

Olga continued: 'Now she was part witch, part demon, unlike a creature that had never existed before, Brynhild was now more alive than before and more reckless, she had failed in her attempt to be reunited with her mother and two sisters, as a consequence of channelling the sceptre' magic, some of the magic's aspects had mingled with her magic, taking on Lillith's hatred of living in the present and the sadness of living in the past from her third sister... Brynhild was cursed in many ways, unable to move on from her sadness or not being able to die since a vampire cannot kill themselves, she vanished and never saw anyone again, forever refraining from lingering in the outside world.'

Olga continued to speak: 'According to the very old story, Brynhild was the first Heretic witch, apparently this story stems from the 7th century AD and that was a long time ago, now the link to the Red Blood Queen and Brynhild is that according to my daughter Voica, the Red blood queen is the oldest living heretic witch to exist, perhaps they are the same person, now remember how I mentioned the Apheseus coven, their coven emblem is a snake that wraps around a sceptre... in the story I just told you, Lillith took the sceptre and went to Wallachia to hide and safe guard it, she went to a place her ancestors came from, a place she had a daughter in secrecy, so that's why the emblem is a snake because Lillith is the founder of the Apheseus coven and in my coven the sceptre was passed from the second coven leader to her descendants, her name was Olga meaning she must have been Lillith's daughter who was named after her grandmother, remember, Gothel had three names, Gothel, Grendel, Olga... the first real Olga the Wise, if she was the daughter of Lillith, she is my ancestor.... Now in the inscriptions I found at the Sacred Grove it said that the Red blood Queen gave the sceptre to the coven leader, if the coven founder was indeed Lillith and the Red blood Queen is indeed Brynhild, it would make sense for the queen to have given the sceptre to the other witch, not because out of understanding but because they had a deep meaningful bond as sisters... this proves that the story of the trinity is true... when Istvan went to serve the Wallachian Voivode's family, he mentioned to me in letters of a man named Lucien... a friend of the Voivode's wife, Vladana... the name Lucien was mentioned in the story as well and he turned Brynhild into a vampire...perhaps when they refer to your brother as demon born, Lucien turned Vlad into a vampire as well...the importance of this is that in the story.'

Olga continued: 'Lucien was mentioned alongside the oldest vampire in the world whom Lucien also probably turned, the oldest vampire who's name is not known, could be the one who was referred to as the oldest vampire Ancestor in the information of the Red blood Queen's prophecy and Siegfried, the oldest wolf Ancestor, I remember when Andreea Szilyagi had once told me that she was a descendant of the oldest wolf, if that is so and Siegfried is the oldest wolf Ancestor, that means that Andreea Szilyagi and her children, Ilona and Jona as well as her sister and her sister's children are all descendants of Siegfried and if Lucien really did turn Vlad into a vampire using his own blood like he did for the oldest vampire Ancestor, there might not be a genetic relation but a sort of blood relation since both vampires were sired from the same blood, this is what the man in the fire had told me about, to find the pieces of the puzzle, if Brynhild did do the prophecy as the Red blood Queen and she sealed the spell with blood magic so that no one could repeat the spell without the Ancestors for the good of the prophecy. However, the time has come to once more perform the spell for the good of all vampires and werewolves but the Ancestors have not shown themselves yet, perhaps they are hiding from the Red blood Queen, they may know more about Brynhild's plans than we do, plans for evil, maybe she doesn't want to repeat the spell but undo it so that vampires and werewolves hate each other again and fight each other to the death, Brynhild's idea of ideal chaos but in order to break the spell she needs to gather all components of the spell, however, she does not have the aid of her friends and since the spell was sealed with blood magic, she requires someone who was either descended from the Ancestors or shares a unique blood bond like a sire bond from vampire to vampire, now Vlad and the oldest vampire are blood sired from the same person, that in itself is enough to represent a blood bond and Ilona Szilagyi is a descendant from Siegfried, it is very convenient that Vlad III and Ilona have recently married and that they have two children, one of the children, I believe it was Hanna Tepes who died mysteriously as an infant...'

Olga said: 'Maybe the babies were switched out and the real Hanna Tepes is still alive and is kept in hiding by the sisterhood to be offered soon as a sacrifice to undo the prophecy... since Hanna Tepes is half of both her parents more than her brother, she alone would be enough to represent blood ties to both Ancestors which is why I am with the Dragon Order, so I could gather more information and allies to stop Brynhild and prevent her from getting the sceptre, because if she is willing to cause chaos amongst vampires and werewolves, she is willing to destroy the world...but recently I got another warning from the man in the fire, he said that he had once worked for the sisterhood and that the Red blood Queen's inside name to her most trust trusted witches is Imperare which is Latin for to rule. I also discovered that the name of Vlad's mother, the name Vladana, also means to rule, that is the meaning in different languages... so I am not sure whether that is somehow connected but perhaps, according to the trinity story, if the Red blood Queen is Brynhild, when she killed herself to resurrect her soul with her sisters one day to be reborn, maybe one of Brynhild's sisters was reborn into the body of Vlad the Impaler's mother, Vladana which would explain the meaning to rule, Brynhild wanted to be re-united with her sister and rule the world but since Vladana died from childbirth, Brynhild is ever more eager to destroy everything.'

Radu stopped rowing, the row boat continued to drift on it's own.

Olga began to tap the edge of the boat with a finger, a wide scowl was to be seen on her face.

Olga assumed: 'But of course you don't believe in anything I just told you...'

Radu crossed his arms and said: 'Well for starters, your theories are incredibly far fetched, almost impossible to be exact, Lucien is not some strange warlock, he is my brother's friend, besides, werewolves, vampires, dragons, they're all creatures from folklore, nothing to believe.'

Olga tapped more incessantly.

She sneered: 'Is that so...I thought you believed me when I told you I was a witch.'

Radu pointed out rather sharply: 'I had to fake it, perhaps you are a witch, perhaps you aren't but I needed to convince you and Dan that I believed in that sort of stuff so that I could find out what I needed to hear... the truth about my heritage.'

Olga's eyes leered at him.

She yelled: 'You immoral, insolent fool, I should have every bone in your body crushed to smithereens!'

Olga's form disintegrated and turned into a pitch black mass that rose up over Radu.

It's deep voice boomed: 'How dare you insult the very existence of witches, you fowl, rude and despicable sack head-'

Whilst Radu recoiled back in sheer fear, the monstrous creature that seemed to be Olga, jerked it's head to peer behind it.

The creature turned towards Radu once more.

It said: 'No bother, I shall let someone else deal with you.'

It said with a snicker: 'I feel so risible, I could laugh my head off if I wanted, we are almost inshore and I can put this tacky dispute behind me!'

Suddenly, the row boat come to a standstill, motionless, it had reached land. The creature hovered off the boat and next a wall of haze appeared so thick that Radu struggled to see through it. Radu rubbed his eyes vigorously but to no avail the haze disappeared before he could make sense of it yet Olga was once more in her human form and in the same apparel she had been earlier, her long robe on and her shawl wrapped around her neck.

Olga stated firmly: 'The sight of you makes me sick.'

With a motion of her hand, she beckoned and said: 'Follow me.'

Radu unwillingly followed Olga off the boat and onto land. Every footstep he made was not his own. Radu however took a look at his surroundings. There was many trees scattered here and there, yet there was no wildlife to be seen, even though it was night time, you'd still expect to hear birds caw or chirp or hear the rustling sounds from shrubs made by predators at night hunting for food but in this grove, there were no sounds to be heard, it was as if the world revolved around this point in time and the other sounds were muffled out.

Radu felt a rush of fear as he felt like many eyes were peeled on him, watching him ever more closely, now more intensely, eyes so sharp as knives ready to cut him up, predator to prey.

But as they came into a clearing, Radu spotted a fire, a strange fire, a luminescent one with an otherworldly colour, around it there were people whirling and twirling about, dancing and swaying madly to the rhythm of the fire and yet there stood a peculiar woman just watching them like a statue frozen in time, as if to convince someone that she was non-existent.

Olga approached the woman. The woman had known Olga was there for her feet flinched and she turned around rather quickly to face Olga although she did not exchange looks with her, her eyes darted straight at Radu.

Radu found that being caught in the gaze of that woman was unbearable. Eyes glinting with a clash of sadness, it seemed as if lightning flashed in her eyes. Eyes so irate.

An icy grin was to be seen on her face. She raised a torch up high so that her face was more visible. Faint blotches of light refined her face. She had Dark brown, sleek, wavy hair that was medium length and she wore a headband that wrapped around her forehead to the back of her head. She was of medium stature and was white skinned. She wore a long draping robe that extended to the bottom of her legs and it was tied together by a sash.

Olga said while interrupting the awkward silence: 'I have brought the man with whom you have wished to speak with.'

Olga glared angrily at Radu and bickered: 'He however will leave you utterly disappointed, Imperare, he has not believed a single word you have told me to tell him.'

The woman stood herself upright and spoke in a clear voice: 'Well, what a shame, you are no longer of use to me, such disastrous disappointment, here I was making such hasty preparations for the ritual.'

Olga noticed that her master wanted Radu to speak so she smacked him in the face.

Radu gave out a low cry.

He stammered: 'Wh-who are you?'

Olga rolled her eyes.

The other woman remarked in a low tone: 'Yes, that indeed is a good question... more like who was I and who have I become, nothing but a dwindling shadow of who I once was... nonetheless...'

She curtsied ridiculously with sarcastic flair and said: 'My name is Brynhild.'

Olga clapped her hands and said: 'It is intriguing to see you address yourself by your real name, Imperare.'

Suddenly, Brynhild seemed void of feelings and said: 'As always I can rely on your immodesty to keep my life imperfect.'

Brynhild turned around and waved to her fellow witches. All of them now stopped dancing and paid the utmost attention to their leader.

The witches chanted: 'Imperare, Imperare, Imperare!'

Brynhild laughed hysterically... Radu was so frightened by that laugh that it seemingly echoed in his mind.

Brynhild: 'All my fellow followers who have joined me on this dark night, this night in which we shall change the world... all of you who have felt hate and false judgement like I had; it is time to undo that and turn the odds around, we shall plunge the world into oblivion, we will succeed so that all mere mortals and other creatures shall feel our pain, that same needless pain that we had been bestowed by our kindred that hated every core of our being... we are the heretics, we are unstoppable, we shall have our dominion!'

The followers cheered on. In the distance another woman came striding towards Brynhild. She wore a hooded cloak and was carrying something that looked like a toddler. It was wailing. As the woman holding the toddler stood in front Brynhild, Radu could recognise the toddler...he was gobsmacked that he saw Hanna Tepes still alive. Radu fell to his knees in disbelief.

He could not believe it... Hanna Tepes was alive, they were going to use her for their ritual... this Brynhild or so called Red Blood queen really existed? That means that everything else Olga had told him was true... that also meant that everyone here except him were witches... but what about the Dragon Order, wasn't Dan III and Olga supposed to meet here in secret to talk... was that a lie?

Radu muttered to Olga: 'What on earth have you done with Dan?'

Olga whispered: 'Do not have the audacity to interrupt this moment unless you are spoken to.'

Brynhild took the toddler from the other woman and spun it round three times mid air. The toddler screeched. Brynhild laughed, it was a long, dry laugh, almost menacing yet soulless. Radu's eyes shifted in fear. He saw in front of him, someone who relished others suffering immensely.

But why? What was this bitter animosity from that woman, as if she resented every fibre of existence... Radu gulped as a tear forced it's way down his face... this imbalance of hatred and sadness, it reminded him of his own brother. Radu shook his head, removing the ridiculous thought from his mind.

Brynhild tossed the toddler upwards, then caught it, the toddler cried.

Brynhild passed the child back to the other witch and said: 'Prepare her for the ritual...Helene, since you are my apprentice, I expect you to perform tonight exceptionally.'

Helene nodded slowly. Her eyes sparked. Helene had ashen brown hair that was slightly curly and blueish grey eyes. She carried the toddler away.

Brynhild glanced at Radu. She turned around and tilted her head.

Brynhild held her hand out in front of herself and said: 'Children born from sin, their saddened hearts cry from within.'

She said: 'You are one of these children.'

Radu swallowed hard and asked slowly: 'What did you and your accomplices do to the members of the Dragon Order?'

Brynhild: 'Well now that you mention this, I did forget that we killed them, before you got here, the people from the Dragon Order did come as agreed, however, they did not anticipate the ambush that waited for them... we did not show mercy, you see it was all part of the plan.'

Radu asked in a stunned manner: 'Plan, what plan?'

Brynhild stated sharply: 'Everything that Olga explained to you earlier, you see, Olga did work for the Dragon Order, because I told her to, Olga went to investigate the origins of the descendants of John Hunyadi because I told her to, all of what Olga did was because I told her to, she is my sister Lilith's descendant, she wishes to avenge the death of everyone from her coven and for that, the Dragon Order is to blame and she wishes to free her son of the tyrant that misguides her son...'

She continued: 'She befriended Istvan Kosovic, perhaps that name sounds familiar... anyway... she did that to uncover his weaknesses because he was the son of the enemy, the son of Morgoth...because of that he was eliminated, as was his brother.'

Radu stammered: 'No, that's impossible... he was beheaded by one of the Ottoman Turks!'

Brynhild laughed and said: 'Poor fool, how do you think the Ottomans found you, your father and brother... Olga disguised herself as a Turkish soldier using her magic and helped the Ottomans find them, she was also the soldier that beheaded Istvan... as for his brother, well, he had married into the Tepes family... I believe he married a certain Vlaadia Tepes, he who apparently, mysteriously died whilst aiding his in law, the Voivode, Vlad II in a war... he was killed by a member of the sisterhood, the man in the fire was the one who had killed him.'

Brynhild: 'Istvan who had become the tutor of Vlad and Istvan's older brother marrying into the Tepes family... that messed with my plan...my plan to plunge the world into oblivion, but I cannot perform such chaotic magic unless I free myself of my curse... after events from the past, my heart had not turned cold at first, at first I still did good deeds, for a while... eventually, being part vampire, I had seen with my own eyes, the hatred that werewolves and vampires shared, back then it tore me apart, so with the help of two men who had been my friends as well as the help of other witches I created a spell so that vampires and werewolves both had weaknesses and they could learn a way of co-existing.'

Brynhild approached Radu and muttered angrily: 'It worked... but the spell ruined me as I had taken all the burden of magic onto myself...in order for such a spell to work it needs a discharge, I bound the spell to a vessel so that it could stabilise, I myself was the only vessel strong enough to withstand the dark side of the spell, but I was cursed eternally, after that, I could no longer perform magic in large quantities... for centuries of suffering in the dark, lacking purpose or existence, I began to tire from my uselessness, I took hold of my own fate and searched for a way to remove the curse from me...'

She continued: 'I found a way but that way was disturbing and seemingly dark, if I reversed the prophecy, the spell of the vampires and werewolves, I could strip myself of this ridiculous curse that irritated me so... I am willing to sacrifice an innocent toddler to achieve my goal... my heart is indeed now cold and harsh but the sacrifice of an innocent life is powerful enough to reverse such a powerful and extreme spell...however I needed to wait till such a child was born, a child that was born of two specific bloodlines, that alone would rid me of any other complications concerning the blood magic of the original spell, yet I still needed the occurrence of the blood moon.'

Brynhild stooped to stare Radu in the eyes; she continued: 'Tonight that long awaited blood moon is here... tonight I can finally set myself free and after this... I am going to destroy the Dragon Order as well as plunge this world into deep oblivion, nobody will stand in my way...all except for one person... which is where you come in... you, Radu.'

Radu gulped and asked: 'Ahem, what am I supposed to do for you?'

Brynhild stood up and said: 'I want you to kill Vlad the Impaler.'

Radu pointed to himself in a skittish manner and asked: 'M-me?'

Brynhild took hold of Radu's shirt and thrusted him upwards.

She said: 'Don't defy me...I might be a witch but I was a battle maiden in my past, I could snap your neck like a twig.'

The witch known as Helene approached Brynhild and said: 'Imperare, we are ready for the ritual.'

Brynhild let go of Radu and said: 'I'll be right there Helene.'

She turned to face Radu and said: 'Vlad the Impaler is the only one who can withstand my most dangerous types of magic, since he was born of the woman who retained a fragment of my old and mighty magic, when he was born after nearly dying, he stole that fragment of magic from his mother Vladana... you see what Olga said was true, Vladana's soul was the soul of my sister who had been re-born into her body, my re-incarnation spell worked back then but Vladana died from childbirth and yet again did I lose the chance at some form of happiness... all because of that rat Lucien...'

Radu attempted to understand: 'You want me to kill my own brother?'

He said: 'If he is a vampire like you witches aim to suggest, how am I supposed to kill someone like that, he isn't exactly human!?'

Brynhild said: 'Well, perhaps you could inform me of some weaknesses.'

She said: 'Vampires weaknesses are for some, sun light but if I lift the prophecy, that will no longer be the case... holy water can weaken their healing powers... wooden stakes, I'm not so sure about that and I can't use my magic because Vlad has immunity towards it!'

Radu said: 'I'm sorry but I don't think I can help you...all of this information is too much to process and besides my brother does not trust me, he is rather paranoid as he hates my guts, besides, if you killed everyone from the Dragon Order that was supposed to come here... I can't trust you.'

Brynhild smirked with a hint of anger: 'I don't need you to trust me... obviously you have not listened to anything I or Olga has said.'

Brynhild said: 'Siegfried fought the dragon and that afterwards will be forgotten by everyone except for me while men still live, yet your brother neither dared to ride into the fire nor leap across it.'

Radu asked dryly: 'What?'

Brynhild made a sword appear. She drove the blade into Radu.

Radu screamed.

Brynhild

Brynhild said: 'You are not of use to me, I see now that Olga was right.'

Radu asked: 'Why on earth did you do that?

Brynhild stifled a laugh and said: 'Only ask for what is best for you to know.'

Radu coughed blood and said: 'Enough with the riddles.'

Brynhild gripped the hilt of the sword and slowly pulled it out.

She smiled at the blade as it shone brilliantly and said: 'This sword I slayed most of my enemies with, the cursed Tyrfing blade, it took me a while to retrieve it from the black sea... I've longed to feel this power again and with this sword I shall kill Hanna Tepes and once I've killed everyone in the Dragon Order with it...I shall have the sceptre of Eterna so that I may erase them from history!'

Radu collapsed effortlessly, sprawled on the moist ground. His eyes peered upwards, watching Brynhild march toward the fire and the other witches... he watched helplessly as Brynhild harnessed the moonlight's energy in the reflective blade. He tried to get up, he mustered up every ounce of strength he had; but to no success, he still was stuck flat on the ground, blood gushing out of his wound.

Suddenly though, thunder clapped in the dark sky, a voice boomed: 'That's enough!'

As if thunder had arms and hands which reached down to the land and struck instantaneously.

Brynhild saw that lightning strike and muttered: 'It's about time...I thought he'd never appear.'

Brynhild said to her witches: 'People, may I present to you, the man in the fire.'

The smoke surrounding the lightning strike dispersed and a man who was literally on fire appeared before the witches.

Brynhild's confidence however wavered when she saw a wolf like creature standing next to the man in the fire.

Helene who stood next to her master said: 'Lukos.'

Helene asked Brynhild: 'What is a werewolf doing here?'

Brynhild said nothing.

The man to whom the witches referred to as the 'man in the fire' said to Brynhild: 'Regina omnium haereticorum... or as your friends call you, Imperare... it's been a while since you banished me to another realm.'

Brynhild muttered: 'Well if it isn't the former fire demon heretic who used to be one of the sisterhood, the one and only, Stark.'

The man's flames flickered consistently.

He said: 'So it seems we remember each other... rather funny, don't you think?... Considering the circumstances where we had last seen each other.'

Brynhild said: 'Leave here now, this does not concern you, if you do not leave, I shall annihilate you, Stark.'

She said whilst pointing the sword in his direction.

Stark took three steps forward.

He exhaled and said: 'Brynhild... I come on behalf of the Witches Covenant under the direct commission of Nikolai Flammel... so you can now presume, there shall be no discussion regarding the new law of the regent, all your acts of crime go against every rule set by the regent's law hence so shall you be damned.'

Brynhild hesitated for a brief moment till she threw back her head. She roared with laughter.

She said: 'Ni-Nikolai Fflammel, that harmless man... the man who was at the heel of the sisterhood for years yet failed to find us let alone stop us.'

Stark walked closer, his boots pounding on the ground. The wolf followed behind him.

Stark said casually: 'You may be a descendant of the first witches but do not forget... I am one of the first creations.'

The man in the fire or Stark, he whom his face could not be glimpsed for even a second within the starved flames... he was not a normal human and his companion the wolf who had an elegant stature yet threatening at the same time, a wolf with dark fur as black as the night sky and had eyes so pale that they might seem ghost like. A distinctive white mark was to be seen on the wolf's sleek back.

Helene stepped forward and held her hand out to Stark, intending perhaps to cast some sort of spell. Brynhild gripped hastily at Helene's wrist and pushed the witch behind her.

A spark of light weakly bounced from the palm of Helene's hand, Brynhild, plunged the sword into the ground, the sword stood straight, patiently waiting for it's master to wield it again. Brynhild knelt down in front of the wolf and stared within it's pale eyes.

The wolf whimpered. Stark directed his glance at Brynhild. He made a glowing chain appear in his hands.

He said: 'Brynhild... your surrender means that you will come along with us willingly... correct?'

Brynhild said to the wolf, pretending to be sincere: 'What on earth are you doing with this traitor... if you had never left my side we could have moved mountains together.'

The wolf replied in a deep voice: 'Why I have never truly left you... all I wanted for you was to be the person you used to be... but I could not side completely with a mad woman who wants to destroy and remove hope from the hearts of all humanity.'

Brynhild said: 'You want me to be the woman who wanted to drown you after you were born...the darkness calls your heart a home as it does mine my child... do not go around telling me who to be when you are ashamed of the part of me that you inherited... my dearest wolf.'

The wolf snapped and growled: 'I came here because I wanted to see you again...but how dare you call me the name that you had given me in the past... my name is Midnight.'

Brynhild stood up and said to Stark: 'No I shall not go freely, I have been plotting all this for centuries alongside my sisters and few brothers... I don't know what Nikolai Flammel has to throw at the sisterhood... I am much more powerful than he will ever be... one can never show up ones elders... I am his ancestor, my blood magic is lethal to him and everyone that is descended from me.'

Stark muttered: 'What is your goal... what are you trying to achieve?'

Olga marched towards Stark and said: 'You need to leave...'

Stark said: 'Brynhild, you claim that you wish to bring oblivion and suffering to this world...but I have reason to believe otherwise...there is one thing that is clear... revenge and self hatred.'

Brynhild winked at him and only returned a cold smile. Olga crossed her arms.

Olga demanded to know: 'What do you mean by self hatred?!'

Stark answered: 'The sisterhood wishes to exact their revenge on those that have or had wronged them... your greatest idol, the witch that all other dark or wronged witches look up to... committed a heinous crime against her own kind.'

Olga stated: 'Imperare would never bruise the honour or harm any of the witches in the sisterhood.'

Stark explained: 'Olga the Wise... the woman with whom I spoke to and tried to reveal the truth yet only to find out that you were on Brynhild's side whilst pretending to be on the side of the Dragon Order, the perfect double agent, you who are the deceiver has been deceived... the one who burned the Apheseus coven to cinders was... me.'

Olga balled her hands into fists. She twisted her mouth and looked angrily at Stark.

Stark continued to explain: 'During the time that I was a part of the sisterhood, Brynhild had trusted me as I was part of the inner circle of the sisterhood witches and warlocks, she entrusted me her deepest thoughts including the pity hatred of her dead sisters.'

He continued: 'You are descended of Brynhild's half sister, Lillith... according to the story of the trinity, the story that is known to the sisterhood... Brynhild was shattered when she heard her sister had been killed by this dragon called Morgoth, towards the end, this sadness caused a wish in Brynhild, a wish to die but in reality that was not the case, she wished to die not just out of sadness but out of hatred as well, she hated her sisters for dying and leaving her all alone... despite having another reason to live...'

Stark glanced at Midnight. Suddenly, a strange draft of wind passed by, a wind that felt cold and remote, a feeling in the air that could be translated as misleading and dull or perhaps as 'intense nervousness.'

A door appeared, an abnormal light glowed around the door like a beacon. A hand appeared and with it a person, this person wore a long sleeved shirt, long pants and also an open coat. As Brynhild eyed who it was, her hands shook, her heart that existed as a dark lump of coal started to burn ferociously, an ember awakening to the heart beat.

Brynhild's voice boomed: 'Lucien!'

She growled: 'How dare you show your face after nearly 756 years!'

Helene took the child from another witch and intended to teleport else where. Lucien waved his hand at Helene. Helene froze on the spot.

Lucien clapped his hands and chuckled.

He said: 'A simple paralysis spell...honestly Brynhild... did you really think you'd get away with your little schemes... I know that you are capable of many things... but even you or someone as powerful as Nikolai Flammel could never stop me.'

Brynhild screamed: 'No!'

Somehow she telepathically created a cut on Lucien's face. Lucien felt for a very distinct, brief moment, the feeling of pain however, in a matter of seconds, the cut healed. Lucien felt with his hand that the wound had healed.

He frowned and said: 'I congratulate you for scraping my face, very few people have done such a feat... well never mind that, I am here for the child that is all.'

Stark stated to Lucien: 'I did not think it proper for the world's most important demon to come all this way to deal with a group of outlaw witches and warlocks.'

Lucien pointed out: 'I could not rely on just Nikolai's warlock and associate to complete the task...besides, these witches are all part demon which leaves some of the jurisdiction to the Hidden Empire.'

Brynhild took her sword and turned to Lucien.

She told him in a serious tone: 'You shall never have this child...just as you continuously deprived me of happiness... I shall keep this child till all the flesh is torn from my bones!'

Lucien said to Stark: 'Besides, this is personal to me... the child might not be of your interest to save but this child belongs to someone that I care about.'

Stark's flames went into an uproar as he said: 'Very well, take the child, me and my accomplice shall deal with the witches.'

Midnight made a strange aura appear around her. She pounced from witch to witch with the speed of light.

Stark's flames wrapped around him till he was completely enveloped by them.

Stark said to Brynhild: 'I shall burn you witches till there is nothing left but ashes, this is not the same evil you had once forced me to do against the Apheseus coven.'

Brynhild stated: 'If you're more powerful than all the witches here then you've always had your own will...do not play it off as being a poor man.'

Stark hesitated at first then said: 'Brynhild, you are correct but we both know that you've always been somehow more powerful than me, besides, back then you had leverage against me.'

Stark disappeared and a large mass of fire encircled the grove... a threatening fire. Voica who was a witch, tried to magically blast water onto the fire as it crept up to her, the flames however would not be beckoned by the water in any way. Voica saw the dead witches and few warlocks. She was one of the last ones standing... it was a stale mate... there was nothing left for a witch like her to do. She raised her hands above her head and created a glowing disc in which the face of whom she thought of... her brother Corvus appeared.

She cried out: 'Corvus, hear my plea, I know who destroyed our coven, search me out if you want to know but right now the sisterhood is being massacred, oh dear I must find mother!'

Voica bolted in search of her mother, the glowing disc had disappeared.

Brynhild looked like she was about to teleport but was stopped when Olga yelled: 'Brynhild!'

Olga summoned using a strange dark magic, a creaky, groaning skeleton that lunged at Brynhild.

Brynhild held her hand to the skeleton and created a shock wave strong enough to rattle the skeleton apart, the bones clattered on the floor, Olga huffed. Brynhild saw the old witch trying to put effort into her magic.

Brynhild laughed at Olga. Olga pointed at Brynhild.

She bickered: 'You, you were the one that conspired against the sisterhood... you destroyed my home by sending that warlock there... don't you feel any remorse!?'

Brynhild answered in an empty tone: 'No.'

A young witch ran to Olga and screamed: 'Mother, we must leave at once!'

She pointed above at the flames that were merging to create a fire dome.

Olga muttered to Voica: 'This is Stark's doing... this is strange magic... we must leave.'

Olga summoned a portal even though it strained her to do so.

Voica asked her mother with worry: 'Mother, why didn't you let me open the portal?'

Olga assured her daughter: 'I may be old and this drastic night of magic may have taken it's toll on me but I'll be alright.'

Olga and Voica proceeded to leave through the portal.

Brynhild scoffed and assumed: 'So this means that the days of the sisterhood are over...perhaps... as long as I live, it will never be over.'

Olga said: 'I no longer choose to help you with your plan Brynhild... I once believed in you... believed in the cause for witches dominion but now you only want revenge... there's simply nothing else left, obviously you are that cursed to not be able to care... you only care about yourself.'

Brynhild asked: 'Does this mean you side with the enemy?'

Olga shrugged her shoulders and replied: 'No, today has proven to me that there is no true enemy for everywhere I see they are always there, the enemy unknown circling me in the midst... this is goodbye.'

Olga went into the portal with her daughter and disappeared.

Brynhild said to herself: 'I do not say goodbye, I will see you again when I kill you for your treachery... even then I shall not say goodbye.'

Lucien tried to remove the force field that Brynhild had cast over Helene and the toddler. His hand touched an impenetrable surface. He knew it was some kind of protection spell. Brynhild and Lucien stood across from each other now.

Brynhild said while looking at her surroundings: 'It's only me, you, the wolf and the annoying fire.'

Lucien said: 'Despite our past, I am willing to let this go... if you come willingly.'

Brynhild said: 'So that head of yours does remember...the centuries of torment you sentenced me to endure when you turned me into a vampire, I am fed up with everyone expecting me to come willingly.'

125

Lucien said: 'Brynhild it is over, your nasty plans have been put to a halt.'

He made a sceptre with the colour of gold and a curious gemstone set inside the top of the sceptre appear.

Lucien hovered the sceptre over his hands.

He explained: 'This has been retrieved from the Dragon Order... I do not know what they were planning with it... luckily, only the inner circle of members know of mythical creatures...then there is you... you want to use this sceptre to erase the Dragon Order from history itself... or once you had stripped your curse, you wanted to store the energy of the curse inside the gemstone of the sceptre.'

Brynhild's smirk twitched, she asked angrily: 'When did you have the time to acquire my sceptre?'

Lucien's finger tapped the pointed top of the stone that was inserted into the sceptre.

He chuckled quietly and said: 'An Actinolite stone.'

Helene's paralysis spell slowly lifted as she could now speak.

She said in a strained voice: 'In Greek Aktis means ray and lithos meaning stone... radiating stone in English it is called Actinolite.'

Lucien casually said: 'Let me briefly explain... it does not matter, this sceptre is going to be destroyed now.'

The sceptre began to spin in a hectic manner, then exploded into multiple pieces. The gemstone however, landed back into Lucien's hand.

Brynhild shouted: 'No!'

Lucien created a gigantic ball of light which turned into a torrent that zoomed forth and blasted Brynhild. Brynhild's protection spell slowly cracked and shattered. Brynhild screeched.

Brynhild's clothes floated to the ground. Brynhild was dead, all that was left of hers was her clothes.

Lucien closed his hand and muttered: 'Something's not right... this was just too easy.'

The flames dispersed and Stark appeared.

He said whilst rubbing his hands together: 'Do not ponder over it... our task here has been completed.'

Lucien nodded slowly in a hesitant manner.

Midnight approached them and spoke telepathically: 'I don't think this brisk mission of ours was a complete success.'

Stark stated: 'Sometimes you have daft senses, wolf.'

A faint voice said: 'How astute of you my dearest wolf......'

Midnight growled: 'Rarr, show yourself... you fiend!'

Lucien said in a self assured manner: 'I knew it!'

He continued: 'You're not dead Brynhild... this is uncalled for!'

Brynhild laughed in a shrill tone.

She said: 'Ahah ha ha... let that annoyance devour you whole for the next time we meet I shall be able to completely annihilate you.'

Stark questioned the voice: 'How did you escape?'

Brynhild casually explained: 'Well originally my clone that Lucien blasted to death using light magic was my escape plan so... you see I had no intention for staying back to get killed with my other witches if something went wrong and it did, so before the entire ritual took place I had created a magic clone that was able to take my place... it was very convincing wasn't it?'

Lucien asked: 'How were you able to do magic that way?'

Brynhild said: 'Simple... the clone was my puppet and I was it's master though working through a clone does have it's limits... the things you all have seen me do was just a taste of my magic... soon all of you will see it's worst... that I promise... so if there is anyway that either of you three should have a fetish for dying, let me know... tah!'

The voice left.

After that, Helene shouted: 'Wait Imperare!'

Stark yelled over her voice: 'She left you here at our mercy...stop bickering and lay your fanaticism to rest Helene!'

Lucien took the child from Helene.

He muttered: 'Such a poor thing...so little yet so many high expectations and dangers are put before you...that reminds me of your father...hmm.'

Lucien summoned a strange door and opened it.

Midnight mentioned to Lucien before he left: 'We have underestimated my mother again... we must put an end to that and her once and for all... in her plans she mentioned wanting to destroy Vlad which I now know why. However, the thing with her is you never truly know what to expect with her... if you care about Vlad... keep a close eye on him.'

Lucien said: 'There is another thing that we must keep in mind... Cyrus.'

Midnight inquired: 'You mean my father's biggest enemy?'

Lucien said: 'Yes... I know where he is... for the last few years he has remained neutral but if he discovers that I lied to him about Brynhild being dead...we will have a revolt from the vampire Ancestor himself... perhaps you should reach out to your father... where is he actually?'

Midnight said in a low tone: 'Me and my father have a difficult relationship... the last thing I heard from other werewolves is that he is somewhere by the Apuseni mountains searching for something.'

Radu who had not been lucid to see the madness unfold, awoke now to see a furry wolf, a strange man who was literally on fire and Lucien holding a toddler?

Radu screamed. Stark noticed him and sighed in annoyance.

He asked Lucien: 'What are we supposed to do with him... a charred body perhaps?'

The flames flickered with slight sarcasm.

Lucien said: 'No... we shall erase his memories, he is still Vlad's brother even if Vlad hates him.'

Radu had a confused and frightened look on his face.

Midnight said to Stark: 'We should report back to the Witches Covenant.'

Lucien said rather stiffly: 'Go... I'll take care of the rest.'

Stark said: 'Alright, we'll teleport back... Lucien... Brynhild's sword disappeared.'

Lucien said: 'So it seems...but without the stone that I removed from the sceptre... Brynhild's sword... that sword is only capable of doing physical damage.'

Stark said: 'I don't understand... her sword you told me it's indestructible a sword from the Gods itself.'

Lucien stated: 'It is quite literally a sword from the Gods... it's power can destroy armies or call upon the dead... a sword that cannot be destroyed in any way nor rebuilt, a sword that cannot be wielded by a nobody... the wielder must be chosen by the sword... a long time ago... when I showed Brynhild how to learn to live as a vampire I had seen that sword... Brynhild claimed a woman had left the sword to the next person who had chosen it... she found a way to amplify the swords powers... an enchanted Actinolite stone... one of a kind.'

Lucien exhaled and continued: 'The first enchanted Actinolite stone in existence...she did not rebuild the sword... she added something to it's guard... a stone set inside the guard of the sword.'

Stark asked: 'Then how did the stone end up in the sceptre?'

Lucien presumed: 'The Dragon Order found the stone and had it placed into the sceptre to amplify it's abilities...'

Stark said: 'Well then the Dragon Order did indeed have the same plan as Brynhild... they wanted to erase each other from history... thank god Morgoth is dead... otherwise the order he had created would have given us a world of pain.'

Stark asked him: 'How did you find the sceptre?'

Lucien said: 'Because of what I overheard from the rumours of Olga the Wise.'

Stark said: 'Lucien... when you appear somewhere again use that demon door of yours... they cannot be traced so easily by witches and so does bypass teleportation.'

Stark raised his hands to the sky and said the following: 'Thunder in the sky, reach down, take us up, bring us high, where I wonder shall we fly, in time we shall find the land to lie.'

The sky thundered, a lightning bolt touched Stark and Midnight after that they were gone.

Lucien muttered: 'Dramatic flare as always.'

Lucien said to Helene who had been watching the entire time: 'Don't worry... I'm sure there's another spot reserved for you by the Hidden Empire's critically insane.'

He shoved Helene through the demon door, he briefly glanced at Radu and said: 'Oh I mustn't forget you.'

He blinded Radu with a strange magic. From which Radu disappeared.

Lucien looked at the empty grove and shook his head, he then proceeded into the demon door and carried the child with him to the underworld. The witches and warlocks who had been killed; their bodies disappeared after Lucien had gone through the demon door. When they were gone there was nothing left but the remains of scattered ashes that were swept by the wind that dwindled amongst the several dark burnt trees but occasionally you'd hear an almost unrealistic tune of laughter prance in that wind.

A voice answered sometimes: 'This is just the beginning of something that has already begun.'

The laughter would come and the voice would trail off into the distance, carried by the wind.

At the end of March, 1456, at Targoviste, Wallachia:

The first rays of sunlight tried to pry it's way into the room via the small pitiful window as Radu jolted upright in bed. He realised that everything had been just a dream... the wolf, a man on fire hah, how creative he was indeed... what a dream that was, absurd and deluded that was what Radu thought. Radu laughed at his ridiculous mind. He dressed himself, combed his hair... you know the types of things someone called Radu the Handsome would do to look good. Right? Radu patted down his clothes to remove any creases... something he could do for hours on end that it seemed like he wished to wage war on his own clothes. He went about his everyday activities... flirting with Ilona's hand maids, pretending to care about Ilona and help with her regent duties. Despite seeing Ilona distraught and barely holding it together... yes, Radu did remember how she suffered from the death of her daughter.

Strangely, Radu's dream involved Ilona's daughter. Nah just a dream right? Not a dream when in fact Lucien had brainwashed Radu and sent him back to the castle where he had been in bed before having gone to the grove. Radu was leaning over a table discussing the regional seats with Ilona and the importance of the regional seat of Poenari castle that is close by to Fagaras but still within the border of Wallachia. It was a good asset to have Radu thought to himself. His brother was smart to have had a castle erected there since it was a good political and tactical spot to have a castle, close to allies but not too far away from Targoviste than it is from Bucharest.

Ilona asked Radu: 'I know Vlad commissioned the build for the castle before the war but the build only started somewhat into the war in 1453... is the castle even finished?'

Radu casually said: 'Most of it is finished but there are a few castle foundations that need modifications.'

Ilona said rather quietly: 'Don't you think it would be wise to have a part of the Wallachian army guard this castle if it's so important?'

Radu asked in a bothered manner: 'What do you mean?'

Ilona had dark circles under her eyes.

She looked at him in a tired manner and said: 'Well, if the Saxons are rebelling and the castle is somewhat close to Fagaras... it will be attacked by them because...'

She nodded to herself in a sheepish manner and pushed a marker across on the map to where Sibiu and Brasov was located.

She ended her sentence with a yawn: 'Because Sibiu and Brasov are shockingly close to the region of Fagaras and Amlash, the Saxons happen to inhabit the Hungarian land of Sibiu and Brasov.'

Radu frowned.

He casually assured her: 'It'll be fine... Vlad is off fighting against the Saxons... they will be kept so entertained by my crazy brother that they won't find the time to get distracted.'

Ilona reproached him: 'Is that what you think of my husband... some dandy parade soldier...what a brother you are... so capable.'

Radu snapped at her: 'I will not be lectured by a woman let alone my brother's wife.'

Ilona said while standing up: 'I may be a woman and I may lack the combat skills of the men in the army but I had basic training so that I could defend myself, my uncle John saw talent in me but because of the fact that I was a woman, my education never went further than that...but still I am a woman... Vlad still decides to come to me for advice and not another man even if he is his brother.'

She barged out of the room.

Radu groaned and dropped ever so pathetically into a chair. He asked himself why he had to come to Targoviste in the first place. There seemed to be this haze in his mind, the more he thought about it, the less sense it made.

Ilona ran to her room and yelled at her maid to leave the room. She sat by the fire place and reached into a basket. Her hands shook as she held a small shirt, something she had embroidered and strewn with those very hands, tears dripped onto her daughters shirt. She buried her face in it and screamed into it, she didn't want anyone to hear her, she was Ilona after all, calm and collected but was she really?

Italy, Florence, 1456 AD:

The day was half way through when a mage named Corvus was waving his hand over a pot of water, the water was moving, a glowing image of everything that happened at the Sacred Grove was reflected on the water. A man who wore rather fashionable clothes for this time and had an extremely modest as well as a stern nature walked up to Corvus and interrogated him.

He asked: 'So after all this time, we finally found information as to why Lucien has been acting so secretively?'

Corvus said: 'Yes indeed, though tapping into the concealing spells to hear and be able to see something was adequately challenging, Lucien truly wanted to make sure no one discovered what happened at the grove, in fact if my sister Voica hadn't sent out that magical signal that tampered a bit with Lucien's spells I would never have been able to break through the magic to see what happened.'

An image of Voica appeared on the water.

Corvus asked him: 'Lord Cyrus, I believe you should see all of it for yourself... there is something that might upset you.'

Cyrus boasted: 'No, why should I be upset... Lucien and I are no longer friends that much is true but I swore like he swore to me, no more lies... so if this has more to do with his new human or vampire pet project named Vlad, that does not interest me or anger me in any way.'

Corvus grinned and said: 'So you say... we shall see Lord Cyrus... please excuse me, I must retire...'

The bell on the shop door rang downstairs.

Corvus said: 'A customer buying more art supplies.'

Cyrus marched towards the stairs and shouted: 'I'll deal with it!'

Cyrus went to the counter to see a young man with chestnut hair observe a vial of crushed powder.

Cyrus asked him: 'May I help you sir?'

He asked again with more suspicion: 'Or can I help a fellow vampire?'

The vampire turned around to face him.

He frowned and said: 'Actually yes you can... if you have a colour that symbolises betrayal.'

Cyrus teased him: 'Why don't you grab a deep red from that shelf over there, I mean it does depend heavily on what you wish to paint put betrayal is a deep thing and red is every vampires favourite colour.'

The other man asked: 'How do you know who I am... a vampire?'

Cyrus said whilst taking a jar that was labelled deep red: 'I know you, you are a very unique vampire, I am pretty sure the oldest vampires have heard of the first known born vampire in existence, Oliver Lothbrok.'

Oliver shrugged his shoulders, passed the money and said: 'Actually I did not come here to talk about myself, I was sent here on behalf of the Demon King himself.'

Cyrus said casually: 'Oh really, now then, does my store not fit the Demon King's imaginary list of regulations?'

Oliver said while taking the jar of paint he had paid for: 'No, he simply wishes to say that he knows that you know and that he will be watching you very closely.'

Oliver waved goodbye and walked out the store though on the way out, he passed a woman who held hands with two children.

Cyrus greeted the woman: 'Ah Odeta, you came all this way for art supplies?'

Odeta complained to her children: 'Leo, Maria, stop it now!'

Cyrus and Odeta held a short conversation from which she and her children left shortly after.

Oliver had only smiled at the children who did not yet understand what they were, neither did their mother.

Later:

Cyrus stormed upstairs and watched the events that Corvus had watched earlier in the water. After a while yelling could be heard from upstairs... an event rarely seen by Cyrus after he tried so hard to rebuild his life from a life time of denial, hiding in the shadows, misfortune at love and being lied to the man he had once considered somewhat of a friend.

He yelled: 'That lying scoundrel, that snide, deceitful, obnoxious idiot, you lied to me!'

He'd then pause and start yelling out other complete nonsense: 'You'll be watching me closely... I've had it with you and your self absorbed poor Demon King trash, I will show you, you flat head!'

Arefu, Wallachia, 1456 AD:

There was an army on its way at the crack of dawn. The men all had degrading looks on their faces. With every step, those looks seemed to sink deeper into their souls. Vlad rode a horse and led his men forth, eventually they would cross the border. They had already passed through Arefu, seen the Poenari castle that was situated on a cliff overlooking the Arges river, this meant they were about to cross the

134

border as they were close to Fagaras. Vlad felt a certain unease take over. He couldn't explain what it was.

On the way out of Arefu, Vlad glimpsed a wild bear.

He came to a halt and got off his horse and shouted: 'Stop!'

He cautiously approached the bear. The bear growled at him. He saw that the bear had an arrow shot close to it's heart. He somehow managed to kneel down in front of the bear.

He spoke in a quiet tone: 'Now what happened to you? Normally I'm not too fond of bears, when I went hunting when I was younger, they'd come and steal what I had felled.'

He stroked the bear's fur and said: 'But for you I'll make an exception.'

The bear's eyes pleadingly looked at him. Vlad seemed to see a part of his own reflection in the eye of that bear. He could not tolerate the suffering of the eyes that were latched onto him, begging for some compassion and understanding. He stood up and retrieved a broad sword from his horse.

He walked back over and said: 'A part of me understands how you feel, all alone in your tangible existence, don't fret, your suffering shall be gone for I will put you out of your misery.'

With one blow to the neck he had ended the bear's life and with that he got on his horse and charged on, for weeks he travelled with his men through to Fagaras and over the main border of Wallachia till they reached a point where they were halfway to Bistri, they made camp on an open plain so that if the enemy approached there would be no landscape advantage since there was nowhere to hide too easily in an open area. No element of surprise so as to say.

In the back of the of wagons that the army had taken all the way with them, they had weaponry which included fire arms, lances, broad swords, bows assembled with arrows, equipment to build tents and so forth, Vlad had indeed prepared ahead for everything... the wagons could even be turned into a proper weapon wagon like the ones he saw John Hunyadi use with triumph in battle.

Transylvania, Hungary 1456 AD,

It was night time. Vlad was feeding his horse some sort of dried food.

He stroked the horse's forehead and said to the horse: 'A-indura, it's been hard, all this warfare, but I promise you on my blood and bones that you shall remain by my side even if you shall be buried next to me my trusty steed.'

The horse stole a piece of food from Vlad. Vlad laughed for a brief moment, he was amused by a horse. He tied the horse to a post.

He said in a saddened tone: 'There are times I wish I had your enthusiasm and your unlimited toleration for things, you get excited about nearly everything... that is why I named you A-indura, in Wallachian it roughly means to endure.'

Vlad was pulled back into the world of reality as someone said: 'Voivode, the blacksmith you requested has arrived with the goods.'

Vlad folded his arms and said: 'As expected, bring me to him.'

The soldier requested that the Voivode followed him if he wished. Vlad entered a tent that smelt like new metal.

Vlad spoke to the two men: 'I gather that these metal suits of armour is like nothing I've ever seen or worn before... hopefully; these cost me a fortune to pay you fools to manufacture.'

Vlad read the mind of the older man and knew what he was about to say.

One of the men wished to speak when Vlad said: 'Before you say something that you're going to regret... think before you speak.'

The other man apologised and said: 'Sorry, my name is Kazaan, my master here who is the blacksmith has a real slick tongue and a habit to be rude, I am but an apprentice, so you'd like to see the armour, here it is.'

He showed Vlad to a pile of armour. Multiple sets of gauntlets, boots, upper body and lower body amour was to be seen.

Vlad asked slowly: 'Kazaan?'

Kazaan asked: 'Yes Voivode?'

Vlad said: 'Nothing, I thought you and I have met before.'

Kazaan said: 'Perhaps Voivode, I mean it is possible that we er have maybe met before, you see my family bloodline could have made it possible before my distant cousin decided to die a martyr or so he thought he did.'

Vlad remembered the memories he had seen in his own mind before he had killed Vladislav a little over two years ago. He knew who this Kazaan was. He was the grand cousin of Vladislav II. Vlad glared at Kazaan. Kazaan shrugged his shoulders.

He told him: 'I am from the Danesti faction if you must know...don't worry I do not possess enough idiocy to cause you trouble.'

Vlad hit him on the shoulder and said: 'I would hope so.'

Vlad froze for a moment. He saw another memory. A woman screaming, he saw people that looked like Ottoman Turks kill the others, there was a young girl who hid a little boy, she seemed to be crying. After she hid the boy in a large basket she was taken hostage by two men and was dragged away. The memory faded.

Vlad shook his head and turned to inspect the armour. Kazaan frowned.

He asked: 'The ore that was used to create all this, what is it?'

Vlad said in a slightly irritated manner: 'It's a secret.'

Vlad turned around to Kazaan and asked him with suspicion: 'Why do you ask?'

Kazaan said: 'It's very versatile, when we transported it here all the way from Bucharest, it rained a lot, there was no damage to any of the equipment... it's like it's rust proof.'

Vlad smiled slightly and said: 'Of course.'

He walked out of the tent after announcing: 'The armour will be worn in the battle against the Saxons.'

When the Voivode left the tent, Kazaan murmured: 'A vicious man our Voivode.'

The older man said: 'Cold and cruel but he does fight for his country with strong conviction.'

A while after that, Vlad had his most talented soldier Ivan and other men join him to devise a plan to launch an attack on Bistri.

Vlad spoke in a clear voice: 'After this conversation, we will pack up camp but keep our spare supplies here, our main supply wagons that are our main convoy shall move closer with us, north east of Bistri there are hills that we can wait out the correct timing to start the attack, doing this we can hide other supplies and Ivan's men shall stay behind there as for the rest of us, we will storm the walls and bring those Saxons to heel.'

Vlad batched wrapped paper onto the table. He unrolled the paper and took a quill and marked a rough layout of what seemed to be a place surrounded by fortress like walls.

Vlad said: 'Here, here and there, the entire place is surrounded by these walls, know your enemy and plan ahead and always have a back up plan, so there are walls... what is the first thing that comes to mind?'

Ivan remarked: 'Challenge of entry.'

Vlad said with a hint of annoyance: 'Very obvious but yes... what should come to mind is that we can't just fly over the walls though that does sound convenient.'

At this statement he smirked.

Vlad said whilst taking a rope from a box: 'This rope has a grapple hook, we can swing the rope upwards and when the grapple hook has hooked itself into the top of the castle walls, we can tug the end of the rope to check for a secure hold. Once the hold has been confirmed, we can then proceed to climb up and over the walls.'

Vlad sensed doubt from Ivan.

Ivan asked: 'But what if there are guards above?'

He asked: 'How do we climb up if they hear or see us before we take action?'

Vlad pounded the table with his hands. He pounded it so hard that the table broke in two.

He said through gritted teeth: 'You seem to deliberately try to get under my skin Ivan... I was going to mention that in due time, it was part of my plan but you had to interrupt me so I couldn't continue... do that again and I will personally chop an entire finger off your hand.'

Ivan cowered under the quick sound of silence.

Vlad said: 'Brilliant, I may continue, so if anyone else wishes to POINT out my plan, I will be much obliged to cut off a FINGER OR TWO.'

Vlad said mockingly whilst appreciating the silence: 'I guess point taken.'

Vlad continued: 'So, in order for us to approach a wall, if there are guards observing from above, a small group of us will go to the other side of the walls surrounding Bistri dressed as civilians with armour underneath and create a commotion, that will draw the attention of the guards from the other side to the distraction; giving the others much needed time to climb over, in addition, we will scale the walls from multiple directions to have more of us in Bistri quicker than the Saxons have time to act, before any of you ask, I have considered the use of a catapult or something else but a mechanism of the sort would make sound and would take a while to assemble.'

Vlad added: 'I have a sort of gut feeling that our combat skills are basic and decent but I do not wish to risk the bloodshed of my own people, which is when we are inside Bistri, we can allow our ruthlessness to run free, but speaking from experience, ruthlessness is important but it is crucial to know when and where to be like that, now my last words of advice is that I have no guarantee that this plan will work but if we never proceed then we shall never find out and the fact that we are trying is displaying our ruthlessness.'

Vlad said: 'Divide and conquer men and prepare yourselves, that is an order, not a request, anyone who does not fall in line, I'd be delighted to have a word with their family so this goes as a HEAD-start for deserters.'

He winked at Ivan and the others and left the tent.

Ivan grumbled: 'Alright then men, you heard the Voivode.'

Ivan was a faction leader in Vlad's army. He had about five years of combat experience and was 20 years old, when he had joined at the age of 16, he had been considered an adult like so many others his age, his father also served the Wallachian army.

Ivan Petrovka was so skilled he could handle a lance and broadsword at the same time though in combat he did have situations were he nearly risked deathly wounds but a bold man he was and driven by strong ambition; though when the Voivode had told Ivan a part of the plan for the expansion of the army which would take place after the battle against the Saxons, Ivan was shocked and disappointed in Vlad's faith in the Wallachian army despite not knowing the facts why the Voivode wanted to recruit peasants and have them join the army as well as create a new social status, free peasants... Ivan could not accept this, he saw how that ruined years of tradition in the Wallachian army and after the battle against the Saxons, a bunch of ludicrous, disgusting and dishonoured peasants would be joining the ranks. Ivan decided to take matters into his own hands and in secret he conspired against his own Voivode. Since he was part Bulgarian and of nobility, he had connections in Bulgaria and sent word of his uprising. Word spread all the way to the Sultan's court. To Mehmed the II to be exact. He and Ivan secretly exchanged letters and cooked up an idea to remove Vlad and place a Voivode onto the throne that was actually in favour of the Ottoman Turks. Ivan had in one of his more recent letters, mentioned a new type of armour that was resistant to rust, versatile like nothing he had seen before. Eventually, Mehmed suggested a way to infiltrate Vlad the Impaler's inner family circle, a person he considered an easy loophole, Radu the Handsome, the one who is least trusted by Vlad would easily side with the ideals of the Ottomans. Ivan was unsure of that suggestion but still managed to pass on a letter to Radu on behalf of Mehmed the second.

After that meeting, the camp was packed up and so the plan proceeded as Vlad willed it. When they reached the hills, the moon gleamed in between the hillsides. From there the plan continued forth. Till Vlad and most of his men arrived at Bistri, the diversion plan worked and the others climbed and stormed the walls of Bistri not wasting a second, the attacks they made struck the victims and wounded instantaneously as if the men were on fire and only when they continued did the fire pause in that moment. Vlad entered via the ajar doors that the others had opened which had been barred shut. He slit throats, stabbed, slashed the Saxons one by one, he tried not to feel any remorse, what he did feel was his blood rush and the dark side claw at his heart.

He thought: 'I promised to fight and fight I shall and once it is over, then I shall be able to return to a place that I call home... I don't want to do this, my heart should not be prey to temptation of letting go, of destroying more than I would with my sinful, damaged conscience, the dark side that Ilona helped me escape, to be better.'

A voice rang in his mind: 'Vlad there is no monster underneath your bed.'

A memory of when Vlad was seven:

Vlad said whilst hiding behind Lucien: 'But I saw something.'

Lucien said to him: 'Well it is what you make of it.'

Vlad asked in a slightly feeble manner: 'So if I think there's no monster, then there isn't?'

Lucien laughed and explained to him: 'No, what I meant is, if you think it's a monster before actually knowing if it is or not, then of course you're bound to be afraid, but you don't have to see it as one.'

The memory dispelled. Vlad noticed how he had kept fighting whilst reliving a memory from his childhood. But he could sense the dark veining that had started to creep from his eyes, now it crawled it's way back till it was no longer seen. What he had felt was an inner blood lust manifest itself. A rage that had stayed hidden until now. Was this his inner vampire speaking? Even though he was part human, part vampire, Vlad never drank the blood of any mortal, he only used his physic powers as a vampire every now and then, before he had lived more as a human, it is not that he considered his vampirism evil for the thing he called his dark side had nothing to do with it, he simply was afraid to lose control of it, especially if someone had ever seen his eyes, his black demonic eyes, he would have a problem... but now in the midst of battle he did not mind to let go for no one paid attention...

The veining tingled in his eyes. He reached for a torch that was lit, took it and marched over to a pile of hay, he then set it alight. The fire started slowly then charged upwards, the flames devouring everything it could till it spread.

Vlad shouted over the sound of flames whilst beheading an enemy: 'Everyone of the Wallachian army, it is over, let us leave and let today be a victory and a lesson for the Saxons not to mess with Wallachia!'

His soldiers saw as others fled from Bistri, they hesitated as they traced with their own eyes, a large area of bodies surrounding the Voivode. In their eyes, it seemed Malevolent, to stand there with a smile.

Vlad breathed in excess. He forced a smile which was so convincing, almost terrifying. The men were compelled to applaud the Voivode out of fear of doing something wrong.

Vlad was about to leave with his men since the fire was tearing at the walls, embers of the fire spread setting new fires when he spotted what seemed to be a girl hiding behind a stack of crates. She covered her mouth to reduce the sound she made. Vlad narrowed his eyes at her. He side stepped and motioned for the girl to come out of hiding. She slowly came out, fear written on her face. Vlad observed his surroundings and saw that his army was waiting in the distance.

He said to the girl, trying to communicate with her: 'Your parents either fled with the others or were killed, sorry but I don't know if I killed them, I killed many, too many to count, now I cannot grant your parent's back their lives but I can do a deed and let you go your ways, I will not hurt you, you may go back to whatever you have left.'

The girl nodded in a timid manner and then made a run for it, after that it was like she had never been there. Vlad cracked his knuckles, sighed and joined his men to return back to the hillside.

Targoviste, Wallachia 1456 AD:

Radu was pondering much over what Ilona had said. She was right. Vlad did indeed seek her counsel more than his own brother... Radu wondered if it was their difficult sibling relationship that led to this. Radu did not care really... or did he? Was he jealous of Ilona? Resentful of the fact that she had some wit and was a woman... jealous of a woman... that's downright outrageous he thought. But what he really was jealous of was the family Vlad had whilst Radu's own wife was probably delusional over the recent incident of the premature birth of their second child, but what about his daughter, Dahlia... what a strange little creature she was indeed... hah a pathetic notion came into mind, love, Radu was always pestering his mother for just even a second of her attention, most of the time she just ignored him then along came a well um a little brother, he could remember the day that his mother seemed so happy, she was brimming with happiness when she found out she was with child.

He had asked her at the age of seven something like: 'Why can't you always be this happy?'

Vladana's face would freeze, she would gaze at him, a timeless stare, perhaps wanting to see right through him then she would look away, smile and laugh once more. As months passed something in Radu's mother changed, it was like she was growing in a certain direction,

Radu thought that a gigantic boulder was growing inside his mother. Radu did not understand how his mother could love a rock more than him. His mother and father named him Vlad. Radu soon discovered his brother was anything but a rock, that was also the same day he swore eternal hatred.

Yes, how he hated his brother... Radu felt as if at every end of every day his thoughts returned back to this. That haze surrounding his mind returned. Confusion plagued his mind.

An anonymous person whispered: 'Radu cel Frumos, I have a letter for you.'

The person edged closer and with a scrawny hand he reached a letter for Radu. The letter was tempting so he snatched it from the person. Radu investigated the letter but when he looked up to see who had given him it, that person was gone. Radu renewed his attention to the letter. He noticed a very fresh newly put seal on the letter smelling strongly of candle wax. This person had been in a hurry to get the letter to him.

Radu added: 'For your discretion, I will read it then.'

He tore open the envelope and gasped at who wrote the letter. The letter seemed abnormal for every word contained a lot of R.

He muttered angrily: 'How am I to read a muddled letter?!'

Then he turned the letter to the back and read a small sentence: Remove the R.

He said: 'Ah so its a matter of secrecy.'

He turned the letter around and imagined away every R that had been placed in the sentence. The letter said:

So you are Radu the Handsome, how intriguing that the mole of the Tepes family had been hiding in Wallachia in plain sight... I am aware of your past and I know how awkward this letter may seem. I am Mehmed the second or as other people call me Mehmed the Conqueror, your brother thinks and acts as if I am a villain, as if everything I do is evil, however, all I ever did was complete my role as the Sultan of the Ottoman Turks... being a leader is hard and it has it's burdens as well as it's fair share of taxing dramas, how is that being evil? Is how I was forced to follow in my father's footsteps evil? It is easy to judge someone's actions after having made them... you too have been judged wrongly as your brother hates you just because he had to become the next Voivode and you didn't, but we both know why you couldn't become the Voivode, don't we? Apparently a person who knew Vlad the second's best kept secret informed me of your past, as you are ashamed, I stand with irritation forever on my mother's pathetic grave. Now Radu, gather that hatred and befriend yourself with the idea of joining the Ottoman Turks in the fight against Vlad, after we overthrow him together, we could place you the title regardless of your heritage, trade between countries could flourish and together we could be invincible. Imagine the things we could achieve. If you consider this send me back this letter with your signature on it.

Mehmed the second.

Radu nodded in appreciation to the letters content but muttered: 'Regardless of my heritage, Vlad the second's biggest secret?'

He said: 'But I will consider it.'

He hid the letter.

Outskirts of Bistri, Hungary Transylvania, 1456 AD:

Vlad and his forces returned to the main convoy by the hillsides north east of Bistri. They made camp for the remaining night. Vlad retreated to his own tent seeking the solace of peace and quiet. Coming to terms with everything that had happened was something he wished to do away from other people, a brief moment of tiredness would seem to everyone else like a huge moment of weakness. He did this not because he was afraid of ruining his reputation since there was nothing to be ruined, especially with the title 'Vlad the Impaler', but what really was the case was that he was the representative of his country, as he must stand for his country, he must also fight for it, he may stand his ground and be his own person but he must give back assurance to his country so that his country would not lose faith in the Vlad they knew.

The Vlad that seemed to the outside world as unhinged, unchecked, ruthless, morbid, truculent, hell bent, monstrous, eternal grudge holder, harsh and insanely straight forward. A person that was never moved to tears. Every now and then, Vlad became self judgemental, through all chaos he seemed to lose hold of himself... the true side of him, perhaps the good that Ilona saw in him, it was then gone which would then take Vlad incredibly long to understand that part of himself again, before that he was lost, he had lost complete understanding of himself and that little part of himself that was able to show a sliver of compassion was gone as well, he would then revert to the version of him that people know as the cruel Vlad the Impaler in absolution. Which is why he acted so exceedingly strict and harsh so that his insanity would give normality...so that Wallachia would not be alienated ever by a slight of their Voivode.

Vlad sat down and rested his chin on his hand and tried to close his eyes. This Vlad was driven to exhaustion. It seemed only like a brief moment of charitable silence till a soldier barged into the tent. Vlad's anger began to boil. He tapped his fingers as he slowly turned to look at who had entered. If looks could kill, that soldier would have been dead the second Vlad's eyes had been set on him. Vlad straightened himself and balled both his hands into fists. He felt like he wanted to explode and set the whole camp on fire or gnash the soldiers head into a wooden post till it split in half... the liberties his cruelty would take if only...he erased the nasty thoughts from his mind and hammered his hatred back in place for the moment. Somehow Vlad was still slightly annoyed but managed to find some correct composure.

He asked the man: 'What on earth is it?'

He added very sharply: 'We only returned from the attack on Bistri a while ago.'

The soldier said: 'The ring leaders of the rebellion that fled from Bistri are now gathering support at Sibiu and Brasov... they are backing a man called Dan the III and Basarab III the Old.'

Vlad sprung up and marched out of the tent.

He shouted at the soldier: 'Silence... I must confront some of my faction leaders first to make a decision, till then keep your mouth shut lest you wish to spread panic in the army and if you don't I'll have your mouth stitched shut.'

He made haste to Ivan and the others. Ivan lead the cavalry units.

Vlad stormed into the tent and said: 'So I heard. What are we waiting for? To invite the Saxons for a dinner party?!'

Ivan said: 'Sir, we were devising a plan.'

Vlad said loudly: 'I kid not Ivan for if we do not act the Saxons will come and then they will definitely not need an invite... there is a time to plan but I feel like now is not the time to dawdle around a table blabbering endlessly about plans like a flock of morons...we must act now to prevent chaos from spreading into Wallachia.'

Vlad vividly moved his hands about and explained to them a random layout of things he had in mind: 'Ivan is the head of the cavalry units, these units ride horses and fast, they will be the quickest to reach Sibiu and Brasov to protect the border of Wallachia, by now the main defences will be prepared to defend the border but it may not suffice, so some of the cavalry will go with Ivan leading them. However, no attack will be launched otherwise Ivan's faction has a higher risk of being attacked before they arrive there, in the meantime, I will prepare a scheme that may or may not convince the Saxons to give up.'

Ivan questioned him: 'That is it, your short plan?'

Vlad said with a hint of annoyance: 'Yes it is and I am unsure if it may work, ruthless as it may seem but I have this feeling that if we don't do anything, we may lose a crucial advantage in this staggering war... do not question me Ivan.'

Ivan said: 'Alright Voivode.'

Vlad said sternly: 'Now go.'

Ivan asked: 'I beg your pardon?'

Vlad shouted: 'Go now with the cavalry to the Wallachian border!'

Ivan nodded with a narrow frown and walked out the tent.

Vlad faced his other faction leaders and said: 'Well don't just stand there like statues, get going, get the weaponry prepared, wagons loaded, notify the men under your command and make sure that certain areas in camp are packed up, the less we have left to do the quicker we can move if need be.'

The men left the tent. Vlad thought about how with just a look of anger in his eyes, he could inspire immediate fear in others.

Vlad retreated to his quarters and began to write a letter. He struggled to write his thoughts as the troubling notions of more looming wars ahead interrupted his mind. He gave his best whilst jotting down the words he had in mind.

He wrote:

I Vlad III of Draculesti and as current Voivode of Wallachia, hereby order that the trade protections that I had granted to the Saxons be stripped if they do not agree to stop this rebellion.

Signed Vlad Tepes.

In a letter that was to be sent to the Saxons he wrote:

By the decree of the current Voivode, your trade protections will be taken away if this rebellion commences further.

Signed Vlad Tepes.

When he was finished, he gave two different messengers each a letter. One he told to take the letter to the Saxons and when bringing it to them he should wave a white flag upon arrival to Sibiu or Brasov to say that he comes in peace. The other he gave to a messenger to bring to Chindia tower in Targoviste and from there the letter will be relayed to his people at his castle in Targoviste. After that both the messengers were sent on their way. Vlad only felt little hope that these letters had a chance of success.

A few days later, Sibiu, 1456 AD:

The Saxons were rather lively and were preparing many of their weapons especially after they had heard what had happened in Bistri from the leaders of the rebellion. Now they were fuming with anger for this Vlad guy and for the Hungarians. First the Hungarians want them there and now they don't? The Hungarians then hire a barbarian who used to protect the Saxons from the Ottomans to kill and bring the Saxons to bend to the will of the Hungarians, practically to do the King of Hungary's dirty work. After all this idiocy, the Saxons had had enough, hence the rebellion so they decided, for their own gain and to infuriate the Voivode to support his enemy the Danesti family of Wallachia. Suddenly a man came riding towards Sibiu. He held up a white flag. The Saxons decided to let him in. They took the letter from the messenger and brought it to their leader. He read it out in a mocking tone:

By the decree of the current Voivode, your trade protections will be taken away if this rebellion commences further.

Signed Vlad Tepes.

The elderly man waved the letter around and burst into a fit of laughter: 'Baaaahaaahaa!'

The other Saxons began to laugh as well and surrounded the messenger. They pulled him off his mount and began poking the man with sharp weapons. They would later strip him of his clothes and etch the German word Arschloch (meaning Asshole in English) over the man's entire body.

Targoviste, Wallachia, 1456 AD:

Ilona was reading a letter she had gotten relayed to her from Chindia tower.

She read to herself: *I Vlad III of Draculesti and as current Voivode of Wallachia, hereby order that the trade protections that I had granted to the Saxons be stripped if they do not agree to stop this rebellion.*

Signed Vlad Tepes.

She smiled a little at Vlad's handwriting. She called on Radu and asked him to look into the current situation regarding the Saxons.

Radu told her in a casual manner: 'There's no need, there are rumours that the Saxons are supporting the Danesti faction to annoy Vlad... if they do that as stubborn as they are, they will not surrender or stop.'

Ilona folded the letter and said: 'Alright, we shall wait for another reply from Vlad.'

Radu bickered: 'We aren't going to act?'

Ilona said: 'We cannot act without the real Voivode's approval or on mere rumours...besides the letter proves something is wrong but we have yet to know as to what extent.'

Radu forced his mouth shut as Ilona was left regent whilst Vlad was away, he was not allowed to argue or go against her. Now he realised how much he really disliked Ilona.

Northeast of Bistri, Transylvania, Hungary, Vlad's army settlement, 1456 AD:

Vlad was deeply enraged on this day. He was greeted by a message sent by the Saxons. A messenger he had sent away with one of his letters, returned dead, a rotting smell with flesh wounds and lovely flies having a banquet but the thing that stood out the most was the mass of words etched into the dead flesh of the body. The same word was repeated. Vlad who had been taught multiple languages knew what this wonderful German word meant, the word Arschloch meant Asshole. Vlad was an Asshole. Vlad saw that the corpse's eyes had been removed and inside the empty eye sockets there were flowers. An attempt of sarcasm? Thought Vlad.

He laughed very loudly and muttered: 'They play a game but I can do it better... today we leave and set foot to the closest Saxon town... let me show them a work of art that they'll remember for a long time to come.'

Wirtsland, Somewhere by Sibiu or Brasov, 1456 AD:

Vlad and his army stormed this Saxon town in such a Brazen manner that the attacks made were completely unexpected. He destroyed the grain, having each and every crop burned and the populace led into captivity. Later, he and his army retreated by St. Jacobs chapel were he had the outskirts burnt to the ground. The next morning he had the people who were in captivity, men and women impaled around the chapel. After all this strife, Vlad was hungry so he had his breakfast surrounded by his impaled victims. His soldiers looked on in horror as he raised his cup to them with a twisted smile. Soon he demanded that the Saxons lay down their weapons and stop the rebellion and cancel their support of the Danesti faction.

The Saxons refused and Vlad felt as if the world was closing in on him. The pressure was mounting, the rebellion elevated. Even the Wallachian Boyars now supported the Danesti family, the Boyars that Vlad had not removed in his purge of Boyars because at the time they had supported him. These Boyars were lords that supported someone and that person then held the title of Voivode, even if a noble family had the Boyars favour and the heirs that follow have some entitlement, if the Boyars simply decided to stop supporting that family, the title of Voivode would easily be removed and given to another from another noble family. A part of Vlad feared that his existence as Voivode would slide and he would fall. The cards were falling from his hands so as to say. After everything he'd been through, everything he had endured... it simply could not end this way, it must not end this way and yet all of Vlad's hard work came tumbling down, all the bloodshed, all the extremism had nothing to account for. There was only one thing he could do, give it everything he had, full throttle, complete ruthlessness and all the wit he could gather, only looking forward, no looking back, death, blood and gore must be the end result.

Northeast of Bistri, Transylvania, Hungary, Vlad's army settlement, 1456:

Vlad was expecting a visit from Michael Szilagyi. The tactician to the King of Hungary had sent an envoy to inform Vlad of his arrival on this day. Michael arrived in a carriage. In the distance, galloping of horses was to be heard. The carriage skidded to a halt. The members of Vlad's army whispered amongst each other as a man dressed in a stately manner opened the carriage door and got out. Vlad walked with long strides towards Michael.

He asked Michael: 'What do you seek Michael?'

Michael had a rather smug look on his face.

With his hand he knocked on Vlad's armour and said: 'I've heard the Wallachian army invented a new type of armour, the King is very interested, in fact he even sent me here to propose a bargain, a trade for some of the armour.'

Vlad felt like ripping Michael's smug look off his face.

He said: 'You tell him for now, no, right now I have other important matters to deal with.'

Michael jerked his head and said: 'Actually that is fine, I did not really come on behalf of that proposal, in truth I am just here to check on the progress of the Wallachian army and report back.'

Vlad said: 'Whatever.'

It was when a certain someone stepped out of the carriage that Vlad's face flinched for a brief moment.

Jona Hunyadi smiled.

Michael glanced at her; he remarked: 'Ah yes, she insisted to come along, something about wanting to hear from you how her sister is doing.'

Vlad shook his head.

Vlad said: 'Follow me to my quarters and I'll inform you of what has been achieved so far.'

When they were finished, Michael commented: 'Seems like multiple accomplishments for your army... okay then I presume I shall be on my way.'

He exited the tent.

Vlad's mind and heart still being captured by the crisis of war, thought to himself: 'The death of others...they aren't trophies, I can't really feel remorse from the people that I killed nor guilt for it is a part of me now, the last thing I feel is hate, hating that I must kill and a small part of me enjoyed it, my dark side but calling war an accomplishment? That's just, just...'

He ran out and shouted at Michael: 'War is not a laughing matter, we either lose our minds or ourselves, we either fight for something or nothing, clinging desperately to any form of hope whilst condemning ourselves to insanity and giving in to our darkest impulses, but we never truly laugh about it because with war, there comes not just the death of our people but the death of our land.'

Vlad added: 'We kill when we must, it is no accomplishment but something that must be done.'

Michael looked at Vlad in disbelief. He had not expected him to say such things since the King referred to him as barbaric, but someone that speaks from the heart like that is no true barbarian.

Michael nodded and walked to the carriage. Jona approached Vlad.

She said: 'It has been a while since I've seen Ilona.'

She added: 'I miss her very much.'

Vlad thought about Ilona and why she didn't write to him. He had been so busy with the rebellion that he forgot about exchanging letters with Ilona. He worried that there might be something going on in Targoviste.

Jona said: 'I thought that if I spoke with you in person that perhaps you might be able to tell me if there's something wrong with Ilona.'

Vlad said: 'I am sorry, she hasn't written to me either... I've just been so caught up in these times that I struggle to keep up with certain things.'

Jona said: 'So from what I overheard, war is terrible on you and everyone here.'

Vlad replied: 'Yes and every now and then, I feel as though the odds are stacked against me but I must-'

Jona presumed: 'Keep fighting no matter what... even if you're out on a limb with an army that's barely scraping by?'

Jona asked him a simple question: 'Vlad, what is it that drives you... motivates you, inspires you to fight like this?'

Vlad thought on it for a moment then replied: 'A while before I was taken hostage by your uncle John Hunyadi, I told myself I wanted to make a difference for the people of my country and Wallachia but now through all this madness, I feel that in this time, I have lost my sense of compassion and understanding, this vow I made turned into instinct that drove me to the edge of my insanity, this instinct forces me to keep fighting, not because I feel that I must, because I know that I must and now because of all the killing, this vengeful killing has become a complete part of me, this dark side.'

Jona laughed: 'Dark side... that's what you call your need to kill your enemies to satisfy your need for justice?!'

Vlad frowned.

He said: 'I'm being genuine and honest with you here.'

Jona calmed down and said: 'Yes I'm sorry.'

She added: 'But whatever the problem is at hand, you'll overcome it, I know you will because that's what I've always known you to do.'

Vlad chuckled and asked: 'You know me that well?'

Jona shrugged her shoulders and said: 'I guess, anyway, I must leave now, my father is waiting for me... let me know when you get any reply from Ilona.'

She wanted to run. Vlad sensed sadness in her. He grabbed her by the wrist and pulled her back.

He said: 'Look me in the eyes Jona, I can't tell otherwise if your display of sincerity is fake or not.'

Jona smiled meekly.

She said: 'It is fake, I do not in the least want to return to Buda, to my idiot husband the King of Hungary as well as being the father of my child and my cousin.'

Vlad said: 'So that is why you are sad, you are to be a mother; what is so strange about that?'

Jona stated: 'You are a man, it is something you would not understand.'

Vlad said: 'Yes but I know what it is like to have children and ponder about their future.'

Jona muttered: 'How did you know that? It is like you can read my thoughts.'

Vlad said: 'Quite literally I can do that, you are not the only one that is different, Jona.'

Jona gasped.

She said: 'Are you a werewolf like me?'

She added: 'Although even though I am a Werewolf I am currently unable to read minds. Maybe it has something to do with my pregnancy.'

Vlad chuckled and said quietly: 'I am far from it, but I am not a complete human, that is all I can reveal to you.'

Jona said: 'Well still I am with child, I may not show yet but I fear that this child will become like me, a werewolf.'

153

Vlad said: 'Only time will tell, like you told me to keep going and figure it out, I am telling you to do the same.'

Jona said: 'It is decent advice.'

Vlad slowly let go of her wrist, for a moment there he felt like holding her back, refusing to let her leave but he hesitated.

However, Jona did not leave without saying: 'Good luck Vlad.'

In that moment, you alleviated my spirit and eased my mind. He thought.

He said as the void of loneliness widened and a gap between him and his heart opened: 'Good luck Jona.'

Somewhere in the Underworld, 1456 AD:

Lucien sat in a chair. He looked into a bowl of water whilst stirring it with his finger. A reflective image appeared. He looked within the image. In the moving image, a man whom others called Dan the third was in a building that looked like a vast chamber. He appeared to be presenting a silver dagger to the others, behind them on the chamber wall there was a huge wall mural of a painted black, winged dragon, next to it was the symbol of a crescent moon and the word Moarte.

The others wore hoods over their faces. Dan placed dried leaves into the bowl that was placed on the altar and emptied a bottle into the dried leaves. He raised his hands to the ceiling chanting some nonsense.

Lucien knew what this man was planning. Since he had destroyed the sceptre and prevented them to use Radu in their attempts to kill Vlad, they now decided to create their own weapon. He also knew what the word Moarte meant, it was the Wallachian word for death.

A voice spoke: 'Lucien.'

Lucien had accidentally knocked over the bowl of water after having been distracted by the voice.

The clear voice echoed: 'Lucien.'

A man appeared as a reflection on the spilt water. Lucien glimpsed the reflection.

A shadowy figure spoke to Lucien: 'I have found that which I require to kill her, there is only one way to ensure that her soul is dead.'

Lucien replied: 'Is that really you?'

He added: 'So that is what you were looking for all this time.'

The shadow cast figure held a small box.

The figure said: 'I will take care of this myself Lucien... do not interfere.'

The figure disappeared and Lucien made a chess board appear on the stone table.

He handled the queen chess piece and said: 'I would not dream of meddling with your murder plots for the Red Blood Queen, yet...'

Borders of Brasov, Hungary, 1456 AD:

Hordes of Saxons were gathering as the rebellion continued. Vlad had the bold idea of secretly moving his army to the shared border that lied between Fagaras and Wallachia. Before this plan, Vlad introduced favourable tariffs to the Wallachian merchants to keep them on his side and in his favour, this worked and Vlad benefited from it in a way that he managed to keep the small but important Wallachian Merchant class on his side. The Saxons were so feisty that they spread false propaganda about Vlad the Impaler, that he was a secret vassal to Mehmed the second. As news of this spread, upon hearing it, Vlad became furious, this fury fuelled his anger further and further, so much so that Vlad forced and battled his way with his army, to Brasov. At the head of a small cavalry force and with speed of lightning he attacked the land that was situated between Sibiu and Brasov, impaling, slaughtering and burning everything in their path and Saxon merchants were tortured and killed slowly. There were wins and losses, however, many Saxons died, Vlad refused to give up and kept going, this rebellion spanned to 1457-1458 (historically 1458-1460). Eventually after much torture, death and chaos, the Saxons finally gave in and were brought to their knees, they pleaded Michael Szilagyi to call Vlad and his forces off, they even willingly surrendered their support of Bogdan the II and Dan III as well as offered to pay 10,000 florins for war damages.

However, just when Vlad felt a narrow feeling of release and victory in his grasp, Mathias Corvinus, King of Hungary, travelled to Sibiu and arrested Michael Szilagyi, his own uncle! He went one step further and backed Dan III, Vlad's enemy. Now once more, the cards fell out of Vlad's hands and he was forced to return to the Wallachian border. He had been so close to ending everything, everything he had sacrificed would have had something to account for but now, nothing. Just nothing. Vlad still could not surrender to this notion, so he stood up again once more to finish the job that had been started. Murdering, plundering, slaughtering till he and his forces broke through the borders of Brasov and charged forth. Tis the season of Gore it was indeed for the gruesome events that followed was that Vlad had dinner with Saxon ambassadors who were force fed by some of Vlad's soldiers. What they were forced to eat was soup served with hacked off limbs from Saxon corpses. Vlad watched on in a bizarrely amused manner. Surrounding them were impaled victims covered in candle wax and set alight as giant human corpse candles for lighting.

Vlad said: 'Talk about a luxury life style.'

One of the men choked on a piece of human flesh.

Vlad roared with laughter and said: 'I remember a piece of poetry from the Germans, it went like this; Kin of kin, blood of blood, we are all of the same flesh and blood, we are one... and shall be forever with the rising sun... how about this instead; Kin of kin, blood of blood, we are one as we eat the toe of a Saxon man.'

He said: 'It is fitting to hear a line from a German poet is it not, especially when it is German people who are being tortured.'

He asked Ivan who stood nearby: 'Quite ironic isn't it?'

He expected an answer.

Ivan quickly answered: 'Yes Voivode.'

Vlad: 'Marvellous.'

Vlad added: 'Ivan, a portrayal of my loyalty when it comes to torturing traitors or annoying bastards.'

Ivan said: 'Yes Voivode.'

Ivan's face flinched a little at the word 'traitor.'

In the coming days, Vlad successfully captured Dan the III during a getaway attempt. The day he decided what to do with him:

Vlad shouted at someone: 'Get me a priest, we need to arrange a memorable departure for our beloved captive.'

Soldiers were digging a wide grave.

Vlad said to them: 'I swear if the priest doesn't come, I'll be his god and pass judgement for him, I'll bludgeon him to death with his own bible.'

He made an accidental pun: 'This is a grave matter, it is interesting that the English word funeral has the word fun in it, that it will be indeed.'

He winked at Dan III who was tied to a wooden post in front of his own grave.

Dan was insane by now. He was rambling on about the Dragon Order and a woman who forced him to do strange things.

Vlad approached him and asked: 'What are you talking about, what on earth has the Dragon Order supposed to do with the recent rebellion?'

Dan yelled in Vlad's face: 'You will be killed, you are an abomination, the Dragon Order will see to it that you will be dead.'

He groaned. His absurd topic changed.

He said: 'She wants you dead, she wanted me to kill you, she will not stop till you are, I failed to kill you, she brainwashed me to do her bidding, that's why I got away, I escaped.'

He giggled; he continued but spoke in a different tone: 'Enemies are circling Vlad, allies shall rise in unexpected places and certain family shall betray you... a pawn in others plans, muwahaha!'

He spoke in his normal tone: 'The dragon is dead another shall rise, it is not over, creatures all over shall tremble in the up rise of the Dragon Order, with my death it will not be over.'

Vlad tried to enter Dan's thoughts, he saw in a memory a boy he called Kazaan and when he tried accessing a memory with a woman who cast some spell over him, the memory immediately crumbled away. That was strange, normally that never happened when he tried to read other people's minds. Dan screeched. Vlad motioned for the priest to commence the funeral service.

The feeble mannered priest did his job and an executioner came forth with a huge shiny axe. Dan saw his own reflection in the axe and gulped. His resolve crumbled.

He said to Vlad: 'No let us start over, I will become your most loyal ally, just don't let me be killed.'

157

Vlad smiled sarcastically.

He said: 'Sure we can start over, easy, as easy as a clean slate.'

He winked at the executioner and repeated: 'Clean slate... chop chop, get going.'

Dan asked in a scared manner as the axe neared his head: 'Hey now wait, what exactly do you plan to do to me now?'

In one swing, the head was off, the head bounced onto the floor and into the grave. The body was tied loose and tossed into the grave. They closed it up and left. Dan's allies were later impaled nearby so that he would not be alone.

December, Wallachia 1458 AD:

After the King of Hungary heard that the man he had supported had been killed by Vlad's forces, he tried to cover up the humiliation he had forced upon the Voivode of Wallachia by organising an incredibly fragile peace. Apparently Vlad had to pay for some of the 'damages' **his** 'campaign' had caused while the Saxons (or what was left of them there?) were 'required' to pay an annual sum to Vlad III to help maintain a 4,000 strong army to help defend the Saxons against the Ottoman Turks. Finally, or what seemed to be final, the rebellion was over. Vlad felt a weight lift from his complicated conscience, all the trouble and challenges he and his not so big army had to face, after everything, at least it was not for naught. He could return to his home after nearly more than two years. He wondered how much had changed by Ilona during the time that had separated them. He wondered if she was alright.

Targoviste Wallachia, 1458 AD:

Ilona sat at Vlad's writing desk. She leaned her head on it. She was sad because none of her letters seemed to reach Vlad for she received no message back, the only letter she received was the one regarding the removal of the Saxons trade freedoms, no personal reply back from Vlad or her sister, it seemed to her as if he was a world away. Nothing was as it used to be and Ilona was falling apart.

Soon after that, remarkably an envoy came and intended to report to the princess about the ongoing war. However, Radu stopped the envoy and asked what the message was.

The envoy said: 'Vlad Tepes has been reported to be alive... in fact he's on his way back to Targoviste.'

Radu sent off the feeble envoy and told Ilona the exact opposite of what the envoy had actually reported. Ilona stood in her room by the long narrow window of the tower. She tapped her fingers nervously on the windowsill. She heard Radu enter the room. She turned to look at Radu. She saw his saddened look which he actually faked. She was fooled by his pretend emotion.

She ran to him and asked: 'What is it...is it Vlad, is he alright?'

Radu shook his head and pretended to be in despair.

He answered: 'An envoy came and told me that Vlad has been found dead on the battle field... I'm sorry Ilona.'

He felt immense joy in Ilona's suffering. His plan he had been creating for two years was finally working it's magic. He had indeed been the one who had intercepted all of Ilona's letters after she had sent them off. He had in secret destroyed all of the letters, none of the letters ever even had a chance of reaching Vlad. Radu was on the correct path in destroying Vlad's life.

Ilona forced a calm look. She motioned for him to leave the room. She locked the door behind her, walked towards the window and stared at the extending drop towards the rocky ground. She climbed up to the windowsill. She felt the wind whip at her, it seemed to call her, pulling at her to follow. Though something held her back.

She looked back at her son's cradle. She felt dizzy, her whole body felt lightweight, she felt like wanting to die, it was as if her entire world had been based on her love for Vlad and never realised it. But her son was a part of Vlad, was it enough to keep living for her son? She smiled and laughed at herself for how stupid and foolish she was. He was enough. She did love her son.

She wanted to get down from the windowsill but an invisible voice laughed: 'Too little too late Ilona.'

A force of wind that almost felt like a hand swept her off the window's edge and she fell to her death. The last thing she thought of was a memory from her child hood.

A man said to her: 'Ilona you must protect this secret with your sister, as you are both my descendants I trust both of you.'

He put a necklace around Ilona.

The memory faded exactly when Ilona was dead. It seemed that the trauma in that moment had unlocked a distant memory from her childhood.

Radu barged open the door and found that Ilona was gone. He looked out the window, then down below, there was Ilona, unconscious on the forest floor. Guards went and retrieved Ilona and discovered she had died.

Radu had a grin envisaged in his mind.

Vlad took a long time to return to Targoviste. When he did, he left his men and hobbled inside the castle. Because of his vampiric powers, he was not wounded just in a weakened state. The people that worked at the castle were astonished as to how Vlad Tepes was unscathed after being involved in an all out war. He was put in his bed chamber to rest. He asked for Ilona to come see him, but was infuriated when he heard from the servants that she had jumped out of the castle tower because she believed that her husband was dead. When he confronted the servants about the matter, they said they had heard Radu speak with Ilona only a few seconds before she fell out of the tower. Apparently, Radu had spoken to her about a message from an envoy. Once Vlad felt better, he summoned the envoy and discovered that the message was that Vlad was alive not dead. After this, Vlad came upon the realisation that his own brother had lied to Ilona and because of that she threw herself out of the tower. To add to it, he found out that his daughter had died from an illness whilst he had been away.

He confronted his brother one day. He stormed into the room and thrusted Radu against a wall.

Radu grinned. He knew his brother found out about the truth as to how Ilona died.

Vlad yelled: 'Why!'

He punched Radu in the stomach and let go of him. Vlad paced back and forth.

He asked: 'I know you are a traitor, I know you hate me but you could have left Ilona out of our sibling feuds, what did she ever do to you?!'

Radu said while pointing to himself: 'I did not kill her, she jumped, it was of her own volition, I merely brought her into that direction, do not accuse me of something that I have not done.'

Vlad said: 'I loved her, more than anything in this life.'

Radu stated: 'At least you got to experience what love felt like, whilst I searched a lifetime without finding it or feeling it.'

Vlad said: 'Yes you did, Ilona loved you, she loved you as if you had been her real brother.'

Radu stood in silence for a moment. He remembered how Ilona always supported his love for clothes and cleanliness, she never seemed to mock him like others did behind his back.

Vlad watched Radu's contemplative look.

He scoffed and said: 'I cannot stay here, this place reminds me of her, it is like the heart has been torn from this place, best I leave before I do anything unpredictable.'

He looked angrily at Radu and walked away.

He decided he wanted to have Ilona's body cremated, he simply couldn't let go of her, selfish as it was. As the body went up in flames, Vlad could not help himself, how the smell of fire invoked various memories from war, all the things he had burnt to the ground.

Vlad left Targoviste and moved to Poenari castle. He spent many lonely days there, kept dull company by his wife's ashes and a painting of Ilona Szilagyi. His little son was kept shut away in another room there. Vlad cried more than he had his entire life, however, one could not really call what Vlad did, crying. When he cried, the tears came out but clinged to his eyelashes. He had to wipe them away. This was not how Vlad had expected to spend his war and rebellion free days.

Eventually, Vlad felt all of this hatred that he held against his brother. After the death of his young daughter and his wife, the only woman he truly loved, he wanted revenge... and no matter how, what or when... no matter how much blood be spilt to achieve this... he would succeed.

In front of Poenari castle, he arose into a black mist and ascended into the pitch black night sky.

His heart cried for the one common soul he had lost and he knew, a woman like her would never exist again. So he decided to take those away from his brother's life. The ones Radu seemed to care for most. A life for a life to end the strife.

Vlad travelled to Turnu and intended to do the most terrible thing he had done yet. But to him, in his strong fit of rage he simply didn't care about some little life even if it was the life of someone whom he had known since he had been a boy. He sneaked into the castle using his mist form. Apparently, because he had been directly blood sired by Lucien himself, he had different powers than that of a cursed vampire. Which is why Vlad could transform into animals or use mist like forms. Vlad crept towards the door of the room that Fenna was sleeping in. He smelled the scent of her hair. He heard her voice. Like a stealthy assassin he turned the cold doorknob and pushed open the door. The door creaked open and he stepped inside the room.

Fenna put back her child into the cradle, after that she turned and saw Vlad standing there.

Fenna chuckled in an absurd manner and asked: 'Um Vlad, might I ask you as to what you're doing here at this time of night?'

Vlad's menacing eyes reflected on the flickering candle in the corner of the room. Vlad closed in on her in a threatening manner. Fenna backed up to the wall and stumbled over the night dresser.

He said in a deep tone: 'You do not know what your monstrous husband has done... as always you continue to linger along in this sad life of his, he turned you into his forever slave.'

Fenna was on the floor now, she got back on her feet and sneered at Vlad: 'You don't have any business insulting my life.'

Vlad shouted: 'I only wanted to live my life in peace, he took my wife away from me, he ruined my trust and dignity... he took it all away!'

Fenna said: 'I have no idea what you're talking about.'

Vlad grabbed her by the shoulders and tightened his grip on them.

He said to her: 'My brother, my own brother lied to me and to my wife... because of that, she's dead... the only one I ever loved is gone... my brother always hated me because he thinks that I killed mother...he thinks that I should never have been born and believes that I am a monster, I will show him what a monster is.'

He clutched her shoulders very tightly now. Fenna starting kicking and punching him, trying to force Vlad to let go of her shoulder's.

She screeched: 'Vlad, you're hurting me!'

Dahlia began to cry. Vlad threw Fenna against the wall in his fit of frustration and anger. She began bleeding on her forehead.

Fenna said in a weak tone: 'Maybe you are a monster... you know what people here say about you... back when you were born they called you the Draculea, the devil... because you should have died but you came back to life, meanwhile there are also rumours circulating that you are a demon that feasts off the dead during the wars...the fact that you returned from multiple wars unscathed and victorious proves that you are a monster.'

Vlad's eyes turned black, as dark as coal and fangs flashed.

He said: 'If I am a monster, then so be it.'

Vlad gripped her at the neck then he thrusted her upwards and held her against the wall.

He said: 'I am the monster that is going to take your life.'

Fenna said: 'So you are a monster... I see, now everything that was a blur now makes sense, Radu was right to be hateful at you.'

Her eyes trembled. She wrapped her hands around Vlad's hand that held her neck. She saw the true Vlad for the very first time, suddenly she realised, she had always been afraid of him. However, this fear seemed to have been distant up until now. In her mind, a blizzard played out before her. Vlad bit her in the neck and drank her blood. Up until now, his inner vampire was hidden by his humanity but now there was no controlling it any more. Vlad was tired from hiding his true nature, he intended to use his power to exact his revenge on Radu. After he had finished with Fenna, he let go of her.

Her shallow body collapsed onto the stone floor. Although he killed Fenna... something he had planned with her was bound to happen. Radu had just arrived at his home. He went inside to find his wife lying on the floor, unconscious. He heaved her up and placed her on the bed. Soon after that, Radu noticed that his daughter was no longer in the cradle. He heard distant crying coming from somewhere in the castle. Following the sound, he entered the more isolated area of the castle. With it, he found a trail of bodies. They wore the clothing of castle workers. Radu recognised that all the servants that had worked there were dead. At the far end of the corridor, stood a figure with a distraught, mental and bloodied face. The dark figure, like a character out of a horror story, going haunting amongst the shadows and darkness. He grinned in a sinister manner and walked with one step towards Radu. Suddenly, just like when people say that life flashes in front of one's eyes, Radu saw Vlad flash toward him. Just like that, Vlad was standing in front of his brother. He pierced a weapon into Radu's stomach. Vlad seemed to have a glare that burned a hole right through Radu's soul. Radu's eyes saw it.

The evil that possessed his brother.

Radu said in a frail tone: 'I beg of you, spare my daughter that you keep hidden... don't just do and take as you please.'

Vlad's eyes turned black again. Black veining began to occur under his eyes. He shoved the weapon deeper.

He said in a cruel sarcastic manner: 'Hurts doesn't it... I'm just repaying the kindness that you gave me... all my life.'

Radu stammered: 'Do you hate me that much... obviously I had no clue that you were so sensitive.'

Vlad was infuriated: 'I hate you... I hate you I-I hate you!'

Radu said: 'I've always felt the same... I've always despised you for all you had... and everyone that gave to you... mother sacrificed herself so that you could live... meanwhile... all she gave to me was nothingness... eternal emptiness!'

Vlad said: 'You could have loved me... why couldn't you love me as a brother should... I am done with you... you are going to die here... may your soul rot and die... here you shall perish!'

Radu said: 'You always had the strength... you should have killed me... when I was blinded by my hatred for you.'

Vlad tightened his grasp on the lance and remembered that he had had a much more undignified death planned for his brother. He tore out the lance and threw it aside. After that he pushed his brother to the ground.

Vlad mumbled: 'Even upon the time of your death... you try to flatter me with your insults and your declarations of hate towards me... now I tell you, my ever so dearest brother... you are and never will be entitled towards such declarations for that is reserved for me.'

A sudden sound of footsteps made Vlad smile.

He announced: 'She is coming... the one that gave your measly life meaning and kindness... she is going to destroy you... that is now her destiny and your fate.'

Radu was too weak to stand up. He saw Fenna approach out of the dark empty corridors. He was terrified of her. She had an expression that was too painful to bear. Walking in her dainty, blood stained night gown. She went up to Radu and pounded her foot onto his back. Radu grunted from the pain of his wound.

Fenna said in a traumatised tone: 'It smells filthy here.'

Vlad said while leaning against the wall: 'Finish him.'

Fenna's eyes widened.

She said in a shocked tone: 'Vlad... no, I can't do that.'

Vlad shouted impatiently: 'Kill him!'

Fenna collapsed like a fragile puppet.

She sobbed: 'No... p-please I can't d-do this.'

Vlad said: 'You will do it... you obey me now... hurry creature of the night... the dark eclipse is coming... I feel my power surging and when that happens, I will have full control of you... however, I want to see you destroy his life force of your own choice... it's what he deserves... the wretch.'

Fenna felt an insatiable hunger. Her body was freezing. She covered her face using her hands.

She screeched: 'What have you done to me!'

Vlad said: 'I somewhat killed you... then used my blood to bring you back... just like what Lucien did to me... but I was born this way... you died to become this way... you are a cursed vampire... or that's what Lucien likes to call them.'

Fenna screeched: 'I'm not dead... I didn't die...'

Vlad's voice boomed: 'Yes you are... now kill him!'

Fenna felt a rush of hatred. Her heart beated heavily. She hated Vlad. For turning her into a monster like he was. But she remembered what her human life had been like. Sad, lonely, dull. That had all been increased now. But there was something else, her hatred at her neglecting husband. Who had been always busy scheming to get back at his brother. She remembered when he left her there in the bed where she cradled the dead body of her child for hours and hours. All she cried for was strength for someone to lean on. The help she longed from the one person she thought she could rely on had not been there. For this betrayal, her hatred took hold of her heart. She pulled Radu towards her. She bit into his neck using her fangs. As she did so, a simple lonesome tear rolled down her cheek.

Radu's life force was weakening. He was blocked out by all.

The only thing that he noticed was the voice of his pained brother: 'As you have taken from me, I shall take from you... whilst you intoxicated yourself with lies behind those castle walls, my life has been stripped bare by you, my infamous brother... I will tarnish and forever stain your soul with endless suffering and misery; meanwhile your wife's honour has been tragically defiled as she takes her place amongst the demon kind.'

Eventually Fenna let go of Radu's body. He was still alive but barely. Fenna gazed down at her hands. She saw the stains of her crime. She began to cry. Vlad forced Radu to drink his blood. He made Fenna watch and threatened her that if she didn't, he'd kill her child that was hidden away in the castle.

Future Radu speaks: 'After that night, I can recollect that was the very night that I was awoken as a different being...Vlad had ruined my life in every way imaginable... he turned my wife into a monster and he made her drain all the life away from me... then he turned me into a vampire so that I could lead an eternal life of misery with the additional hatred of my wife who later kidnapped our daughter and ran away. Vlad told me to flee to the ends of the earth... to live out an eternity of pain and torment of which he'd only tasted a short life time of... so that I would know how he felt and that if he saw me before the time frame of five hundred years, he would kill me. At first I did not understand the point of all of it until now... he had wanted me to suffer like he did and then eventually kill me.'

TO BE CONTINUED

An Unimaginable Beginning and a Journey For a Pooka Hybrid

For as long as Namira could remember, since she was a little girl, she was different from anyone and everything. When she was little her father would tell her stories, of a fabled city called Atlantis, where an unruly, unhappy king named Poseidon lived. When her father would tell her that this was her grandfather, she didn't believe him. Not even when he gave her a family heirloom a locket or necklace which belonged to his mother, which had a trident engraved.

Her mother would say, 'Don't believe everything he tells you.'

She at times would think her father was delusional, but still loved both her parents, with all her heart. When Namira was seven years of age, she encountered a creature she had never seen before. It was a normal day like any other, Namira was woken up by her mother Keera. Her mother had a smile on her face, today they would again venture towards the nearby lake. There her mother and Namira walked among the shore and yellow, golden sands. Until her mother spotted someone in need of help. Keera told Namira to stay put. Namira tried to listen to what her mother had told her, but something she couldn't ignore happened. Just as her mother went off. There was a slight rippling sound of water. Something in the lake was charging her way. The closer Namira went to the edge of the lake, the slower the rippling movements were. Once Namira, stood with both feet planted in the water, the movement suddenly stopped. Namira decided to move out of the water. When two hands grabbed her by the legs. Namira screeched and fell with her backside into the water. She was perplexed at what she saw next. There a boy her age came into view, he had red hair and very pale green eyes.

The boy said, 'Booh!'

Namira looked at him with a condescending look.

'Sorry for scaring you,' the boy said.

'You don't scare me!' Namira replied.

'My name is Ryan, see you around,' he laughed, and dove back into the deep blue body of water.

Namira told herself that she wouldn't let this boy belittle her. So she swam after him and transformed into her mythical form. The water was cold but at the same time refreshing. Namira tried to glimpse the boy when suddenly. A creature which looked like some kind of waterhorse swam her way. Namira somehow sensed that this was the boy that called himself Ryan. She sensed that he was challenging her to a race of sorts. They dashed through the water like turpedos. But in the end, Namira turned out to be the winner. Once they both set their differences aside. Namira and Ryan swam back to the surface and sat on the shore together. They both got talking.

'It seems that you and I are the same but somehow different,' Namira said.

'What kind of creature are you???' they both said at the same time.

They both laughed. Just as they were to about get better acquainted, Namira's mother came dashing towards them.

'Where were you, I told you to stay there, what on earth were you doing, who is this boy???' said Keera in a cautious tone.

Before Ryan could even utter one single word. Namira was grabbed by the arm by her mother who had a furious look on her face.

Once they both arrived home. Keera tried to explain to her daughter that she couldn't just run off like that, without telling her or her father about her whereabouts, especially if she was told to stay there where she was. Keera also told her that under no circumstances was she to see that boy again.

When Namira asked her mother a reason as to why, Keera replied, 'He is a waterhorse, but a different kind. His kind is a creature or species called the Kelpies, who are a deceptive species. They only cause all sorts of pain or trouble.'

Namira asked, 'But why can't we be friends?'

Keera said, 'Because it is as it is, we Pooka's and Kelpie's have been at odds for a long time.'

Namira didn't understand why she couldn't be friends with Ryan. She thought to herself, he is just like me, misunderstood. She had seemed to have found a person or creature who was just like she was. Namira wasn't exactly liked in the pooka community as she was also part mermaid and so was seen was an outsider. She may have looked more like a waterhorse, but on the inside Namira, felt like she had belonged nowhere. Once everyone was asleep, Namira snuck outside, towards the lake, the moons light shimmering downwards. The water reeds, swaying gently back and forth in the wind. Namira stood at the edge of the lake in her night gown. When she started calling out Ryan's name. She waited there for some time, until the sun rose, and she decided to return home. When suddenly, Ryan shouted her name. Namira turned around. She grinned at the sight of him. Ryan got up out of the water and then sat on the sand.

'Are you OK?' Ryan asked.

'Yes,' Namira replied.

'Is it ok for you and me to to be friends of sorts? Is your mother ok with this?' Ryan continued to question Namira.

'Yes,' Namira said.

Even though she had pretty much lied to his face.

'I know what you are, you are a Pooka,' Ryan said.

'And you are a Kelpie,' Namira said.

'I hope we can remain friends, as our kind and your kind, can't seem to get along,' Ryan said in a worried tone.

'I believe we can someday all be friends, and live in some sort of peace among our species,' Namira said in a hopeful tone.

From then on Namira snuck out each night and they would meet at the lake's edge, this was for about half a year. Julian and Keera were naively unaware of this unruly behaviour.

On one of these nights Julian decided to check on his daughter, when he couldn't find her in her room. He panicked and told Keera of the bad news. Keera somehow knew that this had something to do with this boy, Namira had once met. Julian told himself how much he saw of himself in his daughter and now understood in some ways how his father must have felt, when he was on his great adventures. Keera and Julian hurried towards the lake, but Namira was nowhere to be seen. Keera sprang into the water and transformed into her waterhorse form. She searched and scanned each nook and cranny of the lake until, she spotted Namira with that Kelpie boy. She swam towards them and in a fit of fury, charged at Ryan. They fought and fought, until Ryan gave in, he was injured in the process and had a scratch in his face. He looked at Namira in disbelief and in a sluggish manner, swam away, into the darkness. Keera escorted her daughter back to the surface. Where Namira, got angry looks and expressions from both her parents.

Namira broke into tears, 'But I only wanted to be friends with him, why did you push him away?'

Namira sobbed.

'Kelpie's and pooka's can be friends,' Namira went on to say.

Keera said, 'Kelpie's are masters of deception, when the time comes, you will learn to understand, Kelpie's always want something. You may see him again someday and when you do, you will learn to distrust their species.'

Julian agreed with Keera. With that Namira was put to bed. She told herself that she would not forgive her parents for this, and also told herself that she would not forget Ryan. Even though she would not see Ryan for many years to come. One year later when Namira was eight years of age. Her father received an unexpected letter from some Queen of Germany, her name was Monica and the letter was addressed to him. Her father read the letter out aloud.

Dear Julian,

This is Monica, the girl you once knew, a long time ago. I am no longer the person, I once was. I need you to come here, as our daughter Lorelei is in grave danger. Yes our daughter Julian, who is now 13 years of age. It has since occured to me that she is more like you than she will ever be like me. I have never told you this before, but I have never mentioned much of my childhood because I didn't know much about my past either. I have recently done some research here in my family's library and found out that my family is closely related to a line of werewolves. Lorelei our daughter has recently transformed into a werewolf in front of my very eyes. Once we were near the ocean, and suddenly she fell because she had transformed into a mermaid, after we brought her to a drier spot she transformed back into a human being. My husband has seen her transform and has ordered her to be executed, as he now knows that I have been unfaithful. I know my time has come to go. But please come and spare her the misery, of seeing me executed. You know how it feels to lose someone close. Please come before it is too late for her as well.

Your Old Friend

Monica Of Germany

Namira's father had an expression of sadness on his face. In reality Namira's father Julian had almost truly forgotten this woman, he had known 13 years ago. As Keera, Namira's mother heard these news, she was angry with him and never truly forgave him for this.

The next day Julian set off to get his other daughter Lorelei from Germany. Namira didn't see her father for many weeks afterwards. Instead she spent more time with her mother, swimming with her in the lake in her waterhorse/mermaid form. Namira may have been a hybrid but she looked more like a waterhorse than she did mermaid. Namira's hybrid form looked like a black as night horse with dark flowing hair, eyes that seemed pitch black and a tail that resembled a pooka's tail but looked more like a mermaid tail. A mermaid tail that had the same colour like the rest of her hybrid form.

While her father was gone, her mother taught her what it was like being a waterhorse and how she could help people in need. Keera also warned her that she would need to learn how to sense who was good or bad. As well as who wanted help, or didn't want help. During this time Namira was finally accepted more in the pooka community. Namira, thought that she wouldn't see her father ever again, and strangely accepted the fact that it would only be her mother and her by themselves. Just as Namira had settled in with her new lifestyle with her mother. Her father and older half sister had finally returned home. It had been a hot humid summer day. Namira was enjoying the sun's rays on her skin, when suddenly, someone tapped on her shoulder. It was her father. Namira was overjoyed to see him again, after such a long time apart. She hugged him, but over his shoulder saw a girl with dark reddish brown hair and blue eyes behind him. Namira let go of her father and took a few steps back. Keera, Namira's mother dove out of the water behind her. Keera held her daughter in her arms, and looked in utter disbelief at her husband, as she also thought that she would not see him again. Julian smiled at the sight of Keera. But Keera didn't want to go too close to Julian, she wanted to keep some distance for some time.

'So where is your other daughter?' Keera asked in a stern voice.

Julian turned around and told the girl that it would be fine, for her to greet her new adoptive mother and half sister. She wasn't small nor tall, but Keera sensed a special magical aura from her.

Keera moved closer to the girl as she was intrigued to find our more about this girl named Lorelei.

Keera spoke, 'So you are the one called Lorelei. My name is Keera and this is my daughter Namira.'

Keera pointed toward Namira who was standing next to her.

The girl named Lorelei seemed hesitant to move closer to Keera, her gaze kept wandering about and she seemed to be unable to shake off the uneasiness she felt being in the presence of these two new strangers. Lorelei had slightly wavy, dark reddish brown hair and dark blue eyes. She was wearing tattered and old looking rags as well as some worn shoes. Lorelei took a step back toward Julian.

'It's alright you will get to know them in time,' Julian spoke in a reassuring tone.

Namira tried to hide her interest for Lorelei and kept her eyesight lowered.

Namira couldn't stand this any longer and so she left the company of her parents and new sibling. She went home to her parent's cottage.

Namira thought that Lorelei was some sort of competition or sibling rivalry, she also thought that her father was trying to replace her. She didn't understand nor could she fully comprehend why her mother was also now interested in getting to know more about Lorelei.

It took some time for Namira and her mother to get to know Lorelei, the same vice versa. Namira tried her best to get to know her sister she never knew or heard of. But whenever she tried to show any interest, Lorelei would pull back. Lorelei seemed to be a shy and closed off person, who could become better with other people she knew with time. Lorelei spent most of her days in her room, looking out of her window onto the surrounding countryside and lake. Namira asked herself what her sister must had been thinking about, probably contemplating her own existence and why her she had to leave her home country, her

173

family and mother. Namira in some way started to feel sorry for Lorelei. Lorelei must have lost someone close to her; a family member or a friend, Namira muttered to herself. Namira knew that Lorelei had been separated from her mother Monica but that was all she knew about the matter. Someday Namira would find out for sure why Lorelei seemed so sad most of the time, once she got to know her sister a bit better.

As the years went by, Keera formed an unlikely sort of motherly friendship with Lorelei, which Namira sometimes even envied. Her mother always said that Lorelei was some sort of mythical being, judging the letter her father had received. Lorelei was a Mermaid & Werewolf hybrid, but how could she turn into two separate forms? When Namira had asked her father, he said that Monica, the woman he had forgotten about was human, but had a werewolf gene as she was descended from a line of werewolves. Maybe because Monica was human and he was once a mercreature. She inherited both the werewolf, mermaid and human forms, and was able to transform back and forth as much as she wanted. Namira wanted to someday put this theory to the test. When Namira was 15 and Lorelei 20, she invited Lorelei to join her down by the lakeside to which Lorelei hesitantly agreed. Lorelei now had been with her father Julian for seven years. She sometimes asked herself where she belonged, because she was so different from everybody else. That is one thing Namira and Lorelei had in common. Lorelei and Namira both calmly walked down to the lakeside. Namira's mother was out on errands all day, helping people in need, wherever, whenever anybody needed it. Namira was curious as to how Lorelei could transform herself into a mermaid or werewolf. Lorelei would say that sometimes things would be out of her control and she would just automatically turn into a werewolf and then into a mermaid. Namira asked whether she could show her how she does this.

'It will take some time though, as I have to concentrate on what exactly I want to transform into,' Lorelei said.

Lorelei closed her eyes and focused her mind. Luckily she was near the lake, when she transformed into a magnificent mermaid. Lorelei's mermaid tail was a sky blue colour, her mermaid scales shone in the sun. Her human legs had disappeared and she she then proceeded to glide in the water up and down the lake. Namira's eyes opened wide, she stood there for some time until she joined in the fun. After spending the whole afternoon with her half-sister, Namira sat down with her sister close to the shore. They were both discussing their past few years and the memories that they had made with each other.

'Today was a good day, was is not?' Namira asked her sister Lorelei.

Lorelei smiled slightly, looked at Namira then back at the surrounding landscape, she then spoke, 'I just wish that I could say the same for my mother and my little sister.'

Namira's facial expression turned into a slight frown.

Did she just say little sister? She was not referring to me, so who is she referring to? Namira asked herself.

'I know what you are thinking, Namira,' Lorelei said casually.

'What do you mean by that statement?' Namira asked Lorelei.

'I can read your mind. I don't know how or why....I am able to do it for some reason. Nowadays I am able to control this ability even more, however, it does take a lot of practice to fully master this ability,' Lorelei replied confidently.

'You fiend and you never told me.... until now,' Namira chuckled.

Lorelei also laughed and then said, 'I never even entrusted with you the utter fact that I have a sister, which I will probably never see again, because I did not know you too well in the past but I do now. I am not even sure if..... my mother is probably no longer in the land of the living. Because she told me herself that she was being condemned to her death. As for my sister I guess I will never know what has become of her.'

Lorelei seemed sad, but she did not cry, for she had already mourned both her mother and sister for the last few years.

Namira could see that Lorelei needed consolement and so she moved closer to Lorelei and gave her a hug.

That moment only lasted for a few more minutes and Namira hesitated to let go of her sister.

When Lorelei said, 'Do you think that a werwolf is quicker or you on your two legs?'

Namira didn't want to answer this question, she just continued hugging her sister, when she felt something like fur under her hand. Namira shrunk back as she saw a brown-reddish coloured wolf with brown-amber coloured eyes stand before her. She had not realised that Lorelei had just transformed into a wolf creature. Namira was nervous but she knew that her sister had the power to turn into her wolf-form at will and so she no longer was scared as she knew that her sister was the wolf.

Namira got up from the ground, the proceeded to run as she shouted, 'Catch up - big wolf!'

The wolf who was Lorelei ran after her.

That was one of the best days Namira would have with her half sister.

Even though Keera had accepted Lorelei as an adoptive daughter of sorts, the last seven years Julian and she drifted apart, they still lived together however, they would lead their own separate lives. Keera still couldn't accept the fact that Julian never told her about Monica and his other child. Keera noticed that the ravages of time had taken a toll on Julian, as he grew more deranged and delusional by the minute. That is why Namira and Lorelei spent most of the time near the lake.

Until one day, Namira sighted a mysterious looking creature which resembled a Kelpie, swimming in the lake. Lorelei also saw this and dove into the lake. Namira went after her. As both were underwater they again saw the kelpie, diving upwards and downwards, as if it was looking for something. Then as if it was surprised, it turned around and swam off. Namira knew deep down, that this was Ryan, as this creature also had a scar in the exact same place Ryan had when he was injured in the fight. Lorelei's expression was priceless, as she was puzzled by what she had just seen. When they were back on land, Namira explained to Lorelei, what the creature was and who she thought it was.

Lorelei laughed and said, 'Hopefully we won't see him again.'

Namira frowned and went home. A week later Namira was helping some farmer with some chores. When from out of nowhere out of the water a seaweed like figure rose up out of the water and turned into a human form. This creature had fiery red hair and the same pale green eyes Ryan had. To Namira's amazement Ryan acted as if he did not see her and then went on to destroy the farmers house and terrorise the whole village. Namira asked herself what great change had taken place for him to act so notoriously and viciously. Namira decided that she would try to help Ryan, be the person he once was. She searched for him far and wide in the lake's waters, but there was no sign of him. A month later, Namira was helping her mother, catch some fish. When a kelpie swam past them, Namira thought this was Ryan and hurriedly swam after him. Keera knew this was a trap, she shouted for Lorelei to help. Luckily she was nearby. Namira dove into a darkness, the darkest part of the lake she had never encountered before. Then Ryan swam in front of her.

'There you are,' Namira said.

'Here I am,' Ryan said in a husky sarcastic tone.

176

Namira didn't notice a horde of Kelpie's surrounding them. Out of the crowd, the biggest Kelpie, named Zelena came into view.

'Good work my son,' Zelena said.

'Now we will finally set things right, kelpies and pookas will never ever be friends. Like the saying goes an eye for an eye, what your mother did to my son, I will now do to you,' Zelena proclaimed.

Ryan stood there like a servant statue listening to his mother's every command. Namira knew then and there, that the Ryan she once had known no longer existed.

In a glimpse, Lorelei in her mermaid form, intervened and snatched Namira out of this sticky situation. When Namira was back on land, she hugged Lorelei for the first time. Keera ran to her daughter and held her in her arms as Namira wept. From then on, Namira did not trust so easily again. Another year went by, Lorelei was now 21 years of age and decided she wanted to explore and travel the world. She said her farewells to Namira and Keera and left for a new chapter of her life to begin. Namira didn't think that she would miss her half sister, but in the end she did. Namira sometimes contemplated leaving as well. When she was 18 years of age she did that exact thing. She asked her mother whether she would join her, but her mother told her that it was time for her to find her own way in the world and become her own person. Keera had one thing left to tell her daughter before she left. She advised her daughter, that wherever she was or would go. That she should choose a place, where a pooka colony/ clan were nearby. Namira took this infomation to heart, as she did not want to accidentally fall into dangerous hands, such as the Kelpies. Before Namira left, she went by her parent's house to say one last goodbye. But she could not find her father. In a panic, she searched the house top to bottom, but it was as if, the earth had swallowed him whole. Namira left but still felt concerned for her father's safety. As she was about to leave, Namira was puzzled to see some weird soldiers, with golden helmets and armour on which a trident was pictured, and some man with a cover over his head. Namira thought she was seeing things that weren't there when the soldiers and the captive disappeared under the water. Namira didn't think anything of this, as she thought this was a figment of her imagination. Namira left, her past and a new journey begun.

Before she journied away, on her own for the first time ever in her life. She looked upon, the place she was born, grown up and now was about to leave. She sighed turned around and started swimming in a North Westerly direction. She swam, swam and swam. Until it felt like she had swum forever, when she crossed paths with another pooka that had swum by and didn't seem to notice her presence. She followed the pooka, until she had reached a pooka clan. The pooka's here seemed to notice that Namira didn't belong here. But they also noticed that she wasn't a threat and that she also was a pooka which didn't bother them. Namira asked them whether there was a village nearby that they offered help to. The pooka's said yes, and a female pooka with black hair and blue eyes, pointed her to where she had to go. From then on, Namira had settled in a village on the Northern and most Westerly tip of Ireland. Namira decided to explore, who or what lived in this village. There were many farmers, fishing families, a tavern and a local mill. Namira had now explored all what this village had to offer from afar, but now she turned into her human form and wanted to have a closer look at it all. At first she went into the tavern, where everyone stared at Namira. Namira didn't know what the problem was.

She went towards the bar keep, named Bruno, and he said, 'I don't know what you are doing here young lass, but I have never seen a woman in a tavern, if you wish to buy a drink, please talk to my bar maid Clarissa.'

There was a awkard silence in the room. Namira decided to look for this lady Clarissa. She went toward a quieter place in the tavern or the Kitchen area, until she found a small but stately woman with dark blonde hair and pale blue eyes. Hunkered over, picking up pieces of glass, that she clumsily had let fall over.

Namira asked in a curious tone, 'Are you ok, do you need any assistance?'

Clarissa in a annoying tone responded with, 'Is this a joke for you wee lass? I have no time or interest to play games or converse with the likes of you.'

Namira was apalled by this remark, but she persisted.

'I am not playing games with you, I REALLY wish to help you, as it is in my nature to do so,' Namira said.

Clarissa stood there for some time as she was lost for words, then proceeded to say: 'What do you mean, it is in your nature to do so?'

'Well I'm a pooka and as such I help those who need help,' Namira replied.

'My dear, you pooka should stay away from this wretched place, get out while you still can, while I am stuck here in this stinking, horrid tavern,' Clarissa said in a quiet tone.

Clarissa couldn't manage to control her emotions neither her mythical abilities, as she in front of Namira turned into a beastly looking woman, with some sort of black aura surrounding her. Namira was surprised by what she had seen. But couldn't grasp what kind of being she had just encountered. Clarissa turned back into her human form, and saw Namira still standing before her with a puzzled expression on her face.

'What kind of being are you?' Namira blurted out.

'I am what people call a banshee. Please do not tell anyone,' Clarissa whispered.

'Why would I? I am a mythical creature myself, now do you need help or not?' Namira asked in a determined tone.

Clarissa accepted Namira's offer of help, and with time they both became good friends.

Six months went by, and Namira was really now at ease, helping anyone who needed assistance, in a village she now called home. Namira had a long work schedule, each day would start with her helping Clarissa setting up tables, cleaning off surfaces, and serving drinks behind the counter. Then she would continue on helping people near the old mill. Then the last chores of the day, she would help farmers, and fishmongers. On one of these days however, Namira met a fisherman, she shouldn't have helped at all. At first, she helped him, on his farm and his fishing boat. Until he saw her one day dive into the lake saw while she was transforming into a waterhorse. This fisherman named Charles or Stinker Charlie his nickname, from the beginning he had seen her, had a sick and twisted idea about what was only actually Namira's way of helping those who needed help. Charlie didn't care what Namira thought, and after seeing Namira transform, this sick love interest grew into something more, he had to have her, whatever he had to do. There was a grey sky one morning, and also a cold breeze which could be felt underwater. Namira scheduled a visit to charlie's, she greeted him like she always did, and he then got talking about what had to be done for the day, when he suddenly stopped talking and moved his fat repulsive lips towards Namira's face. Namira shrunk back and jolted away. She looked at him in a disgusted and angry way, shook her head, and swam away.

That wasn't the last she would see of the stinker though. Charlie was distraught at this rejection he had just witnessed, and so he went on to set up a revenge plan of sorts, he had the will, but he just needed to find a way to enact a plan. Three years had passed, Namira now was one of the most likeable people and mythical beings in the town. It was funny that she had not been the only mythical being. There was Clarissa the banshee, the town jester who was a rather small man, but Namira thought that maybe he was a human born to be small? Of course there were also the Pooka's. A few weeks ago the Pooka clan had spotted some other being just off the Irish coast. From this description it sounded like waterhorses maybe Kelpie's. Namira remained on high alert at all times, once she had received this important piece of information. During the day she remained mostly at the tavern, behind the counter with Clarissa. This was the place she felt the safest. Most of the days during this time felt like a blur. As Namira had grown more paranoid by the second. Clarissa comforted her, as much as she could. Also reassuring Namira, that if someone wanted to harm her, someone would have done it by now. As Clarissa was worried about Namira. She wanted her friend of three and half years, to feel safe. Clarissa said to herself rather be safe than sorry. So she requested the help, of a banshee she once knew and even was friends with once. This banshee's name was Thomasin.

One day late that evening a hooded figure, came into the tavern.

'Thomasin, it is good to see you,' Clarissa said.

This cloaked person came closer to the counter, asked Clarissa if the coast was clear and then de-cloaked herself. All of a sudden, Namira came around the corner, and asked Clarissa who this was. Thomasin was a tall woman with dark brown flowing hair and blue menacing eyes. She had a vivacious look on her face. She turned around, looked at Clarissa, and gave her a small flask.

She said in a quiet tone, 'You better make sure she forgets ever seeing me here.'

With that Clarissa gave her a small bag of money. Thomasin took the money, cloaked herself and left the premises, hoping that nobody else had seen her.

Namira asked Clarissa what this secretive business was about, when Clarissa uttered some sort of spell, 'You shall forgot the name, the name of which she whence came.'

Namira stood there spellbound, when Clarissa asked her what the woman's name was, Namira would reply, 'I don't remember.'

Clarissa told her that her name was Emily. Clarissa told Namira that the flask she had received, was meant for her. She went on to say, that the mixture inside the glass flask, was a potion, which protected whoever drank it, and that it would protect a person from harm and harming themselves. It was a protection charm of sorts. Clarissa warned Namira that she could not stay any longer, as it was no longer safe to do so. Namira frowned at the idea of leaving the village she had chosen some years ago, and a village where she had finally felt at home. She also liked this village because it reminded her, of the village where she was born, grew up and left. Clarissa warned Namira that the spell would wear off after a day had passed and that Namira should make haste. Namira thanked Clarissa for the potion, but told her there was no need for the potion, as these Kelpie news were probably not real anyway, a false alarm.

Clarissa asked Namira, 'Well if you believe these news to be untrue, why do you stay at the tavern night after night and barricade yourself?'

Namira left the tavern with a hot temper, as she could not stand listening to Clarissa's blabber any further.

It was a dark and cloudy night. Namira was walking along the river, and sat down under some trees. She would only sit there for a few mere moments. Namira was ashamed of her erratic behaviour towards Clarissa, so she decided to go back to the tavern to apologise. Before she would do so, she hastily drank the potion, and made her way back towards the village. Namira could have used the river to swim back to the village but she shrieked at the thought of some Kelpie's snatching her. So she decided to stay in her human form and walk back to the village instead. While Namira was unaware, something bubbled in the river and a seaweed like being arose out of the river. It snuck it's way behind Namira, but was unable to grab her as another Pooka lunged out, and the Kelpie grabbed a different Pooka instead. Namira continued her journey back to the tavern, unaware of the events unfolding.

Ryan had thought to himself, what a waste, when he found out that he had managed to capture someone Namira loved very much, he grinned an insidious grin as he would use this as leverage against Namira. Meanwhile, Charlie was waiting at the tavern, waiting to enact the plan he had so carefully weaved these last three years. It all began when he encountered someone who had been looking for Namira, a waterhorse, a Kelpie. This Kelpie who called herself Zelena, told Charlie of such a magnificent plan which allowed Charlie the stinker to finally get the revenge he so craved. Zelena had planned to wait some time to enact it though, because she wanted Namira to think that the worst was over. Namira had finally arrived at the old tavern, when she opened the door though she saw something that sent chills down her spine. She saw Clarissa who was held by Ryan and her mother Keera who was held by Zelena. Namira almost fainted, but luckily she found a chair to sit and lean on. Namira thought she had seen something that wasn't there, but the reality set in, and her mother and Clarissa were really held captive, by the Kelpie's. Out from behind Ryan, Charlie the Stinker came into view.

He shouted, 'Now finally I get the revenge I have planned since the beginning.'

When Ryan swiftly hit him over the head and let go of Clarissa. Clarissa now stood next to the bartender-table.

'What an Idiot,' Ryan said.

'Let's get down to business,' Zelena said and dragged Keera to a chair and bound her to it with rope.

'You either come with us Namira, or, we kill one or both of your loved ones,' Zelena continued on.

Namira sat there in silence for some time, until she decided to surrender herself to the Kelpie's. Namira asked herself how her mother knew she was in trouble; unless Namira's mother Keera found out from the other pooka's that her daughter was in danger. Not even Clarissa who was help captive by Zelena and Ryan was courageous or confident enough to stand against the two Kelpie's even though she was a Banshee. A Banshee who had a lack of control of her own powers. While the others were speaking and while no one was watching Keera; Namira's mother was trying to untie herself but to unfortunately she was unable to do so as the rope that held her in place was holding her tight to a chair. Keera thought of a way to help her daughter. From afar she could see that Clarissa was standing next to a glass cup that was close to the edge of the bar table. While Keera believed no one was watching, she signalled Clarissa using her hand that was tied back. She tried to point out the glass cup. Clarissa who was being watched by Ryan, noticed the subtle hand signals. She moved closer to the cup, her back facing the table so her hands began to slowly move the cup even more to the edge, til it smashed to the ground. Ryan grabbed Clarissa by the arm and moved her next to Namira.

'Sorry, clumsy me,' Clarissa said in a weary tone.

'Don't play games with me!' Ryan stated in an annoyed tone.

While Ryan was conversing with Clarissa, Keera had no other choice than to tilt the chair she sat on. The chair fell to the side, Keera though managed to grab a piece of glass as quickly as she could. Zelena noticed this and moved toward Keera.

'Can't keep it together Keera? There's no need for these theatrics. It will all be over soon,' Zelena spoke in a sarcastic voice.

Zelena lifted the chair back into its original position.

'Nice try,' Zelena said and smirked.

The ugly looking Kelpie directed her attention back toward Namira. Now with the glass shard hidden in her scraped and bloody hands, Keera was able to free herself from the chair. She quietly moved toward Ryan and punched him in the stomach. Now she managed to also overpower Zelena, by making her trip over her idiot son. Keera pulled Zelena up by the arm and held the piece of glass to Zelena's neck. Ryan who had finally managed to get up again saw something before him that would make him furious and even more vengeful. The glass shard was starting to scrape away at Zelena's neck and blood was starting to pour down to the ground.

'Don't you dare harm her!' Ryan shouted at Keera.

'Like your mother so kindly pointed out an eye for an eye. More like torture for torture. You or your mother will never harm me or my daugther ever again,' Keera said in a vicious tone.

Keera slit Zelena's neck in a cold blooded manner, this instantly killed Zelena, so that she bled out from her neck within a matter of seconds.

Keera urged Namira and Clarissa to get out of the tavern, as she wanted to deal with Ryan and Charlie. Namira and Clarissa left the premises.

Keera locked the tavern door to prevent Ryan and Charlie from leaving the premises. However, as soon as she searched the whole tavern, Keera realised that Ryan was no longer there. Keera did not understand how he could possibly have left the tavern, she did not see him run after Namira and Clarissa. Disturbing thoughts were clouding Keera's mind. Keera decided to focus her attention on Charlie. Charlie who was still in the tavern, on the other hand awoke from his unconsciousness and rambled on like a crazy person. Keera was about to kill this scum of a man, when she noticed, that he no longer remembered who Namira was let alone, who he himself was. It was a case of Amnesia. Keera left crazed man alone and in a hurry ran outside, asking herself where her daughter would go for safety. Keera hoped to find Namira by the safety of the pooka colony, but on her way there she was snatched by Ryan. Namira and Clarissa stood at the edge of the waters, where the pooka colony would reside she hoped that her mother would know where to look for them.

There she waited for many hours, until Clarissa told Namira, that for her own safety she was going to leave, she also said, 'We will always be friends, even if we are far apart, but I cannot stay here any longer, anyway that potion I gave you will wear off soon, why don't you join me?'

Namira declined the offer to join her as she needed to make sure her mother would meet her here at the pooka colony. Clarissa said her farewells to Namira and left with some merchants that often came too and from, from the village. Namira had now waited as long as she could, she knew that if she waited any longer, her protection charm would wear off. But before she could do so. Ryan had appeared, with her mother in his arms.

'An eye for an eye, Namira,' Ryan said.

Keera tried to free herself from Ryan's grasp however, she was unable to do so, in her last moment of sadness she said, 'I love you Namira, but run, escape while you still can.'

With that he broke Keera's neck, right in front of Namira. Namira's mother had died instantly. Tears were flowing down Namira's cheeks. She could not even mourn her mother's death because she trying to find a way of getting herself to safety. Namira tried to run off but had no success in doing so. She had not noticed that she was standing on a slippery surface, so unfortunately she slipped and hit her head on a hard rock surface, and was left unconscious. Ryan was about to exact his vengeance, just as a harpoon like object, was thrown, and dug deep into Ryan's flesh. Into Ryan's spine to be exact. Ryan pulled back, as the pain was too immense, and he was flung back into the river, by the harpoon that had been shot out. It was the Pooka's who wanted to avenge Keera's death. A few Pooka's dove out of the water and pulled Namira onto a small boat. They pushed the boat towards a farm, and sensed that the person that lived there, wasn't bad nor good. But this person would help Namira regain her strength.

This was when Namira had met Patrick, the man she would fall for. He found her lying unconscious in that small boat. He helped her get back to full health. For which Namira was utterly thankful for. She met him at the start of 1505. She enjoyed every minute she had with Patrick, but once she had found out that she was with child, she knew she would have to enact a plan; as she knew that Patrick didn't want children, so she told Patrick that she would leave for London for some time, and return as soon as possible. Once Namira had met Thomasin Patricks's sister, who for some reason hated children, she thought to herself she had met her somewhere before, but she never questioned her otherwise.

From then on she went to London in England and searched for a lady or woman, called the hag, she did this as per Thomasin's instructions or advice. Once she had found the hag she asked herself, why she felt like she had known her from somewhere, but she would never remember who she was. The hag was an old looking woman with grey-white hair. She seemed to have a very small stature and one would think she couldn't hurt a fly. But looks can be deceiving. She lived with this woman for a duration of nine months. This woman would always insist that Namira should call her Clarissa. Until she had given birth to a healthy baby boy with sky blue eyes and small brown curls. It was hard for Namira to leave her one and only child, but she made sure to leave some items for him, in case he ever would like to know anything further about where he came from and who she was. She got someone to paint her portrait with a small engraving, she also left her son whom she named Thomasin, a gold locket, which had a trident engraved on it. She told the hag whose name was Clarissa that if Thomasin ever questioned where he had come from. She should say from Ireland and give him, these family heirlooms, that she had left for him, she left without looking back, as she didn't want to tempt herself, to go back. She left for Ireland, leaving her son with the hag in London. In Ireland another set of unfortunate events would take place, ultimately deciding Namira's fate forevermore. Namira's son Thomasin would grow up, however die at some point in his life only to return back as one of the most powerful beings in the world 'the Grim Reaper'; he would found one of the most important organisations 'the Order of the Grim Reaper'.

Lone Celtic Wolf – Wolf Origins Part 1

Werewolf a term used to describe a human being who turns into a wolf like creature each and every full moon. So it is said in or believed in today's popular culture. But in truth wolves, werewolves or lycanthropes have roamed the world for thousands of years. Many cultures across the world believe, truly believe in the existence of a wolf creature and all are weary of their existence.

I Fane Halfdan am such a creature and now you will listen; learn what I found out further about the wolf origins their existence, history, their beginning, thus the origin of wolves. For I am also descended from these very same monsters and this is not only the story of the wolves, but the story of how I came to meet an acquaintance; now friend of mine a long time ago.

1830, Germany, Lorelei Castle:

As always the sky was grey, with heavy luminous clouds crowding the sky. However it still did not rain. The cool atmosphere lingered into the castle walls. While a lonely young-looking man was attempting to keep himself warm beside a fire he had lit in an old stone oven in the castle's large so called kitchen. The castle he had called home for the last few months used to be in much better shape. Cracks, tears in the walls that showed the age of the old castle. The spiders and their cobwebs now called Fane's supposed birthplace home. A place that had been abandoned about more than three centuries ago. The place was so dusty that Fane struggled not to sneeze. He was shivering under a blanket he had covered himself with and yet he could have tried to warm himself up using a power within him that he still had struggled to control. Fane was a Celtic Wolf. Meaning he was descended from a old, ancient line of werewolves/wolves that stretched back into the year 700 AD. Maybe even farther than that. His mother whose name is Lorelei had died of unknown causes but that is what Fane believed to be true. Fane had come searching here for answers. Answers to the very questions as to why he was abandoned by his mother and the why. Why she couldn't have kept him. The dreadful, lingering questions that Fane would always question himself. But now for Fane it was all pointless. His being here was pointless, just like his very existence was pointless. Fane's hand touched the bare stone walls. The rough texture of the stone was of interest to Fane. As he was fond of building and crafting things out of wood, something he had learnt from his step-father. That is why he was always questioning/contemplating how specific items, furniture, stone work had been crafted.

While Fane was sitting inside the stone castle that was perched on a cliff, in the remote country side. A stranger was making their way towards Lorelei castle. This person was searching for Fane for some unknown reason. An old and odd looking man in fact was travelling toward the castle. He had white hair that went down to about shoulder length and he wore suitable warm clothing for the exceptionally cold weather. The old man went past a river also called the Lorelei river that was situated in close proximity to the castle that started to look like it was crumbling away. Whilst the man was walking in a rather quick pace, a siren's lullaby could be heard in the distance. Attempting to lure the passer by into the river.

'This is the river of Lorelei. The river that takes and let's everything die. Come hear my dear soul. I want nothing more than to greet you that's all,' the siren sung and waived toward the old man.

The man did not move from the path that was winding up toward the castle. He was determined not to make the same mistake he had made once before with a different kind of siren called a Russalka. A siren that came from Russia.

He shouted so that the siren could hear him clearly, 'I am not falling for these kinds of tricks again!'

The siren slightly tilted her head, a sinister smile spread across her face. It seemed that the old fool was not falling for her tricks; so she left the rock she sat upon and dived back into the river.

The stranger finally arrived at the castle's gates. He tried to open them, but then banged on them persistently. Fane who was still inside the castle walls heard this incessant annoying banging. The clanging sound against the gates annoyed him so much that he threw away the blanket that he had used and walked towards the atrocious sound. Fane had heightened senses when it came to sounds, smells and sight. He hated it especially when someone would provoke him in anyway possible. In long strides he quickly made his way toward the sounds origin point.

The man with white hair stood at the gates, as if he was expecting for Fane to show himself. He patiently continued to stand in front of the tall gates made of metal in front of him as he slightly tapped his foot on the ground. The unknown identity would not have to wait much longer though because Fane was speed walking toward him. Fane was now standing in front of the entrance that led inside to the castle. He questioned the very presence of anyone at this gloomy, rundown and crumbling castle. He was suspicious of anyone he didn't know. No one ever came to this part of remote Germany, especially because of the castle's history surrounding the deaths of every noblemen and woman that ever set foot here. Fane hated, no despised the idea of not knowing who was waiting behind those very gates and this made Fane slightly nervous. But he remembered his stepfather's words; that one should always stand one's ground. Fane grasped one of the double doors handles and opened it slightly. Chilly air was rushing into the castle. Fane closed the double door behind him and slowly made his way toward the gates.

Fane peered through a hole in the gate and was unsure as to who was standing in front of the gate like a frozen statue. All he could see was an old looking man with white hair about shoulder length, he wore a long cloak and was carrying a bag of sorts.

Fane was about to open the gate when the other person spoke, 'I am looking for a man named Fane. I have been told by the townspeople in a village near here that he resides.'

Fane spoke in a condescending tone, 'Who is looking for this Fane?'

'Ah yes. I forgot to mention my name. My name is Frances Owen Gregory, but my friends call me FOG,' FOG replied in a hopeful tone.

Fane had an absolute mind blank, he could not remember ever encountering someone named Frances before.

'Does Fane know you?' Fane asked plainly.

It was starting to drizzle and soon it would start to rain endlessly as FOG was about to explain to Fane how he came know him.

'About 25 years ago I crossed paths with him. Of course under very different circumstances. Fane sought out the monster/beast called the Dullahan in Ireland, but that is all I know of this Fane. Now I kindly ask that you'll let me in, as I have something to discuss with him,' FOG explained.

The peculiar looking man that had an odd way about him. The man from England. Now Fane exactly knew who this stranger was.

Fane opened the door. At least he finally knew who was looking for him. But why? Fane told himself.

FOG now saw before him the person he had been looking for. A young-looking man, with slightly wavy, red-brown hair and brown eyes. He was not tall nor small, he was not lean but not highly muscular.

'Well, well. You still look the same. I guess some things never change,' FOG smirked.

Fane looked at FOG with a look of distrust. He encircled him like an animal waiting to pounce on his prey.

FOG knew that Fane didn't trust anyone too easily. Of course he didn't know the why.

'I barely managed to recognise you. I never thought I would see you again. I guess time has not been kind to you,' Fane said in a sarcastic tone.

'Enough of this small talk. It is time to get down to business. But let's get inside first, so we can talk about this behind castle walls,' FOG stated in a quiet tone.

FOG felt like he was being watched by the creatures or sirens that dwelled close by to the castle. That was the reason why he asked to talk further inside the castle.

'Fine, let's head inside' Fane hesitantly said.

Inside Lorelei Castle Germany:

There were few candles lit that illuminated the hall way as they both moved towards the inner sanctum of the castle. A desolate castle that was abandoned aeons ago.

While both of them were walking Fane spoke, 'So what have you been up to for the last 25 years? Any interesting things happen?'

Fane could see that Frances was hesitant to speak of the past. FOG's face seemed to show a sadness. Like an emotion of loss.

'I would rather not talk about it at the moment. As there would be a lot to tell and since I am here to discuss something with you. Let's focus on you and what has been going on for you for the last 25 years,' FOG cunningly replied.

Fane instead now focused on making his way back to the kitchen area of this dilapidated castle and there he would truly find out the real reason for FOG's being here.

They both sat down at a table located in a servants dining area in the kitchen. The fire was still burning the logs that Fane had put in for heating the kitchen. Frances was waiting or wanting to start a conversation with Fane, so he could reassure him that his appearance here was only to help Fane.

Fane now finally stopped looking at the fire that was still glowing very strongly.

He now spoke, 'I am not one to seek the company of others. As I tend to prefer the solace and peace of quiet I enjoy here at the castle. I know it may not seem that way. But I am just not the type of person that is the cheery or positive minded type, like yourself Frances.'

'Me?....A cheery person. Well if that is what you believe to be true, then fair enough,' FOG replied.

FOG spoke again, 'Alright, I am here because I wanted to check on you. I mean after 25 years one can be a bit curious as to what has become of others. I remember the last time that we crossed paths you were looking for answers for some reason and that you didn't want to talk about where you came from. From the looks of it you have found out some of the answers to your questions.'

Fane tried to maintain a calm disposition. However he was currently clenching his teeth and his fingers/claws were etching into the tables wood. FOG noticed that Fane was not one to talk to about feelings or about his life in general. He had an inkling that it would be very hard to help Fane if at all with any problems he was currently encountering.

There was an ever growing silence in the room, one could barely here the burning of the wood, as the embers would jump up and vanish as soon as they appeared. One could hear the annoying sirens singing in the distance, beckoning anyone idiotic and naive enough to come to them, so they could lure them into the cold river Lorelei. One could hear the wind outside and the trees swaying through the force of air beating against their branches.

Fane said in a tired tone, 'I...um. I do not trust so easily and I am very suspicious of strangers. I know we are acquaintances but that was some time ago. I don't even know how you came to find me here. I can't....I just can't do this right now.'

Fane banged his hand onto the table and then almost jumped up from his chair to leave the room. He seemed to be frustrated and anxious. FOG didn't think it would be so hard for Fane to come out of his shell. It seems that whatever Fane had lived or been through still haunted or scarred him to this very day. Frances decided that if he already was here, maybe he should have a look around. Maybe he would be able to help Fane somehow. FOG left the kitchen quarters and stepped into another grand hall which had a long dining table; which probably was used to seat all the noblemen and women in the past. FOG glanced up toward the arching ceiling he could see old and tattered flag or coat of arms; depicting a wolf or wolf-like creature. FOG now looked to a window, which had a coloured mosaic which would reflect its colours into the room when the sun would shine through. The image or artwork depicted a fair maiden which was seated at the top of the tower, she seemed to be crying, as she was being lured to jump into the river by a siren below. This imagery alone gave FOG the creeps and that was weird coming from someone like FOG who had thought he had really seen/witnessed everything obscure, dangerous and wonderful in the mythical/mortal world. FOG decided to search for Fane. He now understood that the only way to be able to help someone like Fane who had such an immense amount of mistrust for others; would be to explain what had happened to him over the years and explain to him what FOG now did nowadays (helping mythical creatures who needed helping).

FOG walked down many corridors, halls. He entered many rooms; somehow he still managed not to find Fane sitting in one the countless rooms in this castle. FOG was starting to grow restless. He had come all this way from Australia using a portal created by a machine to get here. To help an old acquaintance. Indeed FOG knew what it was like to be suspicious of people, especially since his Grandmother only revealed to him the very secret of their family history once he was a Succubus. After that moment he learned himself to be careful with whom he would place his trust. The only friends he truly trusted were Aya and Cleo.

'Fane!....Fane where are you?!' FOG shouted his voice echoing throughout the whole castle.

FOG ventured toward a room which seemed to be the castle's library there he would find the one he was looking for.

Library Lorelei Castle:

Immense towering bookshelves stood side by side. Row for Row, full of a vast collection of books as far as the eye could see. FOG was amazed by the sheer size of this family library. If there was a room FOG preferred it would definitely be the castle library. Whoever built or arranged for the library to be placed here was a book lover or so called bookworm like FOG. FOG loved his books, especially since he had his own collection at home in Hallow Valley. FOG for now at least was in a sort of trance from which he only snapped free from once he saw a scroll lying folded open on a desk nearby. A candle had already been lit and placed on the very same table the scroll was on. FOG moved slowly toward the document and glimpsed what was written on the scroll. Everything was written in German. Luckily FOG could read some basic words, because he had learnt it from his wife Lara in the past. The title of the parchment was 'Familien Geschichte der Lorelei's' - meaning Family story of the Lorelei's. Below the title it stated that the family are descended from a great German legend known only as Siegfried, who was the first known wolf of the family line. FOG glanced downward at a family tree which spanned centuries up until the 16th century and had ended with the name Matthias. Who according to this document was the son of Lorelei and King Erich. This Matthias also had a great-grand cousin named Kurt and a grandmother named Monica. FOG was fascinated and deeply enveloped by the family tree, when he heard clanging sounds coming from somewhere behind him. FOG turned around but saw nothing behind him. He still believed to have heard a sound coming from inside the castle and particularly this sound was coming from underneath his feet. That's it FOG told himself, he had to find out what Fane; if it was Fane, was doing underneath the castle. How on earth though was FOG going to find the entry to the secret room below. FOG scowered the whole library. He scanned his surroundings and looked for anything out of place or out of the ordinary. In this case FOG finally found something that peaked his interest. There was an inscription chiselled into the stone floor it stated 'Loreley or Lorelei'. He touched the stone brick and it moved aside. The ground underneath FOG seemed to shake and move/jolt as brick by brick a stone staircase was revealed, to which one could see a metal door leading to whatever was hidden down below. FOG carefully went down the stairs and tried to open the door. Unfortunately, the darned thing would not open. FOG could sense a magical field of energy around the door and so he place his hand on the handle and absorbed the energy within himself (since he was a Succubus he would be able to do so). Miraculously the door opened and thus FOG now was able to enter this very secretive chasm located underneath the Lorelei castle.

Secretive Family Crypt underneath Lorelei Castle:

FOG now found himself inside a room or chasm like place which resembled a cave. Now he could hear that dreadful clanging sound even clearer than before. He moved toward the light source he could see from afar. He came closer and closer to the small rays of light that were shining through a small and narrow slit underneath another door. It was a large wooden door, which FOG slowly opened.

Fane currently was rampaging his family's almost empty treasure room. He threw old jugs to the side and coins against the wall of the stone crypt. He was so very tired, tired of finding answers which kept leading to more dead ends. He was tired of being here, of coming here a few months ago.

'Why, why must I be so complicated. Why does everything around me.....aaah!' Fane shouted when he was surprised by the appearance of FOG who now stood before him.

'What?...How did you manage to get in here?' Fane asked in a serious voice.

'I used the magical entry, that you used to get in here,' FOG replied.

'You used the same entry? What did you do to open the metal door that is magically sealed shut by a spell only I and my ancestors can use to even get here in the first place?' Fane said trying to keep himself calm.

FOG moved toward Fane. Fane could sense that FOG was unusually calm.

'I never like talking about the past or my past for that matter. But with you I'll make an exception. I am not a mere mortal man you think of me. For I am a Succubus. Which is a type of demon, that can remove energy from physical items and from living things for that matter. Whether that energy be of a magical nature or not. I may look older than I am supposed to look but that could change in an instant if I were to absorb a huge load of energy; for I would revert back to my young looks instantaneously. I only found out about this after I died and came back to life,' FOG explained.

'You actually died?' Fane asked and frowned.

FOG sighed, 'Yes I died and because of that I came back as a demon. I had been a mute-being all my life. Before you ask under what circumstances I died....I uh....my house was torched by reapers who belong to a group called the Order of the Grim Reaper. My wife was taken before and my son was kidnapped by an evil outlaw called Rumpelstiltskin. I still hope to find my son some day. But for now I intend to help you. I help mythical creatures, whether it be to do with the control of their powers, or they need a place to stay themselves. I had asked myself for the last 25 years in fact what had become of you. Until I was reminded by myself that you seemed to be a lonesome, weary person. It seemed like you needed help then and you definitely need it now. I hope that you now believe what I am telling you. For I have no reason to lie.'

Fane who had been rummaging about in his family's crypt, was now quietly standing in one spot in front of FOG. He had folded his arms and he was slightly smiling. One could see that Fane was amused by FOG's explanation. But at the same time Fane's face showed more of a calmness than before. Maybe, it was because he now knew a more probable reason for this acquaintances' true agenda.

Fane spoke in a casual tone, 'Alright. If what you say is true; then I am sorry for my.......my awkward or unusual behaviour.'

FOG replied, 'Now that sounds like an apology!'

Fane's smirk turned into a frown. He was not one to apologise too easily and he definitely did not tolerate being made fun of.

FOG grew silent quickly as he noticed that Fane was once again in a grumpy mood. Now both of them stood there for an unknown amount of time. They were both unsure as to how to proceed with this conversation from here.

'So where do we go from here?' FOG asked in a puzzled tone.

Fane turned away from FOG and then spoke, 'You told me you where here to help me in some way. So I think that is what you are going to do. But.....I guess I ought to do some explaining, as you will only then understand the true reason for my being here. Let's go back to the Family Library as there is something there I wish to explain in more detail.'

Both men went back toward the library. Once both had ascended the last step of the stone staircase that had brought them both to the Family Crypt. The magical stone floor shifted and moved back into place as it had been before; hiding the secret entry point from sight. Fane walked towards the table where the scroll with the Lorelei family tree was. Both Fane and FOG now gazed upon the vast documentation of names that stretched from top to bottom on the parchment. Fane pointed out that he was the last name to be written down on the scroll. The name being Matthias born 1510- but his death was not documented. Meaning that if this Matthias indeed was Fane then he was already 320 years old. FOG was even more clueless than ever, he had not read the exact details on the scroll, as he had only roughly glanced at it. Fane noticed that FOG had an immense amount of questions after having seen the year that was stated on the scroll. But FOG was too nervous to ask them. FOG moved away from the table, and slowly walked toward the door which led to one of the castle's many corridors. Fane who hadn't noticed that FOG had gone, focused his gaze on where FOG had stood. He turned around and he could see FOG leaving the library. He grasped the scroll, rolled it together and followed FOG toward the Kitchen area.

What is he doing now? Fane asked himself.

The Kitchen area was the best maintained area of the whole castle, even the rodents loved it here. Meaning, the mice and the occasional rat. The spiders that had casted their webs just above the kitchen fireplace had managed to catch many insects in their webs. Fane stood next to a dining table while he was watching FOG looking around in his briefcase for something, what he pulled out next though was unthinkable at first.

It was a plant. There was a real solid plant in FOG's bag. Now that was one thing Fane had not expected at all. It was a Viola that looked dainty and fragile. FOG held the plant in his hands and focused on something. All Fane now could see was that FOG was on his knees, but he could not see what he was doing. Fane moved toward FOG, so he could see him much more clearly. FOG it seemed had closed his eyes and was deep in thought. The plant that had so much green before was slowly wilting and withering away right in front of FOG and Fane. FOG opened his eyes. His pitch black eyes were now to be seen. The eyes of a Demon. Fane had met Demons before but he had not expected to see a Succubus taking the life force of a plant. Of all things a plant! The irony, Fane thought.

'Shouldn't your eyes revert back to their normal colouration?' Fane asked plainly.

'Mine still take some time. I haven't been a Demon all too long. So at times I still don't get the hang of it,' FOG replied.

Fane laughed but stopped just as soon as FOG was frowning at him. Funnily enough his eyes were now back to normal.

'Do not get started with asking me why I absorb the life force of plants. I would not want to harm anybody let alone little creatures like mice,' FOG stated.

Fane laughed loudly once more, then said, 'Nothing more to say Frances. Fine with me. Deal with your Demon side just like I deal with my.....my.'

'Wolf side,' FOG replied swiftly.

Fane decided to sit down on one of the chairs next to the dining table. He motioned for FOG to do the same. It seemed that Fane wanted to discuss something with FOG.

'Do you eat any kind of food? Any food at all?' Fane asked FOG out of curiosity.

'Is this conversation only going to be about me or are you going to explain to me how I could help you in any way? Also, to answer your question, I only consume magical energy or any kind of energy from life forms. This is the kind of sustenance I live from. I will only ever eat food if it were needed for some reason. I believe that I have now again answered your question,' FOG said in a stern voice.

FOG who was also seated on a chair began tapping his right foot on the floor. Fane hated the annoying tapping sounds that he could hear each and every time FOG's right foot came into contact with the stone floor; because of his extra-sensitive hearing.

'I only ask because I go hunting each and every night for food and I was wandering whether you ate meat or if demons ate any meat? I mean I have met demons before but only from afar with their funny-looking beady black eyes. Like those eyes that are sown onto creepy-looking dolls' Fane spoke in an amusing tone.

FOG had an empty/blank expression on his face; he then looked at Fane and replied, 'How!?....I don't have a clue as to whether all demons eat food. My kind of demon known as the Succubus live off energy. I am able to consume food if you really have to know this. That is all I can and will reveal to you.'

'Fine. Finally this conversation is starting to gain traction. In an amusing sort of way. Well, let me explain firstly why I am even here in this.....this remnant of my family's past,' Fane stated.

Fane paused for a moment and then continued to speak, 'I was born in the early part of the 15 hundreds (16th Century). I believe that my mother is this Lorelei who was married to a King named Erich. According to this scroll-' Fane stopped talking and placed the scroll on the table.

He got up from his chair and went to get some wax candles which he inserted in a metal candelabra which was already on the table. Fane was then gone again and came back with a spill (which was a sliver/small amount of wood; but one could also use twisted paper). He slowly moved toward the kitchen oven or hearth fire, where he held the spill into the fire, without accidentally burning himself. The spill was now lit; so now the candles could also be lit one by one.

Fane once again sat down on the chair he had use before. He pushed his chair closer to the table and stared at the scroll.

'So this scroll documented the story of a Werewolf line I am descended from. A wolf line spanning at least 10 centuries, maybe even more. I came to this place, this desolated place by working for someone who had further intel into my family's whereabouts. It was all for nothing. As I had falsely believed to find some or any distant relatives here at the castle. Instead, all I came to find was a crumbling, almost torn down looking residence and not one single living relative,' Fane thoroughly explained.

FOG quickly said, 'Fane, does this mean you were an orphan? That would explain a lot.'

Fane raised his eyebrows and his face showed an emotion of anger.

'Frances or FOG or whatever your name is, yes I was an orphan or I came to be an orphan because I was abandoned by my parents. However......that is all I will tell you for now,' Fane replied and stared intensely at FOG.

Now Fane managed to get back on topic, 'To continue on, I found this abandoned castle, with no living inhabitants whatsoever. Except the annoying non-living sirens situated around the castle or the occasional ghosts that still wander the castle grounds and may pop up anywhere unexpectedly. One of the only useful sources of information I did find was this scroll which detailed the long family line I am supposedly descended from.'

FOG had another question in mind, 'How though do you know that you are Matthias since your name is Fane? Because Matthias, the last name that was written on the scroll is the name that you believe to be yourself.'

'Sorry, forgot to explain this to you. I was abandoned and left with a German Farmer's family that lived during the 16th Century. When I five years of age I was told by them that they found me one morning during the year of 1512, whilst they were tending to their crops and that I had a name stitched into a blanket I was wrapped in...the name being.....Matt-' Fane was about to complete the sentence.

'Matthias,' FOG blurted out.

'Yes, Matthias. I had been wrapped up in a white/grey blanket which had my name and a family coat of arms sown into the fabric. The Farmer family took me in as their own for a few years only though,' Fane almost whispered.

'Why did you only stay with the farmer family for a few years?' FOG asked carefully.

'That is a story for another time. Now what I have been planning to do since I have arrived here a few months back is to journey to another place also located in Germany which may shed some further light into my family history. Maybe we will encounter some of the werewolf tribes on our way there,' Fane stated effortlessly.

'Wolf tribes??' FOG remarked nervously.

'Yes the wolf clans that are situated here in Germany. There are a few clan names I can tell you about but that can also be discussed another time. So I think it is now time for us both to get some rest before day breaks once more,' Fane replied.

Fane got up from the chair and walked down a dark, eery looking corridor.

'Wolf tribes; find out more about my family history; what is your name Frances or FOG?' FOG muttered about with himself.

'I heard that!' Fane shouted so that FOG could hear him loud and clear.

Creepy Sleeping Place Lorelei Castle:

There was an unusual calmness or quietness within the castle walls. It was now almost midnight, while FOG was walking back and forth in the bedroom he had decided to stay in for the night. The curtains draping down on the walls were moving slightly and an oil painting depicting a young woman, showed that the woman's eyes were also seemingly opening and closing.

Unfortunately, FOG failed to notice this as he was deep in thought, but at the same time a bit frustrated. First, Fane had not wanted any kind of help or was not even open to the very idea of talking about himself let alone his past; but now he was doing both of those things. FOG was also thinking about what kind of things would await him in Germany's countryside, moreover, the things he would experience on his way to this castle that Fane had barely mentioned. FOG would find out soon enough what castle Fane had meant to visit; to gain more insight into his family history. FOG would have suggested using the portalinator to get to their destination, but Fane being Fane would probably insist travelling on foot. For now FOG would try to get some rest, because he would probably need it. He sat down on the edge of the bed, then grabbed something out of his briefcase, a picture that he carried around with him wherever he went, a sentimental object that pictured his son and wife Lara. It was a family photo they had done, a long time ago. FOG placed the picture that was framed on the table, he closed his briefcase and then finally proceeded to blow out the candle that had been lit. He now was laying on the bed. Now FOG finally could get some shut eye. The small dark brown coloured clock that stood on a table next to the bed, now struck 12, meaning it was officially midnight; now some particularly slightly disturbing events would take place. The curtains or fabric that had hung on the wall was ripped in half, a chandelier that was attached to the ceiling swayed back and forth. Making an annoying dangling sound. A sinister presence was in the room with FOG, an ethereal presence that sought to scare FOG. FOG though was still able to snore away in his bed. The spirit went on to shake the bed, so that FOG would wake up from the rough movements. But there was still no reaction. The ghost was fed up and so in retaliation smashed FOG's picture to the ground.

The breaking of the glass finally woke up FOG who now looked to the picture that now lay on the wood floor with a broken frame and glass.

FOG was about to pick up the picture when from under the bed the spirit jumped out and said, 'Hello!?'

FOG moved backward onto the bed. He was not scared only slightly startled. But then something happened that he had not counted on. FOG noticed that were was an energy, a cold presence behind him. He turned himself around and saw the apparition or one half of the ghost in the middle of the King size bed. The ghost FOG believed to be a woman, had a ghoulish, monstrous smile and the appearance of the ghost looked like she had drowned in or died in water; as the appearance of her ghost skin looked all wrinkled and rotten. The female spirit opened her mouth and had sharp teeth. The spirit moved toward FOG.

FOG shouted, 'Aaaaah!!!!! Euuccch!' as he fell off the bed and onto the hard floor. *Thud!*

He had forgotten to prepare a salt barrier in the event of the appearance of spirit beings.

Meanwhile: Fane was standing in a room that he thought used to be his mother's. When he had arrived here, he found an old journal which had belonged to a woman named Lorelei and the journal entries matched up with the time frame the woman had supposedly lived. Fane didn't even know what happened to the poor woman. As the family tree only stated when she was born 1478 and did not document or go into any details regarding her death. If she even did die Fane told himself. Or maybe she did die and that is why she could no longer look after a little boy named Matthias. Who Fane believed to be himself. Fane was standing in front of a large oil painting of a massive castle out of stone. This is the place he believed to find out more information regarding his family heritage as this was mentioned in Lorelei's journal. Maybe this new link would lead to some further discoveries and finally clear up the events that led to Fane's rather obscure and at times cruel childhood.

Fane was torn out of his deepest thoughts when he heard something in one of the rooms in the castle. Then he could hear objects that sounded like metal clanging to the ground. Fane ran toward that gruelling sound.

'You fiend!!! Aaaah!' Fane could hear FOG shouting about.

Fane ran and ran. Until he finally spotted FOG fighting off a spectral entity he only knew as the crazy ghost who called herself Kristiane. FOG had run into an old armour, which would explain the clanging sounds he had heard before. Now FOG was standing in front of the ghost, waving an old metal sword about like a raving lunatic.

'Kristiane there is no need to scare the living daylights out of this fool. I mean you have had your fun.... I think it is time for you to leave or should I remind you of the magic mirror I found that can trap spirits and only be released by living creatures,' Fane said in a slight menacing tone.

A frightful expression was seen on the spectres and then it dispersed into nothingness.

FOG still stood there perplexed by what he had seen. He looked ridiculous wearing a metal helmet on his head. While at the same time holding a metal sword in his right hand.

'A metal sword FOG? I think you would have been better off using salt to create a salt barrier around yourself,' Fane said while almost laughing.

'That was one hell of a ghost!' FOG shouted.

'She probably belongs to hell itself, don't you think that yourself FOG?' Fane asked FOG.

FOG replied in a careful tone, 'Is that supposed to be funny. Because I said "that was one hell of a ghost".'

Fane only smirked, his eyes seemed to show a hint of amusement and curiosity at the same time.

'Do you know who that ghost was? You seemed to know her name and something about a mirror??' FOG asked and looked quite mind boggled.

Fane slightly smiled again and said, 'Follow me and you shall see.'

They both went toward a room that was located at the top of the Lorelei Castle. But to get there they would have to ascend step for step a winding spiral staircase made of stone. There they would enter a room that had a arching window from which one could view/see the landscape surrounding the castle. The room itself was circular in shape as well as small in size, except for a small stool and a mirror that hung on the wall next to the window. It had a dark oak frame and the glass, well it looked different to other mirrors. Like it had fine hair line cracks in it. But they were so tiny that the mirror almost seemed whole. If one closely kept looking at the glass one could see the cracks disappearing, reappearing and moving. Only an object of a magical nature would be able to do such a thing. There was text engraved into the wood of the mirror which stated 'Der Zerschmetterte Spiegel' meaning 'The Broken Mirror'.

Fane spoke, 'I came across this magical mirror only by chance. After staying here in this castle for the first few nights I was disturbed by the malevolent spirit I found out was named Kristiane. According to the

family tree, that I found much later on, Kristiane was the sister of Lorelei. Meaning Kristiane would be my Aunt. If I am supposed to believe what the scroll states. To cut the story short, I found this mirror accidentally; after hearing a shrill sound and a screaming voice. I decided to find out where this sound was coming from and found the mirror. In that same moment when I had found the mirror; Kristiane was behind me and probably planned on scaring me when she disappeared or disintegrated into thin air. Unbeknownst to me she was trapped in that ghastly mirror.'

Fane stopped talking and pointed his index finger at the mirror.

'I only found out that she was trapped in there after a few weeks, as I could see her in the mirror, staring outward at me persistently. Allegedly, at the time she was absorbed into the mirror she was in a weakened state; because the mirror absorbed her energy. Meaning, the mirror lives off ghost energy or the energy of dead beings/creatures. I managed to help her out of the mirror by smearing a bit of my blood on the glass of the mirror. With that she was quickly released from her prison,' Fane thoroughly explained.

FOG was puzzled by the utter fact that Fane had decided to help one of his distant dead relatives out of an unusual magical mirror that seemed to trap spirits or beings of the same kind. FOG failed to understand the point, as to why Fane would want to have a weird, grotesque and hideous spirit roaming the castle halls at night. Waiting to scare anyone stupid enough or cowardly enough.

'Why release her at all Fane? I fail to understand why you would want her around you at all?' FOG asked quietly.

'I released her from her prison because......because I had thought.....or wanted to find a few, if even just one living relative. Unfortunately, that was not meant to be as all had passed on or so I thought, until I found out that Kristiane was my aunt and so I kind of felt sorry or sad for her. That is why I released her from that mirror,' Fane said in a solemn tone.

FOG gave Fane a pat on the back and said, 'I understand you fully in that respect Fane.'

Fane pulled back; he looked at FOG in disbelief, 'Do not do that again FOG!....and what...how would you understand how I feel?!'

'Well, I lost my family. However, after some time other bonds formed. Friendships, alliances and of course the occasional enemies. Of course one of my dearest friends is Aya who is a Kitsune and Cleo who I welcomed into my family or safe haven family a few years back. She by the way is a were-cat. There are even legends in South America that delve deep into stories about similar creatures called were-pumas or were-jaguars. Maybe, the descriptions are relevant to the clan of were-cats Cleo came from. Who knows for sure? Eh?' FOG joked about.

'How can you compare your adopted family....to a ghost who is actually related to me?' Fane asked FOG.

'No matter if bound by blood or by a notion of mere friendship/camaraderie. There are different concepts to family. I had a family. But they were taken. I am hopeful to find them again some day. However, since they have both gone. I have gained many friends, allies and foes. But I hope you will at least become an ally of mine. So we can help each other and learn from each other,' FOG stated.

'Fair enough,' Fane simply replied.

'How did you even find out that the ghost that was haunting this castle was named Kristiane?' FOG asked in a sceptical tone.

'She kept shouting about like a raving lunatic. Going on about how she was wronged or something like that calling herself 'the wronged Kristiane'. That is all I can recall about finding out what her name was. Anyway, before I forget, Kristiane once before mentioned that this mirror was not here before I came here. So, however this mirror came to be here, it arrived at the same time I did. That is no mere coincidence and that is another reason for me to leave this....this uncanny place,' Fane replied.

'So you believe the ramblings of a more than 300 year old ghost?' FOG asked clearly confused.

'She did haunt this place for more than 300 years. As you yourself have already stated. So, yes I would probably believe what she says. Kristiane is a deranged and at times senile ghost. But she does know her way around this castle. She even stated that she used to haunt this place with another spirit but that he had crossed over a long time ago. Now she roams this place alone. For the rest of the time though she is indeed incredibly crazy and should be left alone. As long as she is left alone she leaves us alone. Though sometimes she does come up with ideas and that is when I remind her of this mirror, where she then flees as soon as she hears the word,' Fane said in response to FOG's question.

'So will you join me in my quest to unravel the secrets involving my family history?' Fane asked a perplexed FOG.

FOG only nodded and both shook hands.

The next morning: Fane's Sleeping Quarters Lorelei Castle:

Indeed it was morning as the first animals joyously awoke to the first hours of daylight. That being the annoying birds singing coming from outside Fane's window. Fane knew it was the right time to wake up as the birds woke him up every morning at the same time, each and every day. Fane yawned and then glimpsed downward where he saw FOG lying on the ground with a pillow under his head. He had decided to stay with Fane as he had not wanted to unintentionally bump into Kristiane again. FOG awoke but for the same reason as Fane because of the racket being made by the birds outside. Both decided to regain their energy somehow either by eating some breakfast or doing what FOG did to restore his own energy. Fane went back to his room he had called home for the last few months. It had been his mother's room. He only knew this because he had found her old, dusty and worn belongings here in one spot. There also was an oil portrait of her hanging in the room. She was no ugly nor too pretty young woman. But for some reason she had not wanted to be part of Fane's life. This made Fane angry. The realisation of the unknown was at times a lot for Fane to wrap his head around. He would have temper tantrums or outbursts or fits of rage would take him over. It was as if he was possessed. Fane now had to focus on the present. He had now packed all of his belongings, that he had carried with him for as long as he could remember. One of those items being the blanket that he was found with. The blanket which had his name and the Lorelei family coat of arms stitched into the fabric. Fane had his belongings in his bag in one hand and he was about to walk out of the room when he for one last time glanced at the oil painting of the Castle he planned on travelling to. The Castle Satzvey located in the west of Germany. An old castle that had been built some time in the 14th Century. There Fane hoped to find more answers regarding his family history. He averted his eyes and left the room for the last time.

Lorelei - Fane's Mother

Satzvey Castle Germany

Lorelei Castle – The Great Hall:

Fane was staring about at the colossal room he found himself in. That being the Great Hall, which was also the biggest room in the whole castle. There was a long dining table; where royals in the past would gather; with numerous many chairs standing around the table. The ceiling arched upward to the top, making the room seem even more massive. There were many windows that would let the light in during the day and a light source that hung from the ceiling that would illuminate everything at night. Fane was still waiting for FOG to show up. He was patiently waiting and waiting. But there was still no sign of the peculiar old-looking man.

FOG who was still clumsily stumbling about and making his way down the corridor toward the Great Hall; came upon something unexpected. He had found an inscription that was etched into the wall by a sharp object. The inscription stated 'This is the river of Lorelei. The river that takes and let's everything die. Look for where the secrets lie. Where the sirens dwell; watch your step or they'll give you hell. The sirens lullaby is the key; don't be scared and do not flee. For you shall seek and find the very thing that will release her from her prison. This is written by the person responsible for her misery. K.' The first part of this passage, sounded somewhat familiar to him; 'This is the river Lorelei. The river that takes and let's everything die.' It was the same thing that the crazed siren yelled to him when he was walking past her. Maybe, this message had something to do with that siren. As well as with Kristiane. Since the last letter inscribed was 'K'. FOG was slowly piecing this riddle together. This made FOG even more intrigued and even more determined to unravelling the meaning behind this message/riddle. FOG opened his briefcase and got out a notebook and something to write with. When he had finally copied down everything. He then placed his notebook back in his briefcase and began walking toward the Great Hall.

Finally Fane could see that FOG had made it to the Great Hall.

'I thought you'd never find the Great Hall!' Fane shouted.

'Growing impatient as ever Fane,' FOG stated in a sarcastic tone.

As always Fane would try to act as if he didn't care about anything nor anyone. FOG still though tried to gain more of an insight into Fane's mind but trying to do so would probably take longer than he thought it would.

The unusual old-looking man spoke, 'Did you notice the inscription that was carved into the stone wall? On my way here I noticed some writing, maybe; probably carved into the wall with a sharp object.'

The younger looking man named Fane replied, 'What on Earth are you going on about?'

Fane was now again more clueless than before. He asked himself where he could have seen anything etched into the stone walls. But in reality he had never seen anything of that nature inside the Lorelei Castle. Fane asked as calmly as he could whether FOG could show him this supposed writing.

FOG stated, 'Sure, follow me.'

Both slowly walked along a long corridor. Fane could notice that FOG's face showed a hint of confusion. FOG on the other hand was adamant that he had come across the peculiar scribbles of writing in close vicinity of where they now stood. Fane was smiling awkwardly, but he was hiding his anger/discontent for FOG within himself. He started pacing back and forth; whilst FOG was staring at the bare stone walls. FOG though remembered that he had written down what was stated on the wall into his notebook. He opened his briefcase and then proceeded to show Fane that he had indeed written down what he had seen. Once Fane read the passage, he believed FOG, as he had heard this peculiar rhyme or song somewhere before. He just couldn't pin point where though. His mind was drawing a blank. This made Fane even more frustrated. Both Fane and FOG did agree on one thing though; they would both have to track down Kristiane. Because she was the only lead they had in this matter, especially since the last letter mentioned in the writing was K.

Lorelei Castle Later that same day:

Again it was almost sun down. Night time was drawing closer. As Fane and FOG were searching for Fane's relative or long dead creepy aunt Kristiane. They searched the castle from top to bottom. They even went down to the secret family crypt, but still no Kristiane. There was only one place they could search. The family cemetery. Both decided they would continue their search there.

On their way toward the cemetery one of them was bound to strike up a conversation.

'So does she only do the spiky/sharp teeth thing for strangers? Or does she scare the living daylights out of anyone who dares to spend one night in this Castle?' FOG asked in a weary tone.

Fane who had been daydreaming somewhat, now again directed his attention at FOG.

'What are you blabbering on about?' Fane asked in a dazed tone.

'Nothing....nothing much,' FOG replied.

'I know that we could have already begun our journey unravelling the mysteries and secrets surrounding your family history. But I guess that there is still an unresolved matter here at the Lorelei Castle,' FOG replied, trying to reassure Fane.

Fane sighed and continued to walk down many steps until they reached the family cemetery that was located behind the castle.

However, all that was left of the supposed cemetery were the remnants of many desecrated grave stones that were scattered about. Some barely had readable names. Some were starting to crumble and others were barely visible or had turned to a pile of stone. It was now officially

night time. FOG felt an eery feeling come over him. Being in close proximity to the cemetery of course didn't help whatsoever. Fane of course didn't seem to mind being in the presence of the dead or be it the long dead remnants of his relatives. They scanned their surroundings, walked past each grave stone, until they came across a grave with the name barely readable. There was centuries worth of dust/cobwebs or dirt on the stone surface; one could still though recognise that this was Kristiane's grave. It seemed though to both Fane and FOG that Kristiane didn't hang around her burial place. So both decided to head back to the castle. When they could hear some harmonious,graceful and yet deeply disturbing singing to be heard from a small chapel that was located next to the small graveyard. Fane ran toward that very sound.

Whilst FOG who was rather sceptical shouted after Fane, 'Wait!' and then ran after Fane.

Small Chapel Lorelei Castle:

Fane was fed up. He had to find Kristiane and question her as to why she never mentioned this song or rhyme. Why did she carve it into the wall for FOG to find. Couldn't she face her own relative? What else is she hiding? What secrets is she keeping from me? All these thoughts were swarming about Fane's mind and yet he surprisingly was not furious with his Aunt. He was however, disappointed in her. For her not telling him, about this......this....whatever this riddle/matter was about. Fane was determined to find out what was the meaning behind this secret/hidden truth she tried to convey to FOG.

Fane was running toward the distant melody that he had heard before. It was the exact same rhyme he had glimpsed in FOG's notebook. He was asking himself why after all this time she had not sung this puzzling song. It was only since FOG was here that she started to sing in rhyme.

The old chapel that was located next to the rather desolate cemetery was also starting to crumble away. Even the holy cross that used to tower above the church now lay on the floor, as even the chapel roof was starting to wear down. There were shadows scattered about around the stone walls of the chapel. Shadows that were being cast by an oddly shaped and obscure tree that closely resided next to the chapel. The moon's light barely illuminating the leaves, which allowed the tree to cast faint shadows. The wind was gently swaying the tree back and forth. FOG was speed walking after Fane. But Fane was already way ahead of FOG. He was about to turn a corner and walk down a small stone staircase when he saw a distant apparition sitting in a far corner, under an arching ceiling, wearing a dark black dress. The creature or Fane's creepy Aunt was unaware that she was being watched. Fane hid or tried to keep himself hidden if only for a moment. He tried to listen in on his aunt's rather loud, harmonious and shrill voice.

'Where the sirens dwell; watch your step or they'll give you hell. The sirens lullaby is the key; don't be scared and do not flee. For you shall seek and find the very thing that will release her from her prison. The love she has lost is the very thing that will release her from her mysticism,' Kristiane sung to herself.

FOG who still had failed to find Fane, was getting closer to the source of the mysterious voice he had heard sing before. Fane saw that FOG was heading his way. He wanted to reach out and grab FOG by the arm; to stop him from being seen by the ghastly looking Kristiane. But it was too late for the spectre known only as Kristiane, lunged outward at FOG. Her translucent black hair seeming electrified. Kristiane who had now also noticed Fane's presence was in some sort of state of shock. It was as if she was terrified of Fane. FOG who was now free from Kristiane's grasp, on the other hand started to laugh. But he would be the only one to be doing so. For Fane this whole commotion was no laughing matter. FOG's laugh started to fade, as well as his smile. Kristiane seemed to be thinking of a way to explain her way out of her rather unexplainable, out of the usual behaviour.

Fane stood his ground, however, he did not seem to be in a happy mood. But neither in a bad mood though. The atmosphere was tense. As Kristiane struggled to explain to Fane what the matter was.

She only stated, 'I am not one to express much emotion. I have.....I had never received much love.....from anyone. I mean....I was left all alone when I was just a naive little girl. Who had not much knowledge of the world. All I know is that I should not have been such a bad person to the one who only tried to reach out.....'

Kristiane showed an emotion of remorse. It seemed that there had been some unfinished business that she had not resolved in her human life. Things she had done that she had regretted doing.

'Now who is this person you are talking about?' FOG asked with a questionable look on his face.

Fane frowned the only person or persons he could recall that Kristiane could be talking about was her husband or her older sister Lorelei. The woman who was Fane's mother. Her death to him was still shrouded in so much mystery and secrecy.

Fane spoke solemnly, 'The only person I believe that she could possibly be referring to would be Friedrich who was her husband.'

Kristiane shook her head and spoke once more, 'No, that is not the person I was meaning to talk of. Not the person I took for granted. The person I wronged was my sister. We were estranged from one another. Because we were separated; the reason for this separation is unknown to me. After, not having seen her for a very long time, since I was little for that matter, I was cruel toward her. I apologise for not telling you this earlier. I only understood what I had done wrong after being a ghost for many centuries now. Having had enough time to contemplate my wrongdoings. I was a power hungry woman, who married Friedrich, through an arranged marriage. This being one of the things a dutiful woman had to do during that time and this is probably still the case today. After, King Erich married Lorelei they had a child together. That being you. Unfortunately, their happiness was not meant to last. King Erich returned to his Castle in the North West of Germany. Where my husband decided to usurp him. Of course as my husband's dutiful wife I had to follow suit. After having gained control of that Castle. My husband also wanted power over Lorelei and her small Castle on a mountain next to the river Lorelei. Being naive I was the one who suggested for my husband to do this. A few days later, we travelled to the Lorelei Castle, after hearing accounts of castle servants stating that the Lady Lorelei had jumped to her death. The Castle though was derelict, empty and seemingly quiet. Soon after my husband was lured into the river by a siren, to his death, and I died alongside him. Because I tried to save his stupid life. Since then I have been haunting this place with my husband for company. Until....until......' Kristiane stopped speaking as she seemed to be unable to continue.

FOG who stood next to Fane, saw how Fane was struggling to keep himself from going insane. Fane had just heard from his dead/ghost Aunt that his mother had killed herself by committing suicide. Again as usual pointless thoughts and questions were crowding Fane's mind. Whenever Fane got too worked up or stressed nothing good came from it. Suddenly, Fane's eyes lit up in blue colours, he started to lean against a wall and was breathing quickly. Trying as hard as he could to control himself he thought of a memory where he would envisage himself as a young boy, learning from his step-father Sinric the first few steps of wood carving. Usually this would be able to calm Fane down. However, FOG who could also see that Fane was trying to keep himself calm, knew that he was epically failing in trying to do so. Fane ran, ran from the only relative he had gotten to know, or let himself know. He tried to get away from a person he had not seen for 30-40 years. A person he in secret respected in some way. His insides were turning inside out. His muscles ached. The ligaments, and bones in his upper and lower body limbs were rubbing against each other, breaking and healing at the same time. To Fane it was obvious that he was transforming of course involuntarily. Since he had found out he had the ability to transform into a wolf creature, he tried so adamantly to learn the art of controlling his wolf form. However, even though he was now more than three centuries old he still at times lacked control. Fane was back in the cemetery and was on his knees. He was in a crouched position, he could hear how his spine was arching and splitting back into place. Fane didn't understand why of all times this was happening to him now. He had been here at the Lorelei Castle for the last few months and had no problems whatsoever.

Though now he lacked the simple ability to control his wolf powers, form and himself for that matter. Maybe it had to do with the utter fact that his Aunt had kept the details of his mothers death from him or that she knew more than she was letting on. It didn't matter now. All that mattered was that Fane would stay away from everyone. As he was now in an unpredictable and dangerous way. FOG who finally managed to find his way back to the cemetery saw Fane on his knees, in a crouched position. Irregardless of how much FOG wanted to help Fane. He knew somehow, that he should leave him to himself, as he would only bring himself and Fane into danger. FOG snuck away to a quiet spot so that he could safely watch Fane from afar. Fane now started to clench his teeth, his finger nails were slowly turning into claws that were clawing the earth because of the pain. Fane knew something was wrong with him. He had turned so often now that it stopped hurting; meaning that what was happening to him was happening for other reasons. Fane slightly shrieked and shouted out in pain so that FOG could hear it from afar. Pain was radiating throughout his whole body. Small and big jolts of stabbing pains. Fur was now covering Fane's back, shoulders, legs and now his whole body had transformed fully into a wolf creature. A rather beautiful silver-grey beast with intriguing light-blue eyes. The wolf was now in full control of Fane and Fane was no longer in control of his inner beast. The were-wolf ran away into a dark night. FOG stood at the edge of a stone staircase. He was amazed and disgusted at the same time, as he had never encountered a wolf transformation. This was a first for FOG. There was nothing the old-looking man named FOG could do and so he was about to go back into the castle when he heard a deep sombre howl coming from afar. FOG smiled but not because he was happy, it was an unsure response he had when he was worried for his friends or acquaintances. One thing FOG was sure about though is that he would find out what Kristiane had tried to explain before when they were all in the chapel.

Inside Lorelei Castle (Library):

It was unusually warm this time of night. According to FOG's watch it was now almost midnight. He went toward a window, only to see that clouds were covering the dark night sky. One could not even see any stars. That was how thick the cloud masses were. Now FOG could even glimpse light flashes coming from the clouds. Meaning that soon the thunder would soon begin. The trees that weren't moving at all, were now being blown back and forth by the wind. FOG was about to leave the window when a huge thunder beam clashed down to earth. The horrendous sound so loud that FOG was left in disarray. Even the ground beneath FOG seemed to be pounded by the immense build up pressure caused by the storm outside. Now FOG was starting to worry for Fane. He was unsure whether he should venture outside and look for him. But the idea of wondering about like a raving lunatic. In a place he had no knowledge of where to go, made him think otherwise. The darkness outside would be enticing for many mythical creatures. FOG though could only hope that Fane would turn up sooner rather than later.

Lorelei Family Library:

FOG had fallen asleep on an old wooden chair. He had forgotten to absorb his daily energy fill and so had to regain his energy through sleep. FOG was still in a dazed state, once he finally noticed what the time was. He woke up quickly. It was 4am. He had been asleep for four whole hours. He checked his surroundings. He checked all the rooms of the castle and even the secret hidden family crypt. There was still no sign of Fane anywhere. It was still drizzling rain outside. FOG in his delirium hadn't even noticed that Kristiane was following him everywhere he went. Basically she was his shadow. Only when FOG sat down on one of the dining chairs that stood around the kitchen table in the Kitchen area of the Castle did he notice a cold presence close to him. He turned his attention only for a short moment to an empty space behind him and was greeted by Kristiane's spirit. FOG was not scared as he was the last time. But he still had not counted on Kristiane being just right there.

He asked her in a quiet voice, 'Have you seen or heard anything from Fane?'

She whispered gently, 'I have not seen him. But that is not what I wanted to talk about with you. I have not been entirely truthful with both of you.'

Kristiane paused only shortly and continued to speak, 'I....Fane's coming here to find out more of his family history.....that was his decision. But there are devious, dark forces at play here....My husband's spirit never passed on...he...his spirit was transferred into a tree by a man....man with evil intentions. The mirror that Fane told you about....the mirror that appeared here shortly after he came here, was brought here by that same man. I do not know this peculiar man's name. All I know is that he had a particularly small stature for a man anyway. I was forced by this person to make Fane do a blood oath. A blood oath, that Fane would not know of. One he wouldn't think anything sinister of. As soon as he touched the mirror with his blood. I was freed, but he was bound to an item that belonged to the small man. An item that resembled a......a ring. I think it was a ring. I had no choice other than do what he wanted. Because he would have otherwise condemned Friedrich's soul to the underworld. He promised me that as soon as Fane would unwillingly turn into his wolf form. Then my husband would be freed from the tree in return. I did not want to do what I did....I did not know that he wanted to harm Fane. I would have....have.....'

'What?! You could not keep your only living relative Fane away from harm. From a raving lunatic outlaw named Rumpelstiltskin?! How could you! How dare you help an insane, psychotic criminal who is wanted by the The Hidden Empire. You helped one of those....people who single-handedly destroyed my life and now you have also destroyed Fane's!!!!' FOG shouted at the top of his lungs.

FOG had heard enough of Kristiane's fairy tales for now.

But at the same time he still was not finished with her, 'What would Rumpelstiltskin want from Fane anyway?'

'He had once said something about power. Yes....something about power. Making him normal....human' Kristiane stated.

FOG's worst fears had been confirmed. That for the first time he had seen a wolf transform. Would be ultimately Fane's last time to physically transform into a werewolf and that wherever he now found himself. He would be vulnerable to almost everything and anyone.

Suddenly FOG's disarray/scattered thoughts came to a halt, as he was questioning himself why Kristiane had not mentioned the very fact as to why she left a message for them both etched into the wall? The message that was the song she had been singing in the chapel.

FOG was in a bad mood but he managed to ask one last question before he would do the unthinkable, something Kristiane would not count on, 'Were you even the one who carved the detailed but puzzling message into the stone wall?'

Kristiane did not want to be confronted by this man named FOG, but she was the one responsible for what now had happened to Fane and so she would have to answer any question that came her way.

Kristiane spoke: 'I was told to keep quiet.....about this whole matter, I regret not having said this earlier but......the small man carved the message into the wall. He asked me whether I knew something like a rhyme or song that was tied into my family history, the Lorelei family history and so I mentioned the song my mother would sing to me, a song that spanned back generations. I didn't know that he would use it as a distraction to catch you and Fane off guard. He told me that, that was the last thing he would need from me other than singing that song to bring both of you to the chapel. I.....can never......'

Out of nowhere, FOG got up from his chair and banged his hand on the table. FOG could not change the past, nor did he want to waste anymore time listening to the endless explanations from Kristiane; he had a plan in mind and it involved doing something in retaliation for what Kristiane had done to Fane. FOG went up a long spiral staircase, towards the very room that Fane had showed him, where the mirror had stood. But it was gone, just like Fane was. FOG went down to the kitchen area again, and rummaged about the food storage section. He found something that caught his attention. It was an old rum bottle. FOG hurried outside with the rum bottle and a sliver of wood that was burning with him to the chapel, toward the tree that was located close by. He had an inkling that Friedrich's spirit was still trapped inside the tree. So this would be the best revenge FOG could get on behalf of Fane. FOG was about to pour some rum on the tree and ignite a fire. Maybe Fane would be able to find his way back toward the castle, as this fire would act like a sort of signal. FOG though was right to think that Friedrich was still trapped inside the tree.

As a man's rather deep and clear voice was to be heard coming from the tree, 'You shall not destroy me!'

'Oh I shall destroy you and it will be a delight to get rid of you,' FOG replied in a sarcastic tone.

The fire was now lit and the tree was now aflame. The first rays of daylight were now to be glimpsed. As FOG proudly stood in front of the glorious fire he had ignited. Kristiane who was angry at FOG, but at the same time accepted that what she had done to Fane was unforgivable, was telling herself that what FOG was doing to her ghost husband was

217

justified. Not only had she betrayed her sister. But now also her only living relative Fane. Her own flesh and blood. Her blood relative. She was not able to go on. All she could now do was try to make up for what she had done. That would be trying to find Fane. But where he now was that was the real question/dilemma.

During the last few hours of the night; nearby woods in close vicinity of Lorelei Castle:

The last few hours were hectic, as Fane's wolf form was scowering about, scavenging for food or prey. Unfortunately a poor deer got in the way and became the wolf's dinner. Luckily no other living souls got hurt. For the first time in a long time, Fane was out of control, when he was in his teens he lacked the self-control to stop himself from turning into his other self. After many years of discipline and practice he was able to turn himself at will. What was happening to him right now, was for reasons unknown to him. He was no longer himself, the wolf within him was raging on. The wolf was making the decisions now, Fane's normal consciousness for now lay dormant, his wolf side however had full control. He would continue to traverse the slightly mountainous and steep geography of the landscape that was in close proximity to his family's Castle. Until Fane's wolf side became tired and bored. It felt alone and was in some kind of pain. The wolf began to howl in a low tone. Slowly and surely Fane's consciousness would awaken once more,

the wolf however, could notice that it's power was fading. The wolf laid itself down, it's blue eyes glowing one last time. The werewolf now found itself in a deep sleep from which it would awake within a few hours time.

Outside Castle Lorelei; next to the Lorelei River:

It was early in the morning but still relatively dark. The sun rose slowly as it always did, however, the moon still was visible from afar. A man was lying on the ground. His clothes were slightly torn and dirty. His whole body hurt and he was slightly trembling. It was Fane. Who had finally awoken to find himself next to the Lorelei river. It was cold and yet the temperature was starting to climb. Fane was so tired and hungry. He tried to get up, but he was too weak to do so. He would have to wait for a few more minutes before he would even try to do so again. He could not remember the events that had unfolded during the last few hours. From afar, Fane caught the attention of an unfriendly creature a siren that sung a rather disturbing song, when FOG had arrived at the Castle Lorelei. This siren begun to sing a melodic tune, that unfortunately Fane was unable to resist. The tune was so beguiling and charming that Fane who was in a weakened stated was caught/mesmerised by the powerful tune he was influenced by.

FOG who was still staring at his masterpiece. Heard the annoying siren/s singing. Mostly he thought to himself. Whenever these annoying sirens sing, is never a good sign. FOG carefully moved toward the singing sounds. Just in case, he already had something like cotton wool stuck in his ears. So that he would not fall for the sirens charms. Like he had almost before in his distant past.

Kristiane knew where Fane was. She glimpsed where Fane was. She decided that she owed Fane for what she did to him and so she would try to help him, to the best of her ghost abilities. The only thing she could do in this case is possess the siren. Kristiane elegantly floated toward the siren. The siren for one moment stopped her charming tune. She frowned, but could not stop Kristiane from possessing her. Fane was for a short moment stopped in his tracks. He was standing in the river Lorelei and was already knee deep. The water was cold but at the same time refreshing. Fane decided that he would get out of the water.

When he heard a weird sound coming from the siren, 'Aaaacchhhh!!!! It's me Kristiane. Get out of the water and away from the siren. I will hold her off for as long as I can. Go now!!!'

Fane looked at the siren in disbelief. He turned and rushed himself to get out of the water. He almost reached the edge of the river bed. When the siren regained control of herself and continued the melody like she had before. Fane again was under her influence. Kristiane was in a weakened state after having possessed another creature. Possession was a thing that took a lot of energy from ghosts. But this possession came with something else. Kristiane was able to look within and connect with the sirens memories. From what she was able to remember the siren that possessed was none other than her sister. Lorelei! How and why was Lorelei a siren? What on earth triggered her to take her own life or to become a siren? Kristiane only knew that Lorelei had taken her own life after a great sadness had happened to her. Maybe it was Fane? Kristiane was in a state where she was unable to do anything until her ghost energy returned to full strength and her ghost form would remain within the Lorelei Castle walls till she would awake once more. FOG on the other hand was able to see Fane walking blindly toward the siren. FOG had enough taken from him in his life, he didn't want Fane to lose his life because of a damned siren. He ran as fast as he could downhill toward the river. He swam toward the siren who was already closing in on Fane. FOG now could see that Fane was in real danger. The siren was holding Fane under the water and smiling a real grim smile. FOG was just close enough to come into contact with the sirens hand. He was about to do something he vowed not to do ever so often and only if he had to. This was a do or die situation. He grasped the sirens hand and siphoned her energy. The siren who was sitting on a large rock, turned to FOG and tried to fight him off. Fane though was now able to breathe again after having been underwater for the last few seconds. He saw how FOG was trying to help him.

Fane shouted, 'No don't kill her. FOG No!!! That's....it's my m-m!'

Fane's response came too late. The siren's skin started to turn black and piece by piece was withering away; until there was nothing left. FOG swam toward Fane who was sitting on the large rock.

Fane seemed to be displeased with FOG.

'What's the problem now? I saved your life!' FOG shouted while trying to keep himself afloat.

'You took away a life,' Fane stated in an obnoxious tone.

FOG was in a perplexed state. What had he done wrong?

Oh, now something was starting make more sense. The siren that was singing the same song as Kristiane. Was Kristiane's sister. FOG had unintentionally killed Fane's mother.

FOG decided to head back toward the castle. Where he decided to unload a bit of the energy he had consumed onto some of the plants he took with him in his seemingly small briefcase. FOG looked out of one of the many windows and could see Fane sitting on the rock where his mother had probably been seated for the last three centuries.

Fane had in those few moments. Even if he had been under the influence of the siren. Felt a connection to his mother. This connection was somewhat familiar to him. Now he felt like he had never known and lost his mother all over again.

He stayed seated on the rock til night came once more. FOG went outside to keep him company, he was sitting at the edge of the river bed. Waiting for Fane to be done with his mourning. Kristiane who had been in some sort of stasis mode, woke up once more and was greeted by someone she had not expected to see. Both spirits hand in hand went outside toward Fane. It was Kristiane and Lorelei. Lorelei seemed to want to say goodbye to her son. Fane noticed the who spirits hovering above him. He somehow knew that one of the ghosts was his mother. One small tear ran down his face. He smiled and waved toward them.

Lorelei spoke, 'I never left you. You were taken from me. Don't let anyone tell you otherwise. I am proud of you. You have grown big but strong.'

Kristiane spoke, 'We have found each other again. Thank you Fane.'

Lorelei and Kristiane hugged each other and disappeared together into nothingness. FOG saw that Lorelei finally got the peaceful ending she deserved. Yet again though Fane was left all alone.

Lorelei Castle; The Next Day:

A few hours ago Fane had finally left the rock where he had been seated for a rather long time contemplating the events that had occurred. However, now something was different. Fane was different. He no longer had his Celtic Wolf powers and who knows if he even still was a mythical creature? The only one who had an inkling in regard to what

Fane would now possibly be was FOG, who had heard a detailed and complicated explanation from Kristiane herself.

FOG and Fane were now seated next to each other in the Grand Hall. Both look tired and miserable. But now what FOG was about to tell Fane, would make Fane feel even more hopeless.

FOG sighed and then spoke, 'Fane......I do not know how I......am supposed to tell you this but you are no longer.....You no longer possess your abilities and strength.....'

Fane's facial expression looked even more tired than before, he now though replied, 'What do you mean by 'no longer possess'?'

'Kristiane told me that........someone who is wanted by the Hidden Empire, for reasons unknown to me has taken your power. This outlaw is the same monstrous, devious mastermind that took from me as well. His name is Rumpelstiltskin,' FOG tried to explain as calmly as possible.

Fane's eyebrows twitched slightly, his eyes seemed fiery.

He banged both his hands on the table and shouted out loud, 'You....mean to tell me that a ridiculous fool named Rump....Rump.....never mind stole my powers to use for his own advantage? Is this what you mean to explain to me FOG?'

FOG had a nervous look on his face. He seemed to be lost in thought for a moment.

When he replied, 'All I know is that your Aunt Kristiane betrayed you to help her ghost husband Friedrich get freed from the tree. She traded your life, your abilities for Friedrich a ghost who was trapped in a tree next to the chapel outside.'

'How exactly was she able to pull off her charade?' Fane asked plainly.

'She made you think that you managed to trap her inside that mirror that appeared shortly after or when you arrived at the Castle,' FOG replied in a confident tone.

Fane was so unsure of himself now. How could he have trusted someone so easily? Someone who was not even a person. A ghost, a relative that he thought would have his back. But as always Fane should have shut off his stupid feelings and emotions. He should have listened to himself. Not the tired strings that were attached to his foolish heart yearning to have a connection with someone. Be it a ghost, who at least was related to him in some way. He should have thought through the whole situation he had found himself him before touching that ridiculous, heinous mirror.

Fane eye's began to look slightly teary, but he managed to keep himself together, 'How could I have been so......dumb, so irresponsible not to see the lies this woman, this ghost was telling me!? She was the one who told me that blood magic, that living beings were able to release ghosts from some dark objects. Like that damn mirror. As soon as I touched the cracked surface of the mirror, as soon as my blood came into contact with the cursed object, I felt something pulsate on my hand. But I guess my goodwill and lack of judgement got the better of me!'

Fane spoke once more, 'I mean why would this supposed outlaw wait so long to take what he wanted? According to Kristiane the mirror appeared only once I had arrived, and the menace only implemented his so called plan after you arrived, FOG. Do you understand what I am trying to imply?'

'Fane.....I....uh, I am not sure why Rumpelstiltskin enacted his plan only once I arrived here to find you. But for now it doesn't matter as we might find out the why someday anyway. Fane don't blame your aunt and don't forget that Kristiane did try to hold off your mother from killing you. She was truly sorry for doing what she had done. Just like I am sorry for.....even if it was accidental...killing your mother,' FOG replied trying to get Fane to calm his temper.

For some unusual reason Fane did manage to calm himself down. Maybe this had something to do with the utter fact that Fane was now more human than anything else. Though there was still an inkling, a spark of the wolf within him. For now though Fane was almost as vulnerable as any mere mortal human. The idea of this scared him almost to the core.

'I.....am unsure, as to where we go from here. I have just lost a huge part of what made me, me. Now I feel broken. Like a broken object that has lost its purpose. Throughout my whole life I have had my powers to lean on. What am I without my wolf side FOG? Aren't I just another low life human? Like every other human out there? Vulnerable and pathetic,' Fane stated in a low voice.

FOG now had a stern expression on his face. He used his right arm and patted Fane on the back.

Then spoke, 'Fane, firstly, not all humans are as vulnerable and pathetic as you make them out to be. Of course I am also referring to myself, as I also used to human. All I can tell you I will go wherever you go, for now anyways. If you need help, or if we need some allies. I know who I will call on to come here. That is all I will tell you for now. One last thing, I will try to help you retrieve what you have lost. The power that Rumpelstiltskin has taken from you. Was not his to take. It does not belong to him. We will get back that ring from him and you shall get yourself back.'

Fane seemed to be content with what he heard FOG say, 'Thanks FOG. I might feel a bit better now. You are good at pep talks, you do know that?' Fane said in a mocking tone

'Don't get started with your sarcastic, smartass remarks,' FOG replied in an annoyed tone.

Fane got up from his chair and now he patted FOG on the back.

He then went on to say as he was walking away from FOG, 'Then let's get a move on then! We will have to visit one of my old employers. She still owes me one, since I worked with her for years.'

'She?! Who are you referring to?' FOG asked in a sceptical tone.

'Maybe sometime in the near future I will let you know her name. For now you will only know her as M,' Fane said and was now out of the Grand Hall.

Outside Lorelei Castle; From afar:

A huge ruin of a small castle was still barely standing on the mountain it was built on. A place, Fane had called his home for the last few months. Castle Lorelei was very much a castle built on Legend, Hate, Sadness and for Fane represented a place of lost opportunity. A home he could have had, grown up in. Had his mother and Father for company. But what Fane had gotten was the upbringing no child should have to endure. He still carried a reminder of his past with him wherever he went. That being the small blanket he was found with, when he was only little. Fane would have been excited to continue his journey to find out the secrets behind his family and its history. But for now these mysteries would still have to remain unsolved.

Fane gazed back on the castle one last time. He would again have to accustom himself to the idea of again having no roof over his head. Again he would be on a journey, trying to take back what he lost in the first place. But he would never forget the Lorelei Castle, neither his Aunt Kristiane, the ghost who had betrayed and helped him. Fane smirked to himself, but at the same time he was somewhat relieved not to be journeying on his own. Of course he would not admit this to FOG, who would be his trusty sidekick the whole time. Both turned their backs on the Castle Lorelei, not knowing if they would ever set foot there again.

Germany Unknown Location 1830:

Again the darkness of night consumed the whole countryside. All living creatures would be asleep, except for the night creatures that would be roaming about such as the night owls who would hunt their prey.

Fane and FOG were seated on the ground around a small fire they had ignited to keep themselves warm. They had set up camp in the middle of a forest that was rather secluded and hidden from prying eyes. But still somehow Fane felt like he was being watched. He could have sworn that he had heard some twigs crunching from afar or the rustling of grass/leaves.

He got up off the ground and looked at the surrounding trees that he had sat amongst.

'Do you think that we are being watched or followed? I have a growing suspicion that we are...that someone is watching us.....right now!' Fane shouted.

'Show yourself. I am waiting for you!!!' Fane continued to announce loudly.

'Stop, making a fool of yourself!' FOG said in a loud voice.

'Why?......Am I bothering you FOG?' Fane asked in a suspicious voice.

FOG seemed to be hiding something from Fane. However, Fane would not let himself get tricked again.

'I mean I am not saying that we aren't being followed and I am not saying that you are seeing/hearing things. But why would someone as cunning as Rumpelstiltskin waste his time by watching us, stalking us?

After gaining the power he wanted. Sorry but that is how I see it,' FOG replied.

'Never mind FOG. I could be getting a bit too paranoid ever since I lost my powers,' Fane said.

Fane still was not entirely sure that FOG was not hiding secrets from him. In this instance he decided to trust FOG, as much as it went against his own nature to do so.

Again many hours passed. FOG and Fane decided to get some rest. Even if Fane didn't try to let himself sleep too deeply. In case of any kind of unusual events that could take place. He kept a sword that he decided to take with him from the Lorelei Castle, close to himself. An old family heirloom or historical family piece from the family crypt. Since Fane no longer was able to use his Wolf powers he would have to rely on his combat skills that he had learned long ago from his step-father Sinric Halfdan. A person Fane admired and respected. The only one person he truly trusted. Until one day he disappeared when Fane was 15 years old. He still did not know the reason to this either. Fane vowed to find out what happened or where Sinric was. *Crunch, crunch.* Fane awoke from a sound close in the vicinity. He sat himself up and could see that FOG was no longer there. Fane who now stood up. Followed a trail he believed would lead him to FOG.

Meanwhile, FOG who was trying to reach Aya through a magical hand mirror that allowed them to communicate was practically speaking to himself, 'Aya.....Aya.....you said you would be joining us tomorrow, but not now. Aya.....don't be up to your usual tricks.....uhhhh.'

Fane was still walking through the forest. Not being able to see a lot if anything didn't help. He kept going straight til something stood in his way. It seemed to be a person. This person was running from him. Fane could barely make out that this someone had worn a ring. Maybe it was the ring that had stolen his powers. Could this have possibly been Rumpelstiltskin? Fane tried to keep up with this stranger. He ran, ran but then stopped as he had to gasp for air. Fane would have been able to keep up when he was still a were-wolf. But now he really was frail in contrast to what he had been. Fane headed back to where he had tried to sleep before. But now Fane could see that FOG was back where he had been fast asleep or so he thought, when FOG awoke and had an uneasy expression on his face, as he stared into the dark space behind Fane. Fane turned and saw a woman stand before him. She seemed to look different than women that were from Europe. That being not European. She had longer than shoulder length black hair. Her brown eyes seemed to hold much energy/liveliness. She was smiling at Fane in a cheeky manner. Fane was about to turn his attention back to FOG. When he was grasped by the arm by the peculiar woman.

'Mmmhm, you seem to no longer be a wolf. I cannot sense an energy, that all mythical beings have coming from you. So what FOG has told me is true,' the unknown person stated.

Fane removed his arm from the woman's hold, he frowned at her and spoke, 'I do not know who you are but it has now come to my attention that FOG is your BFF.'

'BFF??? Fane my name is Aya. I do not know what FOG has mentioned, yet spoken of his friends. However, it is a pleasure to meet you. I have also heard from FOG that you are not one to talk. So may I now get some well needed rest next to you two......never mind....' Aya smirked and tried to see where FOG was.

Fane turned around and asked FOG, 'Do you know this delusional woman?'

'Yes I know who this is. I have already mentioned Aya once before. Of course I never went into any further details. I am also befriended with someone named Cleo. You may meet her some other time,' FOG replied in a seemingly monotone voice.

'Hey.... Don't speak like that about me!' Aya shouted at Fane.

Fane now moved to the side so that Aya would be able to speak to FOG.

'Don't worry my dear friend, for I have not FOG-otten about my not being here before sunrise. But I could not resist the temptation of giving you both a fright....even if my prank did not work,' Aya spoke in a sly manner.

'I am glad your prank has not worked. I am so close to gaining a further insight Fane's psyche. So I don't need any of your usual tricks or jokes. I.....I am not even sure if Fane is still a mythical creature. Ever since he lost his powers....because of Rumpelstiltskin. Thanks for coming anyway. I think we will definitely be needing your assistance because of Fane's current state of mind/situation,' FOG stated in a clear but quiet voice.

Fane stared at FOG and Aya. FOG noticed this, he motioned for Fane to speak if he had something to say.

'I may not be as powerful as I was before. But I can still tell when people are speaking about me. I am not as vulnerable as you want me to think, for I can use my combat skills to defend myself and others. Before we left the castle I took with me this sword that belonged to one of my family members. I am still unsure to which of my relatives specifically wielded the sword. All I know is that it has the letter L engraved at the top. I am unsure whether that letter is designated for a name or whether it is meant to state the first letter of the Lorelei family name. The Lorelei family line, tree or descendants. Me being one of those descended from the first great founders of the Lorelei family....I think that, that is enough history for today,' Fane stated and decided to go to sleep.

FOG and Aya were both unsure why Fane decided to share with them the details surrounding the sword. But one thing they both knew for certain was that they would be slowly gaining Fane's trust and for them that was a good thing.

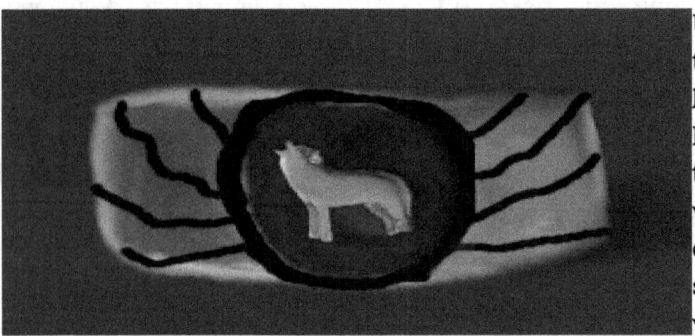 Unbeknownst to the three that being Fane, FOG and Aya; they were being watched from afar, by someone wearing a ring. It was a man with a rather small stature. A creature and outlaw known as Rumpelstiltskin. He was cackling with himself; also telling himself that nothing, nothing would take from him the power he had only just received. He left the three alone and using Fane's power that was contained in the ring, he opened himself a portal that would transport him away to wherever he wanted.

The next day FOG and Aya awoke to see Fane sitting upright on the ground looking at them. FOG and Aya who were still a bit tired. Were taken by surprise, seeing Fane already awake. He seemed to be ready to set off and continue their journey to find what was taken from him.

FOG had one more thing he wanted to give Fane, before they would start travelling once more.

'Here Fane this is for you to keep. Put this in your bag or satchel. It is a magical mirror, which allows for you to speak to others. By just thinking about that other person/mythical creature. As long as the person you wish to contact also carries the same magic mirror. Aya and myself already possess such items. But we got our resident witch Josephine who also lives in Hallow Valley to create another mirror for you,' FOG spoke in a confident voice.

Fane did not know what to think of this trinket. All he could do was nod and thank FOG and Aya for the magical item, he would hopefully would never have to use.

Now Fane, Aya and FOG would be leaving the forest area and continue their journey. FOG and Aya would of course be following Fane. As they would have to rely on Fane's sense of direction and knowledge regarding the whereabouts of this mysterious someone only known to them as M. Fane as usual would be trying to remember the last time he had come across M and the crew of misfits/mythical creatures that worked under M. While they were journeying toward the unknown, FOG and Aya glimpsed the very sword Fane had mentioned. It was a large, metallic broad sword, which had a gemstone inserted close to the handle region. While Fane walked, Aya and FOG glimpsed that this gemstone was glowing. FOG and Aya were definitely not imagining this. As soon as they would set up camp once more they would let Fane know about this interesting fact about the sword.

On one night when all three made camp somewhere in Germany, FOG and Aya told Fane of what they noticed the gemstone do. That it had glowed. Fane didn't believe them until he saw it for himself. FOG offered to hold the sword. As soon as he held it, the gemstone stopped glowing. The same reaction was with Aya, no glow. It was now obvious to all of them that the sword's magical properties would only work for Fane.

After having journeyed for about a week. Fane, FOG and Aya arrived at an old desolate-looking ruin. Only known as Kyllburg located in the North West of Germany. Fane, Aya and FOG decided to wait for a long duration of time. Fane would tell both his new acquaintances that he was waiting for an old friend of his. Someone he had known before going to the Lorelei Castle when he had still believed to find even more substantial evidence in regard his family history. When FOG and Aya asked Fane who this person or creature was.

Fane would say, 'Wait, you will just have to wait. For he shall probably appear soon.'

To that FOG would ask, 'So how would your friend, know of your wanting to meet him here?'

Fane rolled his eyes and sighed, 'Come here and I will show you.'

Aya as well as FOG slowly moved closer to Fane who was getting something out of his bag. It was a piece of stone. A small piece of stone.

Aya began to laugh, then stopped to stay, 'You have hit rock bottom Fane. You definitely have.'

FOG who stood next to Aya, had nothing to say. He believed that if Fane was truly able to communicate with this other unknown person then it could be possible if it was through an interesting way; meaning a possibly magical rock that would allow him to communicate with others.

'Uhhh! This is an enchanted rock that is going to bring me into contact with my vampire friend. Maybe friend is too strong of a word. But he has helped me on more than one occasion and I him,' Fane stated in a fierce tone.

'Vampires. At least something we can deal with. Especially after knowing someone as headstrong as Freya,' FOG accidentally spoke out loud.

'Who is Freya? Never mind, probably another one of your friends?' Fane questioned himself somewhat and looked back at Aya and FOG.

'Freya is a vampire. Who stole something from me. A while back, when I was still human. She did give the thing she stole back. So I guess in that sense we are even. Haven't seen her since I was human though,' FOG replied.

Fane looked about, but for all the time he had already waited and wasted time waiting he decided that it was enough. He told FOG and Aya that they should probably get some shut eye. So that they would all get the rest they needed before they would continue their journey somehow the next day. While everyone was about to get some sleep, there stood a figure hidden amongst some trees. The only one who noticed the presence of this unknown entity was Aya. She had the ability to sense energies and shadows especially now in the darkness of night.

Using her ability over the power of shadows. She used the shadows that the fire cast, and directed them at the unknown entity. Aya's eyesight was directed for now at the unknown entity. This unknown entity was surprised by the shadows that morphed around him. Now the shadows surrounded him and he was being dragged or forcefully taken hostage by those shadows.

Fane awoke to see a huge black mass in front of him. He could see that Aya was currently occupied with keeping this stranger in her shadow prison. Fane could hear something rustling in the trees from close proximity to FOG. It was another shadowy figure. Again Aya tried to use her shadow Kitsune powers and blocked that other unfamiliar presence with her shadow mist that slammed the other opponent against one of the ruin's stone facade that still remained. Fane now only noticed that they were being attacked, for reasons unknown to him. Fane remembered that he had taken that sword with him. He rushed to his bag and grabbed the sword. The gemstone now flashing erratically. With a strong will within him. Fane focused his attention on another attacker coming from another side. All the heinous monstrous entities had one thing in common they were all vampires. First there were two. That Aya managed to fend off for now. One being still in her Shadow cage. Fane however sensed that this was not the last of them. He turned and from afar he could see two eyes glowing. This being ran toward him. In this short moment, Fane drew his sword, as the vampire almost reached him. He sliced the vampire in half. Then he proceeded to beheading the vampire. Shortly afterwards the vampire turned into a pile of grey ash. Fane laughed but was almost blindsided by another vampire that had nearly managed to knock him unconscious. Somehow Fane used his elbow and hit the vampire in the gut region. Then using his sword he was about to strike the vampire in the heart. However, the vampire acrobatically manoeuvred itself out of harms way. Then a stupendous thought came over Fane. Why did not any of these creatures try to kill them? They were only trying to subdue him. FOG who was still asleep did not even wake up by the whole commotion unfolding. Aya was still battling the other monster that she had managed to slam against the tree. But she was struggling to hold on for much longer. Fane could see this. He scanned the whole vicinity to see whether there were any more mythical creatures headed their way and indeed there were. Now they were being surrounded from all corners, from all sides. In one last attempt, Fane unleashed a power from the sword that he had not counted on.

Fane shouted, 'Then come on fight! You cowards!'

He plunged the sword into the earth in a fit of fury and unleashed unworldly powers amongst the old ruins. There were deep cracks opening within the earth, deep and wide openings that allowed for other monsters and the undead to fight on behalf of the one who plunged the sword into the earth in the first place. The hands of skeletons came into the view. They were crawling out of those crevices. Heaving themselves out from the darkness below. One would think that these undead zombies/skeletons would be slow. But alas they were seemingly fast. This army of undead fought with the surrounding enemies that had encircled FOG, Aya and Fane.

FOG had finally awoken from his slumber and stared about. He could not believe his eyes when a zombie or undead creature that reminded him of someone, looked like it was about to attack him. The face of the undead monster, whose flesh seemed to be falling off, was smiling somewhat as it was trying to sense whether FOG was a friendly or not.

The undead scoundrel smiled even more and moved clenched, gritted its teeth. While it was still trying to determine whether to kill FOG or not.

FOG who was sat on the ground was trying to think of ways to get out of this uncanny situation. Either he would get himself out of here and help his friends or he would have to use his Succubus powers once more. The creature seemed to retreat back to its other undead mates. Who were fighting against the true enemy. That being many different kinds of mythical creatures, mostly vampires who were trying to get to Fane for some reason. FOG who saw that Fane was fighting back against the enemy with that sword he had taken with him from the Lorelei Castle, was about to intervene and help Fane. When he was grabbed from behind and abducted into the woods. Aya who had managed to ward off these infidels most of the time, could no longer hold the first one that had appeared. Her powers were beginning to wain, as she finally had to kneel down and she hoped that Fane and FOG were able to get away. Fane who was still battling against the ghastly opponents, failed to notice that Aya had been captured as well as FOG. He well and truly was battling alone. He was on his own, trying to fend off the darkness. Trying to keep himself away from the enemy. Out of nowhere a surprise attack managed to knock Fane unconscious and the undead army of zombies and skeletons, crumbled and fell apart into tiny little pieces. A man or creature with short black hair, grey/beige skin and dark black eyes stood over Fane. Using his foot, he nudged Fane's shoulder and he could see that they had finally captured the one his master wanted.

The grey/beige creature spoke, 'I am sorry my friend that this had to happen. But we all know how hard it is for you to agree to something and so I had to make this decision for you. I for one know one thing, you definitely didn't go down without a fight....'

The grey/beige creature now turned back to its normal state that being normal light skin colour, brown eyes but still that same dark black hair.

'Time to move out. These two are also coming with us,' the man who seemed to be the leader spoke aloud.

The man glimpsed Fane's bag from afar. He picked it up and took it with him. He already had Fane's sword in his other hand. For some reason he took these personal objects with him. He even ordered his other associates to take FOG's belongings with them.

Fane who was being dragged by his arms by two of these vampires, was still unconscious. He was in a deep state of thought. Not knowing what would now become of him.

FOG and Aya were also being dragged in the same direction as Fane, they were just further behind Fane.

They would all remain unconscious for some time.

Unknown Secret Location; Germany:

Everything felt like stone. The floor, the walls. FOG was finally awake from a rather comatose existence he had felt for the last few hours. He still was unsure where now found himself. He did not even know where Aya was. Aya on the other hand was in a metal cage, being kept under watch, by these weird hooded creatures that were supposed to guard her. Fane awoke somewhere even more unexpected. He was sitting at the end of a humongous dining table. Where he saw at the other end of the table another man seated in an equally stately chair. He had dark hair about shoulder length, piercing brown eyes and Fane also noticed that this man was somehow obscure, peculiar, different. The stranger that was seated across from Fane, was drinking from a small peculiar looking goblet. From what Fane could make out it looked like blood. Now Fane also noticed something screaming out from behind the man's chair. Just a few hundred meters away. There was an awkward silence in the colossal room, all one could hear was the sipping sounds coming from the muscular looking man's direction. Close to the man stood someone Fane recognised. It was Max. Maximillian Tillman. The man he had been looking for, just before he had been kidnapped. Fane had been travelling about for the last few days looking for Max, only to be now captured by him. Max who also now noticed that he had been spotted by Fane. Now left the table side and stood next to the stone wall. Where he would be able to listen in on everything.

Fane spoke, 'Max! Max!? I don't know what the problem is but why am I here?' Fane asked with a rather questionable look on his face.

Fane so very much wanted to move toward Max and question him himself, but he was unable to do so, because he was fastened down in the wooden chair he sat in with leather strips that kept his arms in place. The man at the other end of the table could see that Fane was trying to remove the leather straps, or trying to free himself.

The unknown/peculiar man laughed and then proceeded to clap, 'You are one hell of a Lorelei that is one thing for sure. Still trying to free yourself from the chair. It is alright, Max will help you out of it.'

The man motioned for Max to free Fane from the chair. Max moved toward the chair that kept Fane in place. He opened the leather straps and Fane was finally able to move about like he wanted.

Max spoke, 'I apologise for the theatrics, but it had to be done to be sure....'

Fane punched Max in the face.

Max now had a bloodied nose which of course healed up quickly. He was slightly bruised but this would also heal quicker than the bruises of mere mortal humans.

Max stated, 'I think....I deserved that....'

'I think you have earned that for you good behaviour.....' Fane stated in a sarcastic tone.

Fane was about to leave the room and start searching for his friends Aya and FOG. When the man who seemed to be in charge spoke.

'It's not his fault.....I am the one that ordered him to track you down, since you lost your powers....' the stranger replied.

Fane turned to face this unusual what he thought annoying man. He then saw his belongings and his sword on the table. He was about to move toward the table to take what was his when he was stopped in his tracks, by a dark black wolf that was growling at him. Fane moved away from the animal until he was backed into a corner. The creature turned into a mist form and now the man from before was visible again, sitting in his chair. Fane was amazed but at the same time petrified. What kind of being was this man? Was this even a mortal man or something more, something different.

'You may go ahead and take what is yours. I have no qualms whatsoever in releasing you soon. I however, have still a few things I wish to discuss with you,' the creature spoke.

Fane did not hesitate to take the sword and his bag from the table.

'What things would someone like you want to discuss with someone like me? Who....what are you?' Fane stammered.

'My name....is Vlad. Does this piece of information suffice?' Vlad replied in a stern voice.

'Alright, Vlad......my name is Fane.....Half.....' Fane was about to finish the sentence when he was cut off by Vlad.

'Halfdan.....Fane Halfdan....I know who you are already. Why do you think I forcefully captured you and summoned you here?' Vlad smirked and took a sip from his cup.

'Don't worry your friends are fine. They are being confined for their own safety. They will be released as soon as we have finished discussing the precarious situation you now find yourself in,' Vlad continued to speak.

'How on earth did you know that I am related to the Lorelei family? How do you know my name?' Fane asked Vlad plainly.

Vlad sighed deeply and then spoke, 'I... am approximately four centuries old and have met your ancestor whose name is Siegfried. He is my friend and so all of his descendants are also my friends.'

'You are four centuries old? What kind of long-lived creature are you?' Fane replied.

'Isn't it obvious, I am a vampire. However, how I came to be one, is none of your business,' Vlad spoke in an annoyed voice.

Vlad was starting to tap his finger on his chair. He ordered one of his minions to fetch something specific. Something Fane was unable to understand or comprehend.

Meanwhile Stone-Cellar Room:

FOG was still in a tired state of mind. He was in unfamiliar territory. He got up from a seated position. He saw that there was a door, that was being kept shut by some kind of magic. Luckily in this case at least FOG was a Succubus and so he simply put his hands on the door and as usual absorbed the energy within himself. Finally he was out of the room. Now he would try to find out where Aya was being kept prisoner. When he could hear Fane's voice emanating from a room down a corridor and a deep but clear voice was also to be heard. FOG moved toward that door, he peered through a small keyhole and spotted Fane. He tried to listen in on their conversation.

Vlad was concentrated on Fane, until the minion returned with something that looked rather disgusting that was being served on a plate made out of bone. By the looks of it, it looked like a heart. Funnily enough the screaming that Fane had heard before, had stopped.

'Aaah, delicious do you want some? It is delightful to get revenge on one's enemies isn't it?' Vlad asked in a mischievous voice.

Using the cutlery (made out of bone) provided, he used the knife and plunged it in the heart. Then he cut it into pieces and piece by piece slowly ate.

'I am not hungry, Vlad,' Fane replied in an uneasy tone.

FOG could not believe his ears. Did he just hear Fane say Vlad? Did he mean the legendary Vlad Tepes of Romania. Also known as Vlad the Impaler. What would someone as infamous as himself want with Fane? FOG let his curiosity get the better of him. This door also had a magical lock, which he simply opened with his power. Now he was standing on a second level, overlooking the dining place, where Fane stood in front of the legendary historical figure, he had so often read about in so many books. Vlad was shrouded mystery, no one even knew how he looked like and now FOG was able to see that he indeed existed. That this was the man behind the legend.

What an opportunity to meet the legendary Vlad. Fane probably doesn't even know who Vlad the Impaler is. FOG told himself.

FOG hid behind a column. He looked down and now stared at Vlad.

'This is such a hearty meal,' Vlad spoke in a mocking tone.

Suddenly the minion reappeared with something that looked like soup that was being served in a carved out human skull which was made into a bowl. Who knows what the contents of that soup were. Vlad used a spoon that seemed to be made out of bone that was already on the table started eating from the soup. Fane now had made a tantalising realisation that everything that Vlad utilised to eat or drink - the cutlery, the cup, the bowl, the plate were all made out of bone.

'This makes the whole meal even more heartfelt and complements the entree. This indeed is food for thought,' Vlad laughed slightly.

Fane seemed annoyed, however, once he had seen the skull bowl, he questioned himself whether Vlad's intentions were anything but good. Fane hesitantly continued questioning Vlad.

'So what do you want from me?' Fane spoke.

Fane glanced at Max who seemed to be communicating with someone telepathically.

Max moved toward the table and spoke, 'The man known as FOG has escaped. Should we order some.....'

'I already know where he is. Show yourself Frances Owen Gregory, for I have already heard your thoughts loud and clear,' Vlad announced for all to hear.

FOG had not counted on being spotted by the most famous vampire in history. He came out from his hiding spot and smiled awkwardly.

'Come down. I mean you no harm. A friend of Fane is no enemy of mine,' Vlad spoke once more.

'I am sorry to intrude on your conversation,' FOG said as he finally managed to get down a staircase leading to the dining table.

For one moment FOG thought that he was seeing a ghost. Because he thought that Vlad was Lucien. Of course he was seeing things that weren't there. But there were some eery similarities between the both of them. That being their overall demeanour or the authority they had over others.

FOG now stood next to Fane. However, Fane had a perplexed look on his face.

He asked FOG, 'Where is Aya? Pssst, FOG?'

He even nudged FOG but he was in a frozen/catatonic state.

'What did you do to him?' Fane asked in a suspicious tone.

'I have subdued him for the time being. Once we have finished our conversation, he will return to his normal self. However, he will have no recollection of ever being here or meeting me for that matter. Neither will your Kitsune friend Aya,' Vlad stated in a rough tone.

'What?!........Let's get down to business then. What do you want from me?' Fane replied in a defiant tone.

'To help you of course. I will help you track down that one imbecile that has taken your most important asset from you. Your power. I will also get the Grim Reaper to help in this matter, since he has also important assets to retrieve from that same idiot only known as Rumpelstiltskin or the Dwarf King as he is known in some parts of Germany. I am friends with your ancestor Siegfried and I help anyone who is descended from him? Is this alright with you Fane? You do want your powers back or not? I mean Celtic Wolves are a rarity these days, aren't they? Or do you wish to remain a mute-being forever?' Vlad thoroughly explained.

Fane's mind criss-crossed he had so many thoughts/questions. He glanced to FOG who was still standing there as if he was frozen in time. He remembered FOG saying that he was a mute-being once. But he had forgotten what it meant to be one.

'What exactly is a mute being?' Fane asked courageously.

'A mute being is a human with an underlying gene that might cause them to turn into mythical creatures. There have been few cases of this happening. But to say the least, it is amusing to know that there are two beings in this room that both used to be mute-beings. My dear friend Max here and your friend FOG were both mute-beings before they morphed into what they are today. But in their circumstances this only occurred through their tragic deaths. Whilst you have lost your power, you are still part wolf. Unfortunately, you are currently more human. But as soon as we have found that scoundrel Rumpelstiltskin you shall be whole again,' Vlad spoke in a triumphant tone.

Fane definitely wanted to regain what he lost and so he agreed for Vlad to help in retrieving to him his most precious powers. The thing he had relied on his whole life.

Before Fane was about to leave and drag FOG out of the room, Vlad stopped him in his tracks.

Vlad spoke, 'Also I almost forgot to mention. That sword you have there was enchanted to protect only those of Lorelei blood. It glows in the hands of those descended from the Lorelei family. It glows rather strongly in your presence. The sword is your most important weapon against those who seek to harm you. Use it wisely and heed this advice.'

Fane had another question that needed to be answered, 'What is the gemstone on the sword made of?'

Vlad seemed to be slightly smiling he answered, 'The gemstones are predominantly made of the moonstone and the obsidian stone. These two stones combined with another have great protective properties for wolves. Those same stones can also enhance wolf powers and help wolves heal quicker if they were wounded. That is all I will tell you for now. I can tell that you have many questions regarding myself and wolf history. Maybe, I will meet you again one day or you should meet your legendary ancestor Siegfried but for now this is farewell.'

'Wait before I forget, this is for you it is a necklace made out of bone. To be more specific the bones of your ancestors. This item has been magically enchanted; it will shield you from danger, if you want it it's yours,' Vlad said in a rushed voice.

Fane tried to understand what Vlad's agenda was, he did not trust him but he did respect him for his powers as well as his strength.

Fane spoke slowly, 'Sorry to disappoint you, but I have to decline your generous offer.'

Vlad sighed then stated sarcastically, 'Your wish be my command.'

Slowly and surely Vlad turned into mist form right in front of Fane. Until he was no longer there. Even the plate where the heart had been plated on was all gone. As well as the goblet and skull bowl. In essence no remnant of Vlad's was left to be seen not even his bone accessories.

Unbeknownst to Fane, Vlad had magically placed the bone necklace around Fane's neck; it was invisible so Fane would not realise it being there in the first place.

Fane smirked to himself. He could not believe the events that had occurred up until this moment. But what came next would make him almost burst in a fit of laughter.

Fane left through some large, arching, dark, solid oak double doors. Where he could see Aya still caged in a metal cage. Fane went toward one of the vampires guarding Aya.

'Vlad said that once I am free to go. Then my friends are free to go!' Fane shouted at the guard that seemed to be ignoring Fane.

Aya looked up toward Fane, she smiled, she had not expected Fane to consider her and FOG friends. But now it seemed that they now had indeed become friends with Fane. The vampire guards who were still ignoring Fane now quickly reacted after someone they respected in an awkward sort of way came toward them. It was Max.

Max spoke, 'If you don't release this poor woman. You will regret not doing so beforehand.'

He now intensely stared at both guards and smiled a menacing sort of smile.

The guards who seemed to know what Mr. Tillman had been referring to. Moved from their positions and using the keys opened the cage that had kept Aya imprisoned. Now Aya had something she had wanted to do since she had been barred from leaving the cage. Using the shadows that were present in the room, she slammed the guards against the wall. As an act of revenge.

Mr. Tillman clapped his hands and said, 'Bravo.....not what I had in mind but close.'

'What did you have in mind? Stranger,' Aya asked in a confused tone.

'I would have screamed at them in an unbearable high pitch tone....' Max joked but at the same time meaning what he said.

'Why and how so?' Aya still confused asked.

'Well, I am part banshee after all. That's enough small talk, we can continue this conversation at another time,' Max stated swiftly.

'Weren't you able to use your powers to get out of the cage?' Fane asked plainly.

'There was some kind of enchantment, barring me from doing so,' Aya basically explained.

'That explains it,' Fane replied.

'Where is FOG?' Aya asked in a sceptical tone.

'He is right next to me or not?' Fane said but was starting to doubt himself.

'He's here!' Max shouted out loud.

FOG was still standing in the dining room like a wax figure melted to one spot. The mind persuasion powers that Vlad had used on him had still not worn off. But Max had a cunning idea.

'I know something that will awake him right away. But I would advise you to take a few steps back,' Max spoke again in a loud tone.

Fane and Aya took a few steps back. As they believed Max had a reason for them do so.

Max now turned into his other form, his skin turned beige/grey, his eyes were pitch black. He would begin to use a secret weapon, which he kept contained most of the time. He screeched as loud as he could. Being part Banshee of course meant he was able to harness their high pitch screams.

FOG who was now awake from his mind control spell. Now saw before him a terrifying creature, with grey/beige skin and dark black eyes. FOG ran off. He had no recollection of being here in this unfamiliar place. All he remembered was sleeping among the castle ruins the other night and that was that. FOG was running like a lunatic toward anyone or anything familiar. When he spotted Fane and Aya from afar standing next to the front entry of this rather mortifying place.

'Let's get out of here,' FOG stated in a jittery voice.

'What's the problem FOG?' Fane looked at FOG in a questionable way.

'You don't remember coming here, do you?' Aya smirked to herself.

'How.......never mind!' FOG shouted.

FOG turned for a short moment. He could see a young-looking, slightly muscular but obscure looking man with short black hair and dark-brown eyes approaching him. He knew who this was but he was unable to remember a name.

Fane spoke, 'This here is Maximillian Tillman. I worked with him under M. I guess you should know what M stands for. It stands for Medusa.'

First FOG had seen someone he thought was a ghost. But in fact it was someone he had met once before. Under different circumstances of course. Now he also found out that Fane had worked for a mythological creature, famously made evil in most Greek literature and texts? What kind of life did Fane lead? The excitement and stress got all too much for FOG as he fainted right in front of them all.

Fane was surprised that FOG of all times would faint right now.

Aya was not surprised at all. She had known FOG for long enough now, she knew that he had almost fainted in the past. But today was the day on which he finally did faint.

Fane and Aya crouched down and decided to carry FOG with them out of the castle. Surprisingly even Max helped them carry FOG.

Once they were all outside, they put FOG on the ground. FOG would remain in a deep slumber for a few more hours.

'So....what are you still doing here? Go back to the castle and continue serving Vlad' Fane said in a sarcastic voice.

'Don't mock me Fane. Or do you think you would have agreed to meet a secretive leader, at a secretive meeting point here in the south west of Germany. You have a brutally honest and defiant personality. You are stubborn and at some times too headstrong for your own good. Let's agree to disagree. But Vlad's orders are orders and I followed through on them,' Max explained in confident voice.

'How did you come to work for this Vlad?' Fane asked still paranoid with Max.

'Medusa owed Vlad a favour and so in return used me as an exchange/payment of sorts. That is all there is to say....' Max spoke in a calm voice.

'Go back to your servitude,' Fane spoke.

'Vlad freed me from serving him anymore. His last order for me, was that I join you and help you wherever you need it. Based on what I now see before me, you could use all the help you can get,' Max stated.

'Fine,' Fane said in an obnoxious tone.

He held out his hand as a sign of agreement/cooperation. Max and Fane now shook hands. Aya thought to herself, get on with it!

FOG now awoke from his deep slumber once again. He was greeted by Aya's excited facial expression. He sat himself up and then got up from the ground. He saw three faces look back at him that being Fane, Aya and someone who had helped one of his friends, which seems so long ago now. She wouldn't even remember him, FOG thought to himself.

'So can someone explain to me what has happened in the last day or so?' FOG asked in a rather sceptical way.

It seemed that Fane, Aya and Max had a lot of explaining to do.

Tavern; somewhere southwest of Germany:

FOG, Aya, Max and Fane were heading toward a place where they could grab a bite to eat and spend the night.

After hearing what had happened in the previous hours or be it the previous day. FOG was even more mind-boggled than before. Aya on the other hand was still amused by the utter fact that Fane now considered her and FOG friends. She however, did not know what to make of the new unusual traveller that now accompanied them. That being Mr. Tillman. Max noticed that there was a tense atmosphere between Fane and himself, so he decided to keep quiet for now. If only for the next few hours. Fane was leading the way toward a tavern he knew quite well, it was secluded that meaning that it was located in a rather wooded part, farther away from a nearby village. The tavern was small, with a thatched straw roof, and had thick wood white and brown walls from the outside. The wooden sign that hung from a wooden piece off the building stated that the tavern was called the 'Wilde Sau'. Fane and FOG were both chuckling to themselves, as they were the only ones who knew what that meant. Once all of them were inside, the tavern was furnished or kept in a quite cosy state. Fane though seemed to be disinterested in what was in the tavern. Since he was walking toward a private section of the tavern, that being the Kitchen area, where the food would be prepared. Fane was quickly gazing about the room, until he saw

243

something that caught his attention. He moved toward a wall and could hear something on the other side. That something sounding like cheerful laughter from happy customers.

'Damn....they must have changed the entry point,' Fane told himself quietly.

'What entry point?' Aya asked casually.

'There used to be a secret entry. It was....it was right here. Where I am standing. One would have to knock on the wall three times and say the secret phrase/rhyme,' Fane stated in an annoyed voice.

'Fane, I do not mean to sound rude or anything. But why would anyone need to know a secret phrase. Of all places that being a tavern. A place where one should be able to get something to eat, drink and a place to stay the night,' Aya carefully explained.

'This place is not your usual tavern. It is a place not just for humans but also for mythical creatures like ourselves!' Fane replied in a raised voice.

Suddenly some footsteps coming toward them were to be heard.

'Well, you better find a way to get to this other side or there will be one heck of an awkward encounter,' FOG stated in an uneasy voice.

Fane tried to think of how to to find that secret entry point. The phrase that he had used in the past was 'Der Schwein trinkt das ganze Wein,' meaning the pig was drinking all the wine.

Then one would proceed to say, 'Aber der Wolf trinkt den Wein und hat das Schwein zum essen,' meaning but the wolf would drink the wine and have the pig to eat.

Now Fane continued to brainstorm. Until he spotted a barrel with a picture of a pig on it, being chased by a wolf. Fane moved toward the barrel. He gazed down at the barrel to see whether he could make out anything. There was a medium sized gap, under the barrel lid. Fane decided to put his hand through the gap. He felt a lever of some kind within the barrel and pulled it slowly. The images on the barrel began to magically move in a circle around the barrel. Aya, FOG and Max were intrigued but at the same time amused by the theatrics Fane had to conduct to get onto the other side of the tavern. Max who was also at the same time look out, glimpsed a shadow of a person getting closer and closer.

'Der Schwein trinkt das ganze Wein,' phrase was to heard coming from the barrel.

Fane spoke, 'Aber der Wolf trinkt den Wein und hat das Schwein zum essen.'

Magically right in front of them, the barrel disappeared and opened up a passageway. Fane and his accomplices ran through the magic doorway. The wall closed up behind them and for now they were safe. Now though they were yet again standing in front of another obstacle that being a stone/brick wall. In front of them one of the bricks was glowing in gold-yellow colours and one could see an image of a hand print. Fane decided he would now place his hand on the brick wall, when he was stopped by Max.

'Wait a minute. How do you know whether or not this is a trap?' Max asked in a careful tone.

'Let me explain then. When I was still figuring out what kind of being I was or still coming to terms with what I even was. This place we now find ourselves in, was my safe-place. The tavern I have brought you to was a tavern I called home when I was 16 years old. The owner of the place knows me very well. He told me that he wanted a place where mythical creatures could feel at home. Feel like they could belong and have a good time. This tavern has been open for the last three centuries and I believe it will remain so far into the future. But for this one time, I ask you all to trust me, as I have trusted all of you so far,' Fane explained in detail.

Three unsure faces were looking back at Fane.

'Be my guest Fane. You may take this matter into your own hands,' Aya laughed but no one else seemed to laughing at one of Aya's usual puns.

Fane frowned, then sighed, as he placed his hand on the glowing hand print. Fane abruptly disappeared. Max, FOG and Aya now hoping to see a sign that Fane was alright when a golden line came into view, it incrementally grew and seemed to now have the shape of a door. This door opened and Fane was to be seen standing in the doorway.

'Come in! Uhhhm, are you guys coming?' Fane looked at his so called friends with a grin on his face.

Aya, FOG and Max, slowly moved their way forward, from afar they could hear laughter and cheerful sounding voices. Where they would come across some even more obscure and absurd events taking place.

Wilde Sau Tavern; Germany 1830:

This place was vastly different than to where they were before. Firstly, all the walls were made of stone. Secondly, the ceiling was much higher, making the room seem more airy. Fane walked toward the bar. Where mythical creatures would be served by a real-life pig. Of course a humanoid pig named Boris. The wrinkly looking, pink skinned creature looked at Fane with its dark eyes.

'Is that you Fane? I couldn't recognise you at first because.....well, you have finally grown up,' Boris snorted.

'Yeah, I believe so. Ever since I left this place to continue my search for my step-father,' Fane swiftly replied.

Aya, put her hand to her forehead. She looked like she had a migraine, when she asked, 'Can anyone tell me why this place is called the .....Wi....l......d...'

'Wilde Sau?' FOG asked.

'Yes,' Aya complained.

'It means in German 'wild pig'. Does the name now start to make more sense?' FOG said in a sarcastic tone.

Aya punched FOG on the shoulder and replied, 'Smart ass.'

'So who are these strangers?' said Boris the pig.

'Some people I know who are accompanying me on a journey,' Fane stated quietly.

'People I know, pffft....' Aya told herself.

Max gazed about the room while Fane was talking to the owner of the tavern. The tavern was full with many mythical creatures, there was a dwarf-like creature, a tiny fairy, a mysterious woman with brown hair keeping to herself and a competition being held in a corner of the room. There was signage stating that it was a potato cooking competition of sorts and there were lots of contestants shouting at one another. The loudest of them was a masculine looking woman. Max smiled, what an unusual place to come and drink ale?

FOG in this moment was focused on what Fane was discussing with the pig creature.

'So did you manage to find your father?' Boris asked Fane.

'My step-father...you mean my step-father. No unfortunately I never found him,' Fane replied in a solemn tone.

'Then, come and have a drink Fane. I mean nothing better than a jug of beer to ease your sorrows,' Boris replied.

'My sorrows were eased long ago. When I came to terms with being on the run most of my life, on my own,' Fane stated defiantly.

The mysterious woman who Max had seen before, was now inching closer toward Fane. However, she didn't notice that she was being watched by Aya, FOG and Max. The woman decided to turn back, as she felt like she was being watched.

Aya tapped Fane on the shoulder, 'Did you notice that woman before? She seemed like she wanted something from you.'

Fane at present was very tired and kept pinching himself to stay awake, he already had dark rings under his eyes; meaning he was tired.

He spoke in a tired voice, 'I'm sorry if I notice anything at all right now.'

Fane stopped speaking and drank a sip from his beer.

FOG now stepped closer toward Fane. He noticed that Fane was tired and if he continued to drink more ale he would be drunk.

Aya and FOG asked Boris if he had a place for them to stay the night. Which luckily he did. Aya and FOG dragged a tired Fane to his own bed. Afterwards Aya and FOG went to their own rooms. Max however was still in the main room of the secret hidden tavern. He decided to stay away from the bar. Since he had his fair share of problems with alcohol in the past. He was currently seated at a small round, wooden table; where he could listen in on a rather loud conversation from afar.

'This is the best baked potato, not your disgusting shrivelled black disgustingness,' a voice spoke.

247

'Coming from someone who has nothing other than the word disgusting in their vocabulary. You switched the potato dishes and so you are the true scoundrel. But I'll give you a nice surprise to part with!' a woman's voice shouted.

Max turned his head around slightly, however, he could still not see what was going on, he could hear the commotion unfolding behind him. Once he had fully turned himself around it seemed that the other contestants who were at the competition before had already been eliminated, except a muscular looking woman and an old-looking man with a white beard.

He could see that the muscular-looking woman was about to punch the face of the old man. Max got up from his chair and moved toward them.

The muscular-looking, large stature woman had a stern expression on her face, as she looked toward Max who now stood before them.

'What do you want?!' the woman spoke in a vicious tone.

'Yeah! We are in the middle of something!' the old wrinkly man stated.

'How about you both agree on one thing. That both your potato dishes look grotesque. I mean I don't think baked potatos, fried potatos or mashed potatos are supposed to be burnt. Everything you have cooked smells and looks horrendous. Especially your mashed potato dishes looks like.....' Max wanted to continue his descriptive explanation when.

'Don't....you are just making it worse,' the mysterious woman spoke who wore something like a scarf/veil around her head which kept most of her face hidden.

She pulled Max by the hand away from the potato cooking championships.

From afar Max could hear the following:

'He's right your potatos do look grotesque,' the old man spoke.

'Why how about I show you something grotesque! My name's Gerta by the way. So you know the name of the person who is gonna hit you in the guts,' Gerta stated loudly.

So loudly that everyone in the tavern could hear her voice.

The old man who had a German flag stuck on his shirt, decided that the Scandinavian woman was not worth the trouble and so the judges who were silently standing on the side lines decided to make Gerta the winner of the European Potato Championship. Gerta was so happy that she for one short moment turned into her nickur (Scandinavian waterhorse form). A creature with the front body of a horse, but the tail of a fish or those of meerpeople. The whole body of the nickur was coloured a faint grey. What a weird but wonderful looking being, Max thought to himself.

The other contestant who was the old man, turned into a small ugly fairy, it flitted toward the other fairy who Max had seen before, soon after both disappeared into nothingness.

Max now decided to divert his attention to the woman who dragged him toward a darker part of the room. But she was no longer there. All he found laying on a table in close vicinity was two pieces of paper. One stated '*give this to Fane*', and the other '*For Fane*'.

Max snuck toward Fane's room. He indeed was fast asleep as he placed the letter on the table beside Fane's bed. Max returned to the bar, he had hoped to see the funny potato championships continue however, they seemed to be over. Max seated himself on a stool and was about to fall asleep leaning himself against the bar table. When he was startled by the pig creature, he had seen afar from before. The poor pig was drooling everywhere. The pig really was behaving like a pig; how did he even manage to give everyone a clean glass? Max asked himself.

'How did you come to be what you now are?' Max asked in a straightforward way.

'Ah...the old good question. The one about why I am as beautiful as I now am. To answer your question....... I was turned into what I am because I was a drunk fool, that had nothing better to do than go to the tavern each and every day. You see I was not born this way, like I already said before I was made to be this way,' Boris the pig explained.

'Made to be this way? But how?' Max asked.

The were-pig humanoid proceeded to filling Max a tankard of beer and spoke 'This in on the house. So to continue on, once this tavern used to be filled with the ramblings of idiots and the drunkenness of mere mortals. Then a pretty woman came in one night. She would try to help these idiots, idiots like myself make something better of themselves. She did help most of the men who had used to come in and get themselves drunk most of the time. Until she came upon me. I was not poor or anything like that I was a rather well-off merchant that sold items across southwest Germany, however, whatever I made in money, I spent at the tavern for alcohol. To get to the point, on this one night that this woman approached me, she planned on doing a kindness for me, by using one of her magical spells on me to persuade me to better myself. Unfortunately, I felt so bad in that moment I vomited on her shoes. Shortly after she got very angry, that she turned me into what you see before me. Something similar to a warthog or wild pig. 'Die Wilde Sau' yes, the wild pig, that is what I am indeed. Anyhow, after some weeks it was evident to me that this witch was not helping the men who had used to come to this tavern but she was turning them into animals and then butchering them for the dinner plate. After a while she even butchered the owner of this tavern the same way. Many weeks later, there was no further reports of her wickedness and I decided to take ownership of this tavern. This all happened in the year 1524. Somehow the witch must have turned me into an immortal pig, that being one of the only perks being this way.'

'You want to tell me that you are more than three centuries old?' Max asked with his face full of awe.

'Yep....that's about right,' the pig monster spoke.

'Man....well that was one hell of a story. Just as good as what I have seen today......Me, Fane and the other two that are accompanying us, were almost spotted trying to get here to this part of the tavern....I could see his shadow moving closer in on us. I think it was a he....anyway....' Max stated as he tried to look away from Boris's face.

'Yeah I almost saw you guys. That is one thing for sure,' Boris explained.

Max looked back toward Boris and he saw a seemingly normal looking man standing before him. He had dark-blonde hair and brown eyes. He seemed to be in his 30s.

'What where is Boris?' Max asked.

'I'm right here, in the flesh,' Boris replied.

'I thought you were turned into a pig?!' Max said in a louder voice.

'A few years back, I found a kind witch. For some reason she offered me a spell that would allow me to revert back to my human form whenever I wanted. Her name was Josephine,' Boris said and smiled.

'You are one lucky.......guy' Max said and laughed.

Both of them shook hands and drank some beer.

'Let's not get too drunk ever again!' Max proclaimed.

'Yes that's one thing to aim for!' Boris shouted loudly.

While Max was entertaining himself with Boris, Fane was in a deep sleep. He had not had meaningful sleep since they had left the Lorelei Castle. Currently Fane was dreaming. Dreaming about his past when he was a young man aged 15-16 years and he was on the run from some witch-finders. He was running through the woods in the black of night. When he tripped over an old tree stump. Luckily he didn't hit his head; he got back again and continued running. He was gasping for air, as he had been running for a long time. Fane was lucky as he was almost caught/spotted by one of the witch-finders that had caught up with him. It was almost a full moon and Fane could feel the wolf-power within himself. His eyes started to glow. But he would have to keep himself under control. So he would not turn at this moment, as he would lose control over himself and blackout. There was a young girl who magically overpowered the witch finders. She urged Fane to follow her. Fane didn't know who this girl was. He did not easily trust strangers. But now there was nothing else he could do other than follow her. She did help him with the witch-finders. He followed her for some time, when he saw a fire in the distance. A fire that had been lit by a group of people. Fane told himself he would run-off in this moment. When he was confronted by the girl who had been right in front of him for the whole time.

'I can hear your thoughts, loud and clear...' the girl stated.

'You.....you can hear my thoughts? How...why?' Fane stuttered about.

'I am in some aspects like you. Come follow me. We don't bite or anything. The others are just like you and me...different,' the girl spoke as persuasively as possible.

Fane followed the young-girl. Now he was seated next to some other monstrous creatures. Some had hooves and horns. Others looked human, but they seemed to be scarred in some way. Somehow Fane knew that he belonged here. Even amongst these strange creatures.

'My name is Midnight, what is yours?' the girl spoke.

The dream ended abruptly as Fane awoke by some clanging noises coming from outside his door. At least it was now the next day.

While Fane had been dreaming about his past encounters, FOG was battling his own demons. He had been in a deep sleep for a while.

However, he was also dreaming of past events. Involving his wife Lara and son Felix. FOG was standing in a never ending hallway or corridor that had many doors that he could open, leading to different memories involving circumstances he had encountered in his life. As he moved toward the end of the corridor there was a dark black mahogany door. FOG reached out his right hand and slightly turned the door clasp. The door opened and FOG was catapulted into one of his own memories. He now lay asleep alone in bed once more, but this time he was in a place he had used to call home. FOG got out of bed, he noticed that Lara was not beside him, he quickly made his way to his son's room there was also no one there. He moved about the whole house but there was nothing, just the empty shell of a home without the people he loved. He wanted to leave the house. It seemed though that the doors and windows were all jammed shut. A fire began to burn, until FOG was encircled in flames. He tried to peer through but was unable to do so. Before him within the fiery pits of the high reaching fire, shadowy figures were to be seen, depicting a boy taken by a demon outlaw and the reapers draped in their black cloaks, condemning FOG to his fate. FOG began to cough, the fire got closer and closer, until he was no longer there and reduced to a pile of ash.

FOG was forced back to the land of the living as he now awoke because of the same sounds Fane had also heard.

Morning at the Wilde Sau Tavern:

A grumpy Fane awoke to the clanging sounds coming from beyond his door. He was now sitting upright on his bed and was about to leave the room and go complain at the person who was creating the annoying sounds, when he saw a letter, or a piece of paper, folded in half with his name on it.

He grabbed the piece of paper, and unfolded it. It said the following:

Fane, I know as much about you as you do about me. I need to speak to you. Meet me at the tavern. Tomorrow morning as early as possible.

Fane quickly looked out a window that was in his room. He noticed that the Sun had not yet even risen. So it probably was early enough to meet this mysterious someone.

FOG who also awoke from the sounds, decided to leave his room as well. He was out of his room before Fane was and was walking towards

252

Fane's room. When he heard the clanging and banging sounds coming from a door opposite to Fane's door. FOG decided to knock on the door and was then surprised to see someone he had not anticipated to see ever again.

It was Gerta, the potato woman he had met during the same time as he had met Freya who was a vampire. She was holding something that looked like a golden trophy shaped like a potato. Gerta was grinning as she stared at her trophy. On the trophy it stated 'Best Potato Chef in Europe'.

She now looked toward FOG and her smile well turned into more of a grin.

'Ah, it's you Francy......uh....what do you want?' Gerta spoke.

Now FOG remembered why he didn't miss this muscle-tank in the first place.

'I am wanting to know what you were clanging about with and who was creating the ghastly sounds. But I now know who it is. So I better get going,' FOG said in a quiet voice.

Unbeknownst to FOG. Fane had just left his room and was on his way toward the inner sanctum of the tavern.

FOG was startled suddenly by Aya who was also awake 'Is this the one who was banging about?'

'Yes, my name is Gerta by the way. Was only looking for my trophy amongst my things. Going to compete in the International Potato Championships next,' Gerta replied as calmly as possible.

Aya tried to get a sneak peek into Gerta's room but what she saw was enough for her to believe what Gerta was saying. She could see a huge pile of kitchen utensils scattered about the room. Pots and pans stacked up leaning against the wall. There was a pile of potatos, a huge pile of them just laying in another corner of the room. Now Aya also noticed a rotten stench wafting toward her that being a garlic smell.

Aya pinched her nose and told FOG, 'I think we should leave this kind woman alone or not?'

'It was nice to meet you Gerta,' she smiled painfully and went away.

Yes now FOG remembered Gerta's garlic breath. He was about to leave Gerta alone, when he got a potato from her.

'For your garden FOG!' Gerta shouted.

'How did you know that I have a garden?' FOG asked with a questionable look on his face.

'Freya told me!' Gerta replied in a disappointed tone and slammed her door.

The tavern was still dark, at this time in the morning. While Fane decided to seat himself on a chair where he would wait as long as it would take for this mysterious person to show. He was unsure if whether what he was doing now was right. But he would only be risking his own safety and so he just sat there for as long as he needed to. Max had not noticed Fane appearing this early in the tavern. As he was still asleep leaning against the bar table.

Fane stayed seated where he was until he saw FOG from afar. He could notice that FOG had spotted him and now he would also be questioned by him.

'What are you doing here Fane?' FOG asked plainly.

'I am waiting for someone,' Fane replied back.

'It's true....a woman is wanting to meet him here,' Max who had awoken said as he yawned at the same time.

'How would you know that?' Fane asked Max.

'Because she gave me that letter you have probably already read,' Max replied.

'What's the problem? You guys gawking about again?' Aya replied sarcastically.

'There's nothing wrong Aya. Fane is just waiting for someone. Well I guess I'll make myself scarce. I suggest that you, yes you Aya and Max do the same. So that Fane can meet this person in private. Otherwise this person may not show,' FOG stated in a steady voice.

FOG, Aya and Max left Fane to himself.

Many hours passed. Not even Boris the owner of the tavern showed. Fane couldn't even hear any more clanging sounds. The tavern was quiet and seemed so very empty. Fane decided to go and tell his friends to get themselves ready so that they could continue their journey.

Later on: They all were seated around a table in the tavern together, they seemed to be enjoying their late breakfast and were now about to leave the tavern. FOG and Max were conversing with one another about many things, but none of them was about the utter fact that they both knew about something that occurred in the past in regard to someone they cared about, a person who was their friend that being Cleopatra.

Max was the first to mention her name, 'So how is Cleo doing? Since she.....um..lost her memories?'

'She still doesn't remember the events that occurred, or ever having met me, Aya or you before. I am unsure if she ever will remember or recollect anything at all. All I know is that she is fine now and that she is a great help to all of Hallow Valley,' FOG whispered to Max.

'That is good to know,' Max also replied quietly.

'What are you two talking about and since when are you best mates?' Fane asked the two of them.

'We are just getting to know each other better that's all,' FOG said in an uneasy tone.

Aya smirked but she indeed knew what they were conversing about.

Now only in that moment did FOG notice another awkward thing about the tavern. As he saw something that reminded him of Lara's Reapkatcher. Hanging from a nail on the wall.

FOG got up from his chair and asked Boris the humanoid pig why he had something from the Order of the Grim Reaper hanging on his tavern wall.

Boris replied, 'The Reapers like to come here from time to time. To celebrate and arrange parties. I mean even the leader of the Reapers has been here before. I don't know why this bothers you. They just gave me a fake trinket as a thanks of sorts. Sorry if it brings up bad memories for you.'

'I lost my wife because of them.......uh!' FOG said in an angry way.

'Sorry...sorry. I do not mean to ruin your day,' FOG also said and left Boris alone.

On his way back to the table, he saw a lever with a skull in close proximity to the bar. FOG now was asking himself what that was for. FOG was rather annoyed in the moment and Aya could sense this.

While everyone was deep in thought or occupied in some way. A woman entered the tavern. She seemed to be stressed in some way. Her eyes showed a world of pain and longingness to find out more. More about who Fane was. She had only found out about him a few days ago and she was desperate for answers. She had wanted to come earlier but she couldn't because she was being tracked by a hunter. A hunter who specialised in hunting wolves.

The woman could see that Fane was accompanied by the other people she had seen before. She had no other choice than to confront him now and nothing would get in her way. She slowly moved toward them and was then surrounded by many unfamiliar faces looking back at her.

Fane now had an unknown person seated next to him. He was unsure as to how he should begin the conversation.

When the mysterious woman spoke, 'Our father has sent me here. I need your help.'

Fane looked at her in disbelief did she just say our father?

Meanwhile Lorelei Castle:

There was an air of calm at the Lorelei Castle. The living inhabitants including Fane and FOG had all left. Not even the presence of ghosts was noticeable. Except for a few handful sirens that were still singing their charming songs in hopes in luring in passers by. One would be mistaken to believe though that there still were no secrets waiting to be uncovered there. A living inhabitant was still residing at the castle but was about to go on a search for answers.

The events that unfolded as Fane had lost his powers:

In the room that FOG had slept in when he had been scared by Kristiane there was an oil painting of a woman. A woman who seemed to be magically opening and closing her eyes. As soon as Fane had lost his powers, the woman who had been in the painting for about three centuries was released, as a beam of magical power went exactly through the painting she had been trapped in for aeons. A beam of white light came from the painting and she was freed from her purgatory. Not even the famous Rumpelstiltskin had an inkling that he had unintentionally set free this unknown woman. A woman with dark black hair and brown eyes. She was still wearing the same clothing from the medieval ages. She smiled and rejoiced after being released from her prison, however, she did not know what to make of the foreign men who were staying at the castle. She hid from Fane and FOG; she was anticipating their departure.

Once these two men had left the castle, the woman peered out of the window from afar. She smiled, even though an uneasy feeling came over her. Where were her daughters? Her son? How long had she been really trapped in the painting and who had put her there in the first place? For now the only thing that mattered now was that she started finding answers and that is what she would do. She would try to track down the two people who had just left the castle even if it would be the last thing she would do.

TO BE CONTINUED

The Forgotten Child

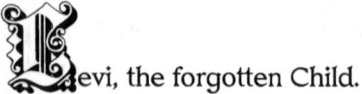

evi, the forgotten Child.

Levi was an odd one ever since he was born. A child born of a rare case. He was a male banshee although a banshee is actually called a 'wailing woman'. His mother though didn't mind him as she saw the potential in her son. But however he remained forgotten by his father (his father was a human) and distant family. Levi was born in 2002 in Australia, was an only child and lacked grandparents. The only one that stood by him was his mother. For eighteen years of Levi's life, his mother trained him to bring out his banshee powers, however, his mother would die trying as she died in 2020, when Levi was almost eighteen years old. Her son being lonely and her wish not fulfilled, Levi became a sad drunk and the love for pubs grew on him.

2 years later: In 2022 Inglewood, Australia, (Levi's present day):

Levi sat on a bar stool, nothing there by him was to be seen other than the fact that he was a drunken fool.

The bartender asked Levi: 'Are you okay, Mate? You don't look so good.'

Then the voice of a woman said from behind Levi: 'Leave the moron be, I'll take care of him.'

The woman's voice was clear but calm. Levi turned his head in struggle to see who was talking. He only made out a figure of a pretty woman with black hair. The mysterious woman heaved Levi off the bar stool and pulled him outside with him leaning on her. Strangely she came to a stop when they were outside and hidden between parked cars. Then next she pulled him off quickly while at the same time she twisted his hand. Levi shrieked out with pain but the woman wasn't finished yet, next she punched him in the face causing him to have a nose bleed. He came to his senses now and could fully see the woman's identity, she was an Asian woman with a pretty looking face but her hands were still made into fists which meant she still had the motive of attacking him again.

The woman folded her arms together and calmed down quite a bit then said: 'Well, say something you stupid drunk.'

Levi giggled to himself and the woman frowned saying: 'My name is Aya Himano, what's yours?'

Levi nodded and said: 'My, my name is Levi Virazio.'

Aya smiled and asked: 'Do you live here?'

Levi answered: 'Yas.'

Aya's eyes revealed mischief and she pointed at him meanwhile shaking her head saying: 'It's yes not yas, man you really are drunk. Anyway, there's a reason why I'm here and that's because I intend to bring you to Fog.'

Levi giggled again and said while Aya was pulling him up onto his feet: 'Who's Fog, Flog, Dog, huh?'

Aya said: 'Never mind and you really are the strangest banshee I have ever met.'

Aya and Levi rode the motorbike on a long trip to a place called Hallow valley and Levi, well he giggled all the way.

Another Beginning of Another End

He stood there for quite some time, as he was trying to comprehend what was happening. FOG was in utter disbelief he had not anticipated to see his son ever again. Standing in front of him was the person he was trying to find. The son he had lost long ago. Now that Felix stood before him, it was like no time had passed at all. However it was not apparent to FOG that time had not only passed by. But that the little boy he once knew was now a confident young man. FOG saw a hint of sadness in his son's face, but also a sigh of relief. They both hugged each other. But what FOG never saw coming was that Felix didn't come alone. For some reason he was accompanied by some other woman and a little girl. He would find out soon enough that she not only was a friend of Aya's, but that she was also family.

Levi had his suspicions about Felix, the woman and the little girl. Why of all times would FOG's son appear again right now? Or the woman that he had come with? Especially just after Hallow Valley had been infiltrated by a complete stranger. It wouldn't matter now. As Levi had more concerning news to share with FOG. Freya was also scratching her head. She couldn't understand why Felix and this other woman who supposedly was Aya's sister of all times would be here now. Freya didn't want to think too much about the matter, only to give herself a headache.

The message that Freya held in her hand, was more important to her and it was important that FOG knew about it sooner than later. Freya went outside, grabbed FOG by the arm. FOG gave Freya an impatient glare. But he somehow knew that Freya would not intercede in his conversation unless she had something important to say. They both now stood back inside the hut. Levi called them towards FOG's office.

'We don't know who or what sent this message,' Freya said in a concerned tone.

'We don't even know what these words say?' Levi said straight afterwards.

'Calm down, I don't even know what you two are talking about,' FOG replied.

Freya handed FOG the piece of paper that appeared out of thin air. FOG read what was written 'Lass die spiele beginnen'.

'REALLY!' FOG shouted.

'What you actually know what this means?' Levi said and smiled awkwardly.

'Yes unfortunately I do. My wife Lara. Umm... I mean in the past my former wife Lara, taught me some German and the words contained on this piece of paper mean 'Let the games begin'. I do not know who would send this to us in the first place,' FOG explained.

Freya, Levi and FOG glanced at each other and a rather eery feeling started to set in.

FOG decided to gather up all his friends or allies and told them to meet him where the huts were. There he would try to explain who he had now found again after all this time. His dearly beloved son Felix. Felix didn't know how to react to all the mythical creatures that supposedly lived in Hallow Valley. However he had seen a lot of them since he had lost his father as well as his mother. Felix was unsure as to how he would have to explain to FOG that he now not only found his son again but also for the first time, had a chance to meet his little grand-daughter. Felix was very curious to find out more about this Aya and if she really was very similar to Osana, Aya's little sister. The first thing Felix would do though is ask his father why everyone seemed to be calling him FOG all the time. 'What an unusual name' Felix thought to himself.

'We are all here today to welcome these friendly new faces/arrivals to Hallow Valley. Please welcome them all with open arms,' FOG announced.

All Hallow Valley's inhabitants seemed to be clapping somewhat. However, their faces revealed what they truly though about these new unexpected people that just showed up here. They probably all thought the same way Levi or Freya did, 'Why are they here of all times? How did they get here in the first place?'

Aya was unsure at the beginning whether the woman that had just arrived was her sister Osana, however, after standing next to her and conversing with her for only a short amount of time she could somehow sense that this was indeed her sibling. FOG had so many questions that he wanted to ask his son. Too many questions. But he knew that his son would need time to adjust being here in Hallow Valley, so he would just have to give his son time. Because as much as it was great to finally be reunited with Felix. They both were overwhelmed by the stress of it all. FOG never anticipated to see his son again. But how did he manage to stay young for so long. 'He must have activated his succubus gene somehow?' FOG thought to himself. One thing however FOG would be unable to keeps his mouth shut about and that was due to the fact that Felix clung to the little girl as if it was... his daughter. It now made more sense. Felix's being here if he felt like he was in some sort of sticky situation. Especially if he now had a young one with him.

Felix though, awkward and straining it would be to explain everything, he knew he obviously had to start somewhere.

Full of doubt he approached the man who is his father. He tapped FOG's shoulder. FOG immediately spun around to face Felix.

FOG randomly muttered: 'This is a disastrously weird situation.'

Felix said: 'You still haven't changed a bit you **sullen clod**...but first I want to introduce you to someone.'

He heaved up the child and held her.

He said to FOG: 'This is Florence Gregory, your grand daughter.'

The girl had Felix's nose but her mother's eyes. She had dark blonde hair.

FOG stammered: 'Gr-grand-d-daughter?'

Felix tilted his head in confusion.

Felix said: 'Yes.'

FOG's eyes lit up with a mixture of surprise and excitement. He seemed as though a statue that might tip over if Aya tapped him, he seemed as though he might just faint.

FOG said: 'You must be proud and as for me, I simply cannot conjure the words but she is adorable.'

Florence just stared at him.

Aya whistled and said: 'Awkward.'

FOG barked: 'Shut up you nuisance!'

Osana who had stood in the back ground was too timid to join in the conversation. She watched the other Asian woman named Aya with interest. She seemed familiar somehow.

Felix motioned for Osana to come over.

He introduced her: 'This is Osana, the mother of Florence.'

FOG said: 'Lovely to meet you.'

Aya interrupted: 'Your name is Osana?'

The woman nodded.

Fog asked Aya: 'Could she be your sister after all?'

Aya spotted a necklace around Osana's neck which had a see through locket that contained a strand of hair.

Aya asked Osana: 'Who gave that strand of hair to you?'

Osana said: 'I don't know really, I can't remember my childhood, I don't know who my mother and father is and I don't know if I even had siblings, everything in my life has been a blur till Felix found me... but what I do recollect is that a woman who named me little fox in my past gave me the strands of hair to keep, I thought this hair was personal so I kept it.'

Aya said: 'You kept it all this time, I'm so proud of you little fox, you are my little sister.'

She glanced at FOG.

She said: 'I knew I would find my sister again through you FOGgy, all roads lead to one.'

FOG grumbled: 'That means that you and I are family now, you are the aunt of my grandchild, why did fate have to do this to me!'

Aya elbowed him and replied: 'That means you won't get rid of me, EVER, I have a feeling we'll have a heap of fun as a family, I can picture it now, you, me, my sister, your son and their kid having a party.'

FOG groaned: 'Yeah I can certainly envisage it, the others at the party meanwhile you plant a fart balloon onto my chair... it will be oh so more fun than the good old days.'

Aya directed Felix and Osana into FOG's hut.

She said to FOG: 'Come on, we have a lot to talk about, well I do with my sister.'

Levi and Freya stood there gaping at FOG.
FOG sighed and said: 'Go to Fogarty farm where Josephine is, maybe, whoever wrote that letter left a magical imprint on it and she can trace it back to something perhaps..... she is the only one here that can do this, she is after all the only witch here in Hallow Valley.'

Someone else was on their way to Hallow Valley. It was Melusine. She decided that she had had enough of keeping all of Rumple's secrets, she had heard of a man named FOG, which stood for Frances Owen Gregory. Just the right man to talk to, of course many mortals and mythical creatures had fallen prey to Rumpelstiltskin's schemes and two sided dark alley deals but this certain man that Melusine had aided and met during their mission in Russia never fell short in strange and unprecedented run-ins with Rumpelstiltskin, the wielder of fate or so people that revered him had called him.

Melusine was nearly there at FOG's hut. When she saw a woman kicking a motorcycle.

'Damn piece of junk, I thought I fixed your engine!' shouted the woman.

She was a woman with brown skin and dark medium length hair that was frayed but neatly tied back. She seemed to have an American accent, she wore a faded black jeans jacket, underneath was a white long singlet with the name of a famous baseball team on it, she wore straight long pants and had unique marks on her wrists unlike anything Melusine had seen before. In the belt of her pants there was a sheathed dagger attached to it, it had a grey blue stone set inside the handle.

Melusine asked the woman: 'Need any help?'

The woman said whilst standing straight to face Melusine: 'No, I'm good.'

A man walked up to the woman and said: 'Ontari, one would think you would know your own way around that thing.'

Ontari said: 'It's not a thing, it's my motorbike that I've had for a long time, it was my mother's.'

The man took a flash light and peered into the engine. He looked at it for a few seconds.

After that, he casually said: 'Well, personally, I think it's not busted, something else must be the problem... but I handle wood not mechanical objects, so I can't help you any more than this Ontari.'

Ontari swallowed with annoyance; she said: 'Thanks anyway Fane.'

Fane scoffed and walked away. Melusine spun a cigarette in her fingers.

She pointed at the motorbike and said: 'Maybe check the battery, perhaps it just needs a new one.'

Ontari huffed and presumed: 'And you know a thing or two about mechanical things?'

Melusine said: ' I'd know enough to make an explosive out of a microwave...not that it's a good thing.'

Ontari bickered: 'Lisa wouldn't be happy if she knew what Aya did to her motorbike.'

Melusine asked: 'Who is Lisa?'

Ontari said: 'My mother... was my mother.'

Melusine: 'Oh sorry I didn't know she was um dead.'

Ontari said: 'Whatever...it doesn't matter... pretty much everyone in my immediate family is dead.'

Aya opened the door of the hut and asked loudly: 'Who the heck are you and what is all this commotion?'

Melusine said: 'I am an old friend of your very old friend.'

Aya marched down to Ontari and said: 'That thing is a thorn in one's side.'

Ontari said: 'It only is because you broke it when I let you borrow it to go and pick up Levi.'

Aya rolled her eyes and said: 'It's not broken, the battery is somewhat dead.'

Ontari grumbled: 'YOU broke it.'

Aya frowned and said with a hint of anger: 'I'm not arguing with you, I know how stubborn you are... I didn't do it.'

Aya said whilst putting two fingers together: 'I can jump start the battery for you.'

Ontari yelled: 'Are you CRAZY, you'll blast the entire motorbike apart with the wrong voltage you damn Kitsune!'

Aya said: 'Relax, I can't control enough voltage anyway, I'm a shadow Kitsune not an electric one.'

Aya created a little flickering, flashing substance in her fingers and applied it to the bike battery. The motorbike roared to life.

Ontari looked gobsmacked; she asked: 'How did you do that?'

Aya shrugged her shoulders and joked: 'You know what, I wouldn't have the FOGgiest idea.'

Ontari frowned.

FOG peered out the door and said: 'I heard that, Aya!'

FOG had spotted a familiar woman. He stood in the doorway now.

He asked: 'Melusine?'

He slowly laughed.

Melusine walked up to him and said: 'The one and only.'

Aya shuffled in behind her.

Aya asked: 'You know this wacky woman?'

FOG lectured her harshly: 'She is a respectable woman, show some manners.'

Aya said: 'Fine, but how did she get here?'

Melusine said: 'I have some valuable information regarding as to who created the virus, I've already shared it with the Hidden Empire to convince them it wasn't Rumpelstiltskin so they sent me here to explain it to all of you.'

FOG: 'Makes sense.'

Aya formed a hand puppet and imitated FOG: 'Makes sense.'

FOG said in a bitter tone: 'I hate you.'

Aya said: 'And I hate you too.'

Fane who had been re-screwing the 'FOG's hut' sign said to Melusine: 'Annoying isn't it... well get used to Aya and FOG head butting like two idiotic old goats, it never stops so they'll keep you entertained.'

Melusine said: 'Don't worry, I'll deal with them.'
She turned around to Aya.

She sang to Aya in an absurd melodic tune: 'You will chill....forget your will, you will chill.'

Aya immediately shut her mouth; she smiled in a dazed manner and said: 'Chill.'

FOG asked: 'Is she alright?'

Melusine said: 'Yes she's fine, I just used a siren song on her.'

FOG said: 'I didn't know you were a siren.'

Melusine pushed him into the hut. Aya skipped into the hut and gently pulled the door shut.

FOG said with a frightened look: 'I don't like this calm version of Aya, to be honest, she is starting to scare me.'

Melusine said: 'My songs can have effects on spirit beings... I don't know why but don't worry it'll stop effecting her after a while.'

Melusine eyed a man in the corner; she asked him: 'Felix?'

Felix turned around and said: 'Melusine... wow I didn't know you were here!'

FOG asked: 'You two know each other?'

Felix said to FOG: 'Yeah, during the time when I was still a child and Rumpelstiltskin had kidnapped me and trapped me in his lair, Melusine found me and spoke to me, she was kind to me during the time of my captivity, she helped me escape from Rumpelstiltskin, after that the OGR found me but that's some of the things I want to tell you.'

Melusine said: 'Well it's nice to know that you found your way in this world kiddo.'

Melusine proceeded to unfold a letter she had pulled out from her jacket pocket and passed it to FOG. FOG took it.

Melusine said: 'That is the evidence.'

Melusine sat down.

FOG read out the contents of the letter:

Hello my fellow friend, Melusine, by now I am presumably dead since I have committed suicide, over the centuries I have resorted myself to absolute madness and insanity, because you are the only person that ever understood my bizarre mind, I've decided to inform you and only you of the truth. The truth that through much experiments on mute beings and scouring the globe in desperate search for answers I have come to the conclusion that it is never truly possible for a mythical creature to become a complete human, the only way to obtain humanity is to be born that way...up to this certain point in time I have made the gruelling decision that if I cannot ever become human, then no human should be allowed to live in such arrogant bliss, I created a virus that will sweep through every land and kill all humans, I wanted to put an end to their humanity and deprive them further of that. Do not worry, mythical creatures will not die of the virus, I designed it that way... if you wish to find proof of all that I am saying go to my hidden lab in Chernobyl in Ukraine, perhaps there are things that will pique your interest Melusine.

Yours regrettably,
Lord Gruesome, A.K.A William Grissom.

FOG's eyes widened as he said: 'Lord Gruesome... the man with the abhorrent mortuary clothes and the ridiculous tacky top hat?

Melusine asked: 'You know him?'

FOG said: 'More like knew him, during a time when I still was a human and my book store in Billows Brook hadn't been burnt to cinders, a strange man came to me and looked like he wanted to kidnap me for his schemes, he did after all experiment on mutant beings, in short meaning mute and they are beings like me, mythical creatures that are born with mostly human DNA.'

Melusine said: 'Yep that sounds like him.'

FOG said: 'In this letter he said he created Covid-19, that means Rumpelstiltskin is innocent regarding the virus... but he also said that the virus was designed so that mythical creatures don't die from it, but what if it mutated?'

Melusine asked: 'What do you mean by mutated?'

FOG explained: 'Me and my friend Cleo, we did some research and found out that there are mythical creatures that have been affected by the virus... though there are no cases of them dying from it.'

Melusine said: 'Well that means that somebody might have gone to Lord Gruesome's lab in Ukraine and tampered with the material and re-planted the virus somewhere for a different second wave of the virus.'

She questioned: 'But who would do something like this?'

FOG: 'Would it be naive to presume that Rumpelstiltskin had a hand in this?'

She said: 'No it wouldn't because Rumpelstiltskin had been affiliated with Lord Gruesome in the past.... which would have confirmed the Hidden Empire's fears on Rumpelstiltskin.'

FOG said: 'Thank you for having shared this information with us Melusine.'

Melusine said: 'I just wonder how this letter reached me specifically.'

FOG said: 'Perhaps you should look into it.'

Melusine got up, shook his hand and said: 'I will and also I'll go and check out that lab...see if I can find it in Chernobyl.'

Aya who had been delirious most of the time snapped out of it and said: 'I have no idea what you two have been discussing but why don't you just check the letter for clues...if someone gives you a letter they want to tell you something but if a mastermind gives you one, they tend to hide the truth in clues.'

Melusine said: 'You broke the hold of my song...never mind that, she's right FOG.'

Melusine placed the letter on a table and turned it over. But she saw nothing. Melusine shrugged her shoulders.

Aya said: 'Wait... that glimmering...can't you see it... it's handwriting.'

Melusine and FOG tried to glimpse what Aya saw.

Aya asked FOG: 'Didn't you say once that, that Gruesome dude was a spirit being, a willow wisp?'

Melusine said: 'It still doesn't make sense why me and FOG can't see it.'

FOG said: 'He must have used the magic light of a willow wisp to burn the words into the letter and because it is a spiritual essence only Aya can see it...but Kitsunes aren't complete spirit beings so that means perhaps I would be able to siphon the energy away.'

FOG put his hand over the letter and his eyes went black. A white energy dispelled from the letter.
After this he took his hand away and his eyes reverted back to normal.

Melusine cried out: 'A word puzzle?!'

Aya cocked her head and said: 'So much for a mastermind.'

FOG said: 'Yes but this could give us the clue to find the lab.'

Melusine, FOG and Aya would try to decipher the word puzzle whilst Felix and Osana who had been talking to each other in the other corner of the room only gave off confused expressions.

What information did the word puzzle contain?

Levi yawned as he and Freya walked up to the door of a small house. Freya knocked gently on the door so as not to break it... Freya had problems every now and then when it came to not breaking things due to her vampiric strength... there was a time when she had tried to reach for a cup... the handle ended up breaking off or when she pulled the door knob on the door to FOG's hut and ripped it off by accident, FOG was furious and ended up asking Fane to replace it. Oh such pain there came with Freya's vampire ability, intense strength, she had more physical brawn than most vampires.

On the floor there was a cute but weird door mat. It featured a flying bat. It said: 'All friends are welcome here straight off the bat.'

The safe haven witch here, Josephine, has had that door mat since she first came here. Then there were statues of angry gnomes chasing after the Leprechauns. There was even a well to the right in the front garden that had a bunch of naughty looking fairy statues stare at you... of course they were only statues, they had nothing better to do than that.

The front garden beds had hibiscus plants and chamomile plants growing all over.

Levi observed it all and said: 'Nice and cosy.'

Freya said: 'Wait till you see the inside.'

A woman opened the door. She had messy tied up blonde hair that had a touch of brown, she wore jeans overalls and underneath, a long sleeved shirt which had it's sleeves rolled up. Her shoes were sneakers. The colour of her skin was white.

She said: 'Oh, I didn't expect you today.'

Freya said while walking in: 'We were sent here by FOG, we need your help regarding a magical letter that appeared to us.'

Levi hit his head on the door frame as he went inside.

He complained: 'Ouch.'

He scratched his dark blonde, short hair and grinned painfully.

Freya remarked: 'I told you to duck your head... idiot.'

Josephine took a stack of books and placed them in the shelves.

Josephine: 'Sorry for the tardy situation but I've been kind of preoccupied lately...so you brought a friend?'

Freya introduced Levi: 'Levi Virazio, the newest arrival here at Hallow Valley.'

Josephine laughed.

She said: 'Yes, the man I helped find, I remember now.'

Levi awkwardly smiled at the woman. His head hit a crystal that was hanging from the ceiling. Now that he noticed, there were a lot of things hanging from the ceiling. Herbs tied down using string and crystals hanging here and there.

Levi pointed at them questioningly.

Josephine explained: 'Yes, um the crystals help draw in cool energy from the outside and utilise it in the inside, it helps regulate the temperature... so hence no fans or air-cons and the herbs are hung up so they are preserved.'

Levi said: 'Not exactly what I imagined under the term witch... I was thinking more like, huge cauldrons, candles everywhere, spider webs, a skeleton hanging here and there, a big, gigantic broom closet and an open roaring fire... and pumpkins wearing evil grins outside instead of the gnomes.'

Freya said: 'I think you are describing Halloween.'

Levi yelled: 'What, no way... that's how you guys celebrate Halloween here... yeesh, I don't want to know how you celebrate Christmas!'

Josephine said: 'Uh no, besides I do have a cauldron, it's a portable one.'

Freya said to Levi: 'I have to do something with her... behave and don't touch anything.'

Freya approached Josephine and said: 'I need you to do a scrying spell to see if you can trace the origins of this letter.'

Josephine closed her grimoire and took the small piece of paper from her. She walked over to a long table that had an array of maps laid out.

Josephine took the letter and held it on both hands. She concentrated. After a few minutes, a cackling sound came from one of the maps. It began to smell smoky. Freya saw that Josephine didn't open her eyes. Blood ran from her nose.

Freya shouted: 'Josephine, wake up!'

Levi tried to rattle Josephine awake. Josephine awoke as the letter started to burn in her hands. Another woman ran towards the pile of maps, grabbed them and threw them outside into the well. All except for one map. A main world map. Where the majority of America had been burned out.

The woman ran back into the house.

She said: 'Sorry but they were burning.'

Freya said: 'It's alright Cleo, or the entire house would have burned down.'

Josephine said: 'I'm sorry, I don't know what happened, normally scrying doesn't work like that.'

Levi said: 'Still we have a clue where the letter came from... from America somewhere... the majority burned out of the map.'

Freya added: 'Yes and the letter burned too, it's gone now.'

Cleo asked Freya with a hint of confusion: 'Does this regard the letter that you and Levi found?'

Freya nodded and passed Josephine a cup of water.

Josephine sat down and drank the cup of water. In the corner of the room, there was Cleo who was experimenting on a device, she was a woman Levi had not met yet, only talked about by FOG, he had talked about a woman who was called Cleo and she was a were-cat as well as was married to someone he had already met, Fane who could turn into a were wolf. Cleo had tied back black hair with light brown skin. She wore a beige button up shirt and wore light blue jeans. Levi was curious to meet her.

Levi asked Cleo who was turning the dials on some device: 'What is that thing?'

Cleo said in a calm manner: 'It's a planetographer, looks fascinating, Josephine invented it, I'm just here checking it out because she asked me to.'

Levi had a puzzled look.

Josephine explained: 'It's a device that can calculate and record the movement and position of every planet.'

Levi stuttered: 'W-what?'

Josephine said: 'You place it into a body of cool water at night or onto the ground during the day and point the spire, the pointy compass bit towards the direction of the sun or moon, then the dials turn and indicate the cycle, positioning of the planets.'

Levi muttered: 'Sure, sounds simple enough.'

Freya remarked in regard to what Cleo was doing as she was deeply immersed by the planetographer: 'Yes, it has Cleo right in her element.'

Josephine's eyes shifted over to a strange object that was covered by a sheet. She closed her eyes in a pained manner.

Freya coughed and said: 'I think it's time we went, the dry sun dew and fox glove reserves are starting to get on my case.'

Freya pinched her nose tightly and tried to walk away from the herbs that had been hanging over her.

Cleo said: 'Wait.'

Cleo reminded Freya: 'I'd still require your help later perhaps, translating something.'

Freya said: 'Alright Cleo, well thanks for the help Josephine.'

Freya pushed Levi out the open door.

Levi asked as they walked down the path: 'There was a French flag in there...why?'

Freya answered: 'Josephine's ancestors came from France but she was born here in Australia... she is under contract of the witches covenant and was appointed here by them... her job is to make medicine for people here and enchant things for others such as moonstones for werewolves, she also uses scrying to help locate others that need help, we then send out people to find those in need to bring them here... that is how you got here Levi.'

Levi joked: 'Wait, was her ancestor the first wife of Napoleon, that Josephine woman, I mean she was French right!'

Freya replied awkwardly: 'Yeah no, I don't think so.'

Levi wondered then asked: 'Why on earth was there a picture of a pig wearing clothes in Josephine's house?'

Freya explained sharply: 'Funnily enough I once asked her that same question, she told me that her ancestor whose name was also Josephine, was a witch that had helped a human pig man called Boris...it's a strange and difficult story to explain... that's all I can tell you about it.'

Freya remarked in her mind: 'Though she's been acting really strange as of lately... I wonder why?'

Their voices trailed off into the distance.

Josephine placed the empty cup away. She went out the back and chucked some scraps out to the chickens. Then she forked some hay into the guinea pig enclosure. She watered the crops, checked the worm farm and tilled a field with Cleo's and Matoko's help in preparation for the next crop season.

Towards the end, Josephine felt exhausted.

As she put the farm tools away, Matoko asked her: 'Are you alright?'

Josephine rubbed the dirt off her hands and said: 'All good here Matoko.'

Matoko took off an apron and stated firmly: 'You know I can sense your emotions...you seem tense.'

Matoko's eyes that always had a usual calm and soothing effect, were now lit up in brown and yellowish colours. She frowned.

She said to Josephine: 'You're hiding something from me, I don't like it when my friends hide things from me.'

Josephine said while going back inside: 'Matoko, I know you are my good friend and you're right, there is something you don't know about, however, I have been sworn to secrecy... I am begging you to understand that.'

The colour in Matoko's eyes faded; she said: 'Very well, I understand, why don't we go inside and I'll make us both a cup of green tea.'

Josephine was inside to find Cleo staring at a mirror. The shards that had once been the perfect inner surface of the mirror floated out in front of the mirror frame. The frame seemed to be old, perhaps made of brass and had been painted black. It was as though a jolt of electricity panged Josephine's heart. The fear gathered again.

Josephine ran over to Cleo and pushed her away from the mirror. Cleo looked frustrated.

She asked Josephine: 'What is this mirror doing here?'

Josephine said: 'I cannot explain, please refrain from making me do so and leave.'

She pointed at the door.

Cleo said in a bitter manner: 'That mirror has an uncanny resemblance to one that Fane had once told me about... besides, it has a dark aura, you shouldn't keep it here in Hallow Valley.'

Cleo left. Josephine sighed. If it was one thing she hated it was lying.

Matoko said: 'So that's what you were hiding.'

Suddenly a black, elegant looking cat appeared out of nowhere.

The cat said: 'Is the big cat gone?'

Josephine lectured her: 'Jo, shut up... Cleo is not a big cat.'

The cat waved her paw obnoxiously at Josephine and said: 'Blah blah blah.'

Josephine asked Jo: 'Whatever, where were you my ever so disgraceful familiar?'

Jo said: 'Meow, you see you may have your rituals as a witch, I have my once in a week ritual as a cat which includes annoying the hell out of FOG's dog and Ontari's dog, plotting to get my revenge on Felicity's pet rat named Rusty, tearing the FOG's hut sign off FOG's hut and counting all the birds in the sky...the last pleasures that remain to a cat like me.'

Jo the Cat

Josephine said: 'So I heard that Fane had to

put that sign back on...you're the one that keeps tearing it down...bad kitty, if you want your share of old birds from the aviary you'd better behave from now on.'

Jo complained: 'I was a wild cat out on the prowl before you turned me into your familiar, I used to be normal as in a cat that can't talk or do weird magic... I hate you.'

Josephine said: 'You mean a normal cat that lived out on the streets and survived on take out food and dead mice... I think I did you a favour you little snitch....now did you get the ingredients that I need or not!?'

Jo levitated a shopping bag labelled 'Mckinley's herbal and co' to Josephine.

Josephine snatched the bag and looked inside.

She said: 'Four dried mandrakes, one Arnica and a bit of Valerian root, good work.'

Jo whined: 'Now give me my payment!'

Josephine retrieved a dead, burnt bird from a drawer and tossed it to Jo. The cat caught it and walked off.

Josephine remarked: 'Just how you like it, a dead bird roasted then seasoned with dill and catnip, then dipped in honey and left to dry... disgusting.'

It was getting late. Matoko had finished her green tea with Josephine. She questioned why Josephine was so worried and caught up in the mirror. It worried her that her long time friend's zealous and kind heart was slipping away. Ever since Josephine had got here, her and Matoko had been close. After the death of Josephine's parents, Marcus and Jane, she was forced to grow up quickly though the witches covenant saw talent in Josephine and recruited her so she was practically raised by them. Her mentor had been a certain powerful witch named Midnight. Eventually she finished her witch studies and had been assigned to this safe haven as every safe haven had one witch.

The entire time that Matoko spent with Josephine, Josephine only glanced at the mirror that was once more covered. The cover of the mirror was special, it could block negative magic and could prevent it from coming from the mirror. Hopefully it was only a matter of time that the Witches Covenant (a sort of council for witches and is supported by the Hidden Empire) would take back the mirror and place it in the newly built vault before it drove her to madness... Josephine would only hope.

Cleo who was still upset with Josephine, was on her way to find Fane. She was annoyed with the fact that Josephine kept a creepy, dangerous mirror that could be the very same one that had hurt Fane in the past. Cleo rarely held a grudge for someone but when it came to something personal or people she cared deeply for, she was the worst with grudges. Fane had been showing Felicity how to hold a mallet and chisel in the correct way. That was one of the ways for the father and daughter to bond. Ever since Fane had made a wooden jewellery box with the name Felicity beautifully etched into the wood and an image of a wolf and a wild cat in the inside and given it to his daughter for her last birthday, Felicity was keen to learn how to make such things.

Fane said: 'You're getting real good at this.'

Felicity said: 'Dad, I'm only learning how to safely hold a mallet and chisel.'

Fane said whilst shrugging his shoulders: 'Well you've got to start somewhere, just like I did when I was a boy.'

He reminisced on when his step father had shown him how to handle and make things out of wood. He also taught Fane how to make things out of metal. Fane smiled a little at those memories. If Fane had a wish it may be a chance to see his step father again and maybe that Felicity and Cleo could meet him. Cleo walked up to Fane and tapped him on the shoulder.

Fane took the mallet and chisel away from his daughter and put them aside, then he turned to face Cleo.

Fane said: 'I thought you were by Josephine checking out that invention that had you so excited.'

Felicity asked in an inquisitive manner: 'So mum, what was the planetographer like?'

Cleo rushed them both and said: 'It was very good...but...'

She knelt down to Felicity and whispered: 'I think it's Rusty's lunch time, why don't you go feed him?'

Felicity said: 'Okay mum.'

She ran off.

Fane noticed Cleo was upset. Cleo stood up.

He asked her: 'What is wrong?'

She explained: 'You know that mirror you once told me about... the one that led to you losing your powers.'

Fane frowned; he said: 'Yes I remember.'

He asked: 'What about it?'

Cleo said: 'I think Josephine has that very mirror in her keeping.'

Fane shouted: 'WHAT!?'

He had a painful, angry look on his face, the one that made him look as though his temper reached boiling point.

Cleo took his hand in hers. She spun a ring that was on his finger. The ring he kept as a memory of one of the most painful experiences he ever had. He even had a scar that looked like deep black veining/scorch marks that ran from his other hand up to his shoulder to mark that same experience.

His eyes turned into a sad blue. Cleo tried to comfort him.

Fane said in an aggravated tone: 'I am going to destroy that mirror.'

Meanwhile, back in FOG's hut:

FOG paced the room back and forth.

Melusine said: 'We managed to put the letters into various words but no possible clue!'

Aya joked tiredly: 'If I do this again for the 200th time I am going to mechanically melt into a miserable heap.'

FOG said enthusiastically: 'Oh come on my friends, we can do this!'

He shouted: 'Groady, another round of coffee please!'

Groady ushered in and said: 'Yes sir, Groady makes best coffee for you three.'

He left and started on the coffee.

Aya groaned: 'No not coffee... FOG, you know I hate coffee and cigarettes and alcohol.'

FOG smiled at Aya's suffering and said: 'Nobody asked you to drink it.'

Aya grinned angrily at FOG.

Melusine smoked her cigarette.

Aya said to Melusine: 'That can't be good for your lungs or vocals... being a Siren.'

Melusine said casually: 'On the contrary I think it gives my songs a bit of an edge....though I appreciate the concern.'

Aya coughed and tried to sweep away the smoke of the cigarette using her hand and said: 'I'm more worried for the health of others here, mine VERY much INCLUDED.'

FOG stated: 'Good riddance Aya, you can't stop being the centre of attention!'

Aya said: 'I'm sorry, it's in my nature.'

Groady came and served the coffee.

Melusine took the cup. She winked at Groady.

Melusine said: 'Thank you, diligent zombie.'

Groady bowed ridiculously.

Aya said to Melusine: 'I wouldn't drink that if I were you.'

Melusine questioned Aya with a hint of annoyance: 'You're not tricking me are you?'

Aya said in a serious manner: 'I may be excellent at pretence but when I tell you not to drink that, I mean it, that coffee is very earthy.'

FOG had already drunken a sip. He had spat it out into the cup.

He yelled: 'Groady, did you use grey water again!'

Groady bolted out the room. He broke his leg during his retreat.

Aya joked: 'Hey, break a leg get it?!'

FOG shook his head.

He said: 'Groady promised me he would get himself stitched back together by Cleo... damn zombie, always breaking his body parts even though he is a Zomon.'

Melusine was embarrassed as she quickly placed her cup back onto the table.

Suddenly, someone knocked on the door.

FOG said: 'Come in.'

Cleo entered the hut and closed the door.

FOG said in a relieved manner: 'Cleo, you're here, finally!'

Aya said: 'Yeah we were at a dead end...now Hallow Valley's genius is here to bring salvation.'

Cleo said: 'Ok I have no idea what you are talking about Aya.'

Melusine explained in a more logical manner: 'I am here with a letter that was sent to me by the man who created the virus, this man left a clue in a puzzle, so far we've managed to put words together but not enough to complete the clue.'

Cleo crossed her arms and interrogated the woman: 'And you are?'

Melusine introduced herself: 'Melusine, the one and only, the one who aided FOG during the mission in Russia, former disciple of Rumpelstiltskin, the one who is mentioned in specific German or French fairy tales.'

Cleo said: 'Ah now I know you... Frances' former travel companion, my name is Cleo.'

Cleo looked at the puzzle. She grabbed the letter and began folding the sections of the puzzle.

Aya said: 'Really so all we had to do the entire time would have been to fold it...'

Cleo said whilst concentrating: 'Yes, it's a fold puzzle, you have to fold it over and over again till the letters are in an array that makes sense... it's hard to describe.'

Aya noted: 'Sort of like Origami... I should have known that.'

Cleo put the folded paper down and said: 'All done.'

Aya leaned over to read it.

It said:

Landthatisdestroyed,awaitingsecretslieintheheartofChernobyltonortheast Dubrovstreet.

Melusine broke it into chunks:

Land that is destroyed, awaiting secrets lie in the heart of Chernobyl to north east Dubrov street.

Melusine said: 'So land that is destroyed, Chernobyl Ukraine because of that nuclear accident, the lab is in the heart of Chernobyl, located north east at a street called Dubrov street...'

Aya asked Melusine: 'Why did that freaky guy choose Ukraine?'

Melusine said: 'William was always drawn to places with catastrophic history... it sounds mental but that was him.'

She stood up and said: 'I'll be sure to go and do some research with a few friends of mine.'

Melusine left the hut.

Cleo asked: 'That was an interesting puzzle... got any more of them?'

Aya and FOG shouted: 'No!'

Cleo laughed at the upset Aya and FOG.

She said: 'By the way, Frances, I came here because I wanted to ask if you knew about that mirror that Josephine is keeping, it's got a certain malicious energy about it and I don't like it.'

FOG said: 'No I didn't know about it, I'm sure it has to do with that witch business.'

Cleo said: 'But still I'm worried and Matoko who is over there frequently hasn't said anything against it.'

FOG said: 'Look Cleo, if it worries you that much I'll go up to the farm later to check on Josephine, she is after all a very good friend to me as well.'

Cleo said: 'Good, now I've got to go and see Freya before she heads off to the underworld... I heard there's something interesting going on in the underworld.'

Aya waved goodbye to Cleo. Cleo smiled a bit and headed out.

The little child that had fallen asleep next to Aya on the couch woke up now.

FOG looked at his wrist watch and muttered: 'Felix and Osana left to go get something to eat instead of Groady's horrible soups... perhaps they'll be back soon.'

Aya reached for a remote and turned on the TV that hung on the wall.

Florence grabbed the remote from Aya and pressed a random button.

The TV spoke: 'Previously on dead men tell no tales, the pirate ghosts...'

The channel changed when Aya switched.

She said: 'No you don't want to watch that stupid series, I mean it's only about a bunch of ghost pirates who get bored on a ghost ship, there's already 200 episodes of that crap.'

Florence squinted at the TV.

The TV spoke: 'Today on mythical trivia we have a few fun facts for you!'

1. 'Did you know that the favourite fruit of dragons is dragon fruit and that of gargoyles is stone fruit?'

2. 'Did you know that only some witches use wands, the novice witches refer to the wand as a crutch to aid them and help them learn how to wield magic, only when they become more skilled can they use their hands.'

3. 'Did you know that witches can spell bind any type of animal into their familiar? The most popular familiars are cats and dogs, logically speaking, witches could turn any animal into their familiar such as ants or elephants but that would be impractical. Any familiar takes on the ability to speak the language of their master and some of their magic. Some familiars can speak Russian!'

4. 'Fairy dust is now an illicit substance in non-fairy entities hands but funnily enough, without it, fairies cannot fly... fairy dust is dangerous to demons as it can paralyse demons, hindering the use of their powers as well.'

5. 'The two best, newest jokes from the OGR, nominated by the Grim Reaper himself are; Hell-o or go to hell and another person says I've already been there!'

Florence looked at Aya. A pleading look.

Aya said: 'Alright, I'll change to the kiddie channel.'
Mr fox appeared on the TV; he said: 'I am fantastic Mr fox!'

Aya gasped and covered Florence's eyes using her hand. Felix and Osana entered the hut and closed the door.

Felix placed food on the table.

He took off his dark green jumper and said: 'You put on our daughter's favourite show.'

Florence was gripping Aya's hand, trying to uncover her eyes.

Aya grumbled: 'You can't let her watch Fantastic Mr fox, it's a disgrace to all Kitsunes!'

Osana was about to change the channel when the TV signal disappeared and the black and white, flashing pixel screen appeared.

FOG said: 'Yes, I've been meaning to have that ley lines router checked, our ley line must have been hijacked... better ring the ley communications intercom hot line to see if anything is wrong.'

An image appeared on the TV. It moved. It seemed to be video. The man on TV giggled. He was of unusual small stature for a man.

He took off what looked like an akubra hat. He winked.

He said: 'G'day, it is Rumpelstiltskin speaking here...yes I am or more like have taken up residence in lovely Australia.'

FOG shouted: 'That little maniac!'

Rumpelstiltskin said: 'Yes this is a recording for your record... hah, never mind that, it has come to my attention that my arch enemy, Lord Gruesome, has decided to create a virus that will wipe out most of humanity, without a doubt, I believe it will do so.'

He continued: 'If you are hearing this, I have probably already been arrested by Hidden Empire officials and have been stuck in a cell in the underworld...it is only due to the fact that someone has ratted me out to the Hidden Empire, a certain witch who is up to no good at all, she is from the Sisterhood....I do not know her motive.'

Rumpelstiltskin said: 'To those who I have wronged...by now you have gotten your revenge but know this... it is not over, and to Lucien I say, the game of ours has reached an end, check mate so to say.... Grandpa.'

He giggled again and said: 'Oh by the way, to my dearest friends down in Hallow Valley, the World Hunt Organisation is not what it seems, something is silently boiling within the organisation in America...did you perhaps already receive a letter saying; 'let the games begin'... if so the great leader, the Oracle has sent it to taunt all of you, bah hah hah... the hunters become the hunted...so if I were you I'd do some research on the Sisterhood and the World Hunt Organisation.'

He waved goodbye and said: 'Farewell, lovelies!'

The video disappeared and the TV signal came back.

FOG shouted at the TV: 'You scoundrel, don't show up on my television ever again!'

He marched to the TV.

Felix grabbed his father's arm and pulled him back. Felix gave him a glare. Florence crawled off the couch. She ran, a purple aura appeared around her then she disappeared.

Felix shouted: 'Florence... no not again!'

Osana opened the door and bolted outside. FOG and Felix as well as Aya torpedoed outside.

The worried mob shouted: 'Florence.... Florence!'

They shouted this repeatedly.

Osana shouted: 'Florence Lara Gregory...come here now!'

FOG asked Felix: 'Florence Lara Gregory?'

Felix said: 'Yes we named her after her grandmother since Osana didn't know the name of her own mother.'

FOG smiled in a sentimental manner. Aya ran up to Osana.

Aya pointed towards a child that was standing in a small body of water.

Felix grabbed Osana and teleported towards the water. Osana somehow magically made the water bend away from her daughter. Felix picked up Florence and went out of the empty space in the water. Osana let go of her control over the water and it sunk back into place.

Florence's clothes were drenched. Florence pointed towards a creature that was standing over on the other side, gazing at them. Felix and Osana stood in awe of the beautiful creature. It was a creature that had the body of a wolf but was smaller than a normal four legged wolf. It had dark, soft silky fur and a long fluffy tail. It had a more small, narrow head and had long whiskers. It had cat like paws but with sharp claws, it was indeed the mixture of a cat and wolf.

Aya noticed who it was. She waved to the hybrid creature.

She said: 'Hi Felicity!'

Another creature that truly was your typical four legged wolf ran up to Felicity, he had silver greyish fur. They then stood together and stared at the others. He eventually motioned for the other one to follow him and they ran off together.

Aya said: 'So heart felt, Fane is teaching his daughter how to control her form.'

A bright, shiny aura appeared around Florence.

FOG asked: 'What is that shiny veil over her...why does it look like a shimmering fox?'

Aya asked in a surprised manner: 'You can see her Kitsune aura?'

FOG said to Aya: 'Yes but I thought you told me only Kitsunes can gaze upon each other's aura.'

Aya said: 'That is true...'

Felix explained: 'Florence is a hybrid, she is half reaper, half Kitsune...because of that she can teleport and her aura can be seen by others, also her Kitsune powers are already present but she can't use them completely.'

Osana added: 'Which is one of the reasons we came here in the first place, we needed help getting her powers under control.'

Florence said: 'I came here because I sensed a funny creature like me.'

FOG said: 'She talked!'

Osana said: 'She can talk, it's not like she's a robot, she's just like me and doesn't talk a lot.'

Aya asked Florence: 'Do you mean the wolf like hybrid creature we had seen? Her name is Felicity.'

Felix put down Florence and together they all walked back to the hut. They all seemed like a strange family indeed.

Meanwhile FOG and the others had gone to the hut:

A dog was ignoring Max completely. The dog walked so slowly as though every paw step was too much pain to bare. Max had tried everything to make FOG's dog Ruby enthusiastic, throwing chew toys, buying dog bones but nothing seemed to please this nit picky dog, she was indeed a 'lady of leisure' so to say and she was a Husky German Shepherd mix. After hundreds of rounds of rough housing and playing

287

chasey with the dreadful, notorious resident cat Jo. FOG had asked Max, to take his dog for a long walk in Hallow Valley to rehabilitate the dog and so after the deed was done, here Max was, finally marching toward FOG's hut.

Remarkably, as soon as Ruby laid eyes on her home, she jetted towards it. Max was out yelling his voice out. Ruby sniffed the door. At this, a familiar man opened the door.

FOG said joyfully: 'Ruby there you are!'

Ruby forced her way past FOG and made haste for the pet bed. She lied down like a proud Diva and went to sleep. FOG frowned at the dog.

Max balled his hands into fists; he fumed: 'I've had enough of these games, doggy... here comes angry Maximillian Tillman!'

He transformed into a shadowy dark figure with grey/beige skin and black eyes.

He crept towards the hut. He had not expected FOG in the doorway.

Max screeched: 'Doggy, nice doggy!'

FOG fainted and was for a brief moment, unconscious.
Max noticed and said: 'Oh dear, I didn't know there were people in there.'

He awkwardly left the spot.

FOG woke up with a spooked expression.

Max retreated to a green house that was located nearby to wait out the tension he might've created.

He hid in a corner of the green house and reverted back to his normal form.

Silly me, he thought to himself. I'm a vampshee, I should know better than to go around screeching at dogs or making people faint!

He had been so lost in thought that there was a girl that he had not noticed straight away. She had light brown hair that was tied back into a thin, stupendously long plat. She wore a green shirt and normal trousers. Max laughed at her hair but was quick to cover his mouth.

A tiny, angry voice said: 'Mind ya rotten manners ye filthy lout!'

The girl turned around and blinked several times as she saw Max.

The tiny man wore a green outfit and had large metal buckles on his shoes; he also wore a tall red hat that was fitted with a large four leafed clover. He sat on the girl's shoulder.

Max observed: 'You're a leprechaun... I thought you'd be bigger.'

He answered in an irritated tone: 'Ye aren't the first moron to notice...don't go thinking ye are a lucky bugger or something.'

He took out a tooth pick and waved it up and down at Max.

His Irish accent was quite dominant. He had red hair and a red beard.

He raved: 'I truly struck gold on idiots this time round, I've got a pot luck with ye now!'

Max defended himself against this uncivilised leprechaun: 'Look here tiny man, I've met fairy species that are kinder than you are, you must be the most rude leprechaun to wander this earth.'

The leprechaun's face turned beet red. He was loaded.
He snarled:'Aye, I am, and when I the grouch am finished with ye, you'll be seeing ya rainbows alright!'

He punched the air in front of him.

The girl grabbed the small man. He was so small he could be held in a human hand.

He bickered: 'Let me go Greta... let me at the buffoon!'

Greta said in a monotone manner: 'Sorry, he has nothing better to do.'

Max said in a more content manner: 'Ah someone polite, finally... my name is Maximillian Tillman.'

Greta introduced herself: 'My name is Greta Funberg and this little man's name is Larry.'

Larry scrunched his face together.

Max burst into laughter: 'Larry the leprechaun...couldn't your parents have chosen you a better name!'

Larry who was clearly upset said: 'Leprechaun's don't have parents, we are born from the magic of pixies, tiny elven folk to make shoes/clothes or keep gold for them...not that it's a bad life...'

Greta explained: 'I am a volunteer here at FOG's green house... what brings you here?'

Max said in contemplation: 'Nothing much, just stowing away for a while till FOG recovers from fainting.'

Greta said: 'I came here after my brother Hans was cooked alive by an evil witch, you see, me and by brother were slaves to our parents mad devotion for the Hansel and Gretel story, hence Hans and Greta, just like me he could turn into a giant squid monster, I hope at least that witch had a fondness for sea food.'

Max frowned; he replied: 'Ooooookay, that's enough detail.'

Greta was a very oblivious, care free and day dreamy person.

She blabbered on: 'I am a descendant of a great Kraken monster and related to a woman called Gerta, also I can talk and communicate with water animals... Larry here got sent here to learn some manners before returning to his Leprechaun cluster... you could say he is so rude that I am his only friend.'

Max plugged his ears and ran out of the green house. He came to a natural decision that the two were more insane than FOG's dog.

Thomasin had finished her mythical creature lessons for the day.

She spent the rest of the evening pondering over the things she had done in the last centuries. She had become so locked in her own world of suffocating memories ever since the Grim Reaper had visited Hallow Valley for the delegate meeting. She had a troubled conscience that weighed heavily on her heart... more than anything in these last past few years she wanted for her nephew to know the truth and that if he wanted to blame anyone for any existing sadness or hatred, he should direct it at her. She sat in a dark corner of the room in her banshee form and cried. The rays of darkness spread across the room.

She threw the necklace with the amber stone at the wall and cried. She regretted it all.

Nevena who was washing out clothes suddenly screamed when she saw blood drip from the linen.
Thomasin ran outside in her human form and hugged her niece.

Nevena said: 'The dragon is dead, another has risen.'

Thomasin promised herself: 'This pain must stop.'

Thomasin's heart beated heavily, her eyes turned pale. She saw a hooded man with a scythe and a dark aura around him have the magic pulled out of him.

A tear flowed from her eye.

She whispered: 'He's going to die again.'

Fane and Felicity had returned to the transformation chambers. The transformation chambers were located further away from the rest of Hallow Valley due to the fact that it was a place for mythical creatures to hide out if they needed to transform into their other form such as some few werewolves who turned every full moon, the types of werewolves that couldn't control their form unlike Fane.

It looked like a huge dome like building, inside there were multiple strong cells built out of indestructible Demonium steel, the steel that was forged using Demonium ore that was mined in the underworld where Hades lives, the ore is formed by the heat of the lava pools and is self replenishing and abundant. It is the most powerful building material known to mythical creatures. It is also heat resistant so it can repel the effects of sun light, good and efficient for vampires. Outside there were signs labelled:

Rules of the Transformation chambers:

1. If you usually lose your clothes because of your transformation, please have spare clothes packed prior to this event.

2. There are noise restrictions, bare in mind that there are others in the chambers as well.

3. Clean up any mess afterwards, say if you are a troll, do clean up loose hairs after your rampage.

4. Bring your own blood supplies or food supplies if you are a ravenous beast, such is not supplied.

5. Zombies will be held responsible for loose body parts, they must sew it back on themselves or take it with them.

6. Spirit beings are not allowed in this facility, it is to prevent them from drifting through walls and to other people who may not want to be seen and want their privacy...

7. If you happen to be a huge giant, troll, ogre or dragon etc., please purchase fairy dust from Josephine and use the dust on yourself to shrink yourself into a human size, if not you will be too big to enter this facility.

Creatures who do not abide by these rules will be punished accordingly.

As decreed and agreed under the *Mythical Transformations Facility Act 2000.*

Fane and Felicity were leaving the facility after they had mocked the rules together.

Fane said: 'So there is the place for you to go if you need to rampage away from others or if you need to transform.'

Felicity said: 'I know, they go there to lock themselves up, to calm themselves down or to transform, but I can control my form so creatures like you, me and mum don't have to go there.'

Fane insisted: 'Yes but I still wanted to show you.'

Felicity looked towards a sloped hill that had an extended gravel path, up the very top there was a high wall.

She asked her father out of curiosity: 'What's up that path, beyond that high wall?'

Fane said: 'Only certain people are allowed up there, FOG and the others say the dragons, trolls, ogres, sasquatches live up there, they prefer to stay separated from the rest of us, besides, they protect the arches.'

Felicity said: 'But dragons have a human form!'

Fane replied: 'Yes they aren't that different to us...but they have had enough negative experience with other mythical creatures, out of sadness and hatred they prefer to live with the bigger creatures.'

She asked: 'What are the arches?'

Fane spun her around to face him. He looked at her.

He asked: 'Listen...do you hear a magnetic howling sound?'

Felicity said: 'Yes I do!'

Fane explained: 'The arches are an array of megalithic pillars that look like arches, they lead to some other place, like a permanent portal, they are the things making that sound.'

Felicity was astounded; she asked: 'What do they lead to?'

Fane said: 'I don't know....come on, it's getting late, we should go home.'

As Fane and Felicity went on their way, she asked: 'Dad, what do you think do all those big creatures eat?'

Fane said: 'Well not the flesh of humans... humans make them more evil than they are for example, the Oni, the Japanese Ogres with horns, sharp claws, blue or red skin and with wild hair, they love Daikon radish and rice, they can't seem to live without it, that's what Aya told me once.'

Felicity asked: 'You're saying the big creatures are vegetarians?'

Fane said: 'Yes basically.'

Cleo was at her and Fane's place, translating a mysterious scripture with Freya.

At the top of the scripture there was an old Norse symbol that Freya immediately recognised. It was a straight line with a tilted line running through the middle of the straight line. The symbol somewhat resembled a cross.

Freya tapped the symbol.

She said: 'Naudh, of the early Nordic rune alphabet, it means in English, Misery.'

Freya read the other text and translated it for Cleo:

'Vaettir are gnomes that live in Iceland, they are respected and revered.'

There was a picture of a small man and woman with dark clothes and wild fuzzy hair.

Freya translated the rest:
'In Sweden and Norway, there are house spirits that protect farmers, families and animals at night. They are called Nisse or Tomte. Nisse have a fondness for horses and like to braid their manes and tails at night time so they are not seen by the household. It is unwise to make them unhappy or they will be prone to break things or tie cows tails together, the best peace offering is porridge with butter, their favourite type of food.'

The rest of the scroll was torn off.

Freya asked Cleo: 'Did you notice this before?'

Cleo tilted her head.

Cleo said: 'No I didn't.'

Freya said: 'I wonder why the Nordic rune for misery is labelled on this scroll, it doesn't fit in with the rest of the content...someone must have added it...'

Cleo said: 'I just ended up having this in my possession.'

Freya questioned: 'Or perhaps it is a sigil.'

Cleo asked: 'What is a sigil?'

Freya explained: 'Witches and warlocks have found a way to create magic symbols that they can simply apply to objects or creatures, most sigils are tracking spells, counter spells or curses... if it is a curse you should get rid of this scroll or place it in Josephine's care.'

Cleo muttered: 'I just wonder what would have been on the torn off bit of scroll?'

Freya debated: 'I'm just worried if someone did place this here to curse you.'

Cleo replied: 'I have other mysterious scrolls that ended up in my possession, they don't contain any weird symbols.'

Freya nodded in relief; she asked: 'May I take this for further analysis?'

She added: 'I think I may know someone who can help...I have a presumption, perhaps this Nordic rune symbol is linked to the history of the old elven folk that lived a long time ago, the ones that Elleswith told me about, the ones that all fairy species are descended from.'

Cleo assumed: 'You'll take it to Oliver won't you?'

Freya said: 'Yes, he is half elven, he may know something.'

Freya took the scroll from Cleo and left.

Just as Levi was about to walk up to Freya. A medium sized cardboard box was hurled at Levi's head.

A grey painted carriage skidded to an abrupt halt. There were spiders hanging around the whole carriage. They swung back and forth rather gleefully and held small tiny lanterns, probably to light the path for the carriage at night time. On the side of the carriage, there was a title painted in a white old fancy style writing which said: GPS postal, 24 hours of unbelievably terrible service. Levi crashed to the floor. He shielded his head using his arms. It throbbed painfully.

Whilst the others sat inside the carriage and drank some grotesque looking green drink as well as feasted on brown dirt cookies, a rude, impatient, sarcastic, deluded looking creature hopped out of the carriage. It was a creature with fuzzy light green fur, as it talked one could see sharp teeth. It had sharp claws and large bat like ears. It wore white/blue apparel that said: 'GPS postal service....so generous and humble!'

It had a high pitched voice that sounded like slow chalk on a chalk board.

It spoke to Freya: 'Parcel for a Cleo Philopetor?'

Freya said: 'Yes.'

Levi said: 'Wait as in Cleopatra...that woman inside just now was...god this place is strange.'

The creature spat as it spoke and Freya had to lean away so as to avoid being spat on.

Freya signed the document.

The creature took the document and said: 'Yap that should be all in order, have a horrible day!'

It smiled a sharp, toothy grin and chuckled as it marched back and jumped into the carriage.

Freya watched as the creatures whipped the death hounds that drew the carriage.

The head creature shouted: 'Barguest, Black shuck, Gurt, Devil's dandy, Wisht hound, Gytrash, full steam ahead!'

The death hounds were tall dogs with black shimmering fur and fiery coal like eyes. The death hounds scratched the floor, then together, they mightily pulled the carriage around the corner. The carriage sped away in an instant and away from sight.

Freya stated: 'That's the GPS postal for you.'
Levi asked in confusion: 'GPS... a navigation system?'

Freya smirked; she explained: 'No, GPS is an abbreviation for Gremlin's Postal Service.'

Levi patted the dirt off his pants; he said: 'This place even has gremlins like from the movies.'

Freya said: 'Not exactly from the films, they didn't become evil by falling into water, now concerning why they are like that in the first place, it's not really their fault.'

She went on to explain: 'Originally, the Gremlins were of the light fairy species not of the dark ones, they lived in relatively isolated forests in England, but when the first world war broke out and their habitat was flown over by war aircraft various times so much so that the Gremlins became infuriated. They began by moving to where the forces kept their air crafts and began causing mechanical problems in the fighter air crafts during night time... but after the first world war, when the Gremlins thought it was over soon after came the second world war and that made them angry that it turned them evil, FOG had once told me that an evolution is possible once in every species of mythical creatures, the gremlins who had once been light fae turned into dark fairies and resorted to completely destroying fighter air craft in world war two and they even moved the air strips or placed gigantic rocks in the way so that planes would have difficulty to navigate, it is rumoured that they even rearranged the patterns of the stars in the sky using their magic so that the pilots couldn't navigate too easily.'

She added: 'During world war two, the humans believed to have seen the gremlins meddle with the planes during the day but they are only rumours...let me tell you a secret Levi, they are true, when some humans thought they were imagining things, the gremlins were actually there... perhaps the Gremlins wanted to be seen so that they could drive the pilots or other people insane... Gremlins weren't always called Gremlins, the humans think their given name came from the combination of Grimm from the brothers grim who wrote fairy tales and Fremlins the name of a popular beer in England during world war two, some others believe their name came from the old English word gremain which means to annoy...FOG had once told me the whole history of the Gremlins.'

She reflected on that memory for a brief moment.

Levi asked: 'So how is it that they came to work here as a um well a postal service?'

Freya said: 'Good question... I wouldn't know, I don't spend a lot of time here except only occasionally... what I do know is they deliver all the letters and parcels that other mythical creatures send them and that they love mud cookies and that green drink of theirs that they make from boiled down fats from trolls toe nails and turnips as well as cabbage...the green gremlins are males and the grey ones are females... a word of advice if you do decide to stay in Hallow Valley, if you talk to them, never correct a gremlin and never partake in Christmas themes, they hate it...I remember when FOG put on a Halloweenmas hat and even though it was not a complete Christmas theme, an entire hoard of gremlins ran after FOG and he ran for dear life...he was too kind-heated to drain the energy from them.'

Cleo ducked her head out the door way and asked: 'What are the two of you still doing here?'

Freya took the parcel from Levi and handed it to Cleo.

She said: 'The Gremlins dropped off this parcel for you... then I was busy explaining to Levi about the Gremlins, don't worry, I'll drop the scroll off to my brother but first I need to talk to FOG.'

Cleo gazed at the parcel. It said: Sender: Unknown. Cleo looked up again to see Freya and Levi walk off into the distance.

Freya and Levi headed back to FOG's hut. Levi was amazed to see white magical orb lights appear everywhere in Hallow Valley as far as the eye could see. It was night time already.

Freya stopped walking and stood across from Levi. She hit him on the shoulder.

Levi said: 'Ouch... what is wrong with you!'

Freya said: 'This is where our adventure ends... I've got something to discuss with FOG and then I'll be off and on my way to the underworld...you've met me, there's a lot of other people left for you to get acquainted with...good luck stranger.'

Levi asked: 'So you're a vampire... how can you walk in the sun?'

Freya said: 'I get asked about that quite frequently, in the past I couldn't walk in the sun, I gained immunity to sun light over multiple centuries but that is only due to the fact of my fortunate sire bond, the vampire that turned me was a hybrid vampire, my sire is powerful so I can walk in sun light as a result, only other vampires who are sired by Nosferatu can gain immunity to sun light over centuries time... Nosferatu is a term to refer to the world's oldest vampires who were sired by the vampire ancestors... the vampire ancestors are the two first vampires in existence and were turned by the Demon King himself...not all vampires gain immunity to sun light... most vampires are descended of a Nosferatu but it has to be a direct, first generation sire bond to a Nosferatu in order to ever be able to walk in sun light, only a small handful of vampires that aren't directly sired or not sired at all by a Nosferatu have gained immunity to sun light... the vampire population consists mostly of lowly vampires as such most vampires cannot go out during the day or morning... however, if they befriend a witch, they can get access to a sun stone that can be enchanted for a vampire, they can then wear it to ward off the effects of the sun for a few hours of every day... other than that it is not possible for a vampire to walk in the sun light unless they are a day walker and are born as a vampire... this has only happened twice in history.'

Levi shook his head and said: 'Wow, there is a lot for me left to learn about mythical creatures.'

He joked: 'If Vlad the Impaler had been a vampire, he would be the world's most famous vampire of all time!'

Freya smirked and said: 'He is, since he is a day walker, a hybrid, that makes him even more world renowned, but no vampire knows where he is at the moment, not even the Hidden Empire.'

Levi blinked multiple times.

He said: 'It seems a lot of history's most famous people had a secret to hide.'

Freya said: 'Perhaps.'

Freya went into the hut. FOG sat on the couch. He held a freeze pack to his head.

He grumbled: 'I could have sworn to have seen Max stand in the doorway, why on earth did I faint? I have seen that banshee form of his before, I am such a fool...ow I did hit my head hard.'

Ruby was off in her corner, dozing in her pet bed.

Felix said: 'Oh relax father.'

FOG: 'Alright alright, it would be sensible of me, but I would still appreciate an explanation from Max.'

Freya who had been watching FOG quietly from afar said firmly: 'FOG, we should talk about what I found out at Josephine's.'

FOG: 'Well go on then, we should not waste any time.'

Freya asked FOG as she saw his upset face: 'What happened?'

FOG bickered: 'You never let anything go, do you? You stubborn, arrogant...'

Felix looked at him. FOG sighed.

FOG explained: 'Very well, today I fainted, now I do not like speaking of the sort of embarrassing incidents nowadays because people like Aya like to make fun of my idiotic stunts.'

Freya said: 'How very FOGgy of you, well I won't make fun of you for sure.'

FOG asked: 'So what did you find out about that mysterious note?'

Freya said: 'Josephine did a scrying spell...but it went all wrong.'

FOG asked: 'Wrong how?'

Freya said: 'Wrong as in it set all of Josephine's maps on fire...then the letter burned away till it disappeared.'

FOG twisted his mouth: 'Oh what an utter disappointment.'

Freya said whilst pulling out a piece of folded paper from her pocket: 'We did discover something.'

She unfolded it and held it up for everyone to see.

FOG noted: 'Most of America is burnt out!'

Freya said: 'This is the main map that Josephine used to trace the origins of the letter, it began to burn at the same time the letter did.'

Aya said: 'So the letter and that map are linked which means that whoever sent it might be in America somewhere and that something bad is happening over there.'

FOG jolted up from the spot.

He said: 'Yes, earlier while you were off, a recorded broadcast from Rumpelstiltskin was shown on TV, he warned us of people called the Sisterhood but at the same time he had come up with a scheme with those very same people then he knew about Lord Gruesome's plans with the virus and he knew about the letter, he even presumed that we should have gotten it by now and that it was sent by the Oracle, the leader of the World Hunt Organisation.'

Freya guessed: 'Maybe it was sent by the Oracle and the World Hunt Organisation is situated in America.'

FOG: 'Rumpelstiltskin said that the World Hunt Organisation isn't what it seems and that the hunters become the hunted, that means the enemy is within the organisation, the Oracle sent the letter so this person is the enemy.'

Aya asked FOG: 'Didn't you say that you and Cleo found reports of mythical creatures that had been affected by the virus, that it had mutated which also means someone had gone to Lord Gruesome's lab to tamper with the samples to mutate the virus...Rumpelstiltskin knew about Lord Gruesome's plans, Rumpelstiltskin knew about the leader of the World Hunt Organisation and her or his plans, what if he had discovered about the Oracle's plans via Lord Gruesome and Lord Gruesome had been in league with the Oracle, the Oracle sent someone to weirdo guy's lab to tamper with the virus, it mutated and the second wave of Covid-19 happened, Lord Gruesome didn't know about the Oracle's true plans because he committed suicide before the second wave was released.'

FOG replied: 'Interesting theory Aya, we'll keep it in mind but we can't just come up to random conclusions.'

Freya said: 'You guys keep pondering and debating this, I have to go to the underworld... it's about time I think.'

FOG asked: 'Time for what?'

Freya said at the door: 'A top secret gathering in the underworld, I hear it is an event that happens there every decade, this time around Oliver asked me to go and help with event planning.'

FOG moped: 'You're lucky your brother is a highly ranked demon official, you get all the inside gossip from him regarding the Hidden Empire and I'm just a lowly mutant succubus even though my grandmother is the grand book keeper of all the Hidden Empire's records and books in the grand Archaium.'

Freya waved goodbye and left.

As Freya was outside now, she summoned a demon door. Since she had been to the underworld numerous times, she was quite skilled in that skill and was able to bring forth the door quickly.

After a short trip, she exited the door and was suddenly at the main parliament section of the underworld. Oliver was there to greet her.

He hugged her and said: 'It's good to see you Freya.'

Freya scanned the area and noted: 'What's wrong with this place, it's as silent as the grave, normally it's all hustle and bustle.'

Oliver summoned a demon door and explained: 'The gathering is held in the void...they left some people behind to monitor the arrivals and to direct them where to go.'

Freya asked herself what the 'void' was. She eyed the strange demon door, it was different to a normal demon door. This one had chains wrapped around the entire door and it's colour was grey and faded. Oliver took a key and unlocked the door. Freya felt a cold chill as she went in the open doorway with her brother. After they went in, the door slammed shut and it faded away.

In an instant, Freya stood on a stone step which led to more steep, cascading steps. Freya's foot had almost slipped if she hadn't balanced herself on the cold stone wall. She felt like a foreigner within this narrow passage, she hadn't been here before in this part of the underworld. Oliver who had gone down a few steps stood there and turned to look at Freya. She had this nervous look in her eyes. Oliver reached his hand out for her. Freya huffed and continued slowly down the steps. There were skulls hanging on the walls. They each had twisted grins and held a ball of fire that seemed to bounce a little occasionally. Oliver smiled and continued the steep passage as well. *Click clack click clack* their shoes went. The stairs kept winding. Freya asked herself if there was an end to the stair case of madness. Finally Freya laughed a little as the reached a clearing. Oliver and Freya crossed a bridge. This room was huge, the ceiling was dark and seemed to stretch out forever. In the middle that was connected by the bridge was a dry, tall, lonely standing tree that seemed to lean in a certain direction. Freya looked underneath the bridge, there was a large cavernous drop that extended downward. It was an absurd feeling but Freya felt compelled to jump into it. She resisted and crossed the bridge with her brother.

They entered through an arch way. There was another passage till at the very end, there was a gigantic door that was covered in vines and had all sorts of ancient looking symbols etched into them. Oliver waved his hands at the door and they sprung open.

Oliver joked: 'Just magic.'

Freya could hear an organ play. It was a haunting melody, so spine tingling that it was guaranteed to make anyone's heart skip a beat. They went inside. Freya saw a sea of people going back and forth. Everything seemed between a mixture of stately and formal.

Freya asked: 'What were those symbols on the door?'

Oliver replied: 'Protection symbols, counter symbols, this room was once used to seal away a very powerful entity, but not any more.'

She said: 'So everyone here is a demon?'

Oliver said: 'Mostly yes but the most important guests have been allowed to invite at least any two people of their choice.'

The doors banged shut by themselves.

Freya said: 'So the honoured demon Oliver Lothbrok decided to invite me.'

Oliver boasted: 'You are my honoured sister.'

Freya rolled her eyes. Aisha who had been mingling in the crowd, wandered over to Oliver. She wore black overalls that seemed fashionable.

Aisha spread out her arms in a greeting; she said: 'Ah you came...my most intelligent student.'

Oliver bragged: 'But I worked for the Hidden Empire before you did so technically I am your teacher.'

Freya frowned over their casual conversation. Aisha glanced at Freya.

She welcomed Freya with a handshake.

Aisha said: 'You must be one of my grandson's friends.'

Freya asked: 'Wait, you're Aisha Gregory, FOG's grandmother?'

Aisha scrunched her face together. Freya frowned at the young attractive woman. She asked herself as to how this woman could look younger than herself... was it because Aisha was a succubus and she could make herself younger any time? Freya felt estranged from her own age even if she was a vampire and immortal.

She said: 'That's what they call my grandson in Hallow Valley, really?'

Aisha added: 'Poor Frances.'

Aisha went on to say: 'Frances told me all about you and the others as well, wow a former viking shield maiden standing here in front of me, you are a living, breathing piece of history my dear...just fascinating.'

Freya said with a hint of sarcasm: 'The forgotten shield maiden, turned vampire and forced to live in exile, yes that would make quite the headline.'

Aisha grinned and walked off.

Freya said: 'She strikes me as a bold, eccentric woman.'

Oliver showed Freya around the massive room.

He pointed at a man and said: 'Leonardo da Vinci, a vampire, his sister Maria, over there is Isabella Drusillia, she is a major vampire influencer, she is also the niece of Leonardo da Vinci...'

Oliver kept showing Freya around.

Aliyah stood next to her father and observed the crowd, she wore a black, long sleeved, long draping dress. She narrowed her eyes at a shadow that was sneaking about amongst the teeming crowd. She gripped her clip board tightly, the one that she used to tick off guests names. She wished to tell her father about it but he was lost in thought. She knew what he was like if he was interrupted. When she was angry with her father, her black ashen hair would frizzle at her hair tips. The pencil that Aliyah had been writing with, tore across the paper and snapped in two. Aliyah decided that next year she would track down her fairy clan, the Peri and spend some time with her relatives. A long time ago, before her father had even met Vlad, Lucien had still spent his days finding a home land for his people, when he had fallen in love with a woman from a fairy tribe, as a result there came Aliyah, though it was against the law for fae species to unify with any demon species due to the remaining conflict that the species shared with their common ancestors, the ancients, so it came to be that Aliyah had been raised by the Hidden Empire, she had spent most of her laid back, distant life cooped up in the underworld. It was all she had ever come to know apart from the sister, Irina Tolski she never got to meet, neither did her father ever explain to her as to why she couldn't meet her sister... answer, she was burned alive, recently she found out the proud outlaw Rumpelstiltskin was none other than her nephew through a bizarre twist of relations, a grandmother that lives so far away that it is out of even her (Aliyah's) comprehension as well as an Aunt that caused all of Lucien's afflictions regarding his pent up rage then there was the abnormal not so much of a family member, not biologically related, the one that everyone called Lucien's blood sired son, Vlad. It is perfectly normal for Aliyah to have the need for a long break.

Isabella stood in the corner of the room. She spun a cup in her hands.

A hooded man who stood next to her said: 'This event is quite petty.'

Isabella nudged him and said: 'Now, now cousin, do behave, we can't have anyone notice your presence.'

The man widened his eyes as he recognised a woman in the crowd. Isabella saw who he was staring at.

Isabella asked quietly: 'Is that Freya Lothbrok...and Oliver Lothbrok, the ones you had once told me about...is it strange to say that they met you before you were born...Sinric.'

Sinric exhaled. He stood silent for a brief moment.

He replied: 'Considering I was born in the year 1477 and the Sinric Freya met lived in the 9th century AD, I can understand that others may find this confusing, but it is just the way it is, Isabella.'

He added: 'She thinks I died and the boy I took care of probably thinks I abandoned him...it's been so long since I have set foot into the real world since I had awoken from my slumber...it's time to come out of the shadows...don't you think so to?'

Isabella replied: 'So it's a good thing I convinced you to come...you missed out on so much Sinric, the boy that you raised, Fane, he has a daughter and someone he loves, he is content.'

Suddenly, the flickering flames that lit the entire room dimmed.

Isabella whispered: 'Of course Lucien invited him.'

Sinric sighed; he said: 'Now I wish I hadn't been convinced to come here with you.'

The heavy doors slowly opened. The man on the organs played the tune again.

Lucien who had been sitting in a high positioned chair shouted: 'Enough already!'

Lucien bickered to his daughter who stood next to his seat: 'Who hired that absolute moron!?'

The man at the instrument shrank back in fear. Lucien waved his hand and made the organ disappear.

Isabella laughed at a tall, wide built golem with an ugly moustache. He seemed to be made of Clay.

But nobody laughed any further when they saw who entered. Two men who wore dark apparel entered. Once the two went through the crowd and up to Lucien, everyone kept talking and gathering. The lights flared up again.

Lucien had a deep, contemplative look on his face. He hadn't noticed a certain someone stand in front of him.

Lucien muttered to himself: 'This day reminds me of her... that I failed to prevent the darkness from taking her... I should have forced her into the underworld and kept her here for eternity...even if it meant to see her sad, she would have been safe and out of Helene's reach...I should have...'

A voice spoke: 'Lucien...'

Lucien opened his eyes and he said: 'Vlad, ah and if it isn't his closest friend, Siegfried here to accompany him.'

Vlad frowned and said: 'Every ten years you summon a bunch of demons down here to celebrate the end of Brynhild's defeat... I have a question for you Lucien...do even half the people here know who Brynhild is?'

Lucien replied to Vlad's remark: 'Vlad, do not act as if I had intentionally gathered everyone here for no particular reason. The whole point of this event originally was to remember the events from the past involving Brynhild and the Sisterhood, in essence the day should be held as a memorial. So that no one would forget the misdeeds that had taken place. However, over time this memorial has turned more into a celebration over the victory of Brynhild and the Sisterhood. To answer your other question I don't believe that everyone gathered here today has forgotten about Brynhild, but some deny she ever existed and others may not have even lived to know the whole story, nor care to know any further about the matter.'

Siegfried replied: 'Don't bother...you mentioned another announcement you wish to make.'

Lucien said in a sheepish manner: 'Yes, the Hidden Empire has finally managed to capture the most wanted criminal ever, Rumpelstiltskin.'

Freya and Oliver had been watching the Demon King and the other two men from afar.

Oliver said to Freya: 'That man there is Vlad the Impaler and the man next to him is the Wolf Ancestor, Siegfried.'

Freya said: 'It is a very impressive gathering that the Demon King put together.'

Oliver explained: 'Yes and it happens every ten years, it is to celebrate the downfall of Brynhild...and also acknowledge all of the demon and zombie lives lost during the dark rebellion.'

Lucien asked Vlad and Siegfried: 'Where is Cyrus...what in the hell is keeping him so long?!'

Vlad and Siegfried exchanged looks and replied at the same time: 'Fashionably late as always.'

Lucien covered his eyes in annoyance; he complained: 'It was part of the agreement that all four of you should come here every ten years...the only one that does a poor job of showing up is Cyrus, Cyrus Sethius...annoying Cyrus...Cyrus Cyrus Cyrus, the more I say his name, the more enraged I get!'

He asked his daughter: 'Aliyah, since Cyrus may not be attending has at least Qamara the Female Vampire Ancestor come to join us today?'

Aliyah said to him: 'Qamara is still not present.'

Someone barged into the room.

A man shouted: 'A PARTY and nobody invited me... how boring, let's **rekindle** this PARTAY!'

A man with fire for hair and embers springing from his fingers grinned at Lucien.

Lucien said while he clenched his teeth: 'Hades!'

Lucien waved his hand at Hades and a big, wide, heavy organ landed smack bam on Hades. Hades was squashed by the organ. Vlad tried not to laugh.

He groaned in pain.

Lucien yelled to the two tall golems: 'Demitri, Fergus, get rid of him before he sets the organ on fire.'

One Golem heaved the organ and carried it out. The other pulled Hades out.

The door closed.

Lucien stood up and spoke to the people: 'I apologise for the irritating delays, I have had all of you gathered here today to celebrate the continuing victory of the fall of Brynhild... as most of you know, she was the leader of the Sisterhood and planned to plunge the world into oblivion...she failed which is only because of the efforts of these two men here...now thanks to the continued efforts of the agents of the Hidden Empire, Brynhild, who had been turned into a statue centuries ago, had been for the last past few years, split into multiple pieces and kept in various places in each continent and is guarded by people of the Hidden Empire....now remembering the dark rebellion and how many countless zombie lives were lost... we will now stand in a moment of silence for them.'

Everyone stood in awkward silence. Freya eyed two Zombies standing nearby. Freya recognised one of them, it was Groady. Freya asked herself why Groady was here.

Lucien clapped and said: 'That's enough, now the final announcement, we have finally managed to capture Rumpelstiltskin.'

All of a sudden, two ugly women with large vulture like wings, talons for fingers and tails flew in with Rumpelstiltskin strapped to a chair. They put down Rumpelstiltskin then flew down and stood next to him.

Oliver explained to Freya: 'Harpies, they're a type of demon, I hear that the Hidden Empire employs them in the asylum to torture prisoners.'

Freya frowned.

The harpies uncovered Rumpelstiltskin's mouth.

Rumpelstiltskin giggled. His giggling echoed throughout the entire room.

Lucien frowned at Rumpelstiltskin and looked down at him: 'Do you have nothing to say for yourself?'

Rumpelstiltskin said: 'No, grandpa, it seems you have not seen the broadcasted message, I have already said all that I need to say and I am resigned to my fate in my cell...however...'

He glared at Vlad and Siegfried.

He said in a sudden stern manner: 'I do have something to say on behalf of someone else...she spoke to me in my mind during the time I was trapped in my cell.'

The harpies planned to cover Rumpelstiltskin's mouth but he bit into the hand of one of the harpies. The repulsive woman screeched.

Lucien shouted: 'Let him speak!'

Rumpelstiltskin smiled fanatically.

He said: 'Thank you, now she told me to tell you that she will be with you shortly...she has a few things to pay you back for Lucien...this goes for your two friends there as well and that your plan to keep her in multiple pebbles forever won't work...sealing her away may have worked up until now but she will soon be put back together again, her statue will be one again...they already have the talisman in their possession...it is indeed all thanks to me!'

Vlad said: 'He is not bluffing...I can sense that he isn't.'

Lucien said: 'I know.'

Lucien said then: 'Bring him away!'

The harpies grinned at Rumpelstiltskin and brought him away.

The crowd was lively again. Lucien spoke to Aisha.

Lucien said to her: 'I need you to check up on all the Brynhild remnant purgatories....that means the one in the Bermuda triangle, the one in the Arctic ocean, one in the Pacific ocean and the one in the Indian ocean.'

Aisha nodded and walked away. She went into the crowd and disappeared. She went out of the room, the large doors closed behind her. But as she was isolated from the rest of the crowd, someone attacked her from behind. Aisha tried to bend her attackers mind but was knocked unconscious.

The person said: 'Rumpelstiltskin kept his part of the deal... even though we ratted him out in the end.'

Someone shouted: 'Stop right there!'

The mysterious woman who had knocked Aisha unconscious noticed the voice of the man.

She made her form look faded; she said: 'If it isn't Maximillian Tillman...if you want to join the theatrics then it is taking place in there.'

Max charged at the woman but failed to do so when he was forced on his knees by an invisible force. He felt as though a ton of sand would fall down on him.

She said: 'Did you really not recognise your blood sire...you fool I am Helene...don't forget that I was the one that turned you into a vampire...as such you cannot harm me as long as I use the unrelenting force on you.'

Helene glanced at Aisha. Aisha's body began to glow and Helene transformed into Aisha. The body stopped glowing.

She smiled menacingly as Aisha and explained: 'Nobody is going to come out here right now because I took on the form of one of their demon employees...duplicating a form is more different than becoming that form, my aura is not detectable now.'

She added: 'The real Aisha there was about to contact the places where the pieces of Brynhild are hidden, then she would have found out that the pieces are no longer there and the demons that were charged with guarding those underwater purgatories were killed and replaced with decoys, soon after she would have reported to the Demon King and the Sisterhood's plans would have been revealed...Rumpelstiltskin spilled the beans enough already.'

She made Aisha's body disappear.

Helene saw that Max was paralysed. She grinned and made her way to the Archaium to retrieve the enchanted stone that Brynhild's soul required to return as a physical form.

Later: Lucien saw the demons exit the room. He was thinking about what Rumpelstiltskin had said. That Brynhild had telepathically spoken to him during the time he had been locked away in the underworld's asylum... the main stone of Brynhild's statue was still kept in the underworld...if each part of the stone had contained a part of her soul, her conscience, would it be possible for a part of that being to have telepathically reached out to Rumpelstiltskin?

Vlad interrupted Lucien's contemplating: 'Your assistant, that woman that you requested to do something, has not returned yet.'

Lucien said: 'My adviser and book keeper, Aisha yes she has been gone for a while and I did sense a strange presence earlier.'

Siegfried asked casually: 'Adviser?'

Lucien explained: 'Yes of the Demon Council...now that reminds me...'

He glanced at Vlad and said: 'I have a proposition for you...to work in my council.'

Vlad frowned. Siegfried chuckled. Vlad glared at Siegfried.

He asked: 'What's so funny?'

Siegfried said with a hint of humour: 'Imagining you working in Lucien's Demon Council seems somehow hilarious!'

Vlad muttered: 'I don't see how that is funny.'

Siegfried said sarcastically: 'Maybe you should invite Radu to join the Demon Council and Fenna too.'

Vlad scoffed and said: 'A nightmare is what that sounds like...in the last few centuries I wished that blithering imbecile was still rotting in his coffin...but because of the excavations those vile humans had to do at Snagov lake, someone went and awoke Radu.'

Siegfried remarked: 'And it's a good thing Radu did awaken and disappear... what do you think would have happened if the humans had found the other secret tomb and they would have discovered a living person who is a vampire, not the dead body of the notorious Vlad the Impaler like expected.'

Vlad debated: 'They never would have found the secret tomb, it was built never to be entered.'

Siegfried noted: 'Yet your brother who has an IQ of a paper cup managed to locate the tomb as well as open it.'

Lucien stopped the two from head-butting.

He mentioned again: 'Just take it into consideration Vlad.'

Vlad said: 'That man, the criminal that you caught... Rumpelstiltskin, I'm glad you caught him, even I had a run in with him in the past...'

Vlad asked: 'He called you grandpa, why is that?'

Lucien had anger burn in his eyes.

Lucien explained: 'It is a rather complicated story I have never told you about, this is only because it stems from one of my deepest regrets, there was once a woman in a village in Russia who was my daughter, under cruel circumstances, she had a child that she abandoned, that child is as we know him today as Rumpelstiltskin.'

A man with a British accent said: 'One of the Demon King's secrets.'

Lucien's voice boomed: 'Jack Bartlett...or should I say Jack the Ripper...get down from there this instance!'

Jack threw back his head and laughed hysterically. He jumped down from the stone ledge that had been carved into the wall above Lucien.

Aliyah frowned and said: 'Jackass.'

Jack smirked. He cocked his head to one side.

He asked in an arrogant tone: 'Who are you calling Jackass, princess?!'

Aliyah's blue eyes turned dark. Black veining trembled underneath her eyes.

She said in a defiant manner: 'You shut up, Ripper!'

Jack sneered at her and teased her: 'What's wrong princess...does your regal nature prevent you from talking?'

She twisted her mouth. She shoved a clip board into Jack's arms. Black butterflies began to flutter around Aliyah, they surrounded her and she disappeared.

Jack cracked his head in place and remarked: 'What a sensitive little princess.'

Jack Bartlett was only one of the most resented vampires in the entirety of the vampire population. His record breaking list of stunts which included having once ripped the head off Lady Hylton and placed it in bed, one night the husband came to sleep and kissed his wife's forehead only to find it was a dead, severed head. It was that same castle in England that was plagued by Goblins. Apparently, it is said that Jack's work inspired the goblins, so they took the head, stitched it's eyes and it's mouth shut then hung it on the door. The husband was shocked, he stumbled out the window and crashed to his death. Of course there are more notable cases of Jack's work such as the killings as Jack the Ripper that made him famous, but these days he has a taxidermist shop for dead creatures in America and steers clear from most crowds... he has a deep infatuation with corpses and fancies spending his time accordingly. If one did see him, his signature clothes was a cap that says: 'You little ripper!' As well as an open, black long waist coat. Underneath he wore a black shirt and grey pants. He had a skull tattoo on his neck.

Lucien angrily pointed out: 'That cap of yours... where on earth did you get that shabby thing?!'

Jack smiled a toothy grin and said: 'But your royal high-ness, I acquired it here in Australia during my vacation...though I must say... the sunshine here is quite unpredictable....don't you get the Australian phrase; you little ripper?'

Lucien gaped at him in disgust.

Lucien asked him plainly: 'What are you doing in the underworld?'

Jack joked: 'I was invited.'

Lucien frowned at him.

Jack explained: 'Oh well it's simple really...someone who turned me into a vampire, who turned them and that person turned them and that person before them and them and them...'

Vlad stated with a hint of annoyance: 'We are aware of how sire lines work, Jack the Ripper.'

Jack said: 'But yes surely enough all of you do understand...bottom line is, the one, the originator of my blood sire's sire line dropped by my business and paid me a rather unexpected visit... I didn't even know that this man was aware that my vampire lineage had descended from him, I believe his name was ah hmmm it was Cy-'

Lucien cut him off: 'Cyrus Sethius?'

Jack replied eagerly: 'Yes something like that... that means I am descended of a vampire ancestor and of a Nosferatu...how miraculous!'

Siegfried said: 'Our old rival is planning something...let's just admit it...he's never up to anything good.'

Vlad argued: 'So that is why he was not here today...considering his intertwined past with Brynhild, I'd say he's in on the game with Rumpelstiltskin.'

Lucien questioned: 'Jack, what did he want from you?'

Jack explained: 'Well just as the Mckinley family specialise in delivering herbal goods world wide to witches, I specialise in bringing deathly objects to deathly people... such as boggart boxes to trap boggarts, dried skeleton parts for ancient or powerful grimoires as such this man propositioned me to build a huge wooden door for him using elm wood.'

Lucien said in an astounded voice: 'Elm wood...of the same trees that fairies have in their forests, the same trees that store pixie dust, or fairy dust underneath from where they grow... how would Cyrus get his hands on Elm wood and why?'

Jack said: 'He mentioned the need to lock someone away, I believe Elm wood has the ability to completely dispel magic... but I didn't get why he needed a door for that.'

Lucien said: 'To build a permanent portal... depending on the doors effects depends on what happens to the people who enter or exit through it...but he needs to lock someone away... Jack, can you recall any other details of this door?'

Jack thought hard then answered: 'Yes there were two symbols I had to burn into the wood, I think it was two old ancient rune symbols, one was a death rune that was used by certain Germanic tribes as for the other it was an old Scandinavian symbol for misery.'

Lucien remarked: 'The mark of the Sisterhood, those two symbols combined...Cyrus knew about that so he is working with the Sisterhood...or what is left of it.'

Siegfried replied: 'Gothel's talisman, the one I used to turn Brynhild to stone, it had those very symbols on it.'

Vlad asked Lucien: 'Where are you keeping the talisman these days, Lucien?'

Lucien said: 'In the Archaium...but Rumpelstiltskin boasted he had helped certain people get a talisman back...perhaps it is the actual talisman which means that everything that Rumpelstiltskin said is true...it also means that there is a traitor amongst the agents of the Hidden Empire.'

Jack cracked his knuckles and said: 'Beats me who is a traitor and who isn't, I want my payment for my valuable information.'

Lucien scowled: 'Why you rotten little...'

Lucien flung some magic energy at Jack. It brushed Jack's face but shot past him.

Jack laughed loudly.

Lucien said: 'You will wait and see...I decide whether you will be paid handsomely or be silenced forever....now bow down in silence and get out of my sight!'

Jack bickered: 'I didn't have to tell you all that...you will hear again of me soon...very soon!'

He shot out the large open doorway using vampiric speed.

Lucien grumbled: 'The next Rumpelstiltskin... better ready a cell in the asylum with Jack's name on it.'

Lucien glanced at a clock that had been floating at the end of the room.

He said: 'I believe the two of you have personal errands to run... I am not going to ask as to what due to Hidden Empire confidentiality... I just hope the stone fragments are still in safe keeping at the purgatories.'

Siegfried muttered: 'Now that was one pointless gathering and for what... to celebrate the fall of Brynhild...yet it still feels as though that happened ages ago.'

Lucien smiled and said: 'That it was indeed.'

Lucien got up from his seat and showed his two guests the way out.

Vlad said as they went out the doorway: 'Lucien, this is farewell, for now... let us know if something bad resurfaces.'

Lucien replied: 'Yes I will, however I need the two of you to do me a favour.'

Vlad and Siegfried exchanged looks with one another.

Siegfried said: 'Well I am no demon so I am not under your jurisdiction but if you need my help what do you need me to do?'

Lucien explained: 'I need the two of you to use your connections to warn those around you...'

He faced Vlad and explained: 'I need you to warn all the vampires that you know...since you are so well known of in the vampire community, I do not believe there to be any issues whatsoever, this is to be wary of people called the Sisterhood.'

He faced Siegfried and explained: 'I need you to also warn your people Siegfried, you should contact all the wolf packs or groups you know and warn them of potential coming hardships.'

Vlad said: 'It shall be done.'

Lucien waved after them and murmured: 'Good, I'm counting on the two of you.'

Meanwhile in the Archaium:

Oliver was showing Freya around the giant library. Freya's eyes darted from one shelf to the other, every surface in this big room was chocked full of curiosities and wonders. She spotted insects flying about that had similarities to fire flies. One landed on Freya's nose.

She asked Oliver: 'What are these?'

Oliver laughed and shooed away the insect.

He said: 'Emberflies, they light up the place when it gets dark...it is said that once the first demons set foot in the underworld, in a place they could call their own. They started to cry embers instead of tears and so the emberflies were born.'

Freya muttered: 'What an unusual story.'

She noticed though that the bugs did light up embers of fire instead of small glowing lights. On the walls, there were velvet tapestries hanging here and there. They seemed to have a story woven into the fabric.

Oliver explained: 'Those tapestries are very old fashioned, I told Lucien that they are off putting but he didn't want to listen.'

Freya pointed up at a woman that was depicted on the tapestry. The woman led a hoard of people towards a body of light.

She asked: 'Who is she?'

Oliver said: 'The saviour, she who ended the final wrath of the Sisterhood and led the first zombie kind to the light, all existing zombies worship her these days... Lucien knew her, a long time ago but he hates to speak of her.'

There came a vibrating sound from above them. Freya gasped. She gazed upon a long array of glowing white vines that stretched across the whole ceiling of the Archaium.

She asked him: 'And that, what on earth is that stuff?'

Oliver answered: 'Nether wart, if collated and put together into a plant formed into long vines, can produce energy here in the underworld, it was originally a foreign plant to the underworld and only grew in the spirit realm, it was introduced into the underworld to help produce a special type of energy that the demons utilise as electricity, because the underworld exists underneath the human world, (the Hidden Empire's Headquarters is exactly located underneath Australia), there is present magnetic energy coming from the earth's core which is why we cannot use magnetite here in the underworld, otherwise there would be way too much conflicting energies, I am aware that in Hallow Valley, Magnetite, the harnessed stone is used to relay energy from that powerful obelisk... I hear it is one of a kind and that other safe havens for mythical creatures have used that invention to follow in Hallow Valley's foot steps.'

Oliver added: 'Well I suppose our entertaining party ends here...I've shown you the Archaium, Freya what do you think of it?'

Freya said: 'It is amazing...you say that all of the books and records of the entire history of demon kind are kept here, so Aisha, your mentor that taught you everything you know is the librarian here, I guess she must protect this place with her life.'

Oliver replied: 'Yes she does, we've never had any break ins before and it's good that way, there's not only precious books here or preserved spells just like the OGR (Order of the Grim Reaper) have in their possession, the Hidden Empire keeps ancient relics trapped away here in a sturdy, robust and hidden vault, even Aisha doesn't know how to open it, the only person that does know is the Demon King.'

Oliver heard someone tearing through a pile of old books. The books were frantically tossed aside.

Oliver pushed Freya away and shouted: 'Who's there?!'

At the raised voice, the unknown person stopped at once and came out from the shadows.
Oliver frowned at whom he saw.

He said in a confused tone: 'Aisha, what are you doing... why are you destroying everything in here?'

The woman was annoyed but still she needed to play along to convince them that she was Aisha.

She scratched her forehead and said: 'Oh silly me, I must have forgotten something here earlier.'

Oliver narrowed his eyes at her and said: 'You aren't Aisha, you are a trespasser, the real Aisha knew this entire place like the back of her hand, she wouldn't knock over book shelves in search for something.'
The fake Aisha dramatically said: 'Fiiiiiiine, you figured it out, yay to you Oliver Lothbrok sorry to disappoint you, but I have already found what I need to awaken Imperare...I was just looking for a certain spell book but that is not here.'

Oliver asked with a hint of confidence: 'Do you mean the book of light...it is not a spell book but a book of prophecies, it has been rumoured to have been around for a long time, hidden in human civilisations, even the most ancient ones.'

The fake Aisha grinned: 'I assumed that would be the case, Rumpelstiltskin's clues as to where the book was were rather ridiculous, now the Sisterhood just takes Rumpelstiltskin for a complete fool, just because his favourite phrase was; 'the book of light will show the way', doesn't mean that he knew where it was located.'

Freya snapped; she asked the woman: 'What did you just say... did you say the book of light will show the way?!'

The fake Aisha laughed menacingly.

She replied: 'Yes Freya Lothbrok, but it does not concern you or me, the only thing that matters is the will of Imperare and the day of final judgement... this time the world shall not be destroyed nor grinded to dust, there shall be no oblivion but divine dominion...the Red Blood Queen shall find her way without the book of prophecies....let me guess... Rumpelstiltskin sent a broadcasted message to Hallow Valley, revealing the things regarding the World Hunt Organisation and the Sisterhood... he had planned revenge on us before he was captured by Hidden Empire officials.'

318

The fake Aisha form seemed to crumble away, revealing who it actually had been underneath the facade.

The woman smiled and said: 'Oh and the Oracle bode me to pass on a message for her to two strangers; that the message, let the games begin was sent personally by her... to all safe havens... you were not the only ones to receive a burning message at Hallow Valley... yes the Sisterhood is working with the Oracle...soon enough, all hunters will bow down to her power and all entities of the universe, their souls will belong to our leader once she has awakened....the virus was mere fore play.'

Freya muttered: 'But that means Lord Gruesome's virus was never meant to mutate... you people are working with the Oracle and Rumpelstiltskin told you all about Lord Gruesome's plans so you sent someone to meddle with the lab samples.'

The woman corrected them: 'Half way correct, actually though, after Lord Gruesome's virus was released and the Sisterhood was told about that man's plans, we used that to our advantage and helped spread the first strain of the virus before we decided to mutate it behind Lord Gruesome's back.'

Oliver demanded to know: 'Why would anyone want to spread a virus at the expense of other's lives... what kind of cruel people would find it in their hearts to do such an ill purposed thing?!'

The woman said: 'The people of the Sisterhood did it to stall for time...to come up with a distraction so that the Hidden Empire and the OGR would be focused on the virus instead, it gave us the time we needed to secretly retrieve the people we needed and the components.'

She waved to them and replied: 'There, that is the message I was supposed to relay, good luck with trying to stop the Sisterhood... farewell.'

She was about to teleport away when she froze on the spot as someone shouted: 'Stop right there Helene!'

She blasted a gigantic fire ball at them. Oliver stepped in front of Freya and activated a type of force field in front of him. The magic fire ball collided with the shield and disappeared.

Helene snickered.

She said: 'Ah so your vampiric ability is to dispel and block physical or magic based attacks... not bad.'

Oliver said: 'I can also regulate how much power someone else's attack has or weaken it...you are not getting out here alive.'

A man behind them shouted: 'Wait, I brought help to stop her!'

Oliver flung a charged spell at her. Strange symbols surrounded Helene. She tried to summon forth magic but failed.

She asked him: 'What is this spell you did?'

Oliver boasted: 'A disarming spell that prevents you from practising magic for a short period of time, you haven't heard of the spell before because I created it, it still needs refining though.'

Freya bolted towards the witch and twisted her arm. Helene only laughed at the pain. Freya noticed the grin on Helene's face. A brief moment of flinching because she let her guard down, Helene threw Freya across the entire room and sent her plummeting head first into a shelf.

Helene pounded the floor with her foot, the floor began to tremble.

She said: 'So Max, you came to aid your allies, you broke free of the unrelenting force but know this, from here on, your efforts are futile.'

Maximillian Tillman said: 'Not exactly.'

Two men emerged from behind Oliver and Max.

One stretched his arms and the other said: 'This better be interesting if you dragged us all the way back here.'

The other man said: 'Well obviously it is of importance if there is a witch of the Sisterhood here, Vlad.'

Vlad glared at Max and said: 'Why didn't you say there was someone dangerous, I could have gotten here in no time using my mist form.'

Max said: 'I did but the two of you didn't take me seriously.'

Freya angrily stood up from the crash site and pulled out a long, wooden piece of bookshelf from her arm.

Helene observed the situation and said before disappearing: 'Interesting gathering here, yet I thought most of the invited people had already left, but to cut to the chase, I am not the one you people shall fight.'

She broke free of Oliver's spell.

She lit up the surface of the floor in front of her using magic and a huge, revolting creature climbed out of the light. It was a lumbering, human like beast that had two large tusks extending from it's face. It had one huge, slimy, disgusting eye that gaped at everyone else, the mere sight of it's squishy eye lid made Oliver and Freya's skin tingle in disgust. It wore fur for apparel.

Helene's laugh echoed in the room even after she disappeared.

Siegfried said: 'Now this will be fun.'

Freya shouted: 'Move now!'

And pulled her brother away from the wrath of the delusional, disoriented creature.

The tall towering, mean looking creature swinged it's hands about rather frantically, trying to smack the 'little creatures' flat.

Max muttered as he sought shelter by a table: 'Definition of madness, this despicable thing seems to love a good shot at whackamole.'

Crash, boom, bang, thud. The whole room seemed to shake and shiver.

Freya's eyes turned black.

She said with a hint of sarcasm: 'If I was so **MUCH** taller then I'd clobber that thing!'

Oliver rolled his eyes; he remarked: 'Silly sister, always taking the 'throw the punch' approach instead of coming up with a plan...how's this for a plan, maybe wear stilts, than you'd be half as tall perhaps.'

Freya scoffed: 'Ha ha, very funny, so what's your plan then... you do know that it's a huge Cyclops that is putting the entire place in disrepair... so much for this archive of history soon to be in shambles... I could have sworn to have seen a Cyclops before in one of FOG's educational books.'

Oliver said: 'Yes a plan... well I didn't count on a Cyclops being here but Aisha would grow furious with me if I didn't protect this place.'

The Cyclops pounded the table that Freya and Oliver had been hiding underneath. It had been crushed to bits. Oliver and Freya got away in time using their vampiric speed.

Oliver realised something important, Freya knew important information regarding the truth about the virus, it was crucial for her to get out of here alive. He summoned a random portal which he knew would lead to Hallow Valley. Freya was pulled towards it.

Oliver shouted to his sister: 'Go back to Hallow Valley and tell your friends what you have found out...that is more important right now...go help FOG warn the other safe havens, spread word.'

Freya remembered that she had given the scroll to him earlier, even though that was the case, she wanted to stay and help him fight.

Oliver sneered: 'You leave me no choice Freya...'

Freya battled against the fluctuating, turbulent wind gusts that Oliver sent toward her to force her into the portal. She pressed her feet hard onto the ground and resisted the wind force as it began to slowly slash her face bit by bit.

Freya shouted at him: 'You are never getting rid of me ever again!'

She looked him in the eye and proclaimed: 'Because you are my brother, viking or no viking, we fight together and go into battle together...because that's what a family like us does, we stick to each other even if the other sibling is royally pissed off by a Cyclops and is a total stubborn douche bag!'

Oliver ceased his magic and said: 'Fine but I hold you to your exact words.'

The consuming portal closed rapidly. Freya sighed in relief till she heard the Cyclops' roar boom loudly. Due to Freya's heightened sense of hearing, it nearly ruptured her ear drums. Freya shouted.

Max interrupted them: 'Sorry but the Cyclops is still there...do we have to kill it, isn't there a way to get rid of it or save it?'

Max remembered all the other creatures he had helped save in the past, he didn't want to see this Cyclops dead, even if he had nearly crushed them all to small smithereens.

Oliver noticed that there was a type of sigil burned onto the shoulder of the creature.

He said to Max: 'There is a way but we need the full co-operation of those two fellow men for this is no normal Cyclops... there is no Cyclops species that has immunity to magic based attacks... my magic won't do much to take down this creature anyway...and opening a portal to send it away could sent it to somewhere, where it will cause mayhem.'

Max asked whilst the tantrum throwing creature was distracted with the emberflies that it tried to swat dead: 'How do you know it is immune to magic based attacks... have you even tried to use your magic against it?'

Oliver explained: 'The mark that the Cyclops has etched onto it's body is artificial, it was planted there, meaning this creature is still under the influence of the witch, but removing it from it's body won't work in any way, it is a sigil, also known as witches poison, a mark that is placed onto a surface, whatever the mark stands for, whatever the effects it does to something or someone, by now the poison has spread to most of the body, that sigil is not normal it is unlike anything I've ever seen before from my studies under Aisha in the past, but something is a bit familiar about that mark, it has slight similarities to a sigil that gives the user magic immunity.'

Vlad asked him with hint of annoyance: 'And you think that means it will be immune to magic based attacks because of your knowledge?'

Siegfried elbow nudged Vlad and said to the others: 'We shall help.'

Max stared at the werewolf that was Siegfried that stood next to him.

Max replied: 'Well you transformed quickly.'

Vlad asked: 'Siegfried, is this necessary, aren't you just as powerful without your wolf form?'

The wolf spoke telepathically to Vlad: 'It's been a while since I've even wanted the opportunity like this, so let me have my fun.'

Max said: 'So we're doing it this way... okay.'

With a simple movement, Max transformed into his true vampshee form. He transformed into a shadowy dark figure with grey/beige skin and black eyes.

Vlad shouted out for all to hear: 'Here comes our one of a kind Vampshee (Vampire-Banshee Hybrid) sidekick.'

Max screeched loudly. A type of special vibrating energy dispersed throughout the room. It reached the Cyclops. The Cyclops bellowed in pain. An entire arm fell off the Cyclops' body and crashed to the floor below.

Max said in a static abnormal voice: 'A banshee's mastered cry is strong enough to even shatter some human bones.'

Vlad teased Siegfried: 'Now what are you waiting for... go fetch!'

The wolf grunted and spoke telepathically to Vlad: 'Don't patronise me.'

The wolf suddenly became invisible. Max became startled.

He said: 'Wait, where did he go?'

Vlad said: 'Being lazy or shying away from battle are we?'

Siegfried said: 'Well join in Vlad, don't be lazy yourself.'

Vlad crossed his arms and said: 'Alright but nothing flashy.....but a bit more fun is called for.'

He disappeared.

Max rose up toward the Cyclops, floating just above it's hand. The Cyclops was now paying attention to Max.

Max said: 'Mind oblivion, my vampiric power that shuts off all functions of the brain, rendering all actions completely useless.'

Freya saw Max create magic pulses from his palm that the Cyclops was exposed to.

Freya grumbled and came to the following realisation: 'That's really not fair, out of all vampires, my power is the most pathetic, I have extreme strength, he can use some power of confusion, that's much better if you ask me!'

Oliver said: 'That's it Freya, you use your power to sweep the Cyclops off it's feet!'

Freya said: 'I can't do that, my vampiric strength isn't that powerful!'

Oliver winked at her, smiled and said: 'It is if you believe in it.'

Freya frowned in the realisation that her brother wanted her to commit to the impossible.

She said: 'Fine but you use your ability to increase my attack power, just in case.'

He said sarcastically: 'Okay.'

She stormed towards the feet of the tall creature and used all her might to heave the feet upwards so the creature would stumble backwards. She felt the sweat on her forehead, but to her amazement, the Cyclops toppled right over.

Oliver raised his hands upwards and concentrated his mind. He imagined a type of wind flow from his fingers, wind that could not be seen nor really felt. A wind that carried power to boost others power, and he could alter that effect using this power of his.

The wolf's (Siegfried's) eyes lit up and from this, a strange beaming source of bright light pierced into the body of the Cyclops, immediately slicing the body into separate halves. The two halves falling onto the Archaium floor.

Vlad laughed and said: 'You just don't want to give up do you?!'

Max yelled at the other two: 'Just put the creature out of it's misery already!'

The wolf spoke in Vlad's mind: 'Aright then, let's end this quickly Vlad.'

Vlad appeared, drifting over the Cyclops and said: 'With pleasure.'

A magical shadowy dome suddenly appeared over the Cyclops. A sound of a loud blast was to be heard.

The body parts or the two halves of the Cyclops that had lain on the Archaium floor, miraculously and eerily glued themselves back together again. Now the Cyclops stood itself upright, then suddenly the hand of the Cyclops was visible and cracked the surface of the shadow dome.

Now the Cyclops was free of the dome that had imprisoned it. The Cyclops should by now have been a ton of sand, but it was quite the opposite.

Oliver exclaimed in shock: 'No, it i-it can't be possible!'

Freya asked with a slightly puzzled expression: 'What shouldn't be possible?!'

Oliver said: 'That ability that Vlad just demonstrated is called taker of life, when used on anyone, that person or creature has their life force completely drained...all that is left of the body is sand... there are no known cases of anyone having ever survived taker of life.'

Freya acknowledged the exact horror of the situation they were in now.

Vlad used his mist form to appear next to Siegfried.

The wolf asked telepathically: 'What happened to you, you look terrible?'

Vlad huffed and said: 'Don't remind me... it's just good that I am a hybrid, my wounds heal far more quickly than other vampires.'

He of course referred to scratches on his face and wounds that looked gnarly, even for a vampire.

Freya thought about what next approach they could take. The entrance to the library was sealed off due to crushed walls or broken furniture that was heaped in front of it. Most people had left by now... what was the chance of anyone finding them or hearing them?

Oliver remembered earlier that the Cyclops had been irritated by the emberflies but why?

Max had tried to use mind oblivion again but was attacked by the Cyclops every time before he even had a second to try to use it.

Max drifted down next to Oliver.

He said: 'Sorry Freya, there's nothing I can do regarding my hypnosis ability... what are we going to do?'

Oliver said: 'It's not possible to teleport in or out of this room, it was built that way to keep impostors out, yet that witch managed to do it... how?'

Whilst Freya and Oliver were debating what to do next, Siegfried and Vlad managed to move the Cyclops to a corner of the room, where it was preoccupied with smashing the emberflies that were flying about.

Freya remembered something FOG had once told her:

It was one day that FOG was organising his books when he blurted out random fun facts of mythical creatures that he had written in his books.

He said: 'Freya, did you know that the Cyclops hate fire, the sight of too much fire can cause blindness in Cyclops... it is also mentioned in the old story regarding the Greek hero Odysseus where he and his men use a burning stake to cause blindness in the eye of the Cyclops.'

Flash back ended.

Freya said to Oliver: 'Oliver... Cyclops hate fire, it's lethal to them!'

Oliver smiled brightly at Freya: 'Yes that's why the Cyclops is always distracted by the emberflies, because they generate fire... Freya, you're a genius!'

Freya said: 'Well FOG is a genius.'

Oliver: 'Never mind that... we know it's weakness now.'

The wolf who had been standing next to Vlad now tried to attack the Cyclops. It created a red spinning orb that extended lines that moved like a whip which slashed the Cyclops repeatedly, upon this, the Cyclops began to scream. Oliver took the opportunity to create a trap for the creature. A spinning fire vortex consumed the Cyclops.

The Cyclops bellowed in pain and it's body fell apart and crashed to the floor.

Oliver said: 'It may not be killed by that spell but it will burn the Cyclops if it tries to place it's body back together again.'

Oliver saw stitches everywhere on the body of the Cyclops.

He ran his hand through his hair and sighed.

Freya asked: 'What's wrong now?'

Oliver said: 'I thought before that there was something unusual about the Cyclops, I was right... it is a Zyclops...a zombie Cyclops.'

Freya: 'Zombie Cyclops.... Sounds very normal sure.'

Grey smoke rose from the body and faded away.

Oliver explained: 'As we all know, zombies are created by using necromancy and a corpse of a creature or human, depending on what the corpse was, depends on what type of zombie it is once the body is awakened and all zombies have the same type of aura, a deathly aura... the reason we couldn't sense the aura of this beast is because the witch had placed a type of cloaking spell, a special one that prevented the beast's aura from being released in any way... also it made it look like a normal creature, it hid the stitches of it's body as well.'

Max asked Oliver in confusion: 'Yes but that doesn't explain why it just won't die?'

Oliver tilted his head and replied to him: 'In that case it would probably be some type of body binding spell... which binds the soul to the body, preventing it from leaving the body... if ones soul cannot leave ones body, it cannot die or be drained which explains why Vlad's ability, taker of life did not work, body binding spells are what heretic witches are known for... as well as the spells they use when it comes to turning their fellow witches into vampires...'

Oliver ended his sentence and glanced at Max.

Max answered in a bothered manner: 'Yes, one of the heretic witches was the one that is responsible for me being a vampire.'

Freya asked: 'What was her name?'

Max answered: 'Helene... I knew her a long time ago, I thought she was my friend and well... she wasn't in the end.'

Suddenly, the Cyclops woke up... it was angry... big time.

The Cyclops burnt head spun around to face Freya. It's one eye stared at her.

Freya noticed how fear rose within her. So much so that it was hard to breathe. Freya coughed and wheezed.

Oliver ran to his sister... all of a sudden, time froze in the room... almost...everything moved in slow motion. A red flashing figure appeared out of a black hole behind her and pulled her into it. After that the gap closed and everything moved normally again... time had been restored.

Oliver ran to the empty space where his sister had stood before she disappeared.

He shouted: 'Freya!'

Meanwhile in Hallow Valley:

Freya fell onto what seemed to be a grassy floor. She was unconscious. Someone turned her round and spoke to her.

The person said: 'Please forgive me Freya...in time you will understand why I took you away from there...things would have gotten far more dangerous for you...I will go and see how your brother is faring... that Cyclops was using it's death stare on you...which could have rendered you in a permanent coma if I hadn't interfered.'

Ontari who had been cleaning the gear on her motorbike nearby, saw a woman on the grass in the distance that looked like Freya.

Ontari felt something amiss. There was a strange pull to an aura that she could not recognise. During her upbringing as a huntress, she was trained in sensing the different type of auras. This aura to her spoke the word 'werewolf'.

Ontari ran toward the woman shouting: 'Freya... you there, you get away from her!'

Ontari saw a normal looking man stand there... but still... she lunged at him, pulling out her keystone dagger.

The man dodged the quick attack and said: 'Wait... you are mistaking me for an enemy.'

Ontari muttered something in another language.

She then added: 'Am I really... are my eyes so blind and ensnaring towards myself, that I would not be able to tell what is reality...then I shall demonstrate my ability to peel the lies away.'

She leaned out of the way and pierced the dagger into his hand. He shook his head in disappointment. He disappeared and re-appeared behind her.

He murmured: 'You tell Fane, that the mirror Josephine has is evil...and to keep a close eye on his family...these are slowly becoming dangerous times.'

Ontari turned around in a startled manner. Ontari realised there was no blood on the dagger... who was this man? She asked herself.

Ontari went to the nearest place where she could get help immediately. FOG's hut. Glowing lights floated about everywhere in Hallow valley as it was still night time. Apparently as Ontari understood it, Josephine, FOG and the others came up with the idea to harness the energy of the resident willow wisps... the lights always appear when it gets dark in Hallow valley as a light source.

Ontari heaved Freya all the way to FOG's hut. She then pounded furiously on the door.

FOG yelled: 'Gaaaaaaaaaaaaaaaaaaaaaaaaaaah!'

He bolted upright on the couch.

He stammered: 'Who-who's there?!'

Ontari said behind the door: 'It's me, Ontari, I need your help, now would be great... I've got an unconscious Freya here.'

FOG shook his head in the effort to wake himself up. He yawned and remembered the nightmare he had, it was where FOG was trapped in a maze that had no end and he was chased by a revolting, drooling grandfather clock monster that kept making this cookoo-cookoo sound which drove FOG insane. Above the maze there resided the evil giant Aya that laughed at him from above, mocking him.

She had joked: 'My you're running away from the clock like it's clock work!'

FOG who was suddenly dressed in a clown suit pleaded: 'Aya, get me out of here please!'

A small black cat and a dog appeared next to Aya. They all laughed together, it was a loud choir of laughter.

FOG clamoured at the wall. He asked himself if the small cat had been Cleo and the dog had been Fane?

FOG jerked his face to see the clock monster approach him; he screeched: 'No!'

The grandfather clock bashed itself into the clown.

Aya mocked him: 'Hey, what's the time old man?'

Dream reflection ended.

FOG shifted his quilt blanket to the side. His sleeping cap that had a puff ball at the end slipped off his head. FOG crashed to the floor after tripping over his slippers. Ontari heard a loud *thud* from inside.

Suddenly a loud trumpet was played inside the hut.

Aya switched on the light switch and said: 'Hey couch potato, I said what's the time old man, I meant to say IT'S TIME TO WAKE THE HELL UP!'

FOG sat on the floor in his sleep apparel with this grouchy look that made you think it might just droop to the ground.

Aya whispered: 'There's an emergency FOG... and um Ontari needs help outside.'

Ontari kicked open the door and FOG saw the unconscious Freya. FOG rushed to aid a friend in need.

Aya cleared out space to lie down Freya. She watched FOG as he placed a hand on Freya's fore head.

Aya asked: 'Can vampires get sick?'

331

FOG replied: 'No... not like mortals do, though vampires aren't invincible and have numerous weaknesses.'

He questioned Ontari: 'Where did you find Freya?'

Ontari said: 'At the outskirts of Hallow valley, she was lying there unconscious and this weird guy stood above her... just staring at her...he had a were-wolf like aura but he had some awfully strange abilities if he was one... his power seemed to be the ability to shift or slow down time.'

Aya reminded FOG: 'Hey wasn't she supposed to be at some fancy demon gathering?'

FOG said: 'Yes Aya, now that you mention it... she was at some secret gathering in the underworld...supposedly with her brother, Oliver... but if Freya came back like this... that means something went seriously wrong there.'

Aya noted: 'Well, we haven't heard anything yet so the demons hopefully have the situation under control.'

FOG replied whilst calming down at Aya's statement: 'Yes, I agree, safe havens are always the first to be notified if something is wrong.'

Suddenly, FOG noticed something reveal itself, visible from Freya's eye lid, her eye seemed pale.

FOG opened her eye lid and remarked: 'We're dealing with something bad here... the effects of a cyclops' death stare.'

Finally, there was more evident feelings of worry shown in Aya's expression.

Aya said with a hint of worry: 'If she doesn't wake up...I'll never get to tell her the new jokes I've kept secret just for her....'

Aya scrunched her face and smiled slightly, she said: 'No, she simply has to wake up... I won't give up on you my some what of a friend...I'm going to stick around till the end...'

She smirked at FOG and said: 'So FOG, whatever we need to get her back to health in no time... you name it and I'll help.'

FOG gulped and said: 'Well that's the problem... not much can reverse the effects of it... the most powerful healing object known to mythical creatures is the medicine or essence of a phoenix...but phoenixes are

332

incredibly rare and there is not one single one living in Hallow Valley at the moment...unless if I drew the damaged aura out of Freya... but that could maybe put me in a sleep instead.'

He muttered to himself: 'But the eye of the Cyclops was often told to have the power of premonitions, not to place people in a coma... only the most powerful or most ancient Cyclops had the death stare ability and they were rumoured to be extinct for centuries.'

Ontari sighed angrily and said: 'Look... I now this is going to sound severe but... if she doesn't wake up, I will end up putting a bullet or my dagger into someone's head and I mean it... I'm dead serious.'

She reminisced on the time Freya had saved her multiple times in the past for her own slip ups. After the death of her grandfather and the untimely, eventual demise of her grandmother due to cancer, Ontari had gone to a dark place. She still believed that she owed Freya a life time repaying debts for as much as she could in her mortal life.

FOG said: 'I understand how you feel but we have to concentrate right now, Ontari.'

Ontari nodded and left the hut, closing the door behind her.

FOG said: 'Hmm, what if the magic of an elven being could heal Freya... that's it... it's the quickest way to save Freya.'

Abruptly, someone bolted into the room and shouted: 'Freya!'

Meanwhile:

In the underworld, after Freya mysteriously disappeared:

Max, Oliver, Vlad and Siegfried tried to avoid the death rays that the Cyclops' eye sent after them. When out of no where, all of the heaps and tons of rubble that had been blocking the door out of the Archaium, was magically flung past Oliver.

Out of the rubble debris, emerged a very enthusiastic and cheesy fire demon called Hades.

He yelled: 'Yeah another party...sign me up!'

Lucien covered his face in annoyance and said: 'Idiot.'

Oliver was shocked at how optimistic Hades was but so much so that it already seemed ridiculous.

Hades turned into a big, fat, round, bulky fire ball and hurled himself at the Cyclops' head.

A voice shouted: 'YOU'RE TOAST!'

After the useless attack that just left the monster's head with first degree burns, Hades stood in front of it in confusion. But launched another attack that consisted out of a huge fiery fist.

He shouted: 'Taste my fury.... CRASH AND BURN you stupid brute!'

Lucien raised his hand towards the Cyclops and undid some spell, then he drew the life force out of the Cyclops, afterwards leaving only a small pile of pathetic, puny brittle bones.

Vlad clapped his hands sarcastically. Lucien glared angrily at Siegfried (Human form) and Vlad who made fun of Lucien's rather corny but effective performance. Behind Lucien a strange creature with dark, rugged, black, slightly scaly skin and wide outspread wings as well as a thin, angry swishing tail, stomped into the room.

The monster rasped: 'Where is that bitch!?'

Oliver stammered: 'Ai-Aisha is that you?'

She placed her hands on her hips and said: 'Of course it's me, Aisha Gregory, who else am I supposed to be?'

Oliver smiled awkwardly at her and replied: 'So that witch pretended to be you.'

Aisha explained: 'Yes, she knocked me unconscious and made me disappear into a musty old closet here in the void... after a while I woke up as this, my true succubus form that I normally revert to when I am in a weakened state or when I transition to a younger age...as soon as I noticed something was wrong, I got Lucien and the useless Hades to follow me here.'

She flicked dust off her rough skin and added: 'And good thing I did before it had killed all of you, that creature, though that bitch, no I mean that witch is going to receive a thrashing if I get my furious hands on her.'

334

She huffed angrily. Poor Aisha, she stood there in ripped and torn clothes in her true succubus form. Oliver remembered how his sister had disappeared without a trace.

Lucien who could sense Oliver's unease said: 'I understand your worry, go look for whomever is the cause of your distress and do me a favour, notify the delegation of safe havens immediately.'

Oliver nodded quickly at Lucien and hurried off into a demon door he had summoned. Oliver didn't want to risk using a portal to Hallow Valley himself, so he decided to use a demon door instead due to the fact that their magic substance cannot be traced or located by a witch. Oliver had this hunch that his sister simply had to be in Hallow Valley. Max wanted to follow after Oliver but was stopped by Lucien.

Lucien said in an earnest voice: 'Maximillian Tillman, you and I have to talk... regarding that Medusa friend of yours.'

Hades joked: 'Oh no, what did Medusa do now...upset another person aside from Athena... wait does Athena even exist?!'

Lucien gave Hades a sharp, angry glare which made Hades shut up.

An ember fly landed on Aisha's finger. It seemed to buzz in a strange language. Aisha was stricken with fear after she had heard what the insect had said to her. In the underworld, demons could use emberflies to send messages to others.

Aisha said to Lucien: 'Sir, sorry to interrupt but there is an urgent message regarding the underwater purgatories... it has been said that the demons guarding the structures have just disappeared and that no stone remnants of Brynhild were found.'

She asked him: 'Was the main stone structure in the underworld moved elsewhere recently because the demon agents have also reported it missing.'

Lucien's eye brows twitched as he said: 'No, it was the Sisterhood, they've been planning this all along and I just played along unknowingly and blind...as always... Brynhild and her band of fanatics are always one step ahead of us...dammit!'

Lucien vented in anger. Large, far extending cracks appeared on the floor.

Max said with hesitation: 'Ahem, maybe we should just calm down now...'

Lucien straightened himself and scolded himself: 'Yes, I should not be overthinking things or making things more concerning than they are.'

Max shrugged his shoulders and replied in the most positive way: 'Look on the bright side...um well I don't know if um there even is a, well um a bright side to this obvious room calamity.'

Lucien sneered whilst someone else smiled sarcastically in the background; he said: 'The good thing is that this room is a replica.'

Lucien did a mysterious swaying motion with his hand and the whole room as everyone saw it seemed to disappear. Virtually it looked like the same room that had been there before... peacefully untouched.

Lucien explained: 'A while back, I feared this room, the Archaium that bares witness to the records of all of the history of the demon kind, would suffer some catastrophe... my gut feeling was right so I had a special type of cloaking spell conceal the room, a special one that actually hid the real room and created a replica of the original.'

He argued: 'But that witch still managed to open the vault.'

Max was in disbelief. He had doubted it for something like this to be even possible.

Max remarked to Lucien: 'Wow you re-vamped the place!'

Someone in the background now had a twisted smirk on their face.

Lucien asked Siegfried with brisk frustration: 'Wipe that smirk off your face...what is so humorous?'

Siegfried explained: 'Well first the 'look on the bright side' phrase coming from someone who is part vampire then the second phrase 'you re-vamped the place'... they are incredibly cringe worthy...no offence to the man who said all that.'

Max gloated: 'None taken...not many people take me seriously nowadays anyway.'

Lucien turned to speak to Max to continue their conversation on Medusa. Whilst Aisha led Vlad and Siegfried out of the Archaium.

Max asked Lucien in a sudden, startled outcry: 'She's what?!'

Lucien replied: 'Medusa was last seen a month ago... after that she vanished from the eyes of all her friends... now you tell me you had no recent correspondence with her... that leaves me to think...and not a good thought either.'

Max replied in a low tone: 'I knew that Medusa was harbouring some sort of pain and as much as I am her friend too, it's wildly hard to admit that even I didn't notice just how distant she was.'

Lucien said: 'Very suspicious... people disappearing... some people don't show up like Cyrus for example...former witches from the Sisterhood break in to steal something, Brynhild's remnant's just are gone... Jack Bartlett reports the build of a strange door that was commissioned by Cyrus himself...and the witches and warlocks of the Witches Covenant grow ever more silent by the day...'

Suddenly, a voice cackled in Lucien's mind.

The voice said: 'You're not ready for what is to come... despite the riddle I gave you.'

Lucien remembered the riddle: *'You must look towards the prophecies that were lost to time. Scattered across the continents of the Earth. There lie answers which hold the key to all your problems.'*

The voice added: 'Find the solution before it is too late... the book of light will show the way.'

Lucien shook his head. He knew the voice had been the voice of his mother.

Lucien stormed to the vault. The door had been left ajar. Everything was still there in the vault. Everything except for Brynhild's Actinolite stone... Why did the sisterhood require that stone? Lucien thought to himself.

Back in Hallow Valley:

Oliver had arrived there. He felt Freya's aura nearby and ran towards it. He bolted inside a hut (having no regard for the person that lived there).

He shouted: 'Freya!'

Aya and FOG stared at the person who stood in the doorway.

Aya had a puzzled look on her face; she asked the stranger: 'And you are?'

FOG stood up slowly as he recognised the young man; he said: 'You're Freya's brother... first time in Hallow Valley....well luckily you are half elven, you can use your healing powers to wake up Freya.'

Aya put a pillow under Freya's head. She had a worried expression. Oliver approached Freya and held her hand. A bright, vibrant white light appeared in the palm that held Freya's hand.

Aya chuckled quietly and asked: 'What is that energy?'

Oliver said in a distracted manner: 'I don't know...some people say my elven healing powers has some kind of soothing effect.'

Aya smiled slightly and replied to him: 'Being in the presence of that energy feels like having fidgety butterflies in my stomach...it feels funny.'

Oliver remarked with a hint of amusement: 'That's the funniest description I've ever heard.'

Aya asked him: 'Have I met you before somewhere... you seem familiar somehow.....my name is Aya Himano?'

Oliver said to her: 'Well maybe... my name is Oliver so that's that.'

FOG had a conversation with him whilst Freya was being healed: 'So what happened in the underworld?'

Oliver hesitated a bit in explaining what had happened. He had a troubled look as he did so. Oliver told FOG and Aya of all the horror that had unfolded in the underworld.

Aya asked again trying not to break into laughter: 'Ok, so a huge, ugly Cyclops broke into the demon library because it was summoned by a witch and the witch stole something from the vault and escaped and you destroyed the Cyclops with the help of a vampire... a wolf ancestor and Maximillian Tillman as well as Hades, a succubus and the Demon King...that sounds like one heck of a story there...sheesh I'm glad I wasn't stuck down there with you.'

FOG: 'What's more important is as to how Freya got here.'

Oliver answered: 'During the fight against the Cyclops, Freya was kidnapped by a strange entity.'

Aya noted to both of them: 'Didn't Ontari say she found Freya unconscious in the presence of a man?'

FOG replied: 'Yes she did...'

FOG had a contemplative look.

Oliver mentioned: 'The Demon King ordered me to notify the Safe haven delegation.'

FOG frowned strongly.

He got up and walked to an intriguing looking device that stood on a small table in the back of the room. Which was also where FOG's small office area was.

Oliver glimpsed the object from afar.

He asked with a hint of surprise: 'Is that a PCB control board of the X100 series?'

FOG commended him: 'That's correct... good eye... it's of the mid generation of the PCB devices... PCB stands for paranormal control board... it enables the user to communicate with various locations across the world simultaneously...this is the most effective way to contact other safe havens without breaching the safe, secure and hidden location of our safe haven.'

FOG seated himself. He wiggled back and forth to be comfortable in the chair. FOG retrieved a hand mirror from a drawer that was underneath the table and inserted it into a slot in the device. He tapped on some keys then the main panel that looked like a ouja board, the piece that looked like a magnifying glass, magically danced on the board, back and forth, from letter to letter, from symbol to symbol. FOG picked up a radio that was connected to the device to listen in.

FOG said: 'On record.... I repeat, this is a message for all safe havens... if you have received a message saying in German 'let the games begin' then be warned, listeners discretion, we are being pulled into dark times...'

FOG went on to explain every detail that he and his friends had uncovered so far, what had happened recently in the underworld, the truth about the virus and that there is danger silently brewing within the world hunt organisation as well as that the location of the lab of who created the virus has been discovered but is yet to be found.

Aya said to Oliver: 'I still don't fully get how that thing works... apparently it can receive voice messages via communications and the letter panel translates the message from any language the message was received in, for example, the PCB can even translate from Morse code to English.'

FOG was about finished when a light lit up and the machine beeped. FOG knew that it only meant when a message had been received by his PCB.

Aya ran up to FOG at the table.

She asked hastily: 'There's a message, what is it?'

FOG changed the radio mode to speaker function. So that Aya and Oliver could hear it.

Someone was yelling in panic in Japanese.

FOG saw the magnifying piece squiggle from letter to letter hectically.

Aya said: 'The person is saying that an evil has come upon them in a safe haven in Japan...they managed to evacuate everyone to a shelter but they need help....'

The message was cut short and the machine fell silent.

Suddenly, there was someone screaming outside. It was a loud cry.

Aya ran outside. FOG left the machine and told Oliver to keep healing Freya and to lock the door of the hut. FOG amazingly didn't stumble over his slippers. He put on his gardening boots and dashed outside.

FOG grumbled: 'When this is over... I'm going to need a sleep vacation.'

A flash of darkness tore across the land in Hallow Valley. The wild *clicking* and *clacking* sound of hooves made the land tremble with fear. The trees bent and swayed in consented despair in the wake of the horse man and horse whom only ever acted as if malice or trauma was in their hearts... if they had one. The horse galloped faster, faster than the ferocious forces of wind ever could be, strips of fire were lit underneath the hooves. Others ran from the creature but FOG and Aya did not because when they had noticed the creature heading towards them, it had been too late.

FOG shouted to Aya: 'We have to get back to the hut now!'

Aya replied: 'I know that FOG but the Dullahan is that close to us... how the HELL did it even end up here now in the first place?!'

FOG shook his head.

Aya pulled out an object from her black jacket. FOG frowned at the object she held. It seemed to be a white painted traditional mask with the face of a fox. Aya strapped the mask to the side of her head.

She grinned and said: 'I had hoped I didn't have to use this new power of mine.'

FOG questioned her: 'Ahem... Aya, what is that thing strapped to your head?'

Aya replied whilst not taking her eyes off the Dullahan: 'A while back, Matoko and a friend of hers brought back this mask from a trip in Japan...they said that this mask is to be worn by a Kitsune, they also said that the old woman who ran the antique store claimed that this was the case, anyway they got the mask from her for free. Since this mask has been in my possession I have somewhat learned to harness the true power of the mask.'

FOG said in amazement: 'That's great!'

FOG added though in realisation: 'But how is a mask supposed to help us against this toxic, hell bent creature?'

Aya said: 'Don't worry FOG... all I need you to do is shut up.'

FOG argued: 'I'd drain the spiritual aura of it but there's one problem... I have restraints on my abilities when it comes to draining the energy of spirit beings...'

Aya scowled: 'Shut up you old fart!'

Aya said as the mad creature charged in their direction: 'Chiyoko, Goman no Kamen.'

FOG felt an eerie fear tug at his heart. Aya grabbed FOG's arm in the final moment as the Dullahan's whip struck Aya and FOG.

The Dullahan came to an abrupt standstill as it saw that it's whip had gone straight through them... It was as if Aya and FOG had become ghosts.

Suddenly a black jaguar like cat sprung out and circled around the creature. The wild cat leered angrily at the horse. Thin white smoke slowly billowed out of the nostrils of the horse.

As Aya and FOG appeared again. Aya's hand twitched slightly.

She smiled brashly and said: 'I think it may take a while for me to get a grip on this new power...I shouldn't be too reckless.'

The horse stood up and moved it's front legs furiously mid air. The horse man crazily clutched onto the rein of the horse. Aya moved her hands in a circular formation as if to reel in shadows around her. Apparently, Aya required only little light to use her powers. Then she used both of her palms to discharge the shadows at the Dullahan which trapped the Dullahan. The cat used it's agile reflexes to lunge at the creature.

The cat's claws scratched the horse's side and left a powerful, torrid, burning wound.

FOG said with a goggle eyed expression: 'This is the absolute first time I have witnessed Cleo use violet claw in her cat form.'

He added: 'Well done Cleo, your power is true prowess!'

The Dullahan suddenly retreated into a portal it had opened.

Later on: After the intrusion of the Dullahan in Hallow Valley, FOG declared an immediate emergency meeting with all his friends at his hut.

Fane, Cleo, Josephine, Matoko, Aya, the conscious Freya, Ontari, Thomasin and Levi were all there. Oliver was there too by his sister. Beforehand, everyone had informed Freya of the events that had taken place during the time she had been asleep.

FOG asked Freya with concern as she sat on the couch: 'Are you alright Freya?'

Freya replied casually: 'I'm fine... don't worry about me... even though my eyes had felt like they were made of stone... just let us get on with the conversation...'

She asked him: 'What exactly is this important meeting for anyway?'

FOG carried on: 'Alright then... so as we all know so far, the Sisterhood is in league with the Oracle, the Oracle is in charge of the World Hunt Organisation and that the Oracle was the one that sent the burning message to our safe haven, the virus was created by William Grissom to wipe out all of humanity slowly, but after William Grissom AKA Lord Gruesome killed himself, Rumpelstiltskin who knew about Lord Gruesome's plans, told the sisterhood about the virus and also where the lab was. The Sisterhood helped spread the first strain of the virus and afterwards they proceeded to mutate the virus... now the virus was all just a useful distraction for the sisterhood...'

He went on to question: 'Now everyone, we must question one thing... what exactly is the Sisterhood planning?'

Freya mentioned: 'The witch that broke into the Archaium, she told me and Oliver that she was from the Sisterhood and that they planned to take over the world, also that Hallow Valley was not the only safe haven to receive a strange letter... all other safe havens got one as well, from the Oracle.'

FOG said loudly: 'So that's why we may have received a message on the PCB from a safe haven in Japan...the Sisterhood is looking for something located in a specific safe haven and because most safe havens are protected by a powerful spell, no enemies can just march straight into any safe haven, they have to find a loop hole, either by sending in a creature that has the ability to warp between time and space itself using a special form of teleportation like the grim reaper...ugh never mind that guy.'

Cleo asked FOG plainly: 'Frances, do you think that this is a plausible explanation for a notoriously known spirit being to be in Hallow Valley... and who are the Sisterhood anyway?'

FOG scratched his forehead at Cleo's question.

Josephine interrupted them: 'The sisterhood is a group of outlaw witches who stand to either dominate or put things into ruin, centuries ago they had been led by a woman that they referred to by three names, the name to outsiders: The Red Blood Queen, to the inner circle of witches: Imperare which is Latin for 'to rule' and her common name: Brynhild... she was the one that is responsible for the Sisterhood's existence... you see, the history of those witches goes back before even the middle ages and all the members are witches and warlocks who are half witch... half vampire.'

343

Fane said in astonishment: 'But that's impossible for a type of hybrid like that to exist unless they are mute beings!'

Josephine said: 'Well they were all killed during the 15th century at the behest of Nikolai Flammel and Brynhild's evil schemes had been brought to an end by the Wolf Ancestor... he turned Brynhild to stone using an ancient talisman that has no known origins... after that, the Sisterhood simply sank underneath the sheet of history itself and disappeared for centuries after that, which is why not just anybody knows who the sisterhood is, most people are simply unaware of the past existence of those witches even to this day...the witches were also called heretic witches due to the fact that they had been shunned by other witch covens and that they had become at odds with their witch beliefs.'

Levi said: 'This just all feels like a sinking ship right now.'

Oliver added: 'I remember having overheard a conversation that Aisha was told by the Demon King to check the status of the underwater purgatories.'

Josephine explained to everyone: 'The underwater purgatories are where Brynhild's stone remains have been stored separately for the past centuries.'

Aya made a raw joke: 'What, a bunch of lonely witches want to glue together a few pebbles to awaken an old, stoned lady who probably has *pretty* solid brain cells by now...come on, those witches need a reality check!'

FOG glared at Aya and said sharply: 'Well if the Demon King is worried that the pieces of Brynhild are missing which is why he had those hiding spots checked in the first place...perhaps the Sisterhood do have the pieces and intend to awaken Brynhild... Aya, your witty joke has just revealed the truth!'

Aya rolled her eyes and said: 'Pfft okay...'

Oliver asked FOG: 'But why does the Demon King remain silent on this...'

Freya suggested: 'Maybe to prevent the spread of panic?'

Cleo asked Freya: 'Haven't you said earlier that this so called Sisterhood wants the Book of Light?'

Freya said: 'Hah, a book that doesn't exist... but yes, the witch that summoned the cyclops did mention a book of light...she even mentioned the phrase 'the book of light will show the way' and also said that it had been Rumpelstiltskin's favourite phrase.'

FOG added to what they had said: 'I also recall in my dealings with that lunatic that he used that phrase as well.'

Ontari thrusted her dagger into the table and said: 'Who cares about that stupid book... what the hell does the sisterhood want from the safehavens?!'

Thomasin who had been cooped up in behind the others decided to speak up now: 'Maybe the power over one of the greatest powers to exist...to shatter the balance of life and death...means to become one with death in order to stand above all the living.'

Levi said to Thomasin: 'Yep, you're not making any sense, at all.'

Thomasin approached FOG and explained: 'I had a premonition recently that the Grim Reaper lost his powers... which is just as good as dying all over again... I could not see who stole the power of the Grim Reaper...but maybe this vision of mine is what may still happen and that this Brynhild woman...what if she is the one to steal his power and what does every safe haven have... a gate way to the spirit realm... but maybe the one in Hallow Valley is more special and leads to something in the spirit realm that the Sisterhood wants in order to steal the Grim Reaper's powers.'

FOG said whilst adding the theory to his note pad: 'Maybe.'

Thomasin said after clearing her throat: 'The reason why I had such a personal premonition of this being is because the Grim Reaper is my nephew.'

FOG's frown sank into a look of disapproval.

FOG coiled his mouth into a frown. Everyone stared at Thomasin in deep seated confusion.

Thomasin shook her head angrily and left the hut.

Aya felt genuinely sorry for FOG; she asked him: 'What's wrong now, Mr. Grouch?'

FOG seemed to ignore Aya's new rather silly nick name for him and said: 'I just feel as though I can't grasp this situation fully enough... the Demon King remains silent... we have yet to hear as to what Melusine has discovered in the lab if there even is a lab... maybe the clues on the

345

letter were a hoax of complete thorough deceit and I don't know what to tell the leader of the Bunyip tribe...I mean of course we all agreed to work together with the Grim Reaper...right?!'

Aya's laughable gaze softened. She placed a hand on FOG's shoulder to console him. She realised he was having an emotional break down.

Aya said to him in a calm tone: 'Don't worry FOG, whatever happens we're all in this together... I know you're passionate about balancing the needs of Hallow Valley and the needs of everything or everyone else at the same time... I'm sure everyone appreciates your efforts...just don't go dragging your head in the ditch.'

FOG smiled and said: 'That's right...now first things first, I'm going to go and talk with the tribe leader.'

But before he left he asked Aya in an over curious manner: 'Why did you wake me up last night with a trumpet... you said it was an emergency.'

Aya cheekily shrugged her shoulders and replied: 'No emergency but it ended up being one in the end with Freya's whole coma thing.'

FOG shook his head at the realisation that the whole trumpet scenario had been another one of Aya's stunts to annoy him... he only hoped that she wouldn't be too meticulous to do that every following night.

After FOG was gone, Aya asked Cleo: 'By the way Cleo... how did you manage to see through my shadow sphere... normally it traps foes to prevent them from leaving outwards and it also darkens anyone's eyesight that stare upon the shadows?'

Cleo smiled casually and explained: 'In my cat form I am able to use a special type of night vision... it is a type of thermal night vision which means that aside from the fact that I can see in the dark with ease, I can see cold and warm colours which help me differentiate between who are human and who are not.'

Aya smirked and said: 'Cool.'

Freya asked Aya with a slight hint of impatience: 'You said there were these jokes that you wanted to tell me?'

Aya's face lit up.

She said to Freya: 'Okay... What is one insult that you don't say to a vampire?'

Freya shrugged her shoulders.

Aya said: 'Well it's bite me because they'll just see it as an invitation...here's the other joke.'

Aya went on to say: 'What do you say to someone from Finland...are you finished?'

Freya frowned angrily. The word 'seriously' was practically written on Freya's forehead.

Later:

Everyone decided that even though strange and dangerous times were circulating... life must move on and so everyone left the hut.

The last thing that had been discussed was the matter regarding the history of the World Hunt Organisation. Ontari had said that before the organisation took on that name, they had been small tribes of people all descended of the Inuit people of Canada and were hunters trained in the arts of killing bad mythical creatures... mostly vampires or werewolves, these tribal people called themselves 'the hunt' and they worshipped and followed their leader whom they called the Oracle, who is always a woman...according to the tribal story... the Oracle is a divine descendant of a strong shaman lineage and can trace their bloodline back to Waheela, the ancestor of every hunter in the modern day version of 'the hunt', the World Hunt Organisation.

After the meeting, Ontari spoke to Fane regarding the mysterious man who had kidnapped Freya and brought her back to Hallow Valley.

After that, Ontari marched off.

Fane thought heavily on what she had told him, this man's message was that the mirror Josephine has is evil and to keep his family safe for there shall be dark times.

Fane was outside of FOG's hut with Cleo. He had already told Cleo about the message. After all, Cleo was the person he confided in the most, who's trust he treasured dearly.

347

Felicity had been playing with little Florence and the two had been watched over by Felix and Osana. Fane and Cleo thanked the two for watching their daughter during the time they had been in the meeting with FOG and the others. Felicity waved goodbye to Florence. Florence smiled with a hint of confusion.

As Fane understood it, Felix was FOG's long lost son... Fane felt a bit suspicious about him but at the bottom of his heart, Fane was happy for FOG, however a part of Fane felt an insecurity about the man Ontari had spoken about. Who was he? Why would he care about his family? Fane thought to himself as they wandered off back home.

Later:
Aya went to go and check on her friends Cleo and Fane.

She saw them sitting outside of their place.

Cleo had been braiding her daughter's hair. Cleo glanced to see Aya standing there.

Fane joked to Aya: 'What a nice surprise this is...we could invite all of Hallow Valley to add to it.'

Aya smirked sharply and said: 'Ha ha, very funny.'

Fane saw that Aya was clutching a wooden object quite tensely in her hand.

Cleo noticed Fane's concern over this and nodded softly. Fane brought Felicity inside. Cleo and Aya spoke for a short time.

Cleo said: 'Ah, typical of you to hold onto that...you always cling onto the past with that wooden fox figure of yours...and what I also know is that when you're in real deep emotional trouble, you bottle it away deep down, it's only a matter of time before the first cracks start to build in that bottle.'

Aya confessed: 'Drat, you got me...yes you're right... it's got to do with someone I haven't seen in a long time.'

Cleo asked her: 'Is it Haru perhaps?'

Aya said: 'Yes, FOG received a message from a safe haven in Japan, there's something bad going on there.'

Cleo pointed at her and smiled; she said: 'The Aya I know would do what her heart tells her to do...then she would try to find the best outcome so as to avoid consequences...that's the wit in you.'

Aya's stress settled down. FOG had been so busy, she didn't want to bother him with her bothered mindset. She remembered that Cleo had a simple way of unifying people or setting aside problems when others could not, she was diplomatic but also a good listener that gave reliable advice.

Aya muttered: 'Then there's that mask...I feel a bit annoyed with myself for having had to use it... but next time, I'll rely on my powers instead, last time was just practice with that mask.'

Cleo asked her out of odd interest: 'What does Chiyoko, Goman no Kamen mean?'

Aya flinched a bit.

She asked with a surprised expression: 'You heard me use the masks chant?'

Cleo wondered: 'So that's what it was.'

She added: 'As I approached the Dullahan in my cat form, I heard you say it.'

Aya explained: 'Well, Chiyoko is actually the true name of my grandmother... in order for me to use the mask, even at half power, I need to be calm like as in tranquil, saying her name to the chant makes me feel more at peace...as for Goman no Kamen...it is Japanese for mask of arrogance...which is the name of the mask at half power...the mask enables the user to become arrogant and allows them to ignore the effects of others attacks or abilities.'

Aya added playfully: 'It's just like your special night vision you didn't tell me about.'

Cleo scoffed and had a slight smile on her face.

Meanwhile in the underworld:

Hades sat at his round table. He was weeping in a hostile manner. Lucien had called him an 'Impolite, heavy-hearted hot headed, fervent monstrosity'. He kept banging the table with his flat hands. All his pretty tea cups fell to the floor. Hades' hair went into raging lunatic mode and swayed violently from one side to the other, the sensitive flames that were clearly upset. Even though Hades enjoyed his occasional tea parties, sometimes all he wished for were real friends... Hades led a lonely life, the only person who technically was his family was Lucien and all his relatives, not that it was an easy thing to explain.

Hades retrieved a bulky, lengthy cloth and blew into it full canon style. He ended up setting the entire thing on fire.

Hades fussed in a mournful manner: 'No...why, my precious cloth!'

Whilst Hades was distracted by his pathetic cloth, an odd light surfaced and swirled about in Hades' crystal ball. The light came to a standstill when it formed into a vividly detailed image. It showed a door that had a glowing rim. The door shook and the door knob rattled with hostility. It was as though a terrorist lived behind that door. Normally this glass-globe was used by Hades so that he could keep an eye on his travelling museum. It was a moving structure that could be anywhere at anytime and was invisible to those it chose to stay hidden from. It was a travelling museum for mythical creatures and Hades simply adored it, he could hoard as much stuff as he wanted as display objects since Hades' addictions were parties, food, tea parties and hoarding random stuff. Lucien hates the building.

The POV (point of view) of what's behind the door:
There was a tiny flickering light in the middle of the room. It was so insufficient that it was meagre. The room was large. People were scattered all over the floor, some were awake.
Two people were speaking in a hushed tone:

A man asked: 'Midnight...why do you think the Sisterhood trapped us here?'

Midnight sighed in frustration: 'I don't know...obviously I have less of a clue than you do, Stark.'

Midnight watched as someone groaned sorely and slowly shuffled toward the only food source they had. It was a tall slender food dispenser filled with old, slimy, onion and leek soup and next to it was a larger dispenser filled with water. The food supply replenished itself every second day as well as the one containing water. For a toilet there was a small toilet where the poo could not be removed from. Grime was spreading on the toilet seat. Occasionally someone would try to scrub away at the toilet with the corpse of a rat or a cloth made of loose clothes or a scrubber made of hair. The toilet had an overhang that consisted of sewn together rags. For entertainment there was an old gramophone that never stopped playing that irritating jazz song. For what seemed for a long time, Midnight and the other witches/warlocks had tried to break the musical object, but every single time the machine magically fixed itself and kept on playing. They even tried to figure out how the rats in the room were able to go in and out of the room...if the rats can get out, why can't they? To their disappointment, they found out that the rats just magically spawned in a corner of the room, they had no way of in or out either. Perhaps ripping out the toilet would reveal a hole made for plumbing...nope nothing and the toilet just moved itself back into place. There were no beds, it really lacked in the furniture department so people had to sit and sleep on the floor. There were no windows or clocks. On the walls that had crumbling wallpaper, Midnight and Stark would etch one line per day that they felt was a day longer that they were trapped... magic could not be used in this room and the door that locked off the entire room was made out of Elm wood, Elm wood dispels and prevents magic...a major bummer for witches. The wood is tough, not the type that could just be kicked down...this type of wood that comes from an Elm tree, could not be hurt using physical means...the only way to destroy the door was to weaken it's powers using a naturally made fire, then it could be broken down but the people who were trapped definitely did not know where they were trapped... even if someone did find them, they would risk burning down the entire

351

building along with them. Obviously, the chance of an escape from this inner hell was highly unlikely.

Stark asked Midnight: 'Perhaps the Sisterhood have motive, maybe they put us all here...all the powerful witches from the Witches Covenant to remove any obstacles in their path for their nasty plans.'

Midnight yawned loudly and said: 'I agree with your speculation....however we must also think as to why they created this room in a way that it keeps us alive...with food and all that...it just doesn't make sense.'

Stark muttered: 'To mock us... by now they are thinking; Hah, we've trapped all the most powerful witches in the world into one place...now we toy with them and torture them forever; those insufferable fools...I feel as though if I stay in this room much longer...I shall suffocate.'

Midnight wondered: 'No, maybe they are keeping us as leverage for something...then they are going to find a way to wake up my mother...Stark if they succeed, the world will be worse than this prison we're stuck in...'

Stark glanced at a rope that hung from the ceiling. The end of the rope had been tied into a noose, the rope was indeed intimidating.

Stark pointed at the rope and remarked with rash sarcasm: 'There is a way out...even if it's not ideal.'

Midnight asked him: 'Can't you use your powers as a fire demon to burn down the powers of this door?'

Stark smirked angrily and said: 'Tsk, tsk, no I definitely cannot...one needs a natural occurring fire as in caused by natures elements or created using natural objects...I am a more magic based entity...so magical fire...we can't use magic in here because of the door in the first place...haven't you noticed that I can only use my human form...I am not even able to set myself up in flames like I usually can.'

Midnight pounded again at the door in brutal annoyance. Trying to use her wolf form would be pointless as the door could not be destroyed using physical means. Despite this, Midnight kept at it with the door; definition of madness is when you keep doing the same thing over and over again in the hopes of other outcomes but have no actual results in the end.

POV (point of view) ended.

Hades was collecting all his broken tea cup shards from the floor. The image of the door had disappeared from his crystal ball.

Meanwhile, somewhere secret, a hidden location:

A woman yelled: 'You useless filthy zombies...gah I have to do everything myself around here!'

The two zombies who looked like their skin was decaying, recoiled back in fear.

The woman fumbled with an electric light in her fingers.

A woman thrusted her arm back and gave her an empty glare; she said: 'It would be best if you didn't waste your time lecturing these low life creatures...the ritual is about to begin...the one you have craved so long for... there is nothing else that made your shallow heart beat than this...or am I wrong Helene... this is what you turned me into a monster for when your greed took over and you said it was my destiny to help return the darkness to the world that I had once stopped with the help of Lucien...don't ever dare forget what I have sacrificed to be here, don't ever forget what our new recruits sacrificed to be here...I pray this Brynhild is worth it because for her even if she lies sleeping, we have knelt down and taken the blade down our throats...we have given up our humanity, even if we have become immortal hybrids.'

Helene fumed: 'You forget your place...I run things here...because of me, the wrath of the Sisterhood lived on through the unnoticed centuries of our existence... Dahlia Tepes.'

Dahlia walked away and said: 'Brynhild is our leader...even if her soul is still in stone, besides, if she awakens, don't forget, her reputation proceeds her.'

Later:

All the witches gathered, there were many, they even came from all different cultures to be here on this special day, the day that the Sisterhood called 'the day of judgement'.

On a raised, round altar lay all the stone fragments of Brynhild. Next to the pieces was the talisman that had turned her to stone as well as a certain enchanted Actinolite stone. The witches began chanting in unison:

'Reverse, reverse, remove Brynhild's curse. All witches come full circle, to perform histories darkest miracle. When the clock strikes nine, we shall awaken the malign, reverse, reverse, remove Brynhild's curse. May the blissful dusk hour of doom return...of that menace others shall learn, reverse, reverse remove Brynhild's curse.'

Dahlia Tepes stood in front of the altar with Helene and a woman that had mysterious looking hair. The three women held hands to strengthen each other.

Slowly, the stones began to shake. Then they pulled each other together to form the body of a woman who was made of stone. After that, the grey colour slowly vanished from the body.

Dahlia let go of both women's hands and said to Helene: 'There, it is done...I have done my part in this mess, let me know when I can perform the spell to infiltrate the safe haven after that ridiculous plan of yours with the Dullahan failed.'

Helene said: 'Wait...perhaps Brynhild wants to speak to you.'
Dahlia replied effortlessly: 'I have nothing to say when there is nothing left to be said.'

Dahlia stormed off.

A voice demanded to know: 'Who do I want to talk to?!'

Helene felt this adrenaline that she hadn't felt for so long, the feeling that made her feel as though she was mere inches away from death. It felt incredible for her. She knew that Brynhild was finally awake. The woman was still flat on the table. She smiled menacingly. Her eyes sprung up.

She laughed and said: 'That's right, I'm back and I'm here to stay...let's have some fun.'

Dahlia retired to her own space in the old abandoned space that the Sisterhood were hiding out in. The room was filled with most peculiar objects. But the thing Dahlia cherished the most was her familiar, Abby who was a raven. Abby was talented, she could speak up to three languages like her master could which were: Italian, English and Romanian. Though she was smart, she was just as clumsy as her master, occasionally crashing into doors and shattering window panes, once she even accidentally flew into her master's cauldron, luckily it was empty!

Abby sat proudly on her perch and cawed: 'So did the plan work?'

354

Dahlia replied to her familiar: 'Yes, everything was a massive success.'

Abby cocked her head and asked: 'Did you even want Brynhild to be awakened?'

Dahlia squeezed her hand over a mortar from which blood trickled into it.

She replied: 'For the last past few centuries I haven't really known what I wanted...for some reason I was drawn to the darkness after Helene turned me into a heretic witch, I couldn't fight against it, it's like I was compelled to give in to the evil deeds that the Sisterhood were known for.'

Abby flew onto Dahlia's shoulder and asked: 'Compelled?'

Dahlia replied: 'In a way that I can't explain.'

Abby speculated: 'So maybe these witches have some mind control over you...'

Dahlia shuddered at the thought that her familiar might be right. Even though she was powerful and she was called the saviour according to demon history, these witches exploited her abilities with ease. Someone knocked on the open door. Dahlia turned to look who it was. It was the arrogant Helene.

Helene asked her: 'Are you preparing the spell for the safe haven ritual?'

Dahlia was forced to answer: 'Yes.'

Helene said: 'Good...I told Brynhild about you...she has high expectations of you now.'

Dahlia said coldly: 'You do understand that if it weren't for me or Cyrus and his vampire friend as well as the efforts of poor Rumpelstiltskin, none of this with Brynhild would have ever been possible.'
Helene nodded slowly and said: 'Well yes, the Sisterhood does appreciate everyone's efforts...it's only a matter of time before the OGR and the Hidden Empire realise what is really going on...I hope they liked my splendid Cyclops friend...took me a while to make him... that was my most difficult job when it comes to making zombies.'

Dahlia blurted out rather angrily: 'Helene... when all of this is finished for the last spell, I intend to leave the Sisterhood... I never have realised it

355

but...I was brain washed by you all these years to serve the Sisterhood as a slave, I was such a precious asset, I don't know how you did it but I've had enough... it's just bitter pain and nothing else left.'

Helene's expression tweaked into sudden fury.

Helene

She shouted: 'Pain?!'

She raved: 'You have no idea what true pain is...the significance and the delicate nature of true pain...I'm not sure if you have ever heard my story before but here goes; I am actually quite old, when I had been a human, I had been born in Athens, Greece and I was the daughter of a philosopher, growing up I was always drawn towards the faith of Athena, the goddess of knowledge and every day as a girl I would go somewhere and pray to the goddess Athena though one day, my father told me to head to the food stalls and buy some food then head straight home to my mother and sister...I did so only to find them both half dead...it was as though the home my family had lived in had become a stained bloodied canvas...I of course was no longer able to escape so I crawled underneath a table...the man who had killed my family had pulled me out from underneath the table.'

She continued: 'He smeared blood on my face and laughed at me...all I could do was scream though the man walked away and left me to cower in a pool of blood...later Brynhild found me and she saved me, later on I found out that the man who had killed my family was none other than the vampire whom we are now working with, Cyrus Sethius... I shall not seek to avenge my family... not for now anyway...he does not even remember me.'

Helene glared at Dahlia with enraged eyes and walked away.

Dahlia muttered to herself: 'Without me you would never have gotten access to the vault, I was the only person that Lucien ever showed how to open it...without me you would never have come up with the idea to trap all of the witches from the witches covenant in a room inside Hades' travelling museum which is right under Lucien's nose so to say but never easy to find...without me that mirror would never have ended up in Hallow valley under false pretences.'

Dahlia cracked her knuckles angrily. A grey, transparent aura of a dragon arose from Dahlia. Though she pulled her aura back within herself to calm herself down. She argued with herself that she must find a way to free herself from Helene's manipulation.

Meanwhile in Hallow Valley, Josephine's place:

Josephine was fixing the binder on one of her older spell books, the binder that she replaced was made from wood off cuts that she had set aside from one of her old trees...according to witch lore it was necessary to bind spell books with something that came from the exact witch's home, apparently it made the spells that were contained within the book more authentic and natural. Suddenly, the cover that had covered the mirror, spookily fell to the ground. Josephine gazed from afar at the mirror. The definition of fright captured on her face. Panic moved her heart beat yet still she gradually approached the mirror. Her finger tips were just mere inches away from the floating shards. She could feel her fingers being cut by the shards even though she had no bruises, all of a sudden, the shards sprang into the base of the mirror, the shards now gleamed as the perfect smooth surface of the mirror. What came next gave Josephine a scare. Her reflection did not move in the mirror. Her own eyes seemed like two cold, sharpened knives staring hungrily back at her. The icy, obsessive discontented, ironic smile of her reflection made her feel sudden disdain for herself. Abruptly, behind her reflection it began to drizzle. Even though Josephine could not feel the rain, she could feel a sheer cold draft flow in behind her. Was this the power of the mirror, to make people insanely sad?

Suddenly, a black maelstrom of mixed energies made Josephine's reflection disappear. Josephine wanted to cover up the mirror but she couldn't. She couldn't do anything, she was paralysed on the spot. Decayed vines crept out of the blackness and extended outwards as though they were arms reaching out towards Josephine as though they were dead plants starved from the light. Black shrivelled up flowers grew on the vines.

A voice spoke:

'Tip toe tip toe, unravels the song of woe, a step in the many dances, your life ends in flashing glances. I shall become you, I am your enemy, I shall be your new me and so this new me shall be in one entity, you are now my possession, I shall breach your mind with aggression.'

A hand shot out of the dark mirror and grabbed Josephine by the neck clutching it tightly. Josephine hit the hand with hers as a strange energy went into her mind. Her eyes rolled upwards. After that she crashed to the floor and the mirror returned to normal. She was now unconscious.

Same day at night:

It was during the hours of night when the pesky creatures only known as the Gremlins from the Gremlin Postal Service aka as the GPS seemed to be making a parcel delivery to someone in Hallow Valley. This time however, their carriage that was illuminated by the little spiders that hang from the sides of the moving contraption were shining brightly, all the odd looking spiders were jingling about in the swaying movements of the rampantly/quick moving carriage being driven by the Gremlin maniacs. The carriage stopped in front of one of the residences situated in Hallow Valley.

One of the Gremlins spoke to the other, 'Yap, this is the residence, where we deliver parcel or should me say parcels.'

Both Gremlins laughed or menacingly screeched at the same time.

The parcels were oddly shaped, one like a pyramid-like shaped object. The other parcel was a smaller flat rectangular shaped box. The greyish coloured, seemingly fat Gremlin opened one of the carriage doors, stepped outside and slowly trudged toward the residence's door. A few steps led up to a door, where the Gremlin decided to place the parcels. On the parcels that were carefully packaged and wrapped up in material similar to thin paper cardboard, there was instructions on the packages in a black colour that stated *Fragile item(s), leave at the recipient's property, do not leave unattended, under no circumstances.*

The Gremlin muttered about with itself, it grew angrier and more annoyed by the second. If only someone or something ruffled it's feathers or so to say ghastly Gremlin fur, this Gremlin would tear everything to the ground if it wanted. The Gremlin pounded on the door, it sounded like the door was going to split into two halves. The Gremlin was disturbed for a mere moment while it was thinking about pointless things, when a young-looking man who was wearing a dark grey bathrobe opened the door. He glared downward and saw the Gremlin standing there. Fane who was awoken by the abhorrent sound that the Gremlin had made on the door, was irritated by the sheer presence as well as the atrocious smell the Gremlin emitted. Since he was a Celtic Wolf he could easily smell the nicest and most unpleasant smells there were in existence and well this Gremlin definitely ticked a lot of unpleasant boxes.

Fane forced himself to smile and asked as kindly as possible, 'What can I possibly do to help you at this hour?'

The fierce looking small Gremlin spoke, 'Yap, just sign here and take parcels.'

The Gremlin shoved a clip board into Fane's Hands.

The creature spoke, 'Sign where it states signature..... very easy peasy.'

Fane was in no mood for these theatrics nor any trouble with the GPS and so he signed the document and handed it back to the Gremlin. The fragile document that looked like it was going to fall apart was now signed.

'Hope you have had a great experience with Gremlin Postal Service, have a nice day!' the Gremlin announced as loudly as possible.

Fane's grin turned into more of an annoyed smile. He left the door open and placed the parcels on a table inside. Then Fane stood in the doorway once more, watching the Gremlin heaving it's fat body into the carriage.

Fane said in a mocking tone, 'Don't have too many midnight snacks and watch out for any water puddles.'

Fane waved goodbye to the Gremlins. Both Gremlins felt like they were being humiliated and so the other Gremlin that had green coloured fur, opened the carriage door and proceeded to throw a rotten egg in Fane's direction. Fane reacted quickly as the rotten egg hit a wall. Fane laughed out loud, he was amused by the reaction the Gremlin's had toward his hilarious remark.

Fane had a big smile on his face as he said, while he was about to close the door, 'Rotten luck you poor Gremlins, you missed.'

The door to the residence was now closed. The Gremlin's both decided that Fane was not worth their trouble. They had completed the parcel delivery like they were supposed to, even if they had rather just thrown the darn parcels out the carriage door like they always did. For some reason they were not allowed to throw any fragile parcels out the door like they did with others, as the sender opted for their premium Gremlin Postal Service plan. Suddenly, the white carriage roared to life, the Hell Hounds awoke from their short slumber and at lightning speed they disappeared from the scene, leaving no trace of their being there. In fact the Gremlin's transport had the ability to also fly in the air. There have been in the past children mistaking the supposed legend that was Santa Claus and his flying sleigh with the Gremlin Postal Service. No one even knows exactly where the Gremlins Headquarters is based. But who knows for sure if they even have one single Headquarters.

Cleopatra who had seen the Gremlin's take off, as well as her husband's sarcastic conversation with them, was now awake as she was asking herself who the parcel was from and for whom it was. She was currently still standing at the window looking out at the surrounding landscape that was Hallow Valley. She could hear the wooden floorboards behind her creaking, she turned around and saw Fane standing there with the two parcels that the Gremlins had delivered.

'Sorry about the whole commotion with the Gremlins. They are an amusing bunch, even if they smell disgusting,' Fane said in an amused tone.

Cleo smiled, she was happy that Fane thought that the Gremlins were funny. They sat down next to each other on the bed.

Fane spoke, 'Unfortunately I have an inkling that this parcel will have no sender information listed anywhere on the inside or outside of the packaging. But regardless who sent this, I think that these parcels are meant for you.'

'I think that you are probably right.......this parcel does seem familiar somehow......' Cleo said whilst staring at the unmistakable shape of a pyramid.

Cleo was deep in thought, she kept thinking of the seeing eye pyramid she had received from Inari, the one that had the power to reveal any mythical creatures true form. Was this the one and same relic? A forgotten object from her past? A past she sometimes wished to forget or wish away. But she could not forget the events that took place in her past lives, that had taken place nor could she forget the family she once had. Cleo felt someone tapping her shoulder. It was Fane who noticed that Cleo was deep in thought.

'Are you alright? You seem a bit glum all of a sudden,' Fane asked in a concerned tone.

'I feel alright.....everything is fine. I think I know what is hidden underneath all of the packaging for at least one of the parcels. I do not want to bother you with this right now.......Why don't we just put this away for now and go back to sleep,' Cleo said as calmly as possible.

It was currently two o'clock in the morning as Cleo and Fane both agreed to get some further rest before the day would come upon them once more. Though as hard as Cleo tried to sleep with a clear mind, memories of her past, assumptions and realisations that circled her mind; she sometimes had this feeling of not knowing what happened to her or how she even got to Hallow Valley in her rather complicated past which still made her sad. All she remembered was that she was brought to Hallow Valley by the man she knows as Max and that she could not remember anything other than her life as someone named Alexene and previous past lives before that in her memories she was still trying to make sense of. She felt like there was a key part of her still missing. A key part of her life as Alexene was missing, she could remember leaving her family, her mother Koaru and her father Naaten. However, she could not remember the exact details as to what led her to come to the decision to leave her family in the first place, a family she had never seen again, unless she had forgotten about seeing them again. Of course Cleo would always shrug off these incessant thoughts as it being all her imagination playing tricks on her.

A few hours later: Cleo awoke from her slumber. She had not slept well at all. The dark rings under her eyes truly showed how tired she was. Cleo looked at a framed picture that was standing on a bed side table showing a picture of herself and Fane, Cleo was holding their daughter Felicity in her arms, when she was only a few months old. Felicity had been wearing little yellow socks and a little dress that was the same colour but had sunflowers pictured on it. Whenever Cleo felt something was wrong or out of sorts with her life she would look at that picture. This made her feel a bit better with herself and would calm the inner thoughts that would occasionally still plague her mind. Cleo clasped her amber stone necklace that hung around her neck. She wanted to make sure she still wore it, because this necklace allowed her to be a long-lived creature without it she would simply age like everyone else.

Cleo cast aside her troubles. Only because a package arrived that reminded her of an obvious past does not mean that that would define the now. Cleo got up from the bed she had been seated on, she left the bedroom and walked down a long hallway toward a kitchen area. She could see that Felicity was already seated at the table and eating her breakfast.

'Good morning Mum, today Dad is going to show me how to make some things out of wood,' Felicity said proudly.

Cleo smirked slightly, patted her daughter gently on the head and said, 'That sounds like you are really enthusiastic about your woodwork studies. Be very studious and safe, my little monster.'

'I'm no monster!' Felicity exclaimed.

'I meant it in a sweet way,' Cleo said as she seated herself on a chair.

'So what did your father make you for breakfast? Let me guess some fried eggs and bacon,' Cleo said and yawned.

Felicity chuckled, her gaze moved toward a pot that was standing on a kitchen island.

'You guessed wrong this time Mum. Dad made porridge. I hope I won't be eating this again too soon,' Felicity replied.

'That's fine, it seems that your father must have been in a hurry to go somewhere. Well at least you have already eaten something. Come on head to your room and do your homework that I had given you yesterday, it is important that you learn all your-' Cleo was about to finish speaking when her daughter interrupted.

'Learn all my mathematics, science, literacy and work on my language skills. I understand completely what you want me to do, but can I play with Rusty afterwards. His cage does need to be cleaned again,' Felicity stated and looked at her mother with pleadful looks.

Cleo said, 'Go on then.'

While Felicity was preoccupied with her homework, Cleo decided to finally open the packaging that contained the parcels that had been sent by the Gremlin Postal Service. Cleo went to her bedroom and grabbed the parcels, then she moved toward a room that was off limits to Felicity. A room that contained relics, parchments or things from the past. It was a place where Cleo could place all things that were for her important to preserve for the future or a place where Cleo would work on things. It was her office as well as her own personal museum, even Fane would at times place things he carved into the room. Things or objects that reminded him of his own past. Cleo gazed upon her and Fane's prized collection of oddities, for instance, the wolf carving that Fane had carved or a parchment that Cleo had collected picturing a map that stated where certain mythical creatures were from. Funnily enough amongst these personal belongings also was a wooden figure of Bastet; this Fane had carved himself for Cleo. Cleo placed the parcels onto a wood table that stood in the center of the room, she now sat in front of the table, she started to unravel the packaging that covered the first parcel. What she saw next would definitely bring up lots of memories. Good that the door was locked shut. As Cleo now was staring intensely at a relic she thought she would never see again nor have in her possession. It was the Seeing Eye pyramid. She had been right all along. For reasons unknown to her this was sent here to Hallow Valley for her. Why had some mysterious sender, sent her this most important relic. An object that was given to her by Inari 2000 years ago. Cleo told herself she would under no circumstances touch the surface of the artifact but Cleo was being pulled toward the pyramid by unknown forces, something about the triangle put her into a sort of trance, she moved closer and closer toward it, til she was on her knees, she could see a golden glow inside the triangle, until finally all her fingertips came into contact with the shiny surface of the object. All Cleo could see was a white flash, and a feeling of clarity came over Cleo. She felt like her inner purgatory had been destroyed. The inner purgatory that made her feel like she was imprisoned within her own consciousness. Out of nowhere there was a knocking sound at the door and Cleo rushed toward the door, as she tried to make sense of what she had just experienced. Cleo opened the front door, she now saw Max standing in front of her.

'Come in I have some good news to tell you and I am not mad with you,' Cleo said in a happy voice.

'I am sorry did I hear that right? What do you mean you are not mad with me?' Max asked in a rather uneasy voice.

'Where are you going? FOG wanted me to bring you to his place. It seems that there is something he needs your help with, Cleo?' Max stated and looked through the open doorway.

'Come in, come in. I need to show you something Max,' Cleo said in a frantic tone.

Max followed Cleo who was already in the house toward the room Cleo had been in before. Cleo pointed at the pyramid in an energetic and enthusiastic manner.

'What....is that what you wanted to show me? I hope you have not done anything stupid,' Max stated in a confused manner.

Cleo frowned and explained as clearly as possible, 'I remember you. I remember everything now, because I touched that pyramid, that object also has the power to retrieve lost memories, as well as reveal a mythical creatures true form.'

'I don't know what you are mumbling on about. I think you are having a case of Amnesia more than anything else,' Max replied trying to sound as sane as possible.

Cleo moved toward Max, put her hands on his shoulders and gazed into his eyes.

She spoke, 'Max do not play me for a fool. I mean it when I said that I remember everything. Meeting Medusa, helping you regain your strength, our adventure in Egypt. I cannot believe that I had forgotten all about these events. I mean I had even forgotten meeting Aya and FOG before I even came to Hallow Valley.'

Max removed Cleo's hands from his shoulders and started to walk back and forth in the room.

'I guess you have regained your memories. I do not know how a trinket like that could do such a thing. But I think I should bring this to FOG for safe keeping, so we can find out what else it can do. I am glad you remember me from before. But I think it would be best if this pyramid stay elsewhere for now,' Max replied in a stern tone and proceeded to grab the pyramid from the table.

'No! I still need to understand why the pyramid was sent to me,' Cleo shouted at Max in a fanatic voice.

After Max's hands came into contact with the pyramid, he collapsed to his knees on the floor. He was in shock, as he could now himself remember a secret hidden memory from his own past, one that he had lost to time itself. Now both Cleo and Max seemed to have both experienced the effects of the pyramid and were both stunned by the memories they had regained after coming into contact with the pyramid. They would remain in that same room for some time.

Same day; Mythical Creature Hut/Place for werewolves, shapeshifters and similar creatures:

Fane was currently trying to explain the differences between born wolves and bitten wolves. The whole group of mythical creatures was seated before him. He had been teaching these new comers for the last few months and most of them did finally understand how to turn at will or how to control where at least they would turn. He would teach other werewolves, shapeshifters and other similar creatures how to control their emotions. Because in all species they one share one similar problem, not letting their emotions dictate whether they would not be able to control that simple urge not to transform.

'What is the difference between a born and bitten wolf?' Fane asked his so called students.

One of them answered, 'One is born of either a werewolf line or one is bitten. I believe that is all there is to it.'

Fane rolled his eyes and then spoke, 'That is all you have learned so far. However, there are some other key difference to do with their appearance or physiology and with their simple genetics.'

Fane paused for a moment because he turned on a projector and pointed it at a pull down projector screen. Images began to be shown on the screen, from time to time Fane would click a button and the next image would be shown.

Fane explained in detail, 'Now as you all know films, TV series have portrayed werewolves as being these not so aesthetically pleasant looking humanoid creatures, or simply they look like wild wolves. In some aspects the belief that werewolves resemble more the looks of wild wolves is more accurate. Also bitten wolves turn every full moon as that is their flaw. Whereas born wolves struggle to control their wolf form when they are young, but once they have it fully under control, that is when they have truly mastered the power of the wolf. Born wolves do not have to turn every full moon, strangely enough though all wolves whether born or bitten have a fondness for the moon, it must be some kind of inner instinct or something like that. It is not all so bad if you are not a born wolf, werewolves that were made into wolves still can have the ability to transform at will, if the ability is diligently practiced. So last question what abilities do werewolves possess?'

Another student raised its hand then diligently answered, 'They have the ability to read minds, they have a keen sense of smell, good sight and are agile hunters.'

'That's about right but werewolves can't read minds, we can communicate telepathically with certain other mythical creatures like vampires and were cats. Now all of you look toward the screen, see here these images show you clearly what the physiological differences are between the bitten and born werewolves,' Fane replied and pointed toward the screen.

All mythical creatures in the hut examined the images and indeed there were some key differences, born werewolves were pretty much the spitting image of wild wolves, but the image depicting bitten wolves showed something similar to wolves but the wolf form was more upright and elongated. The creature had longer legs, arms and it was able to stand upright like a human as well as run on all fours. All mythical creatures were intrigued to find out that not all wolves were the same.

Born Werewolf

Bitten Werewolf

'Now I hope that today's lesson has opened your eyes further to the hidden truths each mythical creature may have within their own physiology. No one should ever make assumptions about knowing something about a subject, not even if they believe they are right. You are all dismissed, the lesson is over for today,' Fane stated as loudly as possible.

Fane seated himself on a chair that was in the hut, he gazed about the hut and looked at the whole room whilst all his students left the hut. He gazed at the images that hung on the walls, showing mythical creatures he had taught and helped over so many years. Sometimes he reflected upon whether any of his students remembered what he had taught them. But in the end that was the student's decision whether they implemented any of the knowledge Fane shared with them. Fane gazed out a window he could see that some of his students were practicing their transformation abilities, one of them turned into an eagle of sorts and the other into a wolf. Fane smirked it seemed to him like sometimes he thought he was the only one of his kind. The illusive Celtic Wolf. A species rarely heard of or seen.

'What is a Celtic Wolf?' a girl aged about 10 asked, that had still been in the room the entire time.

'I guess you are able to hear my thoughts. You must be some kind of psychic type creature,' Fane replied in a curious voice.

'Yes I am a psychic type creature, not that I'll tell you,' the girl answered in a defiant tone.

'Fine, all I'll tell you then is that a Celtic Wolf is a rare type of werewolf that are not seen or heard of. There is nothing special about them, other than that they are longer lived and they have other abilities than those of average werewolves. Now you can go,' Fane said in a irritated voice.

He shoved her out the hut door and closed it shut behind him. Now once more he gazed out the window of the hut and he could see that the girl poked her tongue at him.

'What a nasty little......' Fane managed to say to himself as he hardly even managed to keep himself calm.

He quickly directed his mind to think about other things his daughter Felicity and Cleo; but only for a short moment. As Fane heard a faint sound coming from a desk in the hut. It was coming from a magical handheld mirror he carried around with him everywhere he went. It was kind of like a mobile phone in its practicality.

Fane moved toward the desk, he grabbed the mirror and FOG spoke to him, 'Fane have you heard from Max or Cleo. I sent Max over to your place, as I need Cleo's help. Could you go check on both of them, since I have been unable to reach them for some time now.'

Fane had no second thoughts, he left the hut and took the mirror with him. On the way to his family's place, he walked by FOG's hut and he could hear laughter coming from the inside. It sounded like a child's laughter.

Luckily Fane could quickly listen in to what was going on in FOG's hut.

'Florence, don't....give me the remote. This is not an appropriate TV channel for you,' a feminine voice spoke.

'But me love his hair. It looks so funny,' a child's voice answered.

'Please listen to your mum, give her the remote,' a more masculine voice complained.

'No! No, no no, no, no!' the child's voiced screamed about in a hectic manner.

'Florence Lara Gregory. Give me the remote now! Or there shall be consequences,' the woman's voice spoke in a raised voice.

Out of the blue, a little girl appeared in front of Fane. She had dark brown hair and Asian features. She smiled a little evil, menacing grin, as she noticed she had been found out. Fane could see that she was holding a remote control to a TV set.

Fane spoke, 'You better give that back to your parents. Not even my Felicity did these kinds of stunts, ever.'

'Not until my fun is over!' the little girl said and teleported elsewhere.

From afar Fane was still able to hear the sound of the TV, 'Previously on Mythical Ancients...Giorgio Papadoupolos discovered the ancient ruins of........' after gaining some more distance the sounds trailed off and Fane could no longer hear the TV.

Fane would have helped his friends but now he had another place he had to be. But there was one thing Fane did envy that little girl for her teleporting abilities, because he would have been where he needed to be a lot quicker then. Fane decided to transform into his wolf form so he could then get there even more quickly. Now the wolf was running as swiftly and cunningly as it could, Fane decided to take a short cut toward his house. Until he could finally see his home. He morphed back into his human appearance and opened the front door of his residence. Everything was quiet in the house, except for a television set that was turned on in Felicity's room.

Fane could hear the ghastly sounds of Giorgio Papadoupolos' voice from afar; the voice on TV spoke, 'Yes, yes we can now indeed understand the mysteries of this Mythical Ancient culture and the why.......they why is very important......'

The man's sly and goofy voice disappeared as Fane had turned off the TV.

He looked at Felicity and said to her, 'Don't you ever watch this ever again.'

'Where is your mother, Felicity?' Fane asked his daughter.

'I think she is in her zen room,' Felicity said trying to sound funny.

Rusty the Rat

Fane sighed and was about to leave his daughter's room when he noticed that she was doing something unusual with her pet rat Rusty. It seemed that she had been styling Rusty's hair into an upright bushy kind of hairstyle.

Fane crossed his arms, and began tapping his foot on the ground. Felicity noticed this and began looking upward at her father.

She asked, 'What is wrong now?'

'What on earth are you doing to that poor animal?' Fane said in a serious tone.

'You know that show Mythical Ancients with Giorgio Papadoupolos. I was trying to copy his groovy hairstyle for Rusty. Don't you think it suits him?' Felicity said and held Rusty in Fane's direction for him to see the poor animal's new hair do.

'How long have you been watching this show?' Fane asked casually.

'I am an avid fan, and I have been watching the show, since I can remember,' Felicity replied in a quite voice.

Fane decided that he would watch a few minutes of the Mythical Ancients show so that he could gain an understanding of what it was all about. He grabbed the remote that was on Felicity's desk and turned on the TV. Fane seated himself on Felicity's bed and began to watch the madness unfold on the TV screen.

Giorgio Papadoupolos voice spoke, 'So yes, we have finally discovered proof that the ancient Egyptian civilization could have come to Australia a long time ago. Here is the undeniable proof. See here the hieroglyphs depicted on the stone wall, this here finally shows the evidence to back up my intuitive theory that mythical creatures had come from Egypt to live here long ago. Otherwise why would there be hieroglyphs in this cavernous cave like rock faces hidden behind a mountain? Now all we need to do is understand the why, the why is very important, why did they come here? How long did they stay here? Whatever they were these walls showcased their history and their beliefs. Next time on Mythical Ancients.........'

Cleo and Max were standing in the hallway, looking at what was being broadcasted on the Mythical History Channel. Not even Fane noticed their presence.

Cleo could see images of stone walls that were covered in Egyptian hieroglyphs, that showcased the history of her people the Cat People. She could remember it so vividly as if it was yesterday. All the inscriptions, the history from generation to generation that had existed for 2000 years, had been wiped out sometime in the 1800's. Finally, Cleo could remember what had happened to her cat clan, that had been her home. The home she had known as Alexene.

Felicity spoke, 'Hi, Mum I noticed your scent. The images on the TV looks kind of like how you described your home where you grew up or not?'

'Yes that looks very similar to where I grew up,' Cleo said in a nervous tone.

'But you never mentioned this to me, you only ever mentioned not remembering much of your life as Alexene,' Fane spoke in a confused voice.

The voice on TV spoke once more, 'Don't miss out on next weeks episode!'

Giorgio Papadoupolos ended the show by turning into his true form, that seemed to be a Goblin. He still even had his funky hair do in his mythical form.

Felicity laughed and pointed at the TV.

'That guy is so goofy with his frilled neck lizard hair cut!' Felicity shouted out and then held her own mouth shut afterward as she noticed that everyone was quiet.

There was strong tense environment building up around them all and no one was quite sure how or when to begin the conversation from there. Felicity, Fane, Cleo and Max would remain there in that same place for some time; the eery silence would last until one of them would start speaking.

Florence, Italy:

The city of Florence was bustling with people walking about the city, learning about the revered history behind Florence. What made Florence even more invigorating was the utter fact that Leonardo da Vinci had lived here in the 15th century. A man surrounded by so much

372

intrigue and mystery. Two specific mythical creatures known to history as the two all powerful vampire ancestors were having lunch at a peculiar, strange and shady cafe. The waiters and waitresses were dressed in all black and served their customers with things one wouldn't expect. Of course to the human eye, the delicacies served seemed harmless, something like pasta or one of the national dishes of Italy, the pizza. But to beings that weren't human, this was a cafe to relax and kick back. A place where creatures like Qamara Edazaheresch and Cyrus Sethius could unwind and talk about business. Qamara wore black coloured pants and a beige coloured linen shirt, her hair was bound back as a pony tail. On the other hand Cyrus wore a fully black, formal looking suit, and a white vest shirt underneath. The food served was disguised with a cloaking spell so that it would look normal to humans. If humans wanted to eat at this particular establishment they would be served typical normal human food, expected from a place located in Florence, Italy. The waiters of which some were humans, were unaware of the business going on being conducted by their employer, who of course was a friend of Cyrus'.

The woman named Qamara with lightly dark tanned skin, and long, slightly wavy, dark hair spoke with Cyrus, 'One wouldn't expect the service here to be so slow. Don't you agree Cyrus?'

'We can leave now if the service here is not to your liking,' Cyrus stated casually.

A man with brown hair and brown eyes, dressed in full black attire came their way, he was holding their food for which they had been waiting for.

'Here is the food, I hope you both like it,' the waiter said trying not to have a nervous breakdown.

He placed the food on their table and was about to leave but was grabbed by the hand.

'Maybe this will make you happy somewhat,' Cyrus almost whispered about.

He compelled the waiter to raise his sleeve just a bit. Afterward the waiter, cut his own wrist and blood trickled into a glass Cyrus held, then into a second glass. He told the waiter to cover up his wound and leave them be to eat their main course. The waiter left them alone.

'For you madam,' Cyrus said and smiled.

Qamara did not shown any emotions, she was a being that rarely smiled yet again laughed.

'So let's discuss the intricate details of our success that we have finally managed to resurrect the one and only Brynhild,' Qamara sternly spoke and raised her glass.

'Yes that is one thing to toast to,' Cyrus gleefully replied.

'Now that we have the Actinolite stone in our possession, we can move forward with our new plans,' Qamara said and glared intensely at Cyrus.

'I agree we shall get what we both want. It is funny though that such a stone could bring back Brynhild or Imperare as she is also called,' Cyrus remarked in a sly manner and gazed upon a stone only known as the Actinolite stone.

The stone shining brightly when the sun radiated down toward it.

In close proximity of where both the vampire ancestors were celebrating their triumph, a woman wearing casual clothing; a green t-shirt and dark blue jeans, was watching them both from afar. She had long wavy, dark black hair and piercing blue eyes. In vampire circles she was only known as Isabella. Isabella was speaking to someone on her phone.

'They are here, I think they are up to no good. I have no idea what they are planning. I will leave them be for now but I think we have to take preventative measures soon. Lucien are you there?' Isabella spoke quietly trying not to bring any attention to herself.

Qamara felt like she was being watched by someone not too far away. She looked around at her surroundings but all she could see where the pathetic humans, and of course the city of Florence itself. She tried to hone in on her senses, until she was able to make out a certain voice.

The unfamiliar voice spoke, 'I can't stay here Lucien, I will only bring myself into danger. I am leaving now.'

As soon as Qamara heard the name Lucien, the rage within her started to multiply. Qamara jolted up from her chair and went into the direction where she had heard the voice. Cyrus got up from his own chair and decided to follow Qamara.

Isabella was still fumbling with her phone, trying to put it into her bag as calmly as possible when she noticed faint footsteps coming from behind her. Whoever came toward her had no heartbeat that was noticeable and to Isabella this meant only one thing, she would have to get out of there now, if she wanted to get away. Isabella thought as quickly as she could about what she could do, the footsteps of the two oldest vampires were moving in closer and closer on her. She made a split second decision to hide against a shop wall, because if Qamara and Cyrus noticed any more movement she would be caught right away. Isabella made herself invisible using some magic she had with her. She leaned against the stone wall and made herself as quiet as possible. Any motion whatsoever would send the vampire ancestors in her direction.

'What are you possibly looking for?' Cyrus asked questioning Qamara's judgment.

'I heard someone or something say Lucien,' Qamara said in a frantic voice.

'Wait I do smell something and can feel an aura......a vampire aura,' Cyrus carefully replied.

Isabella put her hand on her mouth, she tried to make herself scarce but it didn't seem to be working as Cyrus now stood in front of her.

Qamara now stood next to Cyrus, both of them gazed at a seemingly empty space before them. Both smiled at each other as they knew there was something there. Qamara grabbed Isabella's neck and now held her in the air. Isabella was no longer invisible.

'Now look what we have found. What are we going to do with you?' Qamara said thinking about her and Cyrus' next move.

In the underworld; the Hidden Empire:

Lucien was staring at an open underground vastness. A desolate vastness, that had a sheer drop, a far reaching drop that surrounded a tree. In the center stood an old dead-looking tree, only known as the dread tree. It was one of three trees in existence known to all mythical creatures, that in combination with two other magical trees would form the famed tree of life. Nobody really knew what immense power all trees together could unleash. But that was not something Lucien wished to speculate at the moment.

Lucien would always seek solace away from the hectic Hidden Empire he had built up himself from nothing, when he was unsure about something. Currently Lucien was awaiting a reply from a text message he had sent to Isabella's phone. Something must have been wrong as he still had not received a reply back for more than two hours. Isabella was a diligent type of person who would almost always reply back straight away. This made Lucien not annoyed, nor mad just plain paranoid. Lucien tried to disregard these pointless thoughts, he had decided he would send another demon agent to the surface to investigate Isabella's disappearance, in the event that something drastic should have happened to her.

Lucien was about to leave this cavernous void, when he noticed the presence of an old friend. It was Vlad who seemed to want to speak with him. Vlad was about to speak when there was a rumbling movement coming from underneath both of them, it felt like a massive disturbance or a shift of the tectonic plates of the earth's crust. Rocks and boulders plunged into the bleak, dark depths below and cracks in the earth surrounded the dread tree from all sides. Vlad & Lucien were both now facing the dread tree, but what they saw before them was far from anything than a dead tree. In front of them stood, a tree with its branches full of hundreds or thousands of luscious, dark, green, glossy, vibrant coloured leaves. The wood of the tree had a very dark brown colour. Lucien neared the tree and now stood amongst the gigantic tree looming above his head.

Lucien was stupid enough to almost touch the tree when Vlad stopped him, 'Are you sure you want to do that? Look here.'

Vlad made Lucien aware of something that seemed to be magically glowing on the tree. It was the unmistakable symbol of the Sisterhood. Lucien now walked around the whole tree and he could see a further symbol, one he knew was for the Order of the Grim Reaper as well as another symbol that was for the Hidden Empire. There were two other symbols glowing immensely in bright white colours on the tree, symbols Lucien could not recognise. Vlad noticed one thing though regarding one of the symbols, one glowed the most and it was the symbol for the Sisterhood.

Order of the Grim Reaper

The Hidden Empire

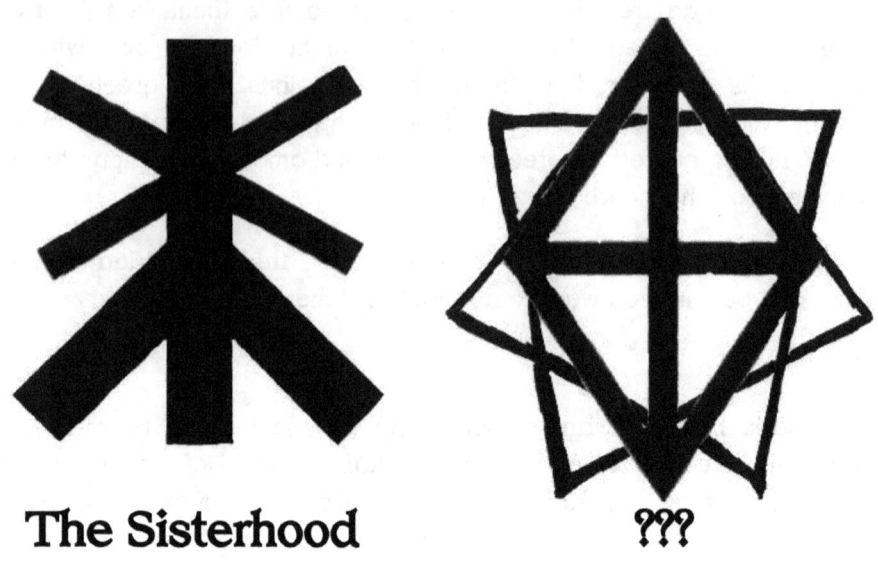

The Sisterhood ???

???

Lucien and Vlad both stood in front of the tree. They both decided it would be best to keep this a secret for the time being. Because if the whole of demon society saw this an unease would spread amongst all demons and weaken the Hidden Empire; not only the Hidden Empire, but all mythical creatures everywhere.

TO BE CONTINUED

Word Glossary – (In Alphabetical Order)

Book of Light:

A special ancient book that has been rumoured to have been around for a long time, hidden in human civilisations, even the most ancient ones. It is a book of prophecies that foretell things to come and that it was written by the Ancients; the Ancients were the god like creatures created by the all mother according to Elleswith's recount in Sing me a song of the dead. Over the centuries the book of light has been rumoured to have disappeared according to mythical creature beliefs but nobody knows where.

Bunyip People:

A group of tribes people native to Australia. They met the Grim Reaper when he was still human. Their leader is a creature called the Bunyip also called the Bunyip-man. The creature is said to have dark fur, a dog-like face, flippers, tusks and the tail of a horse. The Bunyip creature protects the tribe and the land its tribe lives on. However, the Bunyip is not a long-lived mythical creature and so after some time a new leader has to be chosen for the tribe or the role is passed on to the Bunyip's offspring.

Energy capsule:

An object that had been built by Frances (FOG) in his childhood with the help of his best friend Esther. Esther who was a witch later enchanted it. It is now probably still hidden where FOG and Esther last left it. It had the ability to take away energy from someone and afterwards was stored within the device.

Ley-lines Router:

A device that somewhat looks like a small antenna. It is placed on the most middle point of the roof. Mythical creatures use it for their TV to access the special mythical creature channel/s. In essence the router accesses ley-lines which are lines of (magical) power that run along a specific top secret ley-line system or are located closely to very ancient locations/places. If any problems persist with the signal mythical creatures can contact the ley communications intercom hot line to rectify any signal problems.

Ley Communications Intercom Hot line:

World wide corporation that runs the entire Mythical TV channel via analog channel through Ley-lines that reach out to all over the world. They have a 24 hour nonstop telephone service which is the hot line. This hot line is contacted if a Ley-line router needs fixing or if a disrupted Ley-line needs to be checked.

PCB:

PCB stands for Paranormal Control Board and allows the user to communicate with various locations across the world simultaneously. Its design resembles an Ouija board and the control board is like a radio station all in one.

Planetographer:

A device that can calculate and record the movement and position of every planet.

Portalinator:

A device that creates portals using sound waves. The portal it creates can magically transport the user anywhere in the world.

Reapkatcher:

Is a convenient device that was designed and created by the Grim Reaper himself. It is to be used by reaper associates in their work regarding souls. It helps them determine whether the soul is good or bad and is then sent to the veil or the underworld depending on the verdict of the device. The reapkatcher is round in appearance and is of a bronze colour when you are a trainee, the further a reaper advances up the ranks, the colour of the reapkatcher changes to silver, gold, and then gold with some kind of stone decoration. When worn by any head reaper, the stone decoration on the device can glow in different colours depending on the mood of the head reaper who is wearing it but eventually becomes one permanent colour after some time; the colour depends on the head reaper who wears it.

Sceptre of Eterna:

A relic that was made by the Red blood Queen, Lilith and Gothel according to a story that witches tell to their children. It is imbued with the power to erase everything within the world as well as the function to store certain types of energies if it has the Actinolite stone set inside it.

The Descendant:

Is a mysterious device that Thomas Reap built in his young adult years before he had become the Grim Reaper.

The Hidden Empire:

Is the name of the demon empire/society. Mostly is known as a secret society of demons scattered across the world. Their secret world that they can go to is the underworld. All demons accord to the rules of this empire and they are governed by the Demon King Lucien as well as the King's council.

The Order of the Grim Reaper:
Also referred to as the OGR. It was founded by the Grim Reaper, Tom Reap. It is now a major organisation. The reapers job is to help balance the souls that exist between the human world, the veil and the underworld.

The Seeing Eye:
A rather peculiar device that the OGR has in their possession. It is a triangle like, opaque and slightly see through structure with a stone set in it which is called the 'Seeing Eye' and if a mythical creature touches it, it reveals their true identity/form. The Seeing Eye also has the Egyptian Seeing Eye in gold colours on top of its glass surface.

The Sisterhood:
A group of outlaw witches who stand to either dominate or put things into ruin and their leader was a woman called Brynhild. She was the one who is responsible for their existence. All members of the group are half witch, half vampire. The group are the only ones who know how to create vampire hybrids, this thing is normally virtually impossible.

Tyrfing:
Is rumoured to be a sword from the gods (the Ancients). Can destroy armies or call upon the dead as well as that it cannot be

destroyed in any way. According to stories about the last wielder, she was seen channelling magic using the blade but this is only possible if a magic stone is added to the sword. One story of the witches is that it was hidden in the black sea by the last wielder and that its where it still is; others say nobody knows the true location of the relic. Another relic similar to the Tyrfing sword is the sword from the Lorelei family, it is said to have the same or similar powers to the Tyrfing sword and it can enhance powers for anyone who has Lorelei blood in their veins; also shield a Lorelei descendant from harm.

Witches Covenant:

A sort of council for witches and is supported by the Hidden Empire. Was founded by their first and only regent (leader) Nikolai Flammel; the council managed to unify all the witch covens of the world and are basically all the witches on that council are the representatives of all existing witches. They created the law that all witches should swear by, the law that forbids the use and practice of dark magic/necromancy world wide...on the council are only the most powerful witches.

World Hunt Organisation:

Mostly referred to as the WHO organisation. An organisation situated in America that specialises in training humans to kill bad or disorderly mythical creatures. Their leader is always a woman and is called 'the Oracle'.

Would our first book be of interest?

Find out more on our website: www.seeingbeingsisbeli
eving.com

Or find us on Facebook.

www.ingramcontent.com/pod-product-compliance
Lightning Source LLC
Chambersburg PA
CBHW071147100726
47908CB00002B/273